R. Barri Flowers is an award-winning author of crime, thriller, mystery and romance fiction featuring three-dimensional protagonists, riveting plots, unexpected twists and turns, and heart-pounding climaxes. With an expertise in true crime, serial killers and characterising dangerous offenders, he is perfectly suited for the Mills & Boon Heroes series. Chemistry and conflict between the hero and heroine, attention to detail and incorporating the very latest advances in criminal investigations are the cornerstones of his romantic suspense fiction. Discover more on popular social networks and Wikipedia.

Sandra Owens lives in the beautiful Blue Ridge Mountains of North Carolina. Her family and friends have ceased being surprised by what she might get up to next. She's jumped out of a plane, flown in an aerobatic plane while the pilot performed death-defying stunts, and has ridden a Harley motorcycle for years. She regrets nothing. Sandra is a Romance Writers of America Honor Roll member and a 2013 Golden Heart Finalist. Her books have won many awards and she is an Amazon bestselling author.

Also by R. Barri Flowers

Criminal Case Files
Explosion at the Marina

Bureaus of Investigation Mysteries
Killer in Shellview County
Hiding in Alaska
Christmas Bank Heists
Hunting a Predator

The Lynleys of Law Enforcement
Campus Killer
Mississippi Manhunt

Also by Sandra Owens

The Phoenix Three
Dangerous Secret
Dangerous Affair

Discover more at millsandboon.co.uk

CARNIVAL COLD CASE

R. BARRI FLOWERS

DANGEROUS GAME

SANDRA OWENS

MILLS & BOON

All rights reserved including the right of reproduction in whole or in part in any form. This edition is published by arrangement with Harlequin Enterprises ULC.

This is a work of fiction. Names, characters, places, locations and incidents are purely fictional and bear no relationship to any real life individuals, living or dead, or to any actual places, business establishments, locations, events or incidents. Any resemblance is entirely coincidental.

Without limiting the exclusive rights of any author, contributor or the publisher of this publication, any unauthorised use of this publication to train generative artificial intelligence (AI) technologies is expressly prohibited. HarperCollins also exercise their rights under Article 4(3) of the Digital Single Market Directive 2019/790 and expressly reserve this publication from the text and data mining exception.

® and ™ are trademarks owned and used by the trademark owner and/or its licensee. Trademarks marked with ® are registered with the United Kingdom Patent Office and/or the Office for Harmonisation in the Internal Market and in other countries.

First Published in Great Britain 2026
by Mills & Boon, an imprint of HarperCollins*Publishers* Ltd
1 London Bridge Street, London, SE1 9GF

www.harpercollins.co.uk

HarperCollins*Publishers*
Macken House, 39/40 Mayor Street Upper,
Dublin 1, D01 C9W8, Ireland

Carnival Cold Case © 2026 R. Barri Flowers
Dangerous Game © 2026 Sandra Owens

ISBN: 978-0-263-42026-5

0326

Printed and Bound in the UK using 100% Renewable Electricity at
CPI Group (UK) Ltd, Croydon, CR0 4YY

CARNIVAL COLD CASE

R. BARRI FLOWERS

In fond memory of my beloved mother, Marjah Aljean, a devoted lifelong fan of Mills & Boon romance and romantic suspense novels, who inspired me to excel in my personal and professional lives. To H. Loraine (a mermaid at heart), the true and dearest love of my life and very best friend, whose support has been unwavering through the many terrific years together. To the many loyal and lasting fans of my romance, suspense, mystery, thriller and young adult fiction published over the years. A special shout-out goes to a wonderful group of talents whom I have long admired: Carol, Charmian, Hedy, Krista, Lisa, Peggy, Olivia and Sharon. And last but not least, a nod to my superb Mills & Boon editors, Emma Cole and Susan Litman, for the wonderful opportunity to lend my literary voice and creative spirit to the enormously successful Heroes series, as well as Miranda Indrigo, the wonderful concierge, who serendipitously led me to great success with Mills & Boon Heroes.

Prologue

Lynda Boxleitner felt tense as she walked down the sidewalk shortly after midnight. She was scheduled to work at a food truck in a few hours, dishing out corn dogs, tacos and more food items to anyone who wanted them during the Founder's Day festivities that were held each year like clockwork in Reston Hills, Idaho. But before that, she had volunteered to ride in the parade. She was a former high school cheerleader, still shapely and nice on the eyes—if she thought so herself—even at forty-one and three months, to be exact.

Unfortunately, that had proved to be as much a liability as an asset, given the precarious predicament she now found herself in, much as she hated to admit it.

Lynda moved briskly across the concrete, which was damp from the drizzle that was coming down steadily as if it had nothing better to do, matting her long and curly blond hair. She needed to get home, assess the situation and then hope she hadn't gotten in over her head in the worst possible way.

Or had she played her hand just right—much like her late father, Garrison Boxleitner, a former card shark who plied his trade on riverboat casinos once upon a time? She believed she was entitled to be happy just like everyone else. She was an independent woman who had come too far in life to be simply dismissed as an unworthy piece of trash.

She needed to stand up for herself. Certainly no one else was going to. Least of all the powerful man whom Lynda had given everything to, only to receive far too little in return, just empty promises and veiled threats. Or did they go further than that?

Now it was time to turn the tables. But was she being smart about it? Or had she gone too far in making demands that, even to herself, she was beginning to have second thoughts about?

Lynda's reverie was interrupted as she heard footsteps from behind, causing her bold blue eyes to have a quick look over her shoulder. She didn't see anyone. Had she imagined it? Maybe so. And yet her instincts told her someone was watching. Waiting. A real threat.

I have to get out of this rain and inside my apartment, where I'll be safe, she told herself, picking up the pace despite wearing slingback pumps that were uncomfortable on her feet. Her wrap cocktail dress was getting soaked.

It was only in that moment that she began to feel queasy, seemingly coming out of nowhere. This was followed by severe abdominal pains, causing her to flinch from the discomfort. Suddenly, she began to retch the cheeseburger and ranch fries she'd had for dinner.

What's happening to me? Lynda asked herself, frantic, as she tried to remain upright and make it back to her apartment. Someway. Somehow. She thought she heard more footsteps and turned around, but again saw no one. Was she hallucinating? Or flat-out losing her mind?

Something was terribly wrong with her. But what? And why?

Her coordination became impaired as she had trouble maintaining her balance. Blurriness set in like a thick fog for everything around her, and it became hard to breathe.

Just as she was beginning to figure out what was possibly behind her condition, Lynda felt her legs give out from beneath her as if slipping on ice. She fell flat on her face, breaking her nose in the process. But by that time, she had already become numb to her painful ordeal, losing consciousness before ever realizing she had breathed her last breath as the rain fell cruelly upon her lifeless body.

THE DARK SUV had slowly but surely trailed her, making sure to keep its distance. Till she dropped like a sack of potatoes and there was no escaping her fate.

He pulled up alongside the fallen woman, who had given him far more trouble than he wanted. And now she was paying the ultimate price for getting out of line, threatening to disrupt, in a major and unacceptable way, all that he stood for.

Getting out of the vehicle under the cover of darkness, he approached her and checked for a pulse. Happy to see there wasn't even the slightest hint of one, he lifted her up, ignoring the blood that oozed from her broken nose and onto the sleeve of his bomber jacket. He swiftly loaded her into the back of the SUV.

After climbing into the driver's seat, he drove off and soon turned onto a side road in a wooded area. Away from any possible prying eyes, he removed her clothing and shoes while thinking about how much he'd loved seeing her shapely stark-naked body when things were good between them.

Almost too good, in fact.

But that was then. And this was now.

She had gotten way two big for her britches. It left him no other choice than to remind her of just who was calling the shots in this little arrangement between them.

It sure as hell wasn't you, he cursed to himself with a combination of satisfaction and relief. And she had no one else to blame for having her life snuffed out like a candle.

Driving again, he got back on the main road, which soon turned into Hepmore Avenue, where the Founder's Day parade would commence in a few hours, en route to Reston Hills Park.

Getting there ahead of time, knowing he would be participating in the revelries just like damn near everyone in town, he parked but left the engine running.

After dragging the corpse out of the back of the SUV, he deliberately left her in a spot where she couldn't be missed. The sooner her death became public knowledge, the sooner it could lead to an investigation that would have the intended results.

Though, if he were honest with himself, there would be mild regrets and lingering fantasies of what might have been. But he fully intended to get on with his life as though she had never entered and upended it in the first place.

After all, what other choice did he have?

He got back inside the SUV and drove off, content he'd rid himself of a problem that had to be solved without boomeranging back at him in the worst possible way.

RESTON HILLS POLICE DEPARTMENT Detective Mason Sawyer had planned to take off for the better part of Founder's Day and enjoy the yearly celebration with his gorgeous wife, Alyssa, and teenage son, Campbell, knowing just how important quality family time was. Especially in his line of work, when career obligations and professional aspirations tended to win out over a personal life.

But that wasn't happening. At least not yet.

As was often the case at inopportune times, duty called, and he had no other choice but to answer.

A report came in of a naked dead woman found in Reston Hills Park by workers this morning as they were setting up the stage for a concert.

With half the staff off and without needing to be asked by his boss, Lieutenant Gloria Schecter, Mason volunteered to scrub his off day—or at least delay it till further notice—and check it out. As he had serious designs to move up to her position someday, it was always important to show his dependability when others chose to put their own needs first.

As he drove his unmarked vehicle down Hepmore Avenue, Mason knew his wife, loving as she was, would understand. Hadn't that always been true, ever since she chose to take the plunge and marry a dedicated police officer twenty years ago, when they were both in their early twenties? This didn't make him feel any better. He would make it up to her by taking her out to dinner at her favorite restaurant in town. But his son was a different story altogether. Campbell needed that quality dad time to stay engaged, maintain discipline, and keep himself on the straight and narrow path in his life.

I'll make it up to you, too, Campbell, if this turns out to be something other than an accidental death, Mason reflected, scratching into his short black flat-top hair, then smoothing his pyramid mustache. His first thought was that the woman's death could be drug related, knowing that they had a drug problem in Reston Hills, like most big and small towns in the United States. Sadly, overdoses were not uncommon there.

Homicides were, relatively speaking. But he wouldn't jump to conclusions just yet.

Somehow it felt a bit unseemly to kill someone on Founder's Day. As if a killer would take that into consideration prior to ending a person's life.

After he arrived at the park and conferred with the first responder, Jerry Napolitano—an officer around his age and six foot two in height, with brown hair in a buzz cut—they made their way through tall Norway maple and Douglas fir trees to the scene.

Mason took one look at the deceased fortysomething woman and his jaw dropped. Lying awkwardly on her back, her pale white body was exposed for all to see. Blue eyes were open vacantly, her small nose was clearly fractured and discolored, and her full mouth slightly parted as though in total shock that this had happened to her. The long blond hair splayed around her head haphazardly was damp, suggesting she had been there when it was still raining till at least the wee hours of the morning. He noted the reddish-purple marking on her right forearm, which resembled initials.

Mason gulped. He knew her.

Lynda Boxleitner.

They had dated briefly in high school, but she was, quite frankly, more than he could handle at the time, as an attractive cheerleader who had her pick of suitors. It became apparent to him that he was not what she was looking for in a boyfriend for the long term, and both moved in different directions. He'd only spoken to her casually from time to time since then.

Now she was dead.

Mason had a gut feeling that it wasn't a suicide. She didn't seem the type to go there, from what he knew of her. And judging by the positioning of the body, it certainly didn't seem like an accident.

Whether drugs had played a part in Lynda's untimely death remained to be seen.

As did the precise nature of death, which, at the moment, he had to believe was a probable homicide, making the ghastly scenario that much harder to swallow.

Chapter One

Twenty years later

She felt cold, clammy, maybe a little weird and definitely disoriented. But not so out of it so as to not realize she was totally naked.

She couldn't exactly remember removing the knit off-the-shoulder top, ripped straight-leg jeans and flats she'd been wearing.

Yet here she was, and in the park, way past midnight but well before dawn—running almost blindly through the tall, thick trees.

And she wasn't alone.

Someone was chasing her. Someone she knew all too well. And another person, not so much.

They wanted to kill her. To silence her forever.

She wanted to live. But could she realistically outrun them? When they were as determined to catch up to her as she was to evade them with every fiber inside her?

She sucked in a deep, ragged breath—her breathing more and more laborious. Her heart was racing, too, as if wanting to burst through her chest.

What was wrong with her?

What had they to done to her?

She bit back the pain from the blisters on the bottom of her feet from the pounding they took while running across hard dirt and rocks, but she didn't dare slow down.

If only she could get through the trail and find a place to hide from them. Till someone could help her.

Or was it already too late for that, her fate sealed?

As dizziness and queasiness seemed to hit her all at once like a ton of bricks, her thin legs started to give out.

The last thing she remembered before the lights went out for good was that she had gone about things the wrong way. Underestimating her adversary in the process.

And she would never have the chance to rethink her bad choices.

THE FOUNDER'S DAY CELEBRATION, on a Sunday in late June, was in full swing with a colorful parade featuring floats, riders, marching bands, walkers and cheering onlookers as it moved slowly down Hepmore Avenue toward Reston Hills Park, where there were carnival rides—including a Ferris wheel, jumbo slide and a carousel for kids—inflatables, arts and crafts, face painting, entertainers, and business and food vendors eager to market their goods and outdo one another.

Stefanie Nguyen was excited to attend her first Founder's Day event since moving to Reston Hills, Idaho, four months ago from San Antonio, Texas. A Vietnamese American widow at thirty-four, after losing her firefighter husband, Edward Nguyen, two years earlier in the line of duty, Stefanie had made the painful decision to sell their Spanish Colonial home for a fresh start. She was sure Edward would have applauded her decision, not wanting her to dwell on the tragic ending of their marriage and get on with her life as best as possible. To that end, she'd reluctantly removed the wedding ring from her finger, knowing it was time to let go of the past and have a clean slate as a single woman.

Stefanie believed her late parents, John and Brenda Linh, would also have approved of a fresh start for her, having always instilled in her a sense of looking forward rather than backward in terms of making choices that put her needs first and foremost. She'd chosen Reston Hills for its small-town hospitality and traditional values, much like the place where she grew up in Limestone County, Texas. Though her late husband's life insurance, investments and personal savings had provided her the financial means to live anywhere comfortably, Stefanie preferred to work at least part-time, as she had previously. Putting to good use her master's degree in Exercise Physiology from the University of Texas at Austin's Department of Kinesiology and Health Education, she taught yoga three times a week and tai chi twice a week in her new setting, and liked to jog and swim as part of her personal fitness routine.

At the moment, she was enjoying the Founder's Day festivities at the park—which, beyond that, for her, often included hiking on nature trails near and along the banks of the Beeks River. Running a hand through long and straight black hair that fell across her shoulders, Stefanie's small brown eyes regarded the local musicians on the main stage. They were performing everything from country to easy listening to blues to jazz music—much to the delight of those who had gathered around, judging by the foot stomping and hips swaying left and right joyously.

Though she was beginning to feel right at home and had made a few friends since moving there, Stefanie still found herself lonely at times. There had been no one romantically in her life since Edward, save for a date or two that went nowhere. She longed for a day when that might change but wouldn't rush it. When the time was right, she was sure someone suitable would come along.

"Hey, you," Stefanie heard a soft voice say over her shoulder.

She moved her slip-on white sneakers around and looked into the bold green eyes of Bella Reston, whose great-grandfather Arthur Reston was the namesake of the town. Bella, the Founder's Day committee chair, who also ran a private foundation for charitable causes, was the same age as Stefanie, just as slender and about an inch taller. A divorcée—or happily single, as Bella liked to put it—she was gorgeous by any stretch of the imagination, with golden blond hair in a blunt mid-length cut. The two had hit it off after Bella took one of her yoga classes a couple of months ago and later talked her into volunteering to help promote the event and recruit other volunteers to do whatever was necessary to make it a big success.

Stefanie, who was wearing a multicolored split-neck sleeveless blouse and beige twill pants, put a smile on her face. "Hey."

Bella had on a green halter midi dress, which flattered her figure, and wedge sandals. She smiled back and, gazing at the stage, asked, "So, are they any good?"

"They're terrific," Stefanie had to say truthfully. "Definitely keeping everyone engaged."

"Glad to hear it." Bella lifted her dimpled chin. "Let's just hope I can do the same."

Stefanie knew that as the chairperson—with the appropriate genealogy—Bella would be taking the stage momentarily to sing the praises of Reston Hills and its journey to becoming a thriving town in Idaho. "You'll have them eating out of your hands."

Bella laughed. "I don't know if I'd go that far, but it's very sweet of you to say anyway."

Stefanie touched Bella's arm and said, "Hey, it's in your blood. And it's not like you haven't been down this road before." As she understood it, Bella had chaired the committee for the past three years and, given that she'd continued to hold the position, was obviously good at what she did.

"True." Bella took a breath and slipped an errant strand of hair behind her ear. "Well, wish me luck anyhow."

"Good luck," Stefanie told her and laughed. "Not that you'll need it."

"Thanks." She flashed her white teeth. "Hope not."

As Bella made her way to the stage, Stefanie checked her cell phone for messages. There were no new ones. Just as she was slipping the phone back into her pocket, a slender twentysomething African American woman with a blond Afro-puff hairstyle approached her and said in an affable tone, "Hi."

"Hi," Stefanie returned.

"My name's Jasmine," she said, gazing at her with big brown eyes. "I was wondering if you've heard about the Braison Family?"

Stefanie cocked a thin brow. "Actually, I haven't."

"They're a great group of people who love each other, love freedom, love nature and a whole lot more."

"Hmm... Sounds interesting," Stefanie said, for lack of a better response.

"It really is," Jasmine gushed. She pulled out a flyer from her shoulder tote. "You should check it out yourself.

We have get-togethers regularly. I promise you won't be disappointed."

Stefanie took the flyer out of courtesy but didn't imagine it was something she would pursue. Even if she had no problem with camaraderie among like-minded individuals, per se. She had enough on her plate for the time being. "Maybe I will give it a try," she told her nonetheless.

"Cool." Jasmine gave her a toothy smile. "What's your name?"

"Stefanie."

"Well, Stefanie, hope to see you there." She walked away, only to approach someone else with the same obviously rehearsed but convincing lines.

Stefanie watched briefly in amusement as she stuck the flyer in the pocket of her pants, not wanting to litter. She would dispose of it later.

Turning her attention to the stage, Stefanie regarded Bella, who was in the process of charming her audience in a cool-headed, relatable way by masterfully bridging the past to the present on Founder's Day.

"My great-grandfather Arthur Reston had a vision when he founded the town that bears his name, Reston Hills, more than a century ago," Bella was saying. "He wanted this to be a place where hardworking, family-loving, God-fearing Americans could make a good life for themselves—make that *great*—symbolizing the spirit of community that we've all come to love and cherish. My grandfather Malcolm Reston dutifully followed in his mighty footsteps, in promoting the town and its core values. My late father, Stuart Reston, stepped into their shoes with the same dedication. And now it's my turn to make them all proud—and you, too. Let's make sure that the rich tradition we all embody in Reston Hills shall live on as we celebrate another marvelous Founder's Day—"

Stefanie grinned at a job well done by her friend as Bella received applause before leaving the stage and circulating among the townsfolk dutifully while the musicians returned.

I think this is a good time for some me time, Stefanie told herself as she meandered her way through the crowd, seemingly unnoticed by most, who were too caught up in themselves or each other. She headed toward a part of the park near the river that was less likely to be too occupied while the festivities were underway. She had no problem with any mild-mannered wildlife she might encounter. *I won't complain if some western meadowlarks want to sing to me*, she thought wittily.

Just as she started to head down a trail, Stefanie was stopped cold as she came upon a naked body. It was that of a young and slender white female with dark, short hair and small breasts. She was lying flat on her back atop some undergrowth. What looked to be initials were noticeably tattooed on her pale right forearm, as if to make a statement.

Sucking in a deep breath, Stefanie could only imagine how the pretty twentysomething woman had ended up there without any clothes on. But she didn't need much imagination to believe that she was looking at the pallid face of a corpse.

RESTON HILLS POLICE DEPARTMENT Detective Campbell Sawyer sat at the counter of Harriette's Café on Pickford Street, named for its longtime owner Harriette Yardley, musingly sipping coffee with a dash of cream. He probably should have been at the Founder's Day celebration like a number of his coworkers—some on duty, others off—but he figured they could survive without him. Not that he hadn't attended enough of them since he was five years old—probably too many to count.

But it was different now. Or seemed that way. He simply couldn't muster up the same enthusiasm from years past to be an active participant. Even if he was proud to be a member of the community, which was thriving insofar as relatively small towns could thrive. Reston Hills was in Eckerslin County—one hundred and seventy-five miles from Boise, but it might as well be a thousand miles away with regard to its down-to-earth, laidback lifestyle where people largely stayed out of other people's business unless invited in.

He should know. Prior to the last three and a half years, he had lived in Boise, where Campbell worked for the Boise Police Department as a detective in the Criminal Investigation Division's Violent Crimes Unit, Narcotics Unit and Crimes Against Children division at varying times during his ten-plus years with the force. Prior to that, he had attended Boise State University, where he'd received a Bachelor of Science degree in Criminal Justice.

But burnout and a high-stress environment, along with a longing to reestablish roots in his hometown, brought him back to Reston Hills. The fact that there was an opening at the detective level with the Reston Hills PD's Investigation Division, for which he came highly recommended by his former boss, Captain Mick Fernandez, made it a done deal.

Campbell hadn't looked back, having settled into life again in Reston Hills—now at age thirty-six, with few complaints to speak of. He had reconnected with his father, Mason Sawyer, a retired police detective who had a horse ranch not far from town. Though they hadn't always seen eye to eye, the real love and respect had been there throughout. Especially after Campbell had lost his mother, Alyssa Sawyer, a decade ago to breast cancer. He and his father had taken it hard, neither seeming to find the right words to say to each other in dealing with the death. But they had slowly worked their way through and come to terms with it.

Campbell ran a hand through his black hair, which was cut short but was long enough to appreciate. He put the coffee mug to his lips, just below a Dallas mustache. About the only thing missing at the moment in his life was romance. Or something resembling an intimate relationship. Since breaking up with his last girlfriend, Naomi Espelita, while still living in Boise, he'd remained frustratingly single, with only an occasional date here and there to fill the void of loneliness unsuccessfully.

Oh well, I'll just have to wait it out till the right woman comes along and let the chips fall where they may—hoping they fall in the right direction, toward a real future together, Campbell thought, finishing up the coffee.

No sooner had he set the empty cup on the counter when the waitress was before him almost on cue with the pot of coffee in her hand.

"Care for a refill?" she asked, a flirtatious smile playing on her full lips.

Campbell cast his blue eyes at Sarah Huffstetler, in her late twenties and voluptuous inside the tight taupe uniform. She had thick blond hair with parted bangs. They had gone out on exactly one date, which was all it took for him to realize they weren't meant for each other. Though he had expressed this in the nicest way possible, he suspected she may have felt otherwise and had apparently not gotten the message.

He gave a sideways grin and, lifting a hand as if to ward off a blow, responded, "Thanks, Sarah, but I'm good."

She looked disappointed but seemed to recover quickly. "Had to ask."

"I know, and I appreciate the service." Campbell stood to his full height of six feet, two and three-quarter inches, towering over her at just over five feet tall. "See you next time around."

Sarah licked her lips invitingly. "I'll be here."

That's what I'm afraid of, he thought sardonically, but actually had no problem with them being on friendly terms, even a little flirtatious from her end. So long as it went no further than that.

After stepping outside into the fresh—albeit a bit humid—air and bright sunshine, while feeling this was perfect weather for the Founder's Day events, Campbell's cell phone rang. He removed it from the back pocket of his tweed pants and answered in his strong detective's voice, "Yeah?"

"We got a report of a dead naked female in Reston Hills Park," the dispatcher said tonelessly, as if it was no big deal.

Campbell frowned, believing otherwise, as every life was precious to him. Without considering the circumstances of the deceased, he hated the thought that anyone—on this, of all days—should have to die and be deprived of a future and all the positive things it could entail. "I'm on my way," he muttered, walking toward the parking lot.

He climbed into his cypress-gray Chevy Tahoe SUV and headed for the park while wondering if the victim had succumbed to a drug overdose. Or other means of avoidable death. Those were always the worst circumstances, when someone's life was cut short through no fault of their own.

Arriving at his destination, Campbell took a routine peek at the Glock 19 Gen5 9x19mm duty pistol that was concealed in a paddle holster inside his wool blazer. He turned his attention to the festival, which was still in full swing—a good sign, since the community depended on the revenue earned by businesses that used Founder's Day to generate year-round exposure. Not to mention, the last thing anyone needed was to take away from the spirit of the important day in the town's history through tragedy.

Once the cause of death was determined, a period of adjustment could be made accordingly.

Campbell flashed his identification to Officer Eli Gundersen, a twenty-five-year-old rookie who was tall and muscular with red hair in a crew cut.

"We've got a strange one here…" Eli said, a catch to his voice as he rubbed his jawline.

"I can see that." Campbell was inclined to agree as he took a look at the deceased white female laying awkwardly on her back in the nude at the spot, with other officers keeping the public at bay. He guessed her to be in her mid-twenties. She had jet-black hair in a bob style and was maybe five-five or so. There were cuts on her arms, legs and feet that may have come from being in the park naked. But no outward signs of foul play or otherwise significant distress of the corpse.

He zoomed in on her thin forearm and noticed the initials that appeared to be "KB" tattooed on it. That rang an immediate bell with him. Members of a local cult calling itself the Braison Family were being branded with the initials of its controversial leader, Kenneth Braison. Campbell had visited their compound before, investigating reported drug activity that had proved inconclusive. Was she—or had she been—a member of the cult?

"What are your thoughts?" Eli asked curiously.

Campbell couldn't help but think back to a similar case his father had encountered as a police detective twenty years ago that involved a fatally poisoned woman, in what turned out to be a homicide that eventually became a cold case. It had dogged his father for the rest of his career and had never been solved to this day, as far as Campbell was aware. "Well, I'm still working on that," he responded contemplatively. "Any sign of her clothing…or a cell phone…?"

"Not yet." Eli looked off into the distance. "She either ended up here without them, or someone took them after she died."

Campbell pondered this. "Do you know who she is?" Though most people seemed to know one another in a small town, to one degree or another, this wasn't always the case. Especially for those affiliated with the Braison Family, who tended to maintain a low profile in a concerted effort at staying under the radar from law enforcement. Not to mention, the Founder's Day celebration typically attracted visitors from elsewhere.

"Haven't seen her before," Eli answered succinctly. "At least, not that I can recall."

Campbell took that as a no. Or maybe as a newly married man, the officer felt uncomfortable in saying otherwise, as if it made him look guilty of her death just by association. Campbell chose to give him the benefit of the doubt, considering Eli had given himself some wiggle room by not insisting that he hadn't seen her before in any way, shape or form.

Focusing his gaze again on the dead woman, Campbell

felt a touch of familiarity, as if they had crossed paths before, in one way or another. He strained his eyes for recognition. He was usually pretty good at pinning to memory those he'd crossed paths with, even if with little more than a passing glance. But in this instance, he came up empty. Maybe this was the very first time he'd seen her face—and body. And, if so, it would certainly be memorable moving forward.

Campbell turned back to Eli and asked, "Who discovered the body?"

Before the officer could respond, Campbell heard a female's voice say in an elevated tone, "I did."

He gazed out beyond the yellow crime scene tape's established perimeter and laid eyes on a gorgeous and slender Asian woman in her early thirties, with long dark hair. Walking over to her, he got past his initial reaction to her as someone who was totally his type—to the degree that he had any real type, as such—and said professionally, "Hi. I'm Detective Campbell Sawyer."

"Stefanie Nguyen."

Campbell took a moment to gaze into the arresting brown eyes on her heart-shaped face, with a thin nose that was slightly upturned, and a small mouth. He then said evenly, "Ms. Nguyen, can you tell me how you came upon the deceased, if you saw anyone else near the body—and anything more you care to say about this…?"

Stefanie swallowed and replied, with a catch to her voice, "I can try my best."

For the time being, that was about all Campbell could ask for from her. Beyond that, he was more than willing to keep an open mind.

Chapter Two

Stefanie was still trying to come to terms with finding a dead body along the trail. It was quite literally the last thing she'd expected to see when stepping away from the music and other Founder's Day events for a bit of solitude. But here she was, face-to-face with an extremely handsome detective named Campbell Sawyer—albeit on opposite sides of the crime scene tape—who was investigating the mysterious death. She loved his Dallas mustache, which was a perfect fit for his square-jawed features, Greek nose and penetrating blue eyes, as well as the coal-colored hair in a short quiff. He was wearing a dark blue blazer over a light blue checkered button-down shirt and gray tweed pants, along with black monk-strap shoes.

Once she caught her breath, Stefanie met his gaze and said, in a measured tone of voice, "I'd just left the area where music was playing, to be by myself, and was planning to walk down the trail and along the river...when I saw her—" Stefanie glanced in the direction of the body, trying not to freak out. She looked back at the detective. "I never saw anyone near her—only people that were hanging out along the way, seemingly oblivious to what had happened to the poor woman—"

Campbell nodded. "Did you happen to recognize her?"

"No." Stefanie flinched. "I'm not from around here—just moved to Reston Hills four months ago—so I haven't had much of an opportunity to familiarize myself with too many faces as of yet." *TMI*, she thought, but still felt compelled to put it out there.

"I see." He pinched an aquiline nose. "Where are you from?"

"San Antonio."

"Texas?" he said thoughtfully. "Nice state."

"It is," she agreed, missing the state more than she cared to admit but content in knowing the time was right to relocate. She returned to the moment at hand. "I wish I had gotten to know her—the dead woman—and maybe... I don't know, through one means or another, have been able to somehow help her avoid her fate—" *He probably thinks I'm just babbling just for the sake of it and maybe I am*, she told herself, still a little nervous about the situation.

"That would have been great," he said in a gentle voice. "But unfortunately, these things happen—sad as that is—even though none of us ever want it to. Or can control it."

"You're right." Stefanie wrung her hands. "Doesn't make it go down any easier."

"For you and me both," Campbell assured her. "Know that I'll do everything I can to find out who she is and how she ended up dead in the park."

His hard expression told her he meant business. This was comforting to Stefanie, as she felt very much that no one deserved to be humiliated in death. Even if it came by one's own hand, there would certainly have been a trigger to bring her to that point. And if there were nefarious reasons the life was taken away, there was further cause to get to the bottom of it and get justice for the victim.

"I'm sure you're good at your job, Detective," Stefanie

told him instinctively. She looked over his shoulder at the deceased woman and the personnel from the Eckerslin County Coroner's Office, who would remove the body. Gazing back at him, she said evenly, "I just hope she can be at peace when you have your answers."

"Me, too." Campbell reached into his pants pocket and removed a card. "We may need you to come in and give a formal statement. Other than that, if anything pops into your head—big or small—relating to this investigation, call me anytime on either number there..." He handed her the card.

Stefanie took a quick look at the info and nodded. "Will do," she promised.

"Then I'll let you get back to your Founder's Day activities."

She furrowed her brow. "Not sure I'm quite up to that," she admitted, hardly in the mood for fun and frolic after what she'd seen. Instead, she intended to go home. "But thanks anyway."

Campbell flashed her an understanding look and said smoothly, as if he could predict the future, "See you later."

Stefanie couldn't help but feel enthusiastic about the prospect of seeing him again as she watched the detective walk back toward the others on that side of the barrier.

She turned in the opposite direction, in search of Bella, to share the sad news with her. *I almost hate to rain on her parade*, Stefanie told herself, knowing how much Founder's Day meant to Bella as part of her family's legacy. But she would learn about the tragedy sooner or later—as would everyone who lived in Reston Hills—so there was no need to withhold it from her.

STEFANIE PULLED BELLA away from an elderly member of the Founder's Day committee, wanting to be the first to bring her up to speed on the grim discovery as the one true friend she had in town.

"There you are," Bella told her spiritedly. "I was looking for you to see what you thought of my speech—if you could call it that."

"It was wonderful," Stefanie said sincerely. "You would've made your grandfather and father proud." Bella had lost her dad, Stuart Reston, earlier in the year to a heart attack, and her mother, Eloise Reston, years before that to colon cancer. Being without her own parents, Stefanie could very much relate to the pain of their absence in her life.

"Thanks for that." Bella smiled. "Doing my best to keep their dreams alive and make my own come true, to one degree or another."

Stefanie nodded, thinking of her own life and times. "It's really all any of us can ask for."

"So true." Bella eyed her perceptively. "What's wrong?"

After a moment or two, Stefanie answered straightforwardly, "A woman was found dead in the park..."

"What?" Bella cocked a brow. "Where?"

"On a trail by the river." Stefanie sighed. "I was the one who discovered her—naked and no longer breathing—"

"So what happened to her?" Bella asked anxiously. "Was it suicide? Drug related? Or something even worse...?"

"Honestly, I'm not sure," Stefanie responded. "That will be up to the police to determine. Or Detective Campbell Sawyer, more specifically." She pictured him in her mind and wondered if he would need her to come in for that formal statement. Or if they might meet again under more normal circumstances. "He's investigating the strange death."

Bella reacted to this. "Campbell... Figured as much."

"You two know each other?" Stefanie asked, but quickly realized this shouldn't come as a shock to her—assuming that the detective was a local, unlike herself.

"We know *of* each other, is more like it," Bella told her. "We both attended Reston Hills High School, but Campbell was a bit older, so we didn't hang out together or anything. But his father, Mason Sawyer, was also a police detective for the Reston Hills Police Department and was friends with my dad. Campbell decided to follow in his father's footsteps."

"Hmm...interesting." Stefanie fixed her face thoughtfully. "Sounds like someone else I know."

Bella laughed. "I suppose that some things do tend to run in the family, if the will is there."

"True. I just hope that Campbell—er, Detective Sawyer—can get to the bottom of what happened to that young woman..." Stefanie uttered, feeling regret over the life that had ended before its time.

"I'm sure he will," Bella said with confidence.

"Anyway, I'm heading home now. Not in the mood to stick around."

"I understand." Bella nodded her head. "Wish I wasn't obligated to do so, but someone needs to bring others up to date on what happened." She hugged her. "I'll call you."

"All right." Stefanie flashed her a tiny smile and walked off contemplatively.

SHE LEFT THE park in a blue Subaru Legacy sedan and drove down Hepmore Avenue for a couple of miles before turning left on Draker Drive. All the while, Stefanie couldn't get the image of the dead woman out of her mind.

What had happened to her? Could she have really been so strung out on drugs or whatever that she removed her own clothes and died? Or had her death been caused by someone else who had no qualms about having her discovered that way?

Maybe the answers would be forthcoming in short order with Campbell Sawyer on the case.

When she reached Meriotte Road, Stefanie swung left and was soon pulling up to her two-story, two-bedroom rented Craftsman home on a cul-de-sac that sat in front of a wooded area. She'd fallen in love with the place the moment she checked it out, feeling it suited her and reminded her of the house they'd had in San Antonio.

Stefanie stepped inside and onto white oak engineered hardwood flooring. She took a sweeping glance at the open-concept design, with vaulted ceilings and casement windows that offered an abundance of natural light. The ample living room had a stone fireplace and mid-century modern furniture with a separate, similarly furnished dining room. The amazing kitchen included a cozy breakfast nook, an island and quartz countertops. Though she loved making meals on the stainless steel gas cooktop and in the smart convection wall oven, she didn't do it often enough when cooking only for herself these days.

Her attention turned to the wooden U-shaped staircase as her Selkirk Rex cat, Curlie—with her dense cream, black and lavender coat of long hair—came bounding down the stairs. Stefanie knelt to greet her, and the cat leaped into her arms, clearly overjoyed to see her.

Or maybe it was her subtle way of saying she was hungry.

Stefanie decided it was a combination of the two, and chuckled. "Love you, too, Curlie." She petted her head and along the cat's back before setting her down. "Let's feed you," she said, noting that Curlie had already dashed off into the kitchen.

After putting high-protein wet cat food in a bowl and setting it on the floor, Stefanie watched Curlie devour it while she grabbed a bottle of water out of the black refrigerator, opened it and drank a generous amount.

Her thoughts turned again to the dead woman at the park and what may have been behind it—before she found herself pulling the flyer out of her pocket that she had never gotten around to discarding in the trash. Instead of doing so now, she stared at the brief info on the Braison Family. It seemed welcoming enough. And breathed life in its messaging instead of death. Maybe she would check it out sometime.

Stefanie took the flyer with her as she headed up the stairs to wash a load of clothes and make plans for the rest of her day, which had been altered unexpectedly by heartbreak.

CAMPBELL WAS, QUITE FRANKLY, left with more questions than answers after parting ways with the lovely Stefanie Nguyen. The celebratory mood of Founder's Day had dampened, for him at least, with the strange death of the as-yet-unnamed young woman. What circumstances had led to her ending up naked and dead in Reston Hills Park? How long had she been deceased when her body was found? If her death wasn't self-inflicted, who had killed her? And did it have anything to do with the Braison Family cult?

Knowing he would need to exercise a little patience, Campbell took a proverbial chill pill as he drove away from the park. He would need to wait on the autopsy report to learn the exact cause of the woman's death, and pair that with any forensic evidence that might come from the

Crime Scene Investigation Unit that had been dispatched to the scene and could offer some useful findings in the case.

In the meantime, Campbell turned his thoughts to the one who'd discovered the corpse. All he really knew at the moment about Stefanie was that she was relatively new in town—which explained how he'd managed to miss running into her at some point, as he would definitely have remembered if he had seen her before—and originally from San Antonio.

So how did she end up in Reston Hills? Was she there alone? He hadn't seen a ring on her finger. That didn't mean she wasn't hitched. Or without a romantic partner. Any local who was single, available and age compatible would be lucky to have her, if he were basing it on looks alone.

But even beyond that, from what little exchange they'd had, she seemed pretty cool under fire after seeing the dead woman on the trail. Stefanie had even expressed regret in not being able to prevent what had happened, as if she would ever have been able to do so.

It did make him even more curious about her. What was her occupation? He wondered if she could have been a psychologist or counselor, experienced in working with people in trouble. Or did her compassion just come naturally?

Maybe I'll get to ask her these things sometime—and more, Campbell told himself, more than willing to open up about himself in return should the opportunity present itself.

He pulled into the parking lot of the Reston Hills Police Department on Fourteenth Street. When he stepped inside the building, Campbell wasn't at all surprised to see that it was short-staffed, with much of the personnel out in the field. Or taking the day off.

That wasn't the case with Gloria Schecter, chief of police, who was in her office, busy on her laptop. She'd been around since his father was on the force, working her way through the ranks to her present position. She noticed him through the open blinds on her window, acknowledging him routinely with a nod before continuing what she was doing.

Campbell sat on a mid-back swivel chair at a wooden desk in his low-walled cubicle, where he did paperwork on his last investigation of a burglary ring. Juvenile offenders had targeted several local businesses before they were finally apprehended. Another case solved, but whether the perps could learn a lesson from this remained to be seen.

"Hey," Campbell heard a voice say.

He looked up at Detective Georgina Alvarez, who was in her forties, tall and slim, with dark blond hair in a pixie cut.

"Hey," he said. "Isn't this your day off?"

"I wish." She rolled her brown eyes. "Or maybe not. Ted had to work today, so I figured I might as well come in."

Ted Peñaflor was a deputy sheriff with the Eckerslin County Sheriff's Department and Georgina's longtime boyfriend. Whenever Campbell had broached the subject of marriage, Georgina, having once been stood up at the altar, had taken the position of not wanting to rock the boat. Or, in her words, *"If it ain't broken, why would I want to fix it—possibly ruining a good thing?"*

Campbell had hardly been able to argue the point, considering that his previous relationship with Naomi had ended before he could ever put a ring on her finger. Meaning that they probably would have ended up in divorce court. But that didn't deter him from wanting to get married—should someone come along who could put that fever in him.

Georgina was saying, "Just got through taking a statement from a woman who accused her on-and-off-again boyfriend of abusing her—and had the bruises to back it up."

Campbell frowned. "Is he in custody?"

"Not yet. He'd fled the scene by the time officers arrived." Georgina sighed. "He won't get far. We've got a BOLO out on his Ford Bronco Sport Big Bend."

"Good." Campbell hated the thought of any kind of domestic violence. "If he's guilty, he needs to answer for his actions."

"I agree wholeheartedly." She sat at her nearby desk. "Heard you're investigating a naked body found in Reston Hills Park…"

"Yeah." He paused and thought about Stefanie, who'd come upon the corpse. "The dead woman somehow ended up on a trail near the river. Unnamed, for the time being. The death could certainly be described as peculiar—given both the location and lack of any clothing or identifying materials in the vicinity."

"Hmm…" Georgina made a face. "Looks like you have your work cut out for you."

"What else is new?" Campbell tossed at her sardonically. "The answers will be forthcoming soon enough." His only real question at this point was just how satisfactory those answers would be. And where they might lead.

When his shift ended, Campbell headed out in his take-home vehicle. He lived in a two-story, four-bedroom modern farmhouse on Charliss Lane. He'd purchased the place when returning to Reston Hills three and a half years ago, getting a good deal on it from the previous owners. Sitting on three acres of pristine land, he envisioned a place to raise a family someday and enjoy each other's company.

After parking in the driveway in front of the two-car garage, Campbell left his vehicle and walked up to the house. Striding onto the covered porch, which had a natural wood porch swing, he unlocked the door and went inside.

The main floor had high ceilings, a spacious great room, formal dining room, den and primary bedroom—all set on parquet hardwood flooring, with double-hung windows covered by vinyl vertical blinds—with rustic hickory furniture. The gourmet kitchen had granite countertops, its own eating space and all the modern appliances for cooking. Upstairs were two nice-size furnished bedrooms with their own en suite bathrooms, and an extra room that was currently used for storage. There was a wraparound back deck, with lots of room to roam free on the grassy spaces.

Basically, it was everything Campbell could ask for in a home. Well, almost. He wasn't particularly happy living all by his lonesome. Sharing the space with a significant other was high on his wish list. He imagined a beauty like Stefanie Nguyen would fit nicely here. First, he had to get to know her better and see if she was available and had any interest whatsoever in getting to know him—and take it from there.

Turning his thoughts to what to do for dinner, Campbell chose to take the easy way out and got on his cell phone to order a Philly cheesesteak pizza. It would go well with a bottle of beer that was in the side-by-side refrigerator. He could use the time to contemplate why a young woman would end up dead in Reston Hills Park on Founder's Day, of all days.

Chapter Three

The following morning, Campbell drove to work and was at his desk looking at his laptop as the forensic pathologist for the Eckerslin County Coroner's Office, Doctor Jennie Napier, appeared on the screen. In her mid-forties, she had blond hair in a blunt cut and green eyes behind square glasses.

Eager to hear the results on the unnamed dead woman, with the autopsy completed, Campbell asked, "What can you tell me about her?"

Jennie cleared her throat and said evenly, "Well, for starters, the death was a real tragedy, given that it was entirely preventable but happened anyway..." She took a breath. "The autopsy revealed that the decedent ingested a lethal amount of fentanyl that was mixed with carfentanil, a fentanyl analog—dying of acute fentanyl intoxication. The actual cause of death was fentanyl bromazolam—diazepam toxicity, to be exact."

"So, she died of a drug overdose?" Campbell said.

"Yes," Jennie responded surely.

"Self-administered?" he wondered. "Or, in other words, apart from whomever provided the fentanyl, could someone other than the decedent herself have given her the lethal dose deliberately?" He suspected the forensic pathologist would throw the ball back to his side of the court as the investigating police detective. He wanted to put it out there anyway to get her professional opinion.

Jennie remained poised as she answered. "Insofar as the overdose itself, the victim could have ingested the fentanyl voluntarily—or unknowing of the deadly consequences. But there's also good reason to believe that this wasn't an accidental overdose—"

Campbell cocked a brow. "Oh...?"

"There were cuts and abrasions on the decedent's arms, legs and feet, that had bloody blisters as well," she pointed out. "This would seem to indicate that she had been running while naked in the park in the wee hours of Founder's Day—as though away from someone, rather than haphazardly in a drug-abuse haze—hitting branches and shrubbery along the way. Before the fentanyl poisoning took its strongest effect and she lost consciousness, never to wake up."

"Meaning, we could be looking at outright murder," he said matter-of-factly. This included violations of Idaho state law regarding drug-induced homicide, making it a felony to supply fentanyl or any other illicit drugs that led to the death of a person. And federal law that involved the distributing of fentanyl that caused serious bodily injury and death of the victim.

Jennie pushed up her glasses. "That's something for you to determine conclusively, Detective," she told him. "But it does appear that the decedent may well have been fleeing for her life when she died—and, as such, was already doomed."

"That's one way to look at it," Campbell said, gazing at her. Another was that she'd taken a wrong turn, figuratively speaking, putting her on the path in life that could have still been survivable under other circumstances. Either way he sliced it, she'd died way too soon, and Campbell was intent on holding accountable the drug dealer or individual who'd ended the life of a young woman. "Was she sexually assaulted?" he asked.

Jennie shook her head. "There was no sign of a sexual assault."

"Okay." He had to ask, given the way the victim was found and how it could have been a factor in her death.

"Oh, something else caught my eye..." Jennie cut into his thoughts. "I couldn't help but notice that the decedent had the initials KB tattooed onto her right forearm. A boyfriend, perhaps?"

"Perhaps," Campbell went along for effect. He certainly couldn't rule out that the young woman might well have had a romantic relationship with cult leader Kenneth Braison. But the bigger question was whether or not he or his group had anything to do with her death. "We'll see about that and its relevance, if anything," Campbell told the forensic pathologist before ending the briefing.

CAMPBELL PULLED UP the digital case file from the department's Cold Case Unit on Lynda Boxleitner. Twenty years ago, in an investigation led by Detective Mason Sawyer, his father, the forty-one-year-old waitress and former cheerleader at Reston Hills High School was found dead and naked in Reston Hills Park on Founder's Day.

She had a broken nose, and there were other signs of physical duress.

But what had killed her was poison.

According to the Eckerslin County Coroner's Office, Lynda Boxleitner had died from ingesting thallium sulfate, a highly toxic poisonous compound used primarily as an insecticide and rodenticide. Her death was ruled a homicide.

Campbell noted that she had been branded on her right forearm with the letters WB tattooed on it, which were said to be the initials for Wendell Braison, the then-leader of the Braison Family before it was eventually taken over by his son, Kenneth.

Though the elder Braison had long been thought to have been responsible for Lynda's death, Campbell's father had been unable to prove it, and Wendell Braison was never charged with killing her.

And neither was anyone else, Campbell thought, of the case that went as cold as ice. He gazed at the photograph of Lynda Boxleitner, whom his father had dated briefly in high school before meeting and falling in love with Campbell's mother, Alyssa. The picture was of Lynda in a cheerleader outfit from her younger years that showed off her voluptuous figure.

Though he didn't see any clear-cut physical similarities between Lynda Boxleitner and the still-unidentified woman killed at the park on Founder's Day twenty years later, given the similar circumstances that befell the women, Campbell couldn't help but wonder if the deaths weren't connected in some way. Perhaps the apple didn't fall far from the tree where it concerned Wendell Braison, who died seven years ago, his son Kenneth and murder.

I'll need to find out by paying the Braison Family compound a visit, Campbell told himself.

WITH HER HAIR in a high ponytail, Stefanie stood barefoot on a purple mat in the front of her studio on Haegadon Lane for a power yoga class, wearing an orange crop tank and brown high-waist leggings. There were ten women in attendance for the physical and mental exercises, including Bella, who wore a red sports bra and white retro shorts on her toned, long-legged body.

With upbeat music playing, Stefanie took the lead in doing the intermediate routines, happy to lend her expertise to those in attendance. She was still reeling over finding the dead woman at the park yesterday, and could imagine her being part of the yoga class someday had her life not been extinguished.

"Call me anytime," Detective Campbell Sawyer had told her when handing her his card, with respect to the investigation.

I wonder if I should take him up on that? Stefanie asked herself, anxious to learn more about the poor woman's tragic death, as there had been no update on the case from the authorities. Apart from that, it would be nice to get to know the handsome detective—though she realized that might well mean discovering he was married with two children or engaged to the love of his life.

Stefanie frowned at the thought while refocusing on the yoga routines, which everyone seemed to be enjoying.

After the session ended, Bella, wiping perspiration from her brow with a towel, said, "Wow! That was a great workout, mind and body."

Stefanie smiled. "Glad you enjoyed it."

"What's not to like?" Bella grinned. "I'll have to give your tai chi class a try."

"You should," Stefanie encouraged her. "You'd be a natural."

"Hmm...maybe." Bella flung the towel over her shoulder. "Heard anything else about the dead woman in the park?"

"Not yet." Stefanie looked at her, knowing that she had the connections in town to get answers. "How about you?"

"Only that the autopsy has been completed, though the results haven't been released yet to the public." Bella wrinkled her nose. "Guess we'll know when we know how she died and what to make of it."

"True." Stefanie decided at that moment to take the plunge and give Campbell a call to see what he'd learned, for better or worse. She headed to the locker room, pulled her hair from the ponytail and hopped into the shower.

THE BRAISON FAMILY compound was located off South Petriss Road on around ten acres of rural land in an unincorporated area on the outskirts of Reston Hills. It consisted of one big ranch-style house and a number of cabins, where many members of the cult lived. Campbell wondered if this was where the OD victim had stayed before her death. And had someone there supplied her with the lethal fentanyl, making them complicit in the woman's demise?

As he walked past people—mostly in their twenties, thirties, and forties, but some children as well—who seemed almost oblivious to his presence, as though they'd been told to ignore outsiders, Campbell definitely felt out of place. Just as he was sure his father had been when visiting the same compound two decades ago in the pursuit of justice for the victim he was investigating.

Observing a gathering of people surrounding a man whom Campbell recognized as the cult leader, Kenneth Braison, he headed in that direction. He wanted to speak with the one person most likely to give him at least some of the answers he sought.

As his followers parted the way like sheep, Campbell walked up to the charismatic leader. In his early forties and with blue-gray eyes, Kenneth was a couple of inches taller and firmly built, with long, wavy brown hair combed backward, thick brows and a circle beard.

Kenneth brushed his long nose and said curtly, "Detective Sawyer... What brings you to my neck of the woods this time?"

Campbell peered at him and responded with an edge to his voice, "On Founder's Day, a woman was discovered in Reston Hills Park—dead from an overdose of fentanyl."

"Sorry to hear that," Kenneth uttered tonelessly. "Again, why are you here?"

"We think that she was part of the so-called Braison Family," Campbell replied bluntly. "As she was found naked and with no identification—apart from your initials tattooed on her right forearm—I need you to identify her..." Campbell watched Kenneth react to this before he took his cell phone out of his sport coat and pulled up a picture of the initials on the victim's arm. "Look familiar?"

"Yes, it does," Kenneth admitted. He added defensively, "We don't require anyone to do what she or he doesn't want to do. The initials are all about showing you're serious about being a part of our community and not here for games. That's it."

Campbell was sure there was pressure to capitulate, as a way to maintain control over his flock. "I'm not here for games," he pointed out sharply and then showed him a photo of the woman's face in death.

Kenneth took a long look at the decedent's face before sucking in a deep breath, then saying evenly, "Her name is Mia O'Dell."

Campbell took note of this. "How old was she?"

"Twenty-eight. Or so I was told."

"When was the last time you saw her?"

"A couple of days ago," he claimed.

Campbell set his jaw. "Did she live here?"

"Yeah, Mia stayed in one of the cabins when she chose to be at the compound."

Campbell peered at him. "Have any idea how she ended up at the park naked and strung out on drugs?"

Kenneth shrugged. "Wish I could say I did, but afraid not. There are no guards or gates keeping anyone locked in against their will—as opposed to keeping unwanted intruders out. So people tend to come and go as they please. It's better that way." He lowered his chin. "As to OD'ing on fentanyl, we do not use drugs here, Detective, as you discovered the last time we were graced with your presence. We have no control over what people choose to do away from the Braison Family ranch. Apparently, Mia decided to play by her own rules when she was elsewhere…"

"I think she was playing by the rules of whomever supplied her with the deadly fentanyl," Campbell countered straightforwardly.

"You could be right about that," Kenneth said. "But you won't find that person here. As I said, we don't allow drug use or dealing on this property."

"Wish I could simply take your word for that. But it doesn't work that way when investigating a homicide."

Kenneth flinched. "You said she OD'd…"

"She did," Campbell reiterated. "But whoever gave Mia the drugs could be criminally liable for killing her—and won't get away with it."

"Nor should they," Kenneth said in agreement.

But he was too smug for Campbell's comfort. "Where were you in the early hours of Founder's Day?" he asked him directly, in corresponding with the estimated time of Mia's fentanyl exposure and death.

Kenneth answered quickly, "Right here—all night long and throughout the day. We celebrated Founder's Day here at the ranch." He paused. "Or most of the Family did."

"Can anyone vouch for this?" Campbell asked acutely.

"How about everyone?" Kenneth responded with ease. "We had a bonfire and sang songs. It was a real lovefest. Feel free to ask anyone."

Campbell doubted that any of his followers would contradict his alibi. Certainly not any who were still alive. Meaning that he likely wouldn't get very far in loosening any tongues if the man had drugged Mia. Or had taken or followed her to Reston Hills Park.

Campbell thought he might try a different tack. "You mind if I take a look around?"

"Not at all," Kenneth began, then added, "So long as you have a warrant. If not, then I do mind. This is private property, and we like to guard it like Fort Knox from any unreasonable intrusion. I'm sure you understand?"

Only too well, Campbell told himself. Braison was buying time for himself or others to cover any tracks that needed to be covered. That still didn't mean someone there was directly responsible for what happened to Mia O'Dell. But the resistance certainly caused his suspicious meter to shoot up.

"I'm sure I'll be back with the search warrant," he told him warningly.

Kenneth ran a hand across his mouth and glared. "Do what you must."

Campbell held his gaze. "I'll show myself out." He walked away and could feel all eyes on him as if he intended to break up their happy home. Only if there was good reason to. Like being responsible for one death. Or maybe two poisonous deaths crossing two long decades.

KENNETH BRAISON WATCHED intently as Detective Campbell Sawyer left the compound. He seemed full of himself. Just like his father, Mason Sawyer, who had once gone after Kenneth's own father, Wendell Braison. Decades ago, he had been accused of poisoning to death Lynda Boxleitner, a former member of the Braison Family. But the investigation had gone nowhere.

Though Kenneth had long suspected that his father had murdered Lynda—one of his then-lovers—after she had rebuffed his advances, he had denied this till his dying breath. Maybe he simply couldn't bring himself to come clean, not even to his only flesh-and-blood relative. Or maybe his father had been innocent after all and someone else inside the Braison Family, or outside of it, had killed Lynda for whatever reason.

Now Kenneth felt it was like déjà vu. Only this time, Mason Sawyer's son had all but accused him of killing Mia. Though they had slept together a few times, he had more action than he could handle and had no wish to end her life. Nor did he believe any other Family member would dare to do something without his permission that would damage its reputation. Much less, put them under the microscope again in a criminal investigation of that magnitude.

But then, even with his powerful position as the undisputed leader of the Braison Family, did that truly mean that someone hadn't decided to supply Mia with a life-ending drug? And if so, had her death been accidental? Or was there a reason why someone would have wanted her dead?

He headed to his residence for a moment or two of further contemplation, knowing he would need to gather everyone to share the unfortunate news of the unexpected passing of one of their own.

Chapter Four

Campbell was only too happy to invite Stefanie Nguyen for coffee at Harriette's Café after she called him for an update on the investigation. He would have preferred that she was calling with anything she may have remembered or learned regarding the death of Mia O'Dell. But if truth be told, he was willing to meet Stefanie under any circumstances to get to know her better.

Fortunately, she accepted his invitation. A good sign, perhaps. The fact that it happened to be an off day for Sarah Huffstetler was even better. Though Stefanie had absolutely nothing to worry about insofar as his being interested in Sarah, beyond their one date, he'd just as soon not have her serving them and suggesting there was something between them for Stefanie to chew on.

When she came into the café, he waved her over to the booth by the window, thinking that she was definitely a sight for sore eyes.

Standing, he grinned in greeting her. "Hey."

"Hi." Stefanie smiled back.

"Thanks for coming."

"No problem, Detective Sawyer," she said politely. "I had some free time, so…"

"Sit," Campbell told her, and watched as she slid into one side of the booth, then he sat across from her. "Feel free to call me Campbell," he said, not wanting this to be formal, like an interrogation.

"Okay." She smiled. "So long as you call me Stefanie."

"I will." He smiled back, hoping he would get to use the name often.

Almost as if on cue, a short fortysomething waitress with a red shag haircut and round glasses came over with a pot of coffee, filling the two cups at their request.

After she left, Stefanie lifted her cup, took a sip and cut right to the chase, "So, where do things stand in the investigation—if I may ask? Did you find out who the woman is…?"

Campbell tasted his own coffee, having added cream, and responded, knowing it was all about to break, "Her name is Mia O'Dell. She was a local and twenty-eight. An autopsy revealed that she died as a result of fentanyl poisoning."

Stefanie's mouth opened, rueful. "That's awful."

"I know," he concurred. "Unfortunately, the drug epidemic in this country is very real. Even in a small town like Reston Hills, fentanyl use and abuse is a problem. In this case, the victim's fatal overdose, who gave her the fentanyl and how she wound up naked in the park are still under investigation." He didn't want to get too ahead of himself, but he felt that Stefanie, having discovered the body, deserved to be kept in the loop, at least to some extent. "Mia was a member of a local cult when she died…"

Stefanie lifted a brow. "You mean the Braison Family?"

Campbell looked at her with surprise. "You know about them?"

"Only what I've heard, which hasn't been much, really,"

she replied. "At the park yesterday, a member handed me a flyer while doing her best to prop up the group." She met his eyes. "You think they may have had something to do with her death?"

He sipped his coffee, musing. "It's entirely possible," he told her frankly. "So far, we have no proof that the fentanyl came from someone in the Braison Family. Or that the victim used it of her own accord, as opposed to with malice intent. Either way, you might want to stay away from their compound right now to be on the safe side."

"I understand." Stefanie sipped her coffee. "That's not really my type of thing," she told him.

"Good." Campbell didn't exactly mean to pass judgment on anyone who chose to align oneself with a cult. To each their own. But most who did were usually searching for some real meaning to life that might not yield the desired results. Especially if drugs were involved, along with the powers of persuasion that were misused. In this instance, he preferred not to have to compete for her attention with the likes of Kenneth Braison. Or, for that matter, any hot-blooded male who was attracted to her like he was.

Campbell couldn't help but wonder if he wasn't already too late to make a play for her affections. He decided it was best to ask in a roundabout way. "What brought you to Reston Hills?" Or was it who?

Stefanie stared at the question, her expression one of sadness. Then she said, maudlinly, "Two years ago, I lost my husband, Edward—a firefighter—after he was trapped in a wildfire that got totally out of control."

"I'm sorry to hear that." Campbell had nothing but deep respect for those who were willing to put their lives on the line to snuff out dangerous fires. Obviously, in this instance, it came at a high price.

"It was brutal for a while there," she admitted. "Being reminded of the life we had together—before any children could come along—was difficult, to say the least. Things got better over time." She took a breath. "Still, after a while, honestly, I felt I needed a change of pace. This seemed like a great location to make that change—so I sold my yoga and tai chi studio in San Antonio and opened a new one here."

I guess there's no one in her life at the moment, Campbell thought, figuring that after two years of being a widow, she might be ready to start dating again. "Glad you chose to make a home in Reston Hills," he told her, even if that optimism may have taken a hit after finding a dead body. He hoped that wouldn't make her want to flee at the first opportunity to do so.

"I have no regrets," she said, as if reading his mind. "Not counting what I stumbled upon yesterday. Sad as it was, I realize it could just as easily have happened in San Antonio—and, in fact, had more often than I care to admit, as drug addiction and overdoses were an issue there, too."

Campbell admired her courage and ability to put things in a proper perspective, difficult as that may be. "That is something that needs to be addressed nationwide," he told her. "But running from the problem and problems it creates is never the answer for any of us."

"I agree." Stefanie ran a hand through her hair, which was slightly damp, as if she had just showered. "So, I understand that police work runs in your family—"

"Yes, it does." He was surprised to hear her say that and couldn't help but ask, curiously, "Have you been checking up on me…?"

"Of course not." She colored. "Bella Reston mentioned it to me yesterday at the park, after I told her you were investigating the woman's death."

"Bella…" Campbell sat back. "Why am I not surprised? Count on her to be the welcoming committee for newcomers."

Stefanie smiled. "She said you went to the same high school and that your father and hers were friends back in the day."

"The first part was true, though being a couple of years older than her, we didn't travel in the same circles, so to speak. As for the rest, I wouldn't exactly say that our fathers were friends. My dad did do some off-duty work for Bella's father from time to time, like extra security at one of his fundraisers or things like that."

"I see." Stefanie was thoughtful. "So, have you always worked for the Reston Hills Police Department?"

"Just for the last three and a half years," Campbell told her. "Before that, I worked as a detective for the Boise Police Department. Guess I wanted to spread my wings somewhat—even though I was inspired by my dad to go into law enforcement."

She angled her face to the right and asked inquisitively. "Why did you move back home, if you don't mind my asking?"

"I don't." He rubbed his chin and contemplated the question. "It was due to a combination of too much stress on the job, too little return on my efforts, a failed relationship and homesickness." Campbell gazed into his empty cup. "Also, it gave me the chance to get closer to my father, which hadn't always been the case since my mother's death years earlier."

Stefanie gave him a knowing look. "I lost my own parents when I was just a teenager, but cherish all the time that I had with them. I'm glad you took the opportunity to bond with your father while you still could."

"Me too." Campbell found himself liking her more and more with each passing moment. If it were strictly up to him, he could sit there talking with her all day—and even into the night. But he was still on duty and sure she had other things on her plate to do. "Well, I won't take up any more of your time today," he said reluctantly.

"And I shouldn't take up any more of yours," she said with a straight look.

Believe me, I don't mind one bit, Campbell told himself, but responded, "Glad I was able to let you know where things stand at the moment in the investigation."

"So am I." She offered him a smile.

After paying for the coffee, he walked her to her car, where Campbell said tentatively, "Maybe we could do this again sometime?"

Stefanie nodded. "Works for me."

"Okay." He hoped that would be sooner rather than later, but wouldn't push it just yet.

She got into her Subaru Legacy, started it and drove out of the parking lot.

Campbell followed suit in his own vehicle, trailing for a bit before turning in a different direction at an intersection. He wondered where things could go between them, allowing his imagination to run wild for a moment or two, before coming back down to earth. Then he turned his attention to the ill-timed death of Mia O'Dell and the circumstances that may have led up to it. What might his father have to say about this, given the almost eerie similarities to a case he'd investigated twenty years ago?

STEFANIE DROVE DOWN Pickford Street, away from Harriette's Café, glancing up at the rearview mirror to see that Campbell's car was no longer there, as if his vehicle had disappeared into thin air. She almost wished he had followed her home, and they could have talked some more. Apart from getting the scoop on what his investigation had uncovered on Mia O'Dell's death, Stefanie welcomed the conversation beyond that unsettling news. It had been a while since she had opened up like that to a man, and she felt good about this. The fact that he had indicated an interest in seeing each other again, while not necessarily in relation to police work, was something she was totally amenable to. She wanted a full life in Reston Hills, beyond her yoga studio and hanging with Bella. Now was the time to push forward with that and see where she landed.

After pulling up to her house, she went inside and was greeted by Curlie. "Hey, you," Stefanie said, chuckling as the cat lifted it paws onto the leg of her boot-cut jeans. "Looks like you've missed me. Well, back at you."

Picking her up, Stefanie kissed the cat on the top of her head, which Curlie evidently enjoyed. Or at least the attention.

Stefanie fed her and left her alone, while she walked into the living room and took out her cell phone. After sitting on a gray mid-century-modern accent chair, she called Bella for a video chat, wanting to fill her in on the latest in case she hadn't heard.

Bella accepted the chat and said cheerfully, "Hey."

"Hey." Stefanie kept a serious look on her face. "Got a sec?"

"Yes, I'm all yours. What's up?"

"I just met with Detective Sawyer... Campbell," Stefanie told her.

Bella's eyes widened. "Really?"

"Yes, we had coffee at Harriette's Café while he provided an update on the case."

"I see." Bella narrowed her gaze. "What did he say?"

"The woman's name is Mia O'Dell," Stefanie told her.

"What?" Bella looked shocked. "Mia...?"

"I take it you knew her?" Stefanie said, based on the reaction.

"She used to work for my father as his housekeeper," Bella pointed out. "We weren't close or anything, but I'd see her in town every now and then." She sighed. "Now she's dead. How?"

"Drug overdose," Stefanie told her. "Campbell said that she died from fentanyl poisoning."

"That's terrible." Bella's brow furrowed. "Didn't realize she was into that."

"She may not have been," Stefanie pointed out. "Campbell's investigating how she came to have the fentanyl in her system and if the death was accidental or deliberate."

Bella reacted, a thin brow shooting up. "He thinks someone could have intentionally caused Mia to OD on fentanyl?"

"Possibly. Or otherwise played a part in her ending up naked, alone and dead in the park." Stefanie took a breath. "Apparently, Mia was involved with the Braison Family cult. Are you familiar with them?"

"Yes," Bella answered matter-of-factly and as a local historian. "They've been around these parts for decades—started by a controversial and charismatic man named Wendell Braison—attracting those most susceptible to life outside the mainstream. As far as I'm aware, they haven't caused much trouble, apart from occasional skirmishes with the law, and don't seem to be a hot bed for drug activity. But then, what do I know?"

She became thoughtful, prompting Stefanie to ask curiously, "What?"

Bella licked her lips and answered, "Well, I do seem to recall years ago when another woman who belonged to the cult was found dead at the park—on Founder's Day, of all things. I'm sketchy on the details, but I don't believe the case was ever solved..."

"Hmm." Stefanie found that intriguing. What were the odds? "Coincidence?"

"What else could it be?" Bella offered. "Just popped into my head. Let's see if Campbell can reach the right conclusions in the death of Mia O'Dell."

"Agreed." Stefanie had a sense that he would. She could only hope that Mia's fatal drug overdose wasn't nefarious in intent.

After disconnecting from the video chat, Stefanie pondered the tragedy while also wondering if the Braison Family could have been behind it. Or were they truly harmless for the most part, as Bella had suggested?

Maybe I need to see for myself, Stefanie thought. If only to put her mind at ease in feeling a kinship of sorts to Mia, whom she'd happened upon, as though to help her rest in peace, if at all possible.

Chapter Five

Campbell drove down the dirt road off Saldnon Street till reaching his father's horse ranch in Fallon's Creek, Idaho, some twenty miles from Reston Hills. After leaving the police force nearly a decade ago following his wife's death, Mason Sawyer bought the one-hundred-and-seventy-five-acre private property, east of the Caribou-Targhee National Forest. There, he raised American quarter horses, Appaloosas, and Percherons, offered trail rides, and seemed at peace.

Or at least, that was how Campbell saw it as he pulled up in front of the main house behind his father's black Land Rover Range Rover Evoque and a red Hyundai Tucson hybrid that belonged to his longtime girlfriend, Sally Panettiere. He hadn't been able to bring himself to marry again.

Standing in the driveway, Campbell watched as his father and Sally rode up to him on their horses.

Mason Sawyer was in his early sixties and had gray hair in a flow cut and a horseshoe mustache. With his work on the ranch and weightlifting, he had managed to stay in shape since his days on the force. Touching the wide brim of his off-white suede cowboy hat, Mason peered at

Campbell through blue eyes and said tonelessly, "This is a surprise."

"Guess I should've called," Campbell admitted, but he felt that this was something that needed to be discussed in person. So he took his chances. He regarded Sally, a book editor, who was in her late fifties, slender and hazel-eyed, with a blond shullet haircut, wearing an almond-colored straw cowgirl hat. "Hey, Sally."

"Hey to you, Campbell." She showed her teeth. "Believe me, your dad's just as happy to see you as I am."

"She's right," Mason said, leaving no doubt. "You're always welcome here, surprise or not."

"Thanks." Campbell grinned, comforted with the thought but still wishing he had texted him first. He gazed at his father and asked, "Can we talk?"

"Sure," Mason told him. "We'll put the horses in the stables and meet you inside."

"Okay." Campbell watched as they rode off, then he headed for the house. He had a key but rarely used it, preferring not to intrude if uninvited. In this instance, he had his father's permission.

The spacious ranch house was amid mature chokecherry trees with a pond nearby. He unlocked the door and went inside, looking at the open-layout with lots of windows and Western style furnishings on plank flooring. It was the type of place his mother would have loved, had she lived long enough to see it.

But life didn't always work in ways that were understandable. He got that. At least his dad had found a way to move on, and with someone who made him happy in her own right. Just as his mother had.

Twenty minutes later, Campbell was sitting on the back porch with Mason on Adirondack chairs. Both were drinking fresh lemonade that Sally made for them. Resting on the floor, as if with nothing better to do, was Mason's dog, a male yellow Labrador retriever named Hopper.

After a moment or two, Campbell got to the point when he said, "I'm working on a case involving a young woman named Mia O'Dell, who died on Founder's Day from fentanyl poisoning."

"Hadn't heard," Mason said. "Sorry for her."

"So am I." Campbell looked at him. "She was found in Reston Hills Park—naked. The initials KB were tattooed on her right forearm. I was able to establish that they were short for Kenneth Braison, the current leader of the Braison Family cult—"

"Really?" Mason tasted the lemonade as his expression grew more distraught. "Interesting..."

"I had the same reaction, all things considered," Campbell admitted. "I took a look at the cold case that you investigated twenty years ago involving the death of Lynda Boxleitner. The similarities were uncanny, right down to the tattooed initials WB on her forearm—albeit, which were short for Wendell Braison, Kenneth Braison's father. I couldn't help but wonder if the two deaths could be connected in one way or another?"

Mason's brow furrowed. "Two decades is a long time, son."

"But not so long that a killer couldn't have hung around from one murder to let history repeat itself, for whatever reason," Campbell suggested, even if he knew it would be a hard sell. Even for himself.

"I suppose." His father brought the glass of lemonade to his mouth. "One problem with that theory is that Wendell Braison, the chief suspect in the murder of Lynda Boxleitner, died seven plus years ago. Though I was never quite able to nail him, no one else surfaced to the degree that I came to believe I had targeted the wrong man. So unless Wendell found a way to rise from the dead, there's no way he could have been responsible for the latest death. Besides that, Lynda died from thallium sulfate poisoning, as opposed to fentanyl that you say Mia O'Dell OD'd on. Lynda's death was ruled a definite homicide. Apparently, that wasn't the case with Mia's. Doesn't seem to add up."

Though he agreed at face value, Campbell said, "Clearly, Wendell Braison did not kill Mia. But maybe his son picked up where he left off—right down to all but staging Mia's naked body at the park on Founder's Day to practically mimic the death of Lynda Boxleitner. As for fatally poisoning the victim with fentanyl mixed with the fentanyl analog, carfentanil, instead of thallium sulfate, it could be mainly a matter of accessibility. Go with what you have—in abundance these days for practically anyone who wishes to obtain it on the black market. Though the coroner didn't outright declare the death a homicide, she might as well have. Aside from going after the drug dealer for supplying the fatal dose of fentanyl, cuts and abrasions on the victim's arms, legs, and feet indicate that there's a good possibility she was trying to get away from whomever may have given her the drug, as though in fear of her life. That amounts to murder, in my book." *Or close enough to warrant a serious investigation into the death*, he told himself, sipping the lemonade.

Mason jutted his chin. "Have to admit, it smells fishy—the whole thing." He paused. "I assume you've questioned Kenneth Braison?"

"Yes, I questioned him," Campbell verified.

"And...?"

"And the jury's still out on that," he told his father.

"Braison apparently has an alibi for the estimated time of Mia's death. But given that those in his inner circle will likely say whatever he tells them to, I'm not ready just yet to see that as the gospel—till we can get into the compound, where Mia was staying, with a search warrant. It's also more than possible that if Kenneth Braison was the one pulling the strings in killing her, it wouldn't have been difficult to get someone else to do his bidding as a loyal soldier for the cause."

"I suppose." Mason ran a hand across the dog's head. "If the Braison Family is behind both deaths—a generational murder pack of sorts—I hope you can succeed in piecing together where I fell short."

"So do I." Campbell eyed his strained profile. "But for the record, you investigated the Boxleitner murder to the best of your ability with what you had to work with, Dad. No one still around today on the force faults you for being unable to solve the case. Unfortunately, cold cases are a part of law enforcement across the country. Hell, even around the world. We can't solve them all—even if we wanted to."

"You're right about that," Mason said, with a catch to his voice. "Somehow, though—strange as it sounds all these years later—I felt as if I let Lynda down in not being able to allow her the dignity of being able to rest in peace."

"Doesn't sound strange at all," Campbell said. "You and Lynda dated once, giving you a reason to take what happened to her personally on some level. Just as we both had to deal with some things when Mom died—though the cause of her death was quite different." He drew a breath. "Maybe my investigation can make things right for you with Lynda. Or at least give those close to Mia some closure."

Mason pinched the bridge of his nose. "I appreciate that, son. About your mother, too, whom I loved dearly, just as you did—and still miss very much."

"Same here," Campbell told him.

"I kept some info from my investigation," Mason said. "I'll go through it and see if anything comes up that may be of use to you in your case—"

"Okay." Campbell finished off the drink, happy to have his help. He hoped to return the favor by making a more concerted effort to visit the ranch more often, now that he was a resident of Reston Hills again. "I'd better go," he told him, getting to his feet.

Mason nodded. "I'll walk you out."

Campbell grinned at his childhood memories. He'd loved spending as much time as possible with his dad, and those moments had seemed like they would last forever. Till his mother passed and everything seemed to change. Now they were back on the right track, more or less, and trying to start building new memories.

MASON STOOD NEXT to Hopper as they watched Campbell drive off. Having Lynda Boxleitner's strange death brought back to the surface had thrown him for a loop, as he digested what his son had come there to say. The fact that another woman had died pretty much the same way and was left naked in the park like trash was disturbing, to say the least. Having it occur on Founder's Day was all the more troubling.

What was up with that?

Was someone trying to tell him something? Perhaps Lynda or even Wendell Braison—from the grave—wanted to show there was a real connection between the past and present that couldn't be ignored?

Had Kenneth Braison truly decided to walk in his father's shoes, killing one of his followers that he considered uncooperative? Someone threatening the cult's very existence?

Can I really find the answers to Lynda's unfortunate death that have eluded me for over twenty years with the help of my son? Mason asked himself. Or did one death really have nothing to do with the other? He wondered what he had missed and if it could ever turn back the hands of time in delivering justice for Lynda, who didn't deserve to have her life ended that way.

It occurred to Mason that perhaps he had been looking in the wrong direction by going after Wendell. Maybe the same was true for Campbell as he focused on Kenneth Braison. Maybe someone else was the true enemy and was intent on throwing them off the trail.

Or maybe they were definitely on the right track with the Braison Family and only needed to make their case.

When he heard the front door open, Mason turned and saw Sally walk out toward him. Hopper ran up to her.

Sally had a worried look on her face as she regarded Mason and asked him, "Everything all right?"

He thought about it, wanting to just give a pat answer. But knowing how much she had come to mean to him as his partner in life and the closest thing Campbell had to a mother with Alyssa no longer in the picture, Mason regarded his girlfriend and responded truthfully, "Not so much, really. But maybe it can be."

"How?" she asked ill at ease.

He put his arm around her shoulders and replied, "I'll explain inside…"

STEFANIE WASN'T QUITE sure what to expect when she drove through the gates and into the Braison Family compound.

Was it a mistake to go there and try to get a read on presumably the last place that Mia O'Dell had spent her final hours prior to ending up at Reston Hills Park? *Maybe I should leave the sleuthing up to Campbell and the police department*, Stefanie thought. Then she half joked to herself, *What fun would that be?*

Truthfully, she considered this anything but an exercise in fun and frolic. Beyond that, she would just have to play it by ear.

After parking, Stefanie exited the car and was met by Jasmine and a tall, brawny Hispanic man in his thirties with a bald head and crooked nose.

"Greetings," Jasmine said spiritedly. "Stefanie, right?"

"Yes, good memory," Stefanie told her, considering all the people she must regularly try to recruit.

"I make it my business to remember anyone I get a good vibe from," she said sincerely, and looked at the man. "This is Juan."

Stefanie smiled. "Hi."

He didn't smile back, as if resistant to any outsiders. "Hello," he said stiffly.

"Anyway, I wanted to take you up on the invite, Jasmine," Stefanie told her, "and check out the place."

Jasmine beamed. "I'm so glad you did."

"Me too," Stefanie said hastily as she gazed at the stone-faced Juan.

Jasmine took her hand and said, "Come, let me show you around..."

"Okay," Stefanie agreed, watching Juan head off in another direction but still peering at her.

Jasmine noticed and said, "Don't pay any attention to him. He's naturally suspicious of anyone who wants to see what we're all about, as though we're supposed to be closed off to expanding our tent. That isn't the case at all," she argued.

"Cool." Stefanie smiled. She had no intention of joining the cult, but she was most interested in what she could learn about Mia.

After being led around the open country space that included fruit trees, crops and farm animals for a self-sustaining lifestyle, Jasmine introduced Stefanie to a few of the members, then took her to a cabin.

"This is where I live," Jasmine said proudly.

Stefanie took a sweeping glance around the cozy cabin with bamboo flooring and wicker furniture. "Nice," she told her.

"I try to make it as comfortable as possible."

Stefanie smiled softly. "Do you know Mia O'Dell?" she asked evenly.

"Yes, Mia's part of the Braison Family," Jasmine said. "Are you friends with her?"

She doesn't seem to know what happened to Mia, Stefanie thought. *I have to tell her.*

But before she could, a tall and fit bearded man with presence walked into the cabin, and Jasmine said, with eyes wide with admiration, "Kenneth—"

"Hey." He regarded her with a serious look, then turned to Stefanie and said, "I'm Kenneth Braison."

The head of the Braison Family, Stefanie deduced by his commanding presence. "Stefanie Nguyen."

Kenneth shook her hand. "Nice to meet you, Stefanie."

"You too," she told him politely.

"I trust that you've been made to feel welcome to our little slice of paradise?"

"Yes." Stefanie flashed a smile. "Thanks to Jasmine." She looked at her and got a grin in return.

Kenneth fixed his eyes to Jasmine's face and told her intently, "Everyone's meeting in the courtyard in five minutes."

She nodded. "All right."

All three left the cabin, where Juan was waiting outside. Kenneth eyed Stefanie and said succinctly, "Hope you'll come again. Juan will show you out…"

Stefanie glanced at Juan and understood that this was Kenneth's way of telling her it was time to leave, whether she was ready to or not. She looked at Jasmine, who seemed confused, but didn't dare voice an objection. Nor did Stefanie wish for her to put herself at any risk. Especially after what had happened to Mia. Or perhaps because of it.

After leaving the compound, Stefanie wondered if Campbell might be up for having dinner with her. There was only one way to find out.

KENNETH SENSED THAT Stefanie Nguyen was on a fishing expedition rather than truly being interested in becoming part of their family. He'd heard through the grapevine that she was the one who found Mia in the park. So, was she visiting the compound on behalf of Campbell Sawyer, to see if he could connect her death to the Braison Family? Or was it a personal quest by Stefanie to see what rocks she could overturn for her own curiosity?

Either way, Kenneth was not about to let the group his father started be torn apart. Not as he was now the head of the Family. That included making sure that Stefanie stayed in her own lane—as a yoga instructor, he'd learned—if she knew what was good for her.

With everyone now gathered before him, Kenneth sucked in a deep breath and said, with the appropriate remorse, "I have some news to share with you… It's with a heavy heart that I just learned that one of our own, Mia O'Dell, died on Founder's Day from a drug overdose." He watched for a moment as the expected moans and murmurs came from his flock. "She was found in Reston Hills Park. Though I'm sure this comes as a shock to most of you, given that drug use is strictly prohibited on these grounds, Mia may have fallen in with the wrong crowd outside of our reach…and paid the price…"

Kenneth saw this as an opportunity to further separate the Braison Family from outside influences and their decidedly negative play on human nature. If this made them stronger, then all the better. He could only hope that Mia's death wouldn't make its way back to him and everything he stood for. Just as his father had before him.

Chapter Six

"Do you like Vietnamese food?" Stefanie asked Campbell over the phone. Not that it was the extent of what she liked to cook, but it seemed like a nice way to go for starters, if he was interested. But she was also open to other types of meals she was good at making.

"I like every type of food," he said diplomatically.

Good answer, she thought, and asked him, "Would you like to have dinner with me tonight?"

Without pause, Campbell said surely, "I'd love to."

"Terrific. Does seven o'clock work for you?"

"Yes, seven is good."

"Okay." Stefanie thought about Curlie. "By the way, you aren't allergic to cats, are you?"

"Not at all," he said, then added, "Love cats."

She chuckled. "Good."

Stefanie texted him her address while inside her car in the parking lot of a grocery store, where she would need to pick up a few items for dinner now that it had been confirmed.

Two hours later, she had prepared lemongrass chicken thighs, red rice and Vietnamese egg rolls called Cha Gio, to go with white wine and taro rice pudding for dessert.

Hope he likes it, Stefanie told herself after freshening up. She changed into a floral peach-colored midi shirtdress and slipped on wedge espadrilles.

Campbell arrived right on time, grinning as he came in. "You look great," he told her at the door.

"Thanks." Stefanie gave him a once-over, noting that he was wearing a yellow oxford dress shirt, dark gray wool slacks and black loafers. "You clean up pretty nicely yourself."

He laughed. "It's nice to have a reason to every now and then."

"That goes both ways," she admitted, inviting him inside.

Her cat wasted no time cozying up to Campbell's pant leg, as if reuniting with an old friend.

Stephanie said, "This is Curlie."

"Hi, Curlie." Campbell allowed the cat to run around him playfully before scooting off. He looked around. "Nice place you have here."

"Thanks." She smiled softly.

He took a whiff of the food and stated, "Smells wonderful."

"It'll taste even better." Stefanie felt confident enough to be presumptuous in this instance. Till proven otherwise.

"I have no doubt," he told her coolly. "Can I help with anything?"

"You can pour the wine, if you like," she replied, pointing out the brown Shaker-style cabinets where the wineglasses were kept.

"Will do."

As Campbell did that, Stefanie put out the food on the mid-century round wooden dining room table. They sat across from each other on brown faux leather side chairs.

"Delicious," Campbell declared, the moment he bit into a lemongrass chicken thigh.

Stefanie giggled. "Good to know." *Guess I haven't lost my touch after all*, she told herself pleasingly. After he commended her on more of the food, she said to him, "I went to the Braison Family compound this afternoon…"

"Really?" A thick disapproving brow shot up.

She felt the need to explain. "I needed to have a look at where Mia spent her time before what happened to her. And since Bella felt it wasn't a threatening environment for me to be overly concerned about, I went, hoping to get more insight into the life Mia led."

"I see." He scooped up some red rice onto his fork. "And how did you make out on your journey?"

"Not very well, I'm afraid." Stefanie sliced her knife into the Cha Gio. "Before I could make any headway at all with Jasmine—the one who gave me the flyer at the park—Kenneth Braison cut that short. He had a muscular man named Juan escort me off the premises. I don't think it was something I said. Or maybe I didn't say enough to be considered worthy of being a potential member of the Family."

"It was likely neither of those," Campbell told her frankly, forking up a piece of chicken. "I'm guessing that Braison, as the cult leader, is being extra cautious as to who he lets in, while having to look over his shoulder as we investigate the death of Mia O'Dell."

Stefanie angled her face. "So, you still think he may have something to do with it?"

"I certainly can't rule it out at this stage, even if the man can apparently account for his whereabouts when she died." Campbell sat back, pensive. "Wouldn't be the first time a Braison has been at the center of a mystery surrounding a woman found dead in Reston Hills Park on Founder's Day."

Stefanie sipped her wine thoughtfully and said, "Bella mentioned something to me about that. But she didn't provide any details. Are you saying that Wendell Braison, Kenneth's father, was suspected of killing another cult member?"

"Yeah," Campbell said matter-of-factly. "Twenty years ago, a forty-one-year-old waitress and Braison Family member named Lynda Boxleitner was left in the nude at the park, after ingesting a lethal amount of a poison called thallium sulfate. Wendell Braison, who was thought to be romantically involved with Lynda—his initials, WB, were tattooed on her arm—was the chief suspect in her death. But it was never proven. The case has remained in limbo ever since. Though Braison has been dead himself for years now, this story has continued to haunt Reston Hills like a curse."

Stefanie peered at him. "You seem to know a lot about the case…"

Campbell nodded while holding his wineglass. "My father, Mason Sawyer, was the lead detective in the investigation," he told her. "He also happened to have been acquainted with the victim, having dated Lynda years earlier when they were both in high school." Campbell tasted the wine. "Dad did everything he could to find out who killed her and why, but came up short. It was probably the one unsolved case that has stuck with him to this day."

Stefanie took a breath. "If the Braison Family was behind both deaths, do you think it could have been part of a generational ritual?" She had read about this type of thing with other cults and devil worshippers—often involving animals as sacrifices. Could they have taken it much further here, with humans being targeted as sacrificial lambs?

"The thought has crossed my mind," Campbell answered. "But given the twenty years between the deaths, it's more likely that they are linked either by kinship—making the killings personal in nature—or possibly a copycat killer emulating a decades-old murder to carry out another today. At this point, all options are on the table."

"I expected as much," Stefanie said, feeling she may have gotten carried away in her theorizing as a layperson. She dabbed a napkin at the corners of her mouth. She only wanted to see Mia's death solved. If Campbell could solve his father's case as well, then two birds could be killed with one stone, to both of their satisfactions. "Speaking of the table, are you ready for dessert? I made taro rice pudding."

He grinned. "Yes, I've saved enough room in my stomach to take on your pudding. Have at it. I'll help clear the table and refill the wineglasses."

"Okay." She was starting to like him more with each passing moment and wondered what else might be in store for them.

CAMPBELL HAD TO admit that he could get used to having dinner and dessert with Stefanie in a hurry. Sure beat eating alone, as he'd been doing way too often since returning to Reston Hills. The fact that she was a great cook made it that much more enjoyable. To say nothing of just how lovely she was to be around. He liked Stefanie's finicky cat, too, as she'd seemed to take to him just as quickly.

They took their wine goblets with them while sitting on a blue chenille upholstered sofa in the living room.

"So, have you dated much since living in Reston Hills?" Campbell had to ask, even if for selfish reasons.

Stefanie tasted her wine. "Haven't dated at all since moving here," she admitted. "Too busy with other things and lack of interest, I guess." She gazed at him. "Unless you call this a date?"

He didn't hesitate to do just that. "I hope we can call this a date. I'd like that to be the case."

She grinned. "So would I."

"Then that's that." Campbell grinned back at her, seeing this as a positive step in getting to know one another.

Stefanie regarded him. "You mentioned having a failed relationship when you were living in Boise. What happened there?" she probed curiously.

Campbell considered this. He didn't want to keep anything bottled up inside him that could take away from a readiness to move on. "Her name is Naomi Espelita," he said levelly. "Naomi had a lot going for her, including a career as a successful classical musician. Unfortunately, we weren't right for each other. Too little common ground and not enough willingness to meet each other halfway. I wish nothing but the best for her—just not with me."

"Okay." Stefanie let that sink in for a moment. "Do you ever want to get married—if the right person comes along? And have children?"

"Yes, to both," Campbell answered without hesitation. "I'm a big believer in marriage, kids, the whole nine yards. If that right person comes along, I'm there—all the way..."

Her teeth shone. "Nice to know."

"What about you?" Figured he might as well satisfy his own curiosity while they were at it. "Could you see yourself marrying again? And starting a family?"

Stefanie took a sip of wine and met his gaze squarely. "Yes, absolutely. I never asked to be a young widow—but it happened. If a second chance comes along to be a wife again and a mother, I would certainly take it and hope things would work out."

"Okay." Campbell nodded. He wanted to kiss her so badly in that moment but instead talked about what they enjoyed doing outside work. While he mentioned working out at the gym, traveling, reading and riding horses, her hobbies included swimming, watching reality television shows and surfing social media sites. They both liked to jog and hike.

Before he could come back to that desired kiss, Stefanie asked him boldly, "Do you mind if I kiss you?"

Campbell could barely contain his enthusiasm. "Not in the slightest."

They leaned in to each other and exchanged a soft but steady kiss. Though feeling aroused and enjoying the feel of her mouth upon his, Campbell kept his libido in check. He wanted to make sure this was what they both wanted before going further.

"Nice," he murmured after the kiss ended.

"Yes, it was," she seconded with a smile. He left it at that, with visions of more to come.

When Stefanie walked him to the door a few minutes later, Campbell said, "Thanks for dinner."

She blushed. "Thanks for coming."

"Next time, I'd like to return the favor by cooking you a meal," he told her.

"So, you cook, too?" Her eyes lit up. "Hmm… Man of many talents, huh?"

"Something like that," Campbell teased her.

"Then it's a date."

"Okay." He grinned at her.

As he drove away from her house, Campbell felt more than grateful that they'd met at all, though he wished it had been under better circumstances. The last thing he wished upon anyone was to find a dead body—no matter the circumstances. But Stefanie had done just that and taken an interest in Mia O'Dell and her affiliation with the Braison Family. Even if Bella Reston, her friend and a prominent member of Reston Hills society, apparently dismissed the cult as a threat, Campbell was far from convinced. Especially after his father's ordeal in being unable to connect the dots in going after Wendell Braison years ago.

Maybe the more things changed, the more they remained the same. Meaning that Kenneth Braison still had to be considered a person of interest in Mia's death, just as his father was in the death of Lynda Boxleitner.

As such, Campbell felt a professional obligation to protect Stefanie, over and beyond his romantic interest in her, so long as the current investigation remained active. But he wouldn't overstep his bounds in dictating whom she chose to associate with—even if it was members of the Braison Family.

Chapter Seven

At eleven a.m. the following day, Campbell sat at the counter in Harriette's Café beside Detective Georgina Alvarez while they awaited the judicial go-ahead to search the Braison Family compound.

Sarah Huffstetler came up to them with the coffeepot, filling their cups. Ignoring Georgina, she said to Campbell in a syrupy voice, "Hey, handsome."

"Good morning, Sarah," he said to her evenly.

"Heard you were here yesterday with a pretty lady. Anyone I know?"

"I doubt it." *Word travels fast in a small town*, Campbell lamented. He hoped she wouldn't make a scene. "Just a friend," he said tonelessly, even if he was starting to see far greater possibilities with Stefanie.

"We all need friends around here, right?" Georgina threw out with amusement.

Sarah shrugged. "If you say so." She gazed at Campbell. "If things don't work out with your friend, you have my number."

He nodded. "Got it." *I deleted your number right after our one date*, he told himself.

After she left, Georgina chuckled and said, "Looks like

someone has the hots for you, Campbell. Or maybe more than one woman..."

"Nothing going on with me and Sarah," he emphasized. "We went out once and that was it."

"Not sure she realizes that."

"She'll come to terms with it sooner or later." Campbell added some cream and sipped his coffee.

"So who is this other *friend*, Sawyer?" Georgina teased him. "Have you been holding out on us while jumping back into the dating game?"

"Not really." Campbell laughed. "Her name's Stefanie. Met her on Founder's Day at the park."

Georgina cocked a brow. "When?"

"She was the one who discovered Mia O'Dell's body on the trail," he explained, then paused. "We hit it off."

"I see." Georgina grinned. "Good for you. Hope this one is a keeper, just like with me and Ted."

"That would be great," Campbell had to admit, knowing that she and her deputy sheriff boyfriend worked. Though they were apparently not interested in marriage—to each their own. While wedding bells weren't exactly on the docket right now between him and Stefanie, the fact that both were open-minded in that regard could bode well in the future.

Georgina sipped her coffee with two sugars, then asked, "So, do you think we'll find anything incriminating at the Braison Family compound related to O'Dell's death?"

Campbell weighed this. "One can only hope so," he replied, adding more cream to his coffee. "If there's anything at all at the compound in the way of fentanyl or other evidence that can somehow tie Kenneth Braison or one of his followers to Mia's fatal overdose, we'll find it."

"Maybe. Based on past run-ins with Braison, I'm betting that if the Braison Family was involved in her death, they probably covered their tracks well."

Just as Wendell Braison apparently did in managing to skirt the law and his father in the death of Lynda Boxleitner, Campbell told himself. "Our job is to uncover any proverbial tracks if they lead anywhere, or to someone," he countered. "Maybe it's the drug dealer who gave Mia the deadly fentanyl indifferently. Or perhaps she was killed deliberately to keep her from spilling the beans on something or someone who preferred that it went with Mia right to the grave."

Georgina nodded and said, "Let's hope we can give her the peace she deserves—even if she made some bad choices and couldn't pull herself out. If this was out-and-out murder, all the more reason to get whoever was responsible—so no one else has to die."

"Yeah, you've got that right." Campbell tasted the coffee. He couldn't help but wonder if such an unsub could have played a role in Lynda Boxleitner's murder. Could Kenneth Braison have actually killed her instead of his father? Kenneth would have been in his early twenties when she died. Making him more than old enough to have done the deed—either for himself or on behalf of Wendell Braison.

But Dad never mentioned Kenneth as a suspect in Lynda's murder, Campbell told himself. So maybe he hadn't killed her. But that didn't let him off the hook for involvement in Mia's OD death.

When his cell phone rang, Campbell lifted it from the pocket of his blazer and answered, listening to the caller. After disconnecting, he told Georgina, "We got the search warrant. Let's go pay the Braison Family a visit—"

"I'm with you," she said eagerly before they finished off their coffees, paid for them and left the café.

THAT AFTERNOON, STEFANIE SAT poolside on a turquoise chaise longue chair beside Bella as they sipped on cocktails while wearing bathing suits in anticipation of a dip in Bella's resort-like saltwater pool. After her father's death, Bella had inherited and moved into his enormous house—which, to Stefanie, was probably the most elegant home in town—that he in turn had inherited from his father, Malcolm Reston, whom it had been passed on to by his own father, Arthur Reston, the town's namesake.

Stefanie was still reeling from kissing Campbell. She had prompted the kiss, surprising even herself. But it felt like the right time, with the right person. So she'd thrown caution to the wind and gone for it, hoping he wouldn't embarrass her by turning down the request.

Thank goodness he welcomed the invite and was a great kisser, as I suspected, Stefanie thought in her reverie. They'd already made tentative plans for another dinner date, this time at his place. She was excited at the prospect of furthering what they had started.

Stefanie refocused on Bella, who was talking animatedly about the next big project that she was spearheading.

"The Annual Reston Hills Charitable Gala this Saturday will raise money for local theater programs, literacy initiatives and the arts," she said enthusiastically. "It will also be lots of fun with live music, performances, an auction, lots of food and more…"

"I look forward to attending," Stefanie told her while wondering if she could invite Campbell as her guest. Or would he be too busy working on one case or another? That could be something she would simply have to get used to were they to become a bona fide couple. "Maybe I'll even bid on something at the auction—all for a good cause."

Bella laughed. "Or not. Whatever works. You'll definitely be on the VIP list as a good friend—and feel free to bring anyone you want..." She gave her a teasing look. "I'm just saying."

"Thanks for that." Stefanie showed her teeth while making plans to bring Campbell along for the ride. "Can't wait." In the meantime, she could only hope that Campbell and his colleagues wouldn't be left with more dead bodies to deal with. "So, Campbell's looking into whether Mia's death was in any way connected to the unsolved death of Lynda Boxleitner—the member of the Braison Family you mentioned who was found murdered twenty years ago in Reston Hills Park on Founder's Day."

"Really?" Bella batted her lashes. "Seems like a stretch after so many years, but what do I know? Tell me more."

"Afraid I don't have much to tell," Stefanie admitted, flexing her toes. "Only that Campbell's dad, Mason Sawyer, who investigated Lynda's death, found that she, too, was left naked at the park with the initials of Wendell Braison tattooed on her arm and had been fatally poisoned—albeit with a different type of poison than what Mia OD'd on. But since Mia had Kenneth Braison's initials tattooed on her arm and died under similar circumstances, I suppose it's only natural that Campbell would want to see if the father and son could have perpetrated the poisonings for whatever reason as the leaders of the Braison Family..."

Bella sipped her drink. "Well, when you put it that way, it does seem like a good idea for Campbell and the police department to check out if there's any way that Wendell and Kenneth could've used their power to dispose of cult women they viewed as threats to their organization."

Stefanie leaned toward her. "Yeah, as weird as it sounds, I suppose anything's possible till proven otherwise. I'd at least like to see Mia's death solved, for obvious reasons, as the one who found her."

"I'm with you there," Bella said flatly. "As my dad's former housekeeper, Mia deserves justice in any way she can get it. Just as Lynda Boxleitner does. Never too late."

"I agree." Stefanie was hardly an expert on cold cases. Or even hot ones, for that matter. But she sensed that with Campbell investigating the two deaths, anything was possible. She put the cocktail glass to her lips before tossing out casually, "So, I invited Campbell over for dinner last night…"

"Oh, really?" Bella flashed her an exaggerated shocked look. "Didn't see that coming."

"Neither did I, to tell you the truth," Stefanie said before tasting her drink. "But we've gotten to know each other a bit. He seems like a great guy with an interesting background—and someone that, if it continues, could be a good fit for me at this stage of my life."

"Well said." Bella grinned at her. "I say go for it. Campbell and I never connected that way, but I think he's a great catch and so are you, girlfriend. He's lucky to catch your eye—and maybe your heart over time—"

"Hmm…" Stefanie liked the sound of that. "I was thinking the same thing," she said with a laugh.

Bella frowned. "Now, if only I can land the man of my dreams—after my ex, Jeff, turned out to be a dud—or at least someone who can hold my attention more than the blink of an eye."

"I'm sure that will happen sooner or later," Stefanie told her sincerely. "Look at you, you're the complete package. What man wouldn't want to be by your side and all that accompanies that? You just have to be willing to let someone—*the one*—in."

Bella chuckled. "How poetic. You're right, of course. We'll see how it goes. Maybe my knight in shining armor will await me at the Annual Reston Hills Charitable Gala."

"Maybe." Stefanie smiled, wondering if Campbell would prove to be her own knight in shining armor when all was said and done.

Bella suddenly got to her feet, wearing an apple-red halter tankini, and said, "I don't know about you, but I'm ready for a swim."

"Me too," Stefanie told her with a smile. Before she could lift up, wearing a green-and-white cap-sleeve one-piece swimsuit, Bella had already dived into the pool. Stefanie followed her, jumping into the water, anxious to put her swimming skills to work.

CAMPBELL AND GEORGINA arrived at the Braison Family compound, along with additional armed members of the Reston Hills Police Department and a K-9 unit that included drug detection canines, to execute a search warrant on the premises.

They were met at the gate by two men. One Campbell recognized as Juan Barrientos, Kenneth Braison's top sidekick, having encountered resistance from Barrientos during a previous encounter at the compound. The other man was African American, in his thirties and just as muscular, with black hair styled in cornrows and a Garibaldi beard.

Campbell walked up to the men, presented the search warrant and said, "Now, if you'll kindly step aside and let us do our work, we can be in and out in no time flat." *Or longer, if we find reason to stick around for a while*, he thought.

Barrientos gazed at the search warrant, glared at him and said to the other man resignedly, "Let them through."

They both stepped aside as Campbell and Georgina led the way inside the compound, where everyone spread out, while looking specifically for any illegal drugs or weapons on the premises. Of particular interest was the presence of illegally manufactured fentanyl or IMFs, or the detection of fentanyl analogs, such as carfentanil. As well as any evidence they came upon that suggested that Mia O'Dell's death had begun at the compound before ending in Reston Hills Park.

When Campbell approached Kenneth Braison—or actually, more the other way around—the cult leader's forehead was creased in three places as he muttered, "You're back again..."

"I'm sure that doesn't come as a surprise," Campbell shot back. "I told you we'd return with a search warrant, which Juan Barrientos got the first look at." He handed the warrant to Kenneth. "Now it's your turn."

Kenneth barely glanced at it. He sneered at Campbell and said, "Go ahead, look wherever you like. We have nothing to hide. You won't find anything, Detective," he said confidently.

Campbell retorted, "We'll see about that."

"Yeah, right," he said mockingly.

Campbell peered at him. "Mind showing me which cabin Mia O'Dell was staying in before she died?"

"I'll be happy to take you to it," Kenneth replied. "I instructed everyone to leave everything as it was. Wouldn't want you to think we'd tampered with evidence or anything."

Yeah, I bet, Campbell thought as he followed him while directing a K-9 team to join them.

When they arrived at the cabin, Campbell asked Kenneth to wait outside as the search for evidence ensued.

To Campbell, the cabin where Mia had supposedly lived alone was almost too tidy to be believed, leading him to suspect that any potential evidence may have been tampered with. They went through the motions nonetheless, hoping to get lucky.

"Find anything?" Campbell asked the K-9 handler.

Sergeant Vivienne Olmstead, fiftysomething with auburn hair in a flip bob, tightly held the leash of her German shepherd/Belgian Malinois mix canine partner, and said ruefully, "Nothing. No drugs detected whatsoever. At least not inside the cabin."

"All right." Campbell was wearing nitrile gloves as he did his own search through the cabin, with its wicker furniture and standard household items—coming up empty with anything that could tie solidly to the commission of a crime.

Outside, he met up with Georgina, who had the same results. "We haven't come up with any illicit drugs or illegal firearms," she said stiffly.

Campbell frowned. "Looks like they cleared out anything that might come back to bite them," he reasoned, similar to his previous search for drugs and drug paraphernalia that had yielded no positive results. "We'll have to see if we can connect any outside drug traffickers to the Braison Family."

Georgina nodded. "As well as ask around to try and learn who Mia may have been hanging out with inside or away from the compound that may have something to say about what she was up to the day she died."

"Yeah," Campbell concurred, wondering to what extent, if any, the Braison Family was behind the death.

They checked out more places, spoke to a few of the followers—none of whom seemed willing to say much on or off the record—and rendezvoused with the rest of the team, before deciding there was nothing more to do there at the moment.

As they were leaving, Kenneth and his sidekick Juan walked up to them.

Kenneth regarded Campbell and said gloatingly, "I take it you found nothing of use to you, Detective, while searching for answers in Mia's death?"

"Not yet." Campbell jutted his chin, knowing this was precisely what the cult leader had anticipated. "Doesn't mean we won't stop trying."

Kenneth responded, "As you should. Believe me, I'd like to know how Mia ended up OD'ing as much as you. The Braison Family isn't a haven for drugs or drug use—and we wouldn't stand for putting that poison into our bodies."

"If you say so," Campbell said sarcastically.

"I do." Kenneth sighed. "It was the same when my father was at the helm of the Family and *your* father was trying to put the squeeze on an innocent man when another cult member fell prey to poison being put into her system. Wishing for something to be true doesn't mean it is—"

Campbell glared at him, knowing Kenneth had managed to get under his skin by bringing his father into the current case. As well as reminding him about the failure to get the evidence needed to charge Wendell Braison with murder.

Maybe you won't be so lucky when this is over, Campbell thought, and walked away from the cult leader and a hard-nosed Juan Barrientos.

Outside the compound, Georgina pouted and said, "Braison's a real piece of work."

"And probably a lot worse," Campbell told her. "Whether

or not that rises to the level of cold-blooded killer remains to be seen." No matter his dislike of the man, he wouldn't jump the gun by indicting him without the hard evidence to prove his case. *Any more than my dad was willing to do when going after Kenneth's father, even if it meant letting the case grow ice cold*, Campbell told himself as they headed for his vehicle.

KENNETH WATCHED FROM behind the gate as Detectives Sawyer and Alvarez drove off, along with other law enforcement personnel. He hated that they had invaded his territory like they owned the place. But, as expected, they had come up empty-handed. This didn't mean they had gone away for good. As long as Mia's death remained unsolved, the cops figured to be a problem.

"What do you think?" Juan asked, ill at ease, as they walked back inside the compound.

Kenneth ran a hand across his mouth thoughtfully. "I think we need to tread carefully," he answered. "With Mia dead and fingers pointed in our direction, we have to stand strong and not allow them to break up everything my father worked so hard to achieve."

"That won't happen," Juan assured him. "They have nothing, and we have each other. The Braison Family is solid enough to push back anything the police can try to drum up against us."

"I'm glad we're on the same page."

"Always."

Kenneth smiled, putting a hand on his shoulder. "You're a good soldier for the cause, Juan."

"I try my best," he told him.

That would have to be enough, as far as Kenneth was concerned. As was the case for every member of the Family. It was the outside influences that most concerned him. The same ones who may have been responsible for Mia losing her way.

Assuming there wasn't one or more traitors within their midst, deliberately breaking the rules in a misguided attempt to stop the movement. And everything that it stood for.

Chapter Eight

The following day, Campbell drove down tree-lined Pughten Road and onto the luxury waterfront estate of Bella Reston, who, he had to admit, played her part admirably in her family legacy by playing up the core values of the town that bore her great-grandfather Arthur Reston's name.

As Stuart Reston was Mia O'Dell's last known employer—apparently before she became a member of the Braison Family—it seemed a good place for Campbell to start to get some further insight into Mia's life before being recruited and, apparently, indoctrinated by the cult.

Beyond that, as Bella was friends with Stefanie, Campbell thought it was a good thing to win Bella's support in his bid to become closer to Stefanie than he had to anyone in a long time. *I'm sure Bella wants Stefanie to be happy in Reston Hills if I can provide some of that happiness*, he told himself.

He got out of the car, parked not far from Bella's blue metallic BMW X7 M60i SUV outside a four-car garage. *At least I know she's home*, Campbell thought with a grin.

Walking up to the massive two-story brick house with loads of architectural windows, a big swimming pool in the backyard and in a wooded setting, he recalled coming there once as a boy with his dad. Seemed like a place one could only dream of. But his dreams did not go that far at the time.

Or now, for that matter.

The current version of himself realized that it took more than the size of a house to make a home—if the other aspects failed to fall in place properly. Apparently, that wasn't a problem for Bella, having returned to her childhood home with the death of her father four months ago as a single woman after divorcing her husband. Or was it the other way around? The way he'd heard it, Jeff Lacombe, the ex, whom Bella had met in high school, had cheated on her, and that had ended the marriage, with Jeff and his new girlfriend relocating to New Mexico.

Not my problem, Campbell told himself, sure that with all Bella had to offer, she would have no trouble finding someone else to share her life with—just not him. Assuming that wasn't already the case.

After ringing the bell, the door opened and Bella's housekeeper stood there. The thirtysomething medium-size woman with short and curly brunette hair asked, "Can I help you?"

Taking out his badge, Campbell answered, "I need to speak with Ms. Reston," remembering that Bella had reclaimed her maiden name following the divorce.

"Come in," the housekeeper said tonelessly.

Campbell walked into a long hall with marble tile and framed family photographs, and past bifurcated stairs, before being led to the great room and asked to wait. He glanced around at the traditional furnishings, floor-to-ceiling windows and an exposed-brick wood-burning fireplace.

"Hello."

He heard the familiar pleasant voice and turned to face Bella, who smiled.

"Campbell...or should I call you Detective Sawyer?"

He grinned. "Campbell is fine." Especially since he didn't want this to seem like an interrogation so much as an informal chat between old acquaintances, if not friends.

"All right." Bella walked up to him, wearing a sleeveless black wide-leg jumpsuit and flats. "Nice to see you, Campbell. How's your dad?"

"He's doing well, thanks." Campbell appreciated that she asked, remembering that he'd done some work for her father.

She smiled. "So, what brings you my way?"

"Mind if we sit?" he asked, meeting her green eyes.

"Of course. Where are my manners?" Bella eyed a set of maroon Chesterfield chairs angled toward one another by an oval glass table. "Sit."

Campbell sat down and waited for her to do the same before getting right to it. "As I'm sure you're aware, we're investigating the suspicious death of Mia O'Dell."

Bella gave a nod. "Yes, I'm totally aware of that—thanks, in part, to our mutual friend, Stefanie, who's been filling me in on any news she picked up on it. How does any of this relate to me?"

"It doesn't, in so many words," he told her. "But it does your late father, Stuart Reston, albeit indirectly..."

Bella batted her lashes. "I'm afraid I don't follow..."

Campbell explained, "As far as we're aware, Mia's last-known employer was Stuart, who employed her as a housekeeper. We're backtracking her life to try and understand how Mia ended up dead in the park on Founder's Day. Can you tell me anything about her working for your father?"

Bella took a breath and said evenly, "Not too much. I

wasn't living in the house at the time. What I do know is that she was his housekeeper for a few months before he died—seemed as though Daddy had trouble keeping help that lived up to his standards—before he caught her stealing and fired her."

"Really?" Campbell asked attentively.

"That's what I was told," she said, smoothing a brow. "Apparently, it wasn't the first time she stole from him."

"Did he say what she stole or tried to steal?"

"Some of my late mother's jewelry, which he refused to part with." Bella ran a hand through her hair, which stayed remarkably in place. "As well as money that he often had lying around haphazardly."

Campbell leaned toward her chair. "Did your father ever report any of this to the police?" If so, he could easily look it up for more details.

"No, I don't think so. My dad was a private person and preferred not to get the police involved if at all possible." Bella folded her arms. "He chose instead to simply fire Mia. Feeling she was let off easy, she went on her way without a fuss."

"I see." Campbell scratched his jaw. "Had you seen Mia since she was fired?"

Bella met his gaze. "I spotted her on occasion in town—but we never spoke."

"Did your father ever indicate to you any knowledge that Mia was using drugs?"

"No. But I think if he had ever suspected this, Daddy would almost certainly have fired her on those grounds alone." Bella frowned. "As my late mother got addicted to painkillers while battling cancer, my father understood what drugs could do to you. He would never have tolerated substance abuse from one of his employees."

Campbell understood this. He flashed back to his own mother and her courageous battle with breast cancer to no avail. Even with the prescription drugs used to control the pain, they never seemed to be enough, and his mother's suffering really only let up at the end of her journey. He and his father couldn't help but find solace that she was finally at peace—even while missing her more than they could once express properly to one another. Campbell imagined the same was true for Stuart Reston and Bella.

Regarding her, Campbell asked, "Do you have any idea what motivated Mia to join the Braison Family?"

Bella pondered the question, then responded speculatively, "I can only assume that perhaps she was susceptible to their messaging and Kenneth Braison's powers of persuasion. Beyond that, using and abusing fentanyl—before or after—may have weakened her resistance that much more."

"You're probably right on both counts." Campbell still wasn't sure if someone from Braison's orbit—including Kenneth himself—had given Mia the deadly fentanyl. Or if it was someone on the outside. "I don't suppose you would know if Mia was seeing anyone when she worked for your father?"

"Sorry. Can't help you there." Bella pursed her lips. "I hardly spoke to Mia when visiting my dad, and he never mentioned her having a boyfriend, girlfriend or whatever."

"Okay." From what they had come up with thus far, it did appear that Mia was not romantically involved with anyone. At least not outside the Braison Family. But they were still looking into cell phone records that might provide more clues into her final days.

Bella eyed him and said inquisitively, "So, Stefanie mentioned that you were looking into whether there might be a Braison Family connection between Mia's death and the death of the woman at the park on Founder's Day twenty years ago."

"That's true." He didn't deny it, knowing she was around then to remember what had to be big news in Reston Hills on that of all days. "There are some similarities between what happened to Mia and Lynda Boxleitner two decades ago that bear checking out."

She cocked a brow. "I know that Wendell Braison was once considered a suspect in that Founder's Day murder. If he really killed her, do you honestly think Kenneth Braison could have followed his lead in killing Mia as another member of the Braison Family? Why would he do that?"

"People kill for all types of reasons," Campbell pointed out matter-of-factly. "Some are more complicated than others. Some less. Could be that the Braisons felt empowered to do as they pleased to protect what was theirs. Even to the point of murder, albeit decades apart. If neither Braison had anything to do with the deaths, then we'll look elsewhere. Until then, they both will continue to be persons of interest here." *Probably said more than I needed to*, Campbell thought, but somehow felt that she understood, having a vested interest in solving both deaths, if at all possible.

Bella made a face. "If the Braisons were behind the fatal poisoning of *two* innocent women and you're able to prove it, I certainly hope they get what's coming to them. No one should have to die like that. Especially if it was part of a warped cult act of revenge or as some sort of human sacrifice."

"I couldn't agree more about the tragic manner in which they died." Campbell drew a breath. "Time will tell if there is some symmetry here that ties the father to the son—or the Braison Family itself to one or both deaths."

She nodded. "As the sole representative of the Reston family legacy, I do hope you can do right by the town in putting at least Mia's death to rest, if not Lynda Boxleitner's."

"I'll do my best," he promised, then added, to lighten the mood a little, "No pressure, right?"

"Not from me." Bella smiled. "I'm sure you have enough of that from others."

Campbell grinned, welcoming her pressure-free support. He supposed that the most pressure he felt right now, he put upon himself. As his father had before him. He fixed his gaze to her face and said, "Thanks for the chat. I'd better let you get back to your day."

They stood and walked to the front door, where Bella stated, "I'm glad you stopped by, Campbell." She looked at him with a soft smile. "I was hoping to catch up with you and see how the case was coming along—seeing that Stefanie wound up being part of the investigation, as she found Mia's body."

Campbell jutted his chin. "Yeah, that was unfortunate. But it gave me the opportunity to meet Stefanie, who's strong enough to weather what she went through and continue to fit in the community."

"Thanks, in part, to you," Bella told him. "She really likes you, which I'm sure you already know."

"Yeah." Campbell blushed. "I think it works both ways."

"Good to know. Stefanie's heart is in the right place. She deserves a second opportunity to experience love—if it comes her way…"

"Don't we all." He wondered if she was experiencing

this again herself with anyone. Or still waiting for the right person to come along, with her busy life and all.

Once inside his SUV, Campbell pondered just how long it would take for real love to develop between him and Stefanie. Patience was something he was good at and clearly this was true for her as well.

The rest would have to work itself out.

JASMINE ROXBURGH HESITATED as she approached the ranch house Kenneth lived in with his latest girlfriend, Siobhan Froggatt. Siobhan was from London, England, and had been drawn to the Braison Family ever since arriving in the States two years ago, finally working her way to Kenneth's bed when he tired of his prior bedmate—whom Jasmine suspected had been Mia O'Dell.

Now Mia was dead from a drug overdose, and the Braison Family, after a few parting words from Kenneth, seemed to be going about its business as though she was yesterday's news and no longer pertinent to speak about further.

But more troubling to Jasmine was how Mia, whom she'd considered a friend and not a drug user, came to have fentanyl in her system. Did she get it from someone inside the compound? What did Kenneth know that he was keeping from the police?

Jasmine considered the search by the authorities that came up empty yesterday. It went as expected, with Kenneth and Juan seeing to it that anything they had to cause suspicion—including loaded weapons—was well hidden. She'd wanted to speak to Detective Sawyer, but was too afraid to even try, with eyes everywhere and anywhere.

Then there was Stefanie, with whom Jasmine felt a kinship. Jasmine had learned that she was the one to discover

Mia's body. Was that what had brought Stefanie to the compound, before Kenneth sent her away?

Jasmine knocked on the front door, and a follower named Eva opened it. In her early twenties and rail thin with long, stringy blond hair and big blue eyes, Eva asked, "Are you looking for Kenneth?"

"Yes," Jasmine said, second-guessing if it was truly a good idea to approach him directly about Mia.

"Come in." Eva smiled at her. "He's in his office with Siobhan and Juan."

"All right." Jasmine walked alongside Eva on dark hardwood flooring and past farmhouse furnishings in an open-concept layout, knowing that there was never any wandering around the house alone unless you were part of Kenneth's inner circle, which she wasn't.

Eva knocked on the door, and a voice gave her permission to open it. She looked at Jasmine and said, ill at ease, "You can go in now." Eva added, as if feeling it might be needed, "Good luck."

Jasmine smiled softly at her, replying, "Thanks."

When she walked into the big office, which had a large picture window and wooden furniture, Jasmine spotted the three people huddled around each other conspiratorially.

Kenneth broke away and approached her. He asked in a friendly tone, "How can I help you, Jasmine?"

"I was wondering if I could talk to you about Mia?" Jasmine replied tentatively.

"Of course." He looked over his shoulder at Juan and Siobhan, who was a dark-haired, dark-eyed beauty in her mid-twenties, tall and shapely, and told them, "Leave us."

Juan glared and Siobhan pouted as they walked past her. Once they were out of the office, closing the door behind them, Kenneth peered at Jasmine and asked with an edge to his voice, "So, what's on your mind?"

Jasmine suddenly felt tongue-tied as she contemplated where to go from here.

Chapter Nine

In his home office, Mason Sawyer sat on a well-worn, high-backed black leather ergonomic chair at an L-shaped walnut desk that had a small filing cabinet attached to it. His dog, Hopper, sat lazily nearby, rejecting the opportunity to roam free on the ranch.

Spread across the desk were case files from his investigation into the murder of Lynda Boxleitner two decades ago. Though he'd stepped away from police work since retiring—after an injury and his wife Alyssa's death made it too difficult to remain on the force—Mason had never quite been able to rid himself of information on Lynda's mysterious death. It was as though, deep down inside, he believed that he might need to come back to it again once the case was reopened.

He wasn't sure if that was official or not, but Mason believed that his son was hell-bent on clearing up his present-day death of Mia O'Dell by poisoning case in conjunction with the cold case death of Lynda Boxleitner.

Mason felt obliged to do his part to the extent he could as a retiree. He thought, *It's the least I can do in trying to help Campbell piece this together, if the deaths were con-*

nected at all. Not to mention having another crack at solving Lynda's murder long after the fact—once and for all.

But as of yet, he saw nothing while going over the investigation notes, witnesses, evidence and whatnot that he hadn't seen twenty years ago.

All roads still seemed to lead back to Wendell Braison as the most likely culprit in Lynda's death. But that hadn't been nearly enough to make an arrest, much less get a conviction and prison sentence.

But what if I'd been wrong in pursuing Wendell? Mason asked himself, lifting a can of beer and taking a sip. What about Kenneth Braison? Had he overlooked him? Though Kenneth was twentysomething at the time and fully capable of killing Lynda, his alibi of being in Boise when the murder took place had held up. On the other hand, Wendell—who was thought to have been romantically linked to Lynda and manipulative in controlling her and his other followers—was sketchy in his own alibi. But did that make him guilty of murder?

And could Kenneth have pulled a fast one by faking his whereabouts at the time of Lynda's death?

What am I missing? Mason mused, going through the files again. Could another Braison Family member be at the center of both deaths?

Or were Lynda and Mia's poisoning not connected by time? And perpetrated by one or more persons outside of the Family?

When Hopper suddenly got to his feet, Mason snapped out of his reverie as Sally entered the office. She was carrying a plate of oatmeal cookies, his favorite, and said, "Thought you could use a break with some fresh-baked cookies…"

Mason grinned. "That, I could." He watched as the dog

ran up to her, seeking to get a cookie or two himself. "Looks like Hopper feels the same."

"I guess he does." Sally smiled while tossing the dog a cookie, which he caught in midair. She sat the plate on the desk in an empty spot. "So, how are we doing here?"

Mason almost hated to say *not so good*. He had filled her in on what was happening after Campbell paid them a visit. She had been nothing but supportive in his desire to assist his son in reopening the investigation that came with his biggest regret as a police detective.

"Still a work in progress," he settled on telling her. "Could be that I'm only spinning my wheels, going nowhere fast. But it's just as possible that there may be something here that could be a means to one end or another—"

Sally seemed amenable to whichever way this went, kissing the top of his head. Mason was left to wonder if he could ever be satisfied with never knowing who ended Lynda's life—or why?

STEFANIE WAS IN her studio giving tai chi lessons to a group of children. She had once been one of those children in her youth, with her parents encouraging her to develop skills in the ancient Chinese meditative martial art. She hoped to one day teach her own children tai chi, assuming she were so blessed to become a mother someday. The thought of Campbell being the perfect father of those children entered Stefanie's head, making her tingle, though such a possibility was way too soon to get too out in front of.

She came back to reality for now as Stefanie went through warmups with her class of eager learners. This was followed by tai chi short forms, then breathing exercises, or chi kung, while lying down.

The goal, for both children and adults, was to improve

conditioning aerobically, balance and flexibility, and upper-and lower-body muscle strength.

She was satisfied that this was happening and the participants—or in this instance, their parents—were getting their money's worth.

Just as the class had come to an end and the children—wearing white tai chi uniforms like her own—began filing out to their waiting parents, Stefanie was surprised to see Bella strut into the studio. For an instant, she wondered if Bella had thought that it was an adult class today but got her timing wrong. However, as she wasn't exactly dressed for exercise and had designer sunglasses on the top of her head, Stefanie assumed Bella was only stopping by because she happened to be in the area.

Still, Stefanie couldn't help but say jokingly to her, "Here for some beginner tai chi?"

Bella laughed. "Not quite." She flipped back her hair. "Just came from a meeting and thought I'd come by to say guess who paid me a visit earlier today?"

"Uh..." From the look on her face, Stefanie guessed who it might be. But said instead, "Your ex, hoping to somehow win you back?"

"Only in his dreams." Her curly lashes fluttered frivolously. "Actually, it was your boyfriend."

"Campbell?" The name popped out quite naturally, though Stefanie didn't exactly think of him as her boyfriend at this point.

"The one and only," Bella told her, hand resting on a slender hip.

"We're not official right now," Stefanie had to say, though they seemed to be headed in the right direction. She eyed her curiously. "So why did Campbell come to see you?"

"It wasn't to arrest me or anything." Bella chuckled. "He came to talk about Mia O'Dell, who worked for my father as his housekeeper."

"Right." Stefanie was thoughtful. "I remember you saying that."

"Basically, Campbell just wanted to know what I knew about Mia during that time—including possible drug use—and even afterwards when she joined the Braison Family." Bella sighed. "I told him that my father caught Mia stealing and fired her. But I knew nothing about her taking fentanyl, for how long or who gave her the deadly drug. Or, for that matter, how she became indoctrinated by a cult."

"Hmm..." Stefanie wiped her face with a towel. She was surprised that Mia had been a thief. But what did she really know about her, other than that Mia OD'd on fentanyl and was part of the Braison Family? "I'm sure that anything you were able to tell Campbell was helpful in providing clarity to Mia's life, leading up to her death."

"I hope so. But actually, it worked both ways," Bella told her. "Since I had his attention, it gave me an opportunity to pick Campbell's brain on his thoughts about a possible connection between Mia's death and that of Lynda Boxleitner twenty years ago."

"Oh, really?" Stefanie said, regarding her pensively.

"Campbell made a compelling argument that there may have been a link by bloodline and the cult to the two deaths." Bella narrowed her eyes. "I told him that if this proves to be true, then he should certainly do everything he can to bring whoever was responsible to justice. If that boils down to only Kenneth Braison because his father Wendell Braison is dead, then so be it."

"I agree with you there," Stefanie said, wondering if the

Braisons were behind one or both deaths. Or were there other culprits responsible?

Bella looked at her and stated, "By the way, we talked about you, too."

"Me?" Stefanie batted her lashes with surprise.

"Basically, we both agreed that you're a lovely, wonderful person who deserves a second chance at love, wherever it may be and with whom—him, for instance."

Stefanie colored. "Thanks for the show of support." *And thank you, too, Campbell, for seeming to really care for me.*

"Anytime." Bella showed her teeth. "I know you'd stick up for me were the shoe on the other foot."

"Absolutely," she assured her. "Well, I'd better jump in the shower. I'll catch you later."

"All right." Bella pulled the sunglasses down and over her eyes. "I still want to learn tai chi one of these days."

"Whenever you like," Stefanie promised with a smile before heading for the locker room, thinking about Campbell and where things could go between them.

CAMPBELL WALKED INTO the office of Police Chief Gloria Schecter. Pushing sixty, she was slim in her uniform and had ash-blond hair in a piecey pixie cut. She had been a lieutenant when his father worked in the department and served as his boss.

Sitting in a brown leather chair at an adjustable-height corner desk, Gloria looked at him through oval glasses with blue eyes and said levelly, "Detective Sawyer…"

"Chief." Campbell took a couple of steps forward. "As you know, I'm looking into the Mia O'Dell death on Founder's Day."

"Yes—she OD'd, right?"

"Yeah," he responded, "and may have been helped—over and beyond tracking down the dealer—"

"Uh, okay..." Gloria sat back. "So, where are we in the investigation?"

Campbell regarded her. "I'm checking out the possibility that Mia's death could be connected to the death of Lynda Boxleitner twenty years ago, which my father was investigating."

Gloria leaned forward, interest piqued. "Are you, now?"

"Both were found naked at the park on Founder's Day, poisoned to death, and with a tattoo on their right forearm that bore the initials of the Braison Family leaders—Wendell Braison and Kenneth Braison, accordingly." Campbell took the liberty of sitting on an armless fabric guest chair across from the desk, then continued, "Since you were my dad's lieutenant then, I was wondering if there's anything you can remember about the Lynda Boxleitner homicide case that might help with the investigation?"

Gloria pushed up her glasses thoughtfully and replied, "I assume you've spoken with Mason about this?"

"Yeah, we've talked," Campbell confirmed. "He's told me what he remembered and is digging through some old files on the case. I've also checked with the Cold Case Unit and am looking to see if anything clicks."

Gloria drew a breath and said deliberately, "I remember when Lynda Boxleitner was dumped at the park, after having been fatally poisoned and disrobed by presumably her killer. We investigated the homicide thoroughly, led by Mason—Detective Sawyer—but couldn't quite make the case for pinning the murder on the number one suspect—"

"Wendell Braison," Campbell finished.

"That's correct," Gloria told him. "Wendell had his fair share of supporters, but not in this department. We went strictly by the book and believed him to be responsible for the death. We tried to get the necessary evidence to make an arrest." She frowned. "But it didn't work out, unfortunately."

That's obvious, as Dad has never gotten it out of his system, Campbell thought. "Were there any other serious suspects?" he asked, though knowing from his father and his own research into the case that no one else stood out that fit the bill.

Gloria backed this up. "No one that we could lay a finger on," she stated. "And with Wendell Braison maintaining his innocence until his death—though we had serious reservations about that—I guess that's why the case went cold over the years. Till now."

"If Braison didn't kill Lynda Boxleitner," Campbell speculated, "it means her killer could still be alive in the community—and targeted Mia O'Dell as a follow-up, for whatever reason. The different poisons used in the deaths could be strictly a matter of accessibility in different eras."

"Perhaps." Gloria planted her arms on the desk. "Or we could have *two* killers and only one still alive—and out for blood."

"True." Campbell tried to keep an open mind, though wanting to do right by his father and believe Wendell Braison was behind the lethal poisoning of Lynda Boxleitner. If this could be proved.

"You might want to talk to Officer Jerry Napolitano," Gloria told him. "He was the first responder when Boxleitner's body was discovered and may have some thoughts. Jerry's still on the force. Unfortunately, he's currently on the Big Island of Hawaii right now, celebrating his thirty-fifth wedding anniversary with his wife, Orla."

"I'll catch up with him when he gets back," Campbell

said, seeing no reason to disrupt his trip by calling. Especially since he doubted Napolitano would have much more to offer than Campbell's own father in the investigation into Lynda's death. "Thanks for your time, Chief," he said, standing.

Gloria nodded. "If O'Dell's death is in any way, shape or form associated with Boxleitner's murder, I'd love to be able to close both cases in one fell swoop. If not, getting to the root of why Mia O'Dell had to die will have to suffice. In the meantime, my door's always open."

"I'll remember that," Campbell said, knowing that his father, who had spoken highly of her as always having his back during his years on the force, felt the same way.

After leaving the office, he exchanged a few words on the investigation with Georgina, who had taken a strong interest in Mia's case. Turned out that Brandy Peñaflor, the sister of Georgina's deputy sheriff boyfriend, Ted Peñaflor, had been dealing with opioid use disorder—or opioid addiction—off and on for years. As this hit too close to home, Georgina wanted to try to get Mia's drug supplier off the streets, at the very least.

Campbell was on the same page there, though he hoped to connect a few more points in the scheme of things that could tie together two poisonous deaths.

After leaving the building and stepping into the sunshine, he called Stefanie, wanting to invite her to dinner. He hoped she didn't have other plans.

"Hey," he said when she answered.

"Hey." Stefanie's voice had a pleasant cadence to it.

"If you're free, I was wondering if you'd like to have dinner with me this evening at my place?"

"Of course," she said quickly. "I'd be happy to join you for dinner."

"Cool." He grinned while heading toward his SUV. "Is six okay?"

"Yes, perfect."

Actually, you're perfect, Campbell thought, believing this from everything he'd come to know about her. He considered briefly asking if he could pick her up at her place but decided against this. He didn't want to make her uncomfortable in any way. "I'll text you the address."

"All right."

After he did so, Campbell climbed into his Chevy Tahoe and headed for the grocery store, en route to home, while contemplating what to cook. He imagined that Bella had already spoken to Stefanie about his visit to her estate, where—aside from talking about his latest case and Mia's checkered history as a housekeeper for Bella's father, Stuart Reston—they had shared kind words about Stefanie. She and Bella really seemed to have hit it off. Just as he had with Stefanie. He hoped that they would be able to move the needle in continuing to make progress in their relationship. So long as he didn't blow it with the dinner, Campbell was optimistic in that regard.

Chapter Ten

Admittedly, Stefanie felt downright giddy as she drove onto Campbell's property, taking note of the green, hilly acreage. She envisioned children playing and running across it merrily. Along with their doting parents watching their offspring with boundless joy.

Okay, so maybe I'm putting the cart ahead of the horse with this vision, Stefanie thought. She took a breath. Best to let things play out naturally and not assume that she and Campbell were already a match made in heaven. For now, it was just dinner—albeit a second date—and no guarantees of scrumptious desserts to leave a lasting taste in either of their mouths.

Stefanie got out of her car and approached Campbell's farmhouse. With her hair loose, she wore a sleeveless indigo denim dress and black T-strap sandals. Campbell was waiting for her when she arrived at the front door.

"Hey." He flashed her a mouthwatering grin.

"Hey." She smiled back, taking in his formfitting terracotta piqué polo shirt, beige twill chinos and brown boat shoes.

"Come in," he told her enthusiastically.

Stefanie stepped into his house and was even more impressed with the layout and rustic furnishings than she was with the land it sat on. Or at least equally so. "You have a beautiful place here," she remarked sincerely.

Campbell smiled. "Thanks. It's probably a bit much for just one person. Guess maybe I was thinking ahead—"

She grinned musingly, reading between the lines. "I see."

"Food's ready to be served," he said. "I can give you the grand tour later."

"Sounds good."

"Hope you like fish?"

Stefanie picked up the scent of the grilled halibut. "I love fish," she told him.

"Good to know." Campbell grinned. "I added tomato vinaigrette to the halibut, to go with grilled vegetables, lemon-herbed rice and whole wheat bread. There's red wine, fruit punch, water and/or coffee. Whatever suits your fancy."

She smiled. "Everything sounds tasty," she confessed. "I'll have the red wine."

"You and me both," he said flatly. "So, make yourself at home and we'll eat."

They sat kitty-corner from one another in the dining room at an aspen log table on ladder-back chairs. Stefanie had to commend Campbell for the meal. "It's really good," she marveled, which was an understatement.

"Glad you like it." He gave her a slanted grin. "Picked up a few recipes from my dad and his girlfriend, Sally. But mostly, I suppose the cooking comes naturally—if I'm motivated enough."

She giggled, slicing a knife into the grilled halibut. "I guess you were," she teased him.

"Yeah, I can certainly say unabashedly that I wanted to

leave the right impression on you," he said with a laugh, then bit off a piece of bread.

Stefanie scooped up some lemon-herbed rice. "You've succeeded." She put the rice in her mouth, savoring the taste, and wondered what other tricks he might have up his sleeve.

Campbell tasted his wine. "So, I suppose Bella told you that I dropped by to talk about Mia O'Dell?"

Stefanie nodded. "I knew that Mia was the housekeeper of Bella's father," she told him. "But I didn't realize that she was stealing from Stuart Reston and was fired as a result. Not that I would've known this. Still, it kind of came as a shock. Sad, too."

"I agree on both counts," Campbell said. "Especially if losing her job was what led Mia to join the Braison Family—which may have played a crucial role in her use of fentanyl that resulted in her fatal overdose of the drug."

Stefanie's brow creased. "That would be awful, if one bad thing led to another," she stated soberly.

"Of course, whatever her own culpability was, Mia didn't deserve what she got for the bargain." Campbell stuck his fork into the grilled vegetables. "And neither did Lynda Boxleitner. The deaths occurred two decades apart—but under very similar circumstances..."

Stefanie gazed at him. "Do you still think that the two deaths are connected in some way to the Braison Family?"

Campbell sat back contemplatively, then replied with a catch to his voice, "My gut instinct says yes. But the facts, as they are currently, may tell a different story. I suppose I'll just have to keep digging till the right answers surface one way or another. In the meantime, I have someone else who's occupying my attention these days..."

Feeling the weight of his steady gaze, Stefanie couldn't

help but color as she asked playfully, "And who might that be?"

"You, Stefanie," he said clearly and concisely.

Her cheeks reddened with satisfaction. "You're occupying my attention just as much these days, Campbell," she stated candidly.

He grinned. "Good to know."

She thought this was as good a time as any to mention the gala to him. "I've been invited by Bella to the Annual Reston Hills Charitable Gala on Saturday. She's organizing it to raise money for various local causes. I'd love it if you could come as my guest..." Stefanie paused. "I know that as a police detective you probably don't have the luxury to plan anything too far ahead—"

Campbell interjected. "I'd be delighted to go to the gala as your guest, Stefanie. I'll make the time. Having been to a previous gala for guard duty, more or less, it should be fun to attend recreationally, and it's certainly a worthwhile event."

"I think so—and thanks." She showed her teeth, happy to have him accompany her to a public outing.

He echoed those thoughts, saying, "Glad to spend more time with you wherever I can."

"I feel the same," she assured him.

Before Stefanie knew it, they had leaned in to each other and started kissing. The powerful effect it had beyond her lips was instantaneous, causing her entire body to quaver.

Campbell pulled away from her swollen lips, and Stefanie, looking deeply into his eyes, asked in earnest, "Do you want to take this to your bedroom?"

"Yes." His voice was raspy. "But only if you do?"

"I want to make love to you," she responded point-blank. *How could I not, with the way you make me feel?* But she still needed to be responsible. She wasn't currently on birth control. "Do you have protection?"

"Yeah, I do," he assured her succinctly.

That was good enough for Stefanie as she rose from the table. She grabbed his arm and pulled him up toward her and uttered with anticipation, while knowing in her heart the timing was picture-perfect, "Then let's do this..."

STEFANIE WAS ANXIOUS as she stepped inside the large primary bedroom. She glanced at the hickory furniture before her eyes rested on the king-size copper-panel bed, with a dark green quilt coverlet and two large pillows. *Nice*, she thought as her gaze shifted to Campbell, who hadn't taken his own gaze off her, as though hypnotized. The notion turned her on even more.

He cupped her cheeks, and they began to kiss passionately, as Stefanie felt light on her feet. She felt the rigid contours of his body pressed against hers. Just as she had lost herself in the moment, Campbell pulled away.

"Be right back," he said on a breath.

"Okay." Stefanie watched as he went into the en suite bathroom. She started to undress, feeling strangely unabashed, while eager to see the whole of him, and to touch and be touched by him. In her heart, she knew that this was something that needed to happen—and she very much wanted it to.

When Campbell returned, he was holding a condom packet, tossing it on the bed. He peered at her and said desirously, "You're gorgeous—from head to toe."

Stefanie blushed. "You think?"

"Without a single doubt," he doubled down on it, and began removing his own clothes. They fell to the parquet floor one piece at a time as she took in his flat chest, rock-hard abs, long legs and strong feet. In between, his full manhood was clearly ready for her. As she was for him.

"I need you," Stefanie uttered, sotto voice, reaching out to him.

"I'm all yours," Campbell responded, scooping her up in his arms and carrying her to the bed.

"And I'm yours," she told him, eager to proceed on that meeting of the minds with their bodies.

Lying on the cotton sateen sheet, Stefanie waited for him to fall into her arms, half atop her, which he did. Their mouths locked for more deep kissing, and she could hear the patter of his heartbeat. Or was it her own? Either way, the craving within her was insatiable.

This only built in waves as Campbell explored her body blindly with long, nimble fingers, their lips never parting. As he stimulated her taut nipples and private parts, she nearly screamed with pleasure. Instead, she simply lay back and enjoyed it for as long as she could, before her needs went beyond that.

"Make love to me, Campbell," Stefanie demanded, stopping what he was doing, her own delight notwithstanding.

"Are you sure you're ready?" he asked selflessly.

"More than ever!" Her voice rang with determination. She went a step further, grabbing the foil packet and ripping it open. Then she took out the condom and put it on his erection, leaving no doubt as to what she wanted from him. Now.

Heeding her call, Campbell took over from there. He propped up on an elbow and calmly positioned himself between her legs. They locked eyes lasciviously as he slid slowly inside her. Stefanie adjusted her body to him and they began to make love. She planted her feet on the bed while urging him to go deeper and deeper.

As he capitulated to her wishes with abandon while fighting back his own urges, Stefanie climaxed, crying out. Her body quavered wildly as she kissed him—breathing in his enticing masculine scent—she'd nearly forgotten how good it felt to react to a man's intimate attention. She sucked in a deep breath but knew this wasn't over. Nor did she wish for it to be.

Wanting Campbell to reach his own heights of pleasure, Stefanie cooed to him, "Your turn. Let's get there together—"

"All right." Campbell sighed. He flipped her around so that he was on the bottom, and held on to Stefanie's hips firmly. She moved gradually onto him and picked up the pace as he cupped one of her buttocks and they rocked and rolled their way toward his satisfaction.

When Campbell's orgasm came, he let out a primordial grunt and his body shook. He turned them back around so Stefanie was beneath him and experienced a second climax as they soared to sexual heights like eagles in human form, in search of something rewarding that they had seized upon in their mutual pleasuring.

Afterward, both spent, they lay side by side, collecting their breaths while coming back down to earth for a safe landing. Stefanie wondered how Campbell felt, physically and mentally, now that it was over. Any regrets?

As if to alleviate any concerns on her part, Campbell laughed and said sincerely, "Wow! You were truly amazing."

Coloring, Stefanie breathed a sigh of relief. "So were you."

"Some things in life are worth waiting for. This definitely qualifies."

She chuckled. "I'd have to agree with you there. It was

certainly a good thing to wait for this to happen—and then achieve the desired results."

"Amen to that." Campbell laughed, then kissed her shoulder. "Next time, though—now that the sense of urgency was met—I'd like to take it nice and slow so that we prolong the intimacy as long as we can while enjoying the pleasures of sex."

"Mmm..." Stefanie tingled inside at the notion, that there would be a next time. "You'll get no argument from me there."

"Good." He kissed the top of her head. "I hate arguing, especially where it concerns matters of the heart."

"Me, too." She liked hearing him think of sexual relations between them as relating to the rhythm of their hearts.

Stefanie also wanted to see this as the start—or continuation—of something special that had lots of upside for the future. Maybe it was truly their destiny to meet the way they met, to lead to what just happened and could happen beyond. Campbell took her into his arms, and she fell asleep on that sweet thought.

AS HE GOT up the next morning, Campbell could not deny that Stefanie had more than measured up to any fantasies he'd had about going to bed with her. Beyond the hot sex, the chemistry between them in general was undeniable. The fact that the two of them both seemed to be on the same page—now that they had gotten that first night of intimate relations out of their system—in forging ahead, gave him hope that he might finally have found someone that pushed the right buttons in what he wanted from a partner for the long term.

Stefanie had done just that in no time flat. Campbell

watched as she was still sound asleep—lying on her stomach beneath the coverlet, her face pressed sideways against the pillow while looking absolutely beautiful—no doubt needing some rest after their sexual escapades had worked their way into a second round that was even more frenetic and all-consuming than the first.

He was still in reverie mode when Stefanie opened her eyes. Yawning attractively, she looked at him and asked, "How long have you been awake?"

Campbell grinned and responded, "Just long enough to be able to appreciate how hot you look sleeping in my bed."

Stefanie blushed. "You would say that."

"I only tell it like it is," he said truthfully, knowing that she was checking him out as well, still in the nude. "I was about to hop into the shower. If you need a little more shut-eye, I can wake you afterwards and make us breakfast."

"I'm good," she said, rubbing her eyes. "Why don't I join you in the shower and then we'll have breakfast?"

"Okay." He smiled, picturing them fooling around in the shower while putting the soap bar to good use. This turned him on. As did much about her. Even while in the back of his mind duty still called, as he tried to solve at least one case of a fatal OD under mysterious circumstances. Which may or may not be associated with a similar incident that occurred way before his time.

Chapter Eleven

Campbell pulled into Chao's Auto Repair on Sixteenth Street. He was hoping to find Irving Quinaz, a thirty-two-year-old auto mechanic with a criminal record that involved drug dealing. According to a bartender at the Kieke's Nightclub on Lour Avenue, Mia O'Dell was identified as having been there on the Saturday night before Founder's Day and leaving with Quinaz. The location itself was pinpointed as a result of cell phone data that revealed Mia's cell phone—which was still missing—had pinged close to the nightclub a short time prior to her estimated time of death.

It was the last time the phone was on to record her location before it went dead. Considering the timeline and circumstances, Campbell definitely suspected Quinaz was a person of interest in supplying Mia with the fentanyl mixed with carfentanil that killed her. If this was the case, was it an unintentional lethal dose? Or did he willfully kill her—perhaps at the behest of someone else? Such as Kenneth Braison?

Stepping into the auto shop garage, Campbell spotted—working under the hood of a Buick Enclave—a man who fit the description of Irving Quinaz's mug shot. When he looked up, Campbell saw that he had brown eyes and brown hair in a high fade style, was of medium build and about six feet tall.

He regarded Campbell and asked nonchalantly, "Can I help you?"

"Are you Irving Quinaz?"

"Yeah, who are you?"

Flashing his identification, Campbell replied coolly, "Detective Sawyer, Reston Hills PD. I'd like to ask you a few questions about Mia O'Dell—"

Quinaz jutted his chin. "What about her?"

So, he's not denying that he knows Mia, Campbell told himself, stepping closer to the suspect. "She died on Founder's Day from a drug overdose. Do you happen to know anything about that" —Campbell watched his uneasy reaction— "as the man identified seen leaving the Kieke's Nightclub with Mia on Saturday, the night before she wound up naked and dead in Reston Hills Park?"

Quinaz knitted thick brows. "Look, I heard about that, but I had nothing to do with it, okay? We met at the club, hooked up in the back of my Toyota Highlander and went our separate ways. Never saw her again. End of story—"

Campbell peered at him. Even if plausible, he wasn't quite ready to leave it at that. "Did you provide Mia with fentanyl during this hook up?"

"No—definitely not!" Quinaz insisted.

"You have a record that suggests otherwise," Campbell put forth.

"I was a kid when I got involved with the wrong people at the wrong time in the drug culture." Quinaz blew out a loud breath. "I did no time and have kept my nose clean ever since. Wherever Mia got the fentanyl, it didn't come from me."

Campbell mulled that over. He had always believed in second chances—for both mistakes made and romance. Maybe Quinaz deserved the benefit of the doubt. Or not.

"Did Mia ever mention anything to you about the Braison Family?"

Quinaz met his eyes. "Yeah, she said she was a member but might be getting out of the cult."

"Did she say why?"

"Only that it wasn't everything it was cracked up to be...and that something better was maybe about to come her way." He scratched his head. "She didn't say what that was. And I never asked."

Campbell couldn't help but wonder what that was all about. Was that the fentanyl-carfentanil combo creating an unrealistic fantasy in Mia's head before she OD'd on it? Or could she have found herself a sugar daddy outside the cult—who maybe she tried to blackmail and then paid the ultimate price?

Or was Kenneth Braison determined to keep her in the fold, whatever it took? Even if it meant making an example out of her in wanting to break free of his hold as a cult leader.

Campbell cast his eyes on the mechanic and asked him straightforwardly, "What time did this hookup between you and Mia end?"

"Around midnight," Quinaz answered with no runup.

"Hmm. And what did you do after that?"

"I drove home," he insisted.

"What about Mia?" Campbell asked, noting that the nightclub was less than a mile from Reston Hills Park. "Did you see her with anyone else?"

Quinaz shook his head. "She just walked off." He paused. "Thought about asking if she wanted a lift. But I had the feeling—don't ask me why—that she either already had a ride or had other plans that didn't involve me..."

"Okay." Campbell wasn't necessarily sold on his story but couldn't dispute it as yet. He considered the possibility that Mia had gotten a ride with either a known or unknown person. Or may have walked to the park and could have been followed there. Or someone was waiting for her at the park, or she encountered them randomly—and was handed the lethal drug combo.

Maybe surveillance cameras can give us something, Campbell thought. He looked Quinaz in the eye and said warningly, "If I have any further questions, I'll be back."

"Fine by me," Quinaz said with a shrug. "I'm not going anywhere."

Campbell walked out of the garage, believing that it was likely a dead end with the mechanic, while providing more food for thought otherwise. He got in his SUV and drove off, wondering if Mia could have somehow gotten in over her head through one means or another. Over and beyond her exposure to fentanyl.

JASMINE WASN'T QUITE sure who to trust as she walked around the compound, trying to avoid eye contact with anyone who might become suspicious of her and report this to Kenneth or Juan. She did her best to appear as unbothered as possible when it came to Mia being dead from a drug overdose. After all, it seemed as though most of the Braison Family members had come to terms with her death, as if it was just something that happened and not their concern.

But Jasmine saw it differently. She didn't believe that Mia would knowingly ingest fentanyl, putting her life on the line. Not to mention disappointing Kenneth—if, in fact, he wasn't the one who'd handed her the fentanyl in the first place. At least on the surface, he appeared adamantly against drug use on the property.

Yet beneath the surface, Jasmine feared that the Braison Family was pretty much capable of anything. Even murder, if anyone dared to challenge Kenneth's authority. While making it appear to be a self-inflicted overdose.

Was this what had happened to Mia—who could be headstrong and independent-minded, unlike most of the followers? Had she been murdered to keep her silenced forever? Had she learned secrets that made her a liability?

Jasmine sucked in a deep breath as she forced a smile at this follower and that one, but kept her mouth shut. Why hadn't Kenneth been more forthcoming when she expressed her concerns to him about Mia and her totally unexpected and premature death? Why did he, instead, blow her off and go through the same old Braison Family principles as a way to avoid the subject?

Did someone in the Family have it in for Mia—with or without Kenneth's knowledge or consent—and coax her into OD'ing and being left naked and humiliated at the park?

Jasmine wondered if Stefanie might be able to provide her with any answers, if only for her own peace of mind. And to help her decide if she wanted to remain a member of the Braison Family. She and Stefanie had exchanged phone numbers, with Stefanie encouraging her to call if she ever needed to talk—almost as though this was expected of her.

I'll do it—give her a call and maybe we can meet up somewhere away from prying eyes and talk, Jasmine told herself. She glanced over her shoulder as if someone were watching her. While no one stood out, she spotted Siobhan, who tried to pretend she was too busy on her cell phone to notice her—but never seemed to miss a beat when being on the lookout for anything she could report back to Kenneth or Juan. Jasmine couldn't help but wonder if Mia had felt the same way. Before disaster struck like a tornado.

IN HER LIVING ROOM, Stefanie sat on the copper-colored MCM chair, watching television. Or at least she was trying to, gazing at the fifty-five-inch smart TV on the wall. It was hard to concentrate with Curlie on her lap trying to decide whether to be still or spry, per her cat nature.

Beyond that, Stefanie couldn't help but think about her night of passion with Campbell, awakening desires in her she never knew she had. The way he reacted to her touch, kisses and more, she believed that he, too, was feeling it. So yes, she believed that they had started dating officially, more or less. This scared her as much as exhilarated her, as venturing into new territory in a Reston Hills relationship with sex as a part of the equation meant moving into the next phase of starting over as a widow.

Was she really up for this? Would Campbell protect her heart as she needed in forging ahead and making the most of the opportunity that they had both been afforded?

And would she be able to give him everything he needed in a woman, lover and friend as he traded in his single status for becoming boyfriend material?

Stefanie looked even further ahead at the prospects of matrimony, children, meeting Campbell's dad and his partner—and how this all might play out—if she and Campbell remained serious about each other over the long haul.

There you go overthinking things again, Stefanie admonished herself. She would not go there. *Just let things happen as they're meant to—or not*, she thought, enjoying the ride in the meantime.

Curlie grew restless and jumped from her lap onto the floor, where the cat then ran off to be by herself. Stefanie chuckled with amusement, then turned back to the TV screen to focus on the old romance movie she was trying to watch.

When her cell phone rang a few minutes later, Stefanie removed it from the pocket of her denim shorts and saw that the caller was Jasmine, from the Braison Family. Answering the call, masking her surprise, in spite of having invited Jasmine to do just that in getting more info from her on Mia, Stefanie said cheerily, "Hi, Jasmine."

"Can we meet...to talk?" Jasmine asked, sounding tense.

"Of course." Stefanie pressed the phone closer to her ear. "Where?"

"How about Reston Hills Park?"

"That's fine," Stefanie agreed.

Jasmine said, ill at ease, "I'll wait for you near the south entry to the river walk..."

Before Stefanie could say anything else, the phone had disconnected.

NEEDLESS TO SAY, Stefanie's interest was piqued as she drove to the park. Had Jasmine learned something about Mia's death that she needed to get off her chest? Something that Jasmine wasn't at liberty to say at the Braison Family compound under the auspices of Kenneth Braison?

After reaching Reston Hills Park, which brought back unsettling memories from Founder's Day, Stefanie parked in a lot on the south side and went to look for Jasmine.

She found her quickly enough, as Jasmine came out of

the woods, wearing the shoulder tote Stefanie remembered from when they first met.

Jasmine said in an uneven tone, "Thanks for coming," and gave her a hug as if they were old friends.

"Sure." Stefanie offered her a disconcerting look. "What is it?"

Jasmine looked over her shoulder, as if expecting someone to come and attack them at any moment, before eyeing her warily and responding, "Let's move away from here…"

Stefanie nodded. "All right."

They made their way onto the tree-lined walkway on the banks of the Beeks River and ambled along.

After a long moment or two, Jasmine faced Stefanie and batting her eyes, said expressively, "You were the one who discovered Mia's body in the park on Founder's Day?"

"Yes," Stefanie acknowledged. "It was shortly after you handed me the flyer that day. I was actually hoping to talk to you about that when I visited the Braison Family ranch. But then Kenneth and Juan kept that from happening…"

"I know." Jasmine nodded, wrinkling her nose. "I was shocked to hear about Mia's death—and especially the way she died…"

"Are you saying she wasn't using drugs…fentanyl?" Stefanie asked.

"Not to my knowledge." Jasmine wrung her hands nervously. "That's what is so weird about this. Why would Mia OD on fentanyl…unless she was unaware it had entered her system?"

The same thought had crossed Stefanie's mind more than once. She regarded Jasmine and asked, "So, you think someone—maybe from inside the Braison Family—gave the drug to her deliberately? And if so, for what reason?"

Jasmine chewed on her lower lip. "I've asked myself

that," she muttered. "All I can think of is that Mia may have found out something that put her at odds with the Family. Especially if she threatened to expose publicly whatever she knew. Kenneth would never have allowed that to happen—"

Stefanie swallowed thickly and asked, "To the point of killing her to keep Mia's silence?"

"Honestly, I wouldn't put it past him," she said uneasily. "Kenneth would do anything to protect whatever secrets he had. Or could otherwise ruin what he and his father, Wendell Braison, had built over decades." Jasmine drew a sigh. "I just don't know..."

"Have you spoken to anyone in the Family about this?" Stefanie wondered.

"I tried talking to Kenneth, but he just dismissed my concerns as if they had no merit whatsoever. I wasn't about to speak with any other members of the Braison Family, only to potentially put myself at risk..." She looked behind them and back at Stefanie with frightened eyes. "Even now, I'm taking a big risk in talking to you about this..."

"You know, you don't have to go back to the compound," Stefanie stressed to her. "If you feel your life is in danger—"

"I do...but I don't," Jasmine told her. "They think that I'm here passing out more flyers—" she lifted a few out of her tote bag to illustrate and then put them back in it "—in trying to recruit new followers. Which is why I need to get back, before they start asking questions..." She sighed. "Most of Kenneth's followers are there for the right reasons. That includes me. I don't want to mess things up for them by airing my suspicions to the authorities..." She paused, then admitted, "I did try to talk to Detective Sawyer when the police searched the compound, but was unable to do so without being seen by others."

Stefanie gazed at her. "I can certainly speak with Detective Sawyer, if you like," she volunteered.

"Would you?"

"Yes. But without any hard proof to support your suspicions—and mine, frankly—I'm not sure he will be able to do much in terms of putting pressure on Kenneth and the Braison Family."

"Too bad." Jasmine furrowed her brow. "Kenneth knows how to cover his tracks well, so I guess we're stuck."

"Not necessarily," Stefanie argued as they continued to walk. "The police investigation into Mia's death is still ongoing. Don't underestimate their ability to get to the truth—one way or another..."

Jasmine nodded. "Hope so. For Mia. She wasn't perfect—who is?—but she really did want to make the world a better place in her own way. Just as I do."

"Don't we all," Stefanie said idealistically. Unfortunately, the world would always be a dangerous place for some more than others. But that didn't mean there was any harm in maintaining a positive attitude, at the very least. Even if being in a cult was not the way for her to go. And apparently was a wrong choice for Mia, too.

Jasmine said warily, "Anyway, I have to go."

"All right." Stefanie touched her arm. "Please be careful—and don't try to do anything that will put you at risk..."

Jasmine nodded. "I won't," she promised and took Stefanie's hands. "Pray for Mia's soul, as I will."

Stefanie agreed to this, then watched as Jasmine scurried off, disappearing into the woods.

Chapter Twelve

On Saturday evening, the Annual Reston Hills Charitable Gala, held at the Menakerr Center on Sallis Way in downtown Reston Hills, was in full swing. A five-member band was onstage performing live upbeat music, with author book readings, performances by talented children, an auction to raise money for local programs and enough interesting food choices to go around.

Stefanie felt slightly out of her element as she stood in the auction room, wearing a lilac cap-sleeve gown with strap sandals. Her hair was in chignon. Standing on one side of her was Campbell, who was resplendent in a crisp gray suit and tie over a baby blue shirt, worn with black oxfords. On the other side was Bella, who was stunning as always, in a sleek, black one-shoulder ponté knit gown and matching pointed-toe pumps. Next to her was Bella's date for the gala, Russell Kercheval, a fortysomething pro golfer, who was tall and slender, with wavy salt-and-pepper hair in a side-swept style. He wore a black tuxedo and black derby shoes. According to Bella, it wasn't serious.

Stefanie took her word for that, knowing that Bella seemed content at the moment to play the field while putting her efforts into being the perfect ambassador for Reston Hills.

Bella, one arm tucked beneath Russell's, flashed her teeth at Stefanie and Campbell, and asked, "Hope you're having fun?"

"Absolutely," Campbell said in an upbeat voice, holding a flute of champagne.

"I feel the same," Stefanie assured her, wanting the gala to be a big success.

"Me too." Russell grinned and kissed Bella on the cheek. "Always fun to be in your company, Bella."

"Then we're all in agreement." Bella laughed, seeming to soak in the compliment. "Now, let's see if the auction can bring in some big bucks for the right programs and causes…"

"I'm happy to do my part," Stefanie told her, "with my donation of free yoga and tai chi lessons for two winning bidders, respectively."

Campbell pitched in, "As am I, having offered a free trail ride for two at my father's horse ranch in nearby Fallon's Creek."

"They're great donations!" Bella's face lit up. "And should fetch some nice bids."

"As should the free golf lessons that I was happy to donate," Russell said, as if not wanting to be outdone.

"Another winning ticket for would-be golfers," Bella exclaimed. "Thank you, Russ."

He beamed. "Anytime."

After Bella made her way to the podium, with Russell close behind, Campbell commented, "She really is made for these civic duties and keeping her great-grandfather's town alive and well, with a bright future."

"True." Stefanie smiled and sipped her champagne. She

couldn't help but wonder if their own future had brightness written all over it. They seemed to be headed in the right direction, giving her reason for being optimistic.

She wished she felt the same way about Jasmine Roxburgh. If it were up to Stefanie, she would just as soon see Jasmine leave the Braison Family. But clearly this was something that she was reluctant to do, as if Kenneth and company had a hold on her that Jasmine couldn't break free of.

I can only hope that she protects herself from harm, even if that means getting out of there, Stefanie thought. She wondered if this was what had proved to be Mia's downfall—being unable to escape danger. Even if it was staring her right in the face. Till it was too late to prevent her own death.

Campbell got her attention when he asked Stefanie, "I heard music coming from the ballroom. Can I have this dance?"

Stefanie didn't necessarily consider dancing to be her strong suit, but with Campbell she felt she was up for just about anything. So, she responded readily, "Of course. Let's go dance…"

CAMPBELL WAS ONLY too happy to get Stefanie on the dance floor to a nice slow and sensual torch song the band was playing. It gave them an opportunity to show off as one of the newest couples in Reston Hills—competing, he suspected, for that honor with Bella and Russell, who seemed really into each other. Campbell wasn't at all surprised to see that dancing with Stefanie, her head resting comfortably on his shoulder, seemed entirely natural and she felt damned good in his arms in a public setting.

To say nothing of how wonderful she felt in a private setting, where only they could see what one another brought to the table in terms of affection and intimacy. He could only imagine how much more they had to offer to each other, while reaping the benefits left and right. North and south. East and west.

"You're pretty good at this," Stefanie told him, bringing Campbell back into focus with the moment at hand and the gala, which looked to be an enormous success for the community.

He held her a little closer as they danced, and replied, "I could say the same for you. Guess that means that we make one hell of a couple on the dance floor."

"That, we do." She laughed. "And not so bad off the floor as well."

Campbell chuckled, in total agreement. He kissed Stefanie, tasting the champagne off her mouth. "You've got that right." Honestly, he could dance the night away with her every night—given the way their bodies molded together in total harmony—were there not other things both had on their plates.

As it was, for him, there remained the Mia O'Dell case to solve. There was still a question as to who supplied her the fentanyl-carfentanil concoction. And whether or not it was for nefarious reasons, over and beyond the illegality associated with drug dealing that resulted in a death. Until these things could be answered, there would be no rest for the weary as far as the case was concerned.

Along with that, Campbell still could not shake the feeling that Mia's death was connected in some meaningful way with the death of Lynda Boxleitner—apart from, or perhaps in conjunction with, both women being members of the Braison Family. Or maybe he was reading this wrong and only wanted that to be true as a way to clear up both his case and the cold case his father left behind.

When the song ended—too soon, as far as Campbell was concerned—Stefanie suggested they head back to the auction to see if Bella presented anything that might be worth bidding on for them.

"I'm game for that," Campbell responded.

Stefanie smiled. "Good. Maybe later, we can get in another dance or whatever you'd like to do."

"Sounds good," he said wistfully, taking her hand as they headed out of the ballroom.

THAT NIGHT, THEY WENT back to Stefanie's house and wasted little time before ending up in her bedroom. Campbell took one look around at the attractive MCM furniture, then zeroed in on the bamboo-platform queen-size bed with an aquamarine comforter. Picturing Stefanie beneath it, naked and ready, got him aroused.

"So, what's next?" he teased her after pulling her close to him.

"Um…" Her lashes batted flirtatiously. "Any suggestions…?"

"Yeah, I have one." Campbell cupped her cheeks and kissed her lips. He loved the softness of them.

"Just one?" she uttered into his mouth.

He grinned desirously. "For starters."

They kissed again. Minutes later, hot and bothered, they were in bed and deep into foreplay. After Campbell slipped on protection, mutual stimulation slowly but surely turned into lovemaking, where each gave as much—if not more—than they received, stretching well into the night.

Running his hands through Stefanie's long hair while they made love was a turn-on for Campbell all on its own.

As well as hearing her cry out when an orgasm caused her body to respond spasmodically. His climax came shortly after and was equally intense, his breathing heightened during the peak moment of satisfaction.

Stefanie giggled from atop him. "You're insatiable. Or maybe I'm the guilty party here."

Campbell laughed, enjoying the weight of her against his body. "I think we're both into each other enough to make a full confession," he said jokingly.

"I agree." She leaned over and gave him a long kiss, before rolling off him.

While they lay there catching their breath and allowing their heart rates to get back to normal, all Campbell could think of was that this was something he never wanted to see end. But it went beyond that. He was starting to feel something akin to love, even if it still needed a bit more time being spent together. But his gut instinct told him that Stefanie was a special woman who was roping him in like one of his dad's quarter horses. And he didn't mind her being at the reins one bit.

ON SUNDAY MORNING, Stefanie sat with Campbell at the Notton Street Café. They were waiting for Jasmine, who Stefanie had managed to talk into slipping away from the Braison Family ranch and speaking with Campbell about her suspicions surrounding Mia's death.

Maybe nothing will come out of it, Stefanie told herself as she drank her coffee. But at least Campbell was open to an informal chat with Jasmine—the one person from the cult who seemed willing to speak her mind about its inner workings and how this may have played a pivotal role in Mia's lethal overdose—considering that Jasmine was panicked at the thought of meeting with Campbell for an official interview.

Stefanie thought, *Can I really blame her?* After Mia's death and the hold Kenneth Braison seemed to have over his followers, challenging his authority was a risky venture at best. And could prove to be a fatal move at worst.

Fortunately, Campbell took this into consideration as he welcomed an insider's perspective on what she knew and didn't know about the Braison Family. And Kenneth, in particular.

For her part, Stefanie felt an obligation to bring the two together, since Jasmine had reached out to her for help. At least it felt that way when reading between the lines, irregular as they may have been.

Stefanie sipped more coffee as she gazed at Campbell and thought about their latest night of passion and what it meant in moving ahead in their relationship. She was all in with him in seeing where this went. He had made her believe that he felt the same way and wanted this to work out, well beyond the red-hot sex between them. This gave her confidence that their journey had only just begun, with lots of blue skies and symmetry ahead for them.

Campbell met her eyes and grinned. "You're gorgeous," he stated once again, as though he couldn't help himself.

Stefanie blushed. "I never tire of hearing that," she had to admit.

"Good, because I intend to keep reminding you of one of the many great elements that has me hooked."

"Umm..." She gave a soft smile, allowing that to sink in graciously.

Clutching his coffee mug, Campbell said, thoughtful, "So, do you think Jasmine is coming? Or was she prevented from doing so by the Braison Family?"

Stefanie suspected that the second question was more rhetorical in nature, even if a legitimate concern. "I know she wants to talk to you, even if she's afraid to do so. I can call her, if you want…"

Before he could respond, Campbell's own cell phone rang. He removed it from the side pocket of his blazer, glanced at it and said, "I better get this—"

Stefanie nodded and looked on as he listened to and spoke with someone from the police department. He exchanged a few more words as a distressed expression spread across this face, then told the person he was on his way and disconnected.

"What is it?" Stefanie asked, peering at him.

"Some disturbing news…" Campbell sucked in a deep breath and answered soberly, "An African American female's body has been found in Reston Hills Park." He ran a hand across his mouth. "The dead woman has tentatively been identified as Braison Family member Jasmine Roxburgh…"

Stefanie's jaw dropped as the gravity of what she'd just heard weighed on her. Jasmine dead? How? Had someone from the Braison Family come after her to prevent her from talking to Campbell? Or was there another reason why she, like Mia, was now dead?

CAMPBELL WOULD HAVE preferred to take Stefanie back to her house en route to the crime scene. But, as he expected, she would have none of it—insisting on accompanying him to the park. She had blamed herself prematurely for Jasmine's death. He had strongly pushed back against that, certain that whatever the cause—especially if criminal in intent—the onus would lie on entirely whoever was responsible. Stefanie had acquiesced to this, more or less, even as Campbell contemplated the latest casualty to befall a member of the Braison Family.

He glanced at Stefanie in the passenger seat and warned nevertheless, "Let's not jump to any conclusions."

She blinked. "If you mean beyond the fact that Jasmine's dead, I'll try not to."

"All right." Campbell felt that was the best he could hope for, for the time being. He turned back to the windshield, wondering if it had been wise to agree to meet with Jasmine clandestinely rather than in a police interview room. But since she had already spoken with Stefanie and might have had something useful to offer in the investigation into Mia O'Dell's death, it seemed like good idea. Particularly when Mia was reluctant to go on record officially with potential repercussions from the Braison Family. Campbell could only wonder if Jasmine had found herself caught in such a trap with no way out.

When they arrived at Reston Hills Park and got close to the area where the body was discovered, Detective Georgina Alvarez was waiting there to greet them.

"Hey," she said flatly, having been the one to identify Jasmine after discovering a tote bag with her driver's license near the scene where her body was found.

"Hey." Campbell introduced Georgina to Stefanie and vice versa, knowing that the detective was aware of their ongoing personal relationship. "Stefanie and Jasmine were friends," he said, to explain Stefanie's presence at a potential crime scene. "We were supposed to meet with Jasmine at a diner this morning to address her concerns about the Braison Family and Mia O'Dell's drug overdose." He frowned. "But she never showed up..."

"I doubt she ever had a chance to." Georgina sighed heavily. "Judging by her body—which was discovered by a woman who was walking her Finnish Lapphund dog—I'm guessing that Jasmine's been dead for at least a few hours."

Stefanie's brow creased. "How?"

"That'll be up to the coroner to determine," Georgina replied.

Campbell nodded and cast his eyes at Stefanie. "You'll need to wait here." Aside from it being a possible crime scene that didn't need to be disturbed, he saw no need to subject her to having to witness firsthand—up close and personal—another dead body.

Stefanie gave him an understanding look. "All right," she uttered meekly.

He moved away from her, alongside Georgina, and headed toward the decedent, who was lying near a trail on the other side of the park from where Mia was discovered.

"There she is…" Georgina muttered.

Campbell trained his eyes on the nude body of Jasmine Roxburgh. She was lying on her side on the grass in a fetal position—almost looking like she was taking a nap, with part of her blond Afro acting as a pillow. Her toenails had green polish on them. There were no outward signs of trauma. He noted the initials KB tattooed onto her right forearm, as if to remind him that Jasmine was a certified follower of Kenneth Braison—which may have cost Jasmine her life.

Campbell remarked instinctively, "I suspect that Jasmine, like Mia O'Dell, OD'd on fentanyl and carfentanil."

Georgina nodded. "I was thinking the same thing. Once the coroner's office confirms this, the next question is, where did she get the drug or drugs, and was she a victim of drug abuse—or deliberately murdered?"

"Yeah." Campbell gazed again at the attractive young woman whose voice had been forever silenced for one reason or another. "It's not a stretch to believe that however this plays out, Jasmine's death is tied to Mia's and their involvement with the Braison Family." *And, by extension, the murder of Lynda Boxleitner*, he told himself, sensing that the parallels could not be rejected out of hand. Even when the proof had yet to be established.

"I'm in agreement with you there," Georgina said firmly. "We just need to get the goods on Kenneth Braison or his cohorts to make the case."

Campbell jutted his chin. "If it's there, we'll uncover it…" He turned to where Stefanie was still standing—anxious, no doubt. "I need to go fill her in."

"Do it." Georgina nodded. She put a hand on his shoulder. "Sorry she's being put through this—again…"

"Me too." Campbell wished that weren't the case, but it was the hand both he and Stefanie had been dealt. Now they needed to see it through—for better, hopefully, or worse.

Chapter Thirteen

The area where Stefanie had been forced to remain while Campbell went to view the body had been cordoned off by police. She could only lament at the thought that Jasmine had died all of a sudden, if true. The same day they were supposed to meet up with Jasmine to talk about her concerns regarding Kenneth Braison and his cult possibly being complicit in Mia's death, Jasmine had been found dead, too?

What gives? Stefanie asked herself, pacing as she awaited Campbell's return. *This is getting too weird.* How could this happen? Could the two deaths be entirely coincidental and therefore unrelated? Or were they definitely related?

And could they be tied to a cold case homicide that Campbell's father had investigated?

As Stefanie pondered these questions, she took a breath and looked up to find Campbell standing there, gazing at her, having come across the barricade tape.

"Hey," he said in a low voice.

She met his eyes and asked, "What did you find out?"

Campbell hesitated, rubbing his jawline. "Jasmine appears to have died under similar circumstances to Mia…

right down to having her clothes removed. The autopsy will show if she OD'd on fentanyl or another lethal drug."

Stefanie put a hand to her mouth as she envisioned Jasmine lying there and then switched the ghastly image to Mia. "In talking to Jasmine, I didn't get the impression that she was a drug user."

"Maybe she wasn't," he entertained.

"So, we're talking about murder?"

Campbell lowered his chin. "We'll see about that," he responded ruminatively. "Don't want to get ahead of myself by speculating. But clearly, Jasmine's mysterious death—coming when and how it did—is cause for concern."

For me, too, Stefanie told herself, putting it mildly. She said, ill at ease, "The Braison Family has a lot of explaining to do. Or will Kenneth Braison try to worm his way out of this death of one of his followers, too…?"

"If Braison or his Family are culpable in any way for Jasmine's death—or Mia's, for that matter—they'll have to answer for it, one way or another," Campbell promised, leaving it at that. He put a gentle arm around her shoulders. "I'll take you home."

Though she wanted to stick with him every step of the way in the investigation, Stefanie understood that she needed to stay in her own lane and allow him to do the police work. All she could do was hope he could get the right answers on why Mia and now Jasmine were dead seemingly without legitimate reasons.

CAMPBELL FLASHED HIS ID as he stood at the gate to the Braison Family compound, under the watchful eyes of Juan Barrientos and a hefty, bald guard, over six feet tall with a moon-shaped scar on his cheek.

"I need to see Braison!" Campbell said sharply.

Juan smirked. "Uh, Kenneth's kind of busy right now. What is this all about?" he demanded.

"You'll know when you know," Campbell retorted, glancing at the other man, preferring not to give Braison a heads-up on the nature of the visit.

Juan seemed to think about offering resistance, but thought better of it as he got out a cell phone from the back pocket of his jeans and put it to his ear. "There's a detective here to see you..." Campbell watched him listen expressionlessly, then Juan hung up and muttered, "Follow me..."

They left the other man standing guard, and Campbell was led to one of the cabins. Kenneth stepped out of it with two attractive and slender young blond-haired women, who grinned at him coquettishly, then scattered as the cult leader approached them.

Kenneth peered at Campbell and said snidely, "This is becoming rather habit forming. To what do I owe this pleasure, Detective Sawyer, *this* time around?"

Meeting his hard gaze, Campbell answered succinctly, "Another one of your followers, Jasmine Roxburgh, was found dead this morning in Reston Hills Park—"

Kenneth's countenance changed. "What?"

"She was naked and, apparently, left there to die..." Campbell faced Juan, who seemed impassive, then turned back to the cult leader. "An autopsy will show if there were any drugs in Jasmine's system that may have contributed to her death. Or any other explanation for what happened to her—"

After sucking in a deep breath, Kenneth stated somberly, "I'm frankly stunned to hear about Jasmine's death. She was a valued member of the Braison Family...as was Mia..."

"Now both women are dead," Campbell said, an edge to his voice. "And under circumstances that I would call highly suspicious."

"Believe me, I feel the same way," Kenneth argued. "So does Juan. We're family, and what hurts one of us, hurts us all. I wish I could tell you why either of them had to die, but I can't. I can only say that Jasmine, like Mia and every other member of the Family, are free to go outside the compound whenever the spirit moves them. In fact, we encourage members to step into the real world and its many problems as often as they like—so that they can better appreciate what we offer to the contrary in what I see as a much better world within this space we've created here." He scratched his circle beard. "I fear that both Jasmine and Mia were influenced by those on the dark side, and it took them down a very dark path of no return—resulting in drug abuse and suicidal behavior."

Braison's almost too smooth an operator, Campbell thought. Only he wasn't buying it. At least not the notion that the two deaths had nothing to do with the Braison Family and everything to do with the outside world and its negative influences. As far as Campbell was concerned, all roads in this investigation still led back to the cult's compound. In one respect or another.

He narrowed his eyes at the two men and said, "Once the estimated time of death is established, I'll need to know where you both were—and, for that matter, every member of your Family."

"Not a problem," Kenneth said. "Nothing to hide. Neither of us have stepped outside the compound for the last twenty-four hours, at least."

"That's right," Juan backed him up. "We've been

swamped with one thing after another in trying to keep things running smoothly. Anyone can vouch for that."

"Anyone but Jasmine Roxburgh and Mia O'Dell." Campbell rolled his eyes. "They somehow seemed to have slipped out unnoticed—and apparently, with little concern about their health and well-being away from this ranch—while ending up naked and dead in the park all by themselves. Doesn't really sound like a close-knit family who have each other's backs to me when the going gets tough—as in death."

Kenneth furrowed his brow and spat out, "You don't know what you're talking about—any more than your father did when he tried to railroad my father by looking for darkness—but only finding the light within the Braison Family orbit. We're not the enemy, Detective, no matter how much you want to make us out to be this radical group of misfits and weirdos. Now, unless you're here to arrest me, I suggest you be on your way and track down whoever is responsible for either Jasmine's or Mia's deaths—if they weren't self-inflicted. You won't find the person on this ranch…"

That's still open for debate, Campbell told himself, in spite of the cult leader's words to the contrary. It stung to insinuate that his dad was out to get Wendell Braison without just cause. As it did to imply that Braison's son was merely the misunderstood victim of a witch hunt. Or warlock.

All things considered, Campbell preferred to believe that there was something to the Braison Family involvement in the mysterious deaths of three women spanning two decades. He intended to keep up the pressure on Kenneth Braison and his cult to find answers—till he was satisfied that they were barking up the wrong tree.

Campbell shot him a cold stare and said curtly, "If you have nothing to hide, then you have nothing to worry about with this investigation. But if the evidence indicates otherwise, then you've got a real problem that this compound won't protect you from." He took a breath and added thoughtfully, "And just for the record, as a police detective, my father was only doing his job—going wherever the case led him. The fact that it was never solved doesn't mean he wasn't on the right track. Or that the same track has come full circle in bridging the past with the present investigation..."

Campbell left it at that and walked away from the two men, wondering if he would be any more successful in establishing a clear link to the Braison Family in Jasmine's and Mia's deaths than his dad had been in making the case in linking Wendell Braison to Lynda Boxleitner's murder.

KENNETH WAS FROWNING as he observed Campbell Sawyer exit the Braison Family property, a swagger to the detective's step. It was bad enough that another one of his followers, Jasmine, had died so soon after Mia's death—and apparently under similar circumstances. Worse, though, was that it put the Family—and him, in particular—under the microscope. Much like when his father was at the helm two decades ago and became the target of an investigation that went nowhere—but his father had never quite been able to get out from beneath the specter of being an alleged murderer.

This didn't set well with Kenneth. Whether or not his father, Wendell Braison, had actually poisoned to death Lynda Boxleitner—one of his many bedmates—and gotten away with it was irrelevant in present day terms. Wasn't it?

His father, whatever his faults, deserved to rest in peace, just like his mother did.

But Kenneth wondered about his own peace of mind while still among the living. Would the detective continue to hound him, hoping to pin two deaths on him while tarnishing the intent and reputation of the Braison Family? Or would the investigation veer off in a different direction and Campbell, along with the meddlesome yoga instructor he was bedding, Stefanie Nguyen, leave well enough alone? So they could finally go about their business and mission as a family without further interference.

Juan interrupted his thoughts by asking scornfully, "So, do you think the detective is going to lay off us?"

"Only when he has good reason to look elsewhere," Kenneth answered truthfully, rolling his long fingers through this hair. "But he doesn't have nearly enough smoke to start a fire. Otherwise, Campbell would be making arrests. He's got nothing..." Or at least not enough substance that Kenneth felt would ultimately hit the mark.

"Yeah, I'm thinking the same thing," Juan muttered, scratching his head. "They're looking for scapegoats within the Family—instead of going after outsiders who hate us and must have targeted Jasmine and Mia to make examples out of us."

"Perhaps..." Kenneth set his jaw. "Gather everyone to meet in front of my house. I need to share with them the unsettling news of Jasmine's untimely death. More than that, though—after what's happened to her and Mia, I think we may need to put more restrictions on coming and going... And maybe even start instituting drug testing to keep members of the Family from both danger and succumbing to some of the evils of society—"

"I agree." Juan nodded. "I'll get on it."

"Good." Kenneth patted the shoulder of his most loyal follower, with Siobhan, his current bedmate, a close second. He would need them both while navigating troubled waters in the riverscape.

THAT AFTERNOON, STEFANIE SAT in a booth with Bella at the Reston Hills River Pub on Third Street, as they sipped on mojitos.

"It sucks," Stefanie admitted, laying her sorrows out, not wanting to hold them in with the tragedy of Jasmine's death weighing on her.

"I know." Bella grimaced. "Especially since it seemed like Jasmine had something on her mind when she agreed to meet with you and Campbell. Someone must have wanted to prevent that meeting from ever taking place..."

"Right?" Stefanie sighed. "She was suspicious about Kenneth Braison—if not the entire Braison Family. Yet Jasmine was either too afraid or too brainwashed in the cult to break away altogether." Stefanie took a drink.

"Isn't that how it goes with these cults?" Bella pointed out. "They say all the right things to rope you in—perhaps convince you to give up your life savings and self-respect—then mess up your mind so you lose sight of what's right and what's wrong. If Jasmine—and maybe Mia as well—had decided they had enough of the Braison Family, that might have been the catalyst for Kenneth going after them. If it turns out that Jasmine, like Mia, died from a drug overdose, this will prove my point."

"Mine, too," Stefanie concurred, thinking about the conditions of which both died. "Both were without clothing, as if to make some type of morbid statement from their deaths to anyone else who would dare go against the cult..." Would Campbell reach the same conclusion? Or was there more to the story of the disturbing victimization than met the eye?

Bella tasted her cocktail and commented, "It is a bit bizarre... Just like it was when Lynda Boxleitner was found dead in a similar fashion on Founder's Day twenty years ago. It rocked the community and had people whispering and pointing fingers at the Braison Family. And even though Wendell Braison managed to avoid prosecution for the homicide, many people—including Mason Sawyer—never believed him to be innocent. The same may be true for his son, Kenneth Braison, who's fiercely protective of the Braison Family brand, whatever that entailed. The apple never falls too far from the tree, as the saying goes..."

"That's what they say," Stefanie agreed, though she was striving to keep an open mind as more details unfolded regarding Jasmine's death. "We'll just have to see what the investigation uncovers and just how deep within the Braison Family this could go—if anywhere at all."

Bella nodded. "I'm sure that Campbell and the entire police department are committed to doing their job and reaching the proper conclusions—whatever they happen to be and however long it takes—while giving the citizens of Reston Hills some much needed resolution to this unwelcome drama that they can live with."

"You're right about that," Stefanie said, offering her a smile of mutual support. "I need to take a step back and give Campbell the space he needs to figure this out."

"Probably a good idea." Bella held her hand. "You're my best friend, Stefanie. The last thing I want is to see you swept up in the Braison Family deeds and misdeeds—putting you in any type of danger."

Stefanie squeezed her hand, happy to see that she felt

that way about her in such a short period of time since taking up residence in Reston Hills. "I feel the same way about you—we're besties," she told her.

"Nice to know." Bella's eyes lit up and she lifted her glass for a toast. "Cheers."

"Cheers." Stefanie grinned. She thought about her feelings for Campbell, which went well beyond camaraderie—and was sure he recognized this and was on the same wavelength. Beyond that, she would take any real friendship she could get in this new environment. Even if it meant sharing Bella with anyone she chose to romance, such as her current beau, Russell Kercheval, whom she insisted was only a work-in-progress at the moment.

Bella finished off her drink and said, "Next round's on me."

"You're on," Stefanie agreed, more than happy to take her thoughts off Jasmine and the sad way she'd ended up—dead in the park.

Chapter Fourteen

On Monday morning, Mason took his favorite quarter horse, Dodge, out for a solo ride. Sally was at work, but probably wishing she was away from her desk at a local publishing house on the south side of town and riding with him as she loved to do. He loved spending as much time with her as possible. Maybe they would get hitched someday. Or maybe it was best not to mess up a good thing while still holding on to the memory of his late wife, Alyssa.

As he rode down the trail with his well-worn Stetson hat on tightly, Mason couldn't help but wonder about his son's love life. He wouldn't mind seeing Campbell settle down and marry someone who could appreciate what he had to offer, and vice versa, while maybe bringing children into the world to keep the bloodline going and making him a doting granddad.

His mind turned to the cold case that the murder of Lynda Boxleitner had turned into after all these years. It still bugged him that he hadn't solved the case. He was sure that the answers were staring him right in the face. Only he had been unable to visualize what he was seeing.

He imagined the same was true with Campbell, who

was busy trying to piece together his own cases of strange deaths involving naked young women. The latest one that was found at Reston Hills Park with similar characteristics was obviously patterned after the OD death of Mia O'Dell. What was that all about? Were both women simply drug addicts who were given a bad batch of drugs? Or was something more sinister at play here?

And did either death have anything to do with what happened to Lynda and the commonality involving the Braison Family? Or had the passage of time meant that the similarities were just strangely coincidental rather than someone with an agenda in mind to bridge the gap in the deaths?

As he headed back toward the house, Mason intended to take another hard look at his case files on Lynda's murder and, once again, see if anything stood out that might give him a new sense of direction. Perhaps he could help Campbell in his current investigation.

CAMPBELL WAS AT his desk, with Georgina standing over him, as Jennie Napier, the forensic pathologist, was visible on the screen of his laptop to provide them with the autopsy results on Jasmine Roxburgh.

"What do you have for us?" Campbell asked intently, sensing what she might say.

Adjusting her glasses, Jennie responded evenly, "Similar to the recent autopsy on Mia O'Dell, the decedent, twenty-five-year-old Jasmine Roxburgh, died from acute fentanyl intoxication—or fentanyl bromazolam, diazepam toxicity—the result of overdosing on a lethal amount of fentanyl mixed with its analog, carfentanil."

Campbell's brow furrowed, though she had confirmed his suspicions. "I have reason to believe that Ms. Roxburgh—a friend of Ms. O'Dell—was not doing drugs.

Much less, fentanyl or carfentanil," he said, leaning on Stefanie's observation and intuition regarding the cult member. "That suggests to me that someone may have knowingly given Jasmine the fentanyl concoction for the purpose of killing her..."

Georgina pitched in, "It's hard to fathom that someone who just lost a friend to fentanyl would willingly follow in her footsteps by OD'ing herself."

"I understand where you're coming from." Jennie twisted her lips thoughtfully. "I'm assuming you share the same suspicions about Ms. O'Dell's fatal overdose being a case of outright murder?"

"How could we not," Campbell replied matter-of-factly, "given the similarities in the way they died—naked and in the park..." He peered at the forensic pathologist. "What can you tell us about the external condition of Jasmine's body?"

Jennie responded levelly, "The decedent had some scratches on her arms and legs, and blisters on her feet—as well as some bruising on her upper body, suggesting a physical struggle with someone in the process."

Campbell interpolated, "Someone that Jasmine may have been trying to escape from, but failed before, during, or after the fentanyl went to work on her system—in what amounts to, at the very least, a drug-induced homicide?" *If not cold-blooded murder*, he thought.

"Yes, that would be my thinking on the decedent's final minutes of life," Jennie said solemnly.

"Were there any signs of sexual assault?" Georgina asked interestedly.

"No—none that we could ascertain during the examination," she said.

Campbell took note of this, which lined up with the

same confirmation in Mia's autopsy—that she hadn't been raped or otherwise sexually victimized. This indicated to him that neither Braison Family member was targeted for sexual criminality. But may well have been targeted for their common association with a cult and any attempts by the women to reject the teachings or conformity to the status quo.

When the conversation on the autopsy results ended, Georgina looked at Campbell and asked, "So, what do you think?"

He held her gaze and took a breath, before answering bluntly, "Someone obviously wanted both Jasmine and Mia dead for one reason or another..." Campbell mulled this over. "We could be looking at a serial killer—inside or outside the Braison Family."

Georgina's brow shot up. "You think so?"

Knowing that the FBI defined two killings at minimum—with as many as three when counting Lynda Boxleitner's death—as constituting serial murder when certain characteristics were present, which this qualified as in Campbell's book, he responded. "It's certainly something we need to consider, given the manner of death and discovery of Jasmine and Mia in less than a week—as though a serial killer's modus operandi—as an indicator that this is just getting started."

"Hmm...that's a scary thought," Georgina uttered, jutting her chin.

"I know, right?" Campbell sat back in his chair, pondering the concept. "While we need to keep an open mind on all possibilities, Kenneth Braison remains at the top of the list of suspects as the killer—serial or not—for either directly supplying and/or administering the lethal drugs or through his powerful reach with loyal and obedient followers as the head of the Braison Family."

Georgina sighed. "Meaning, whichever way we slice it, we still have our work cut out for us if we're to prevent more lethal overdoses…and homicides."

"Yeah, agreed." Campbell was blown over at the parallel thoughts, unsettling as they were. Moreover, he was determined to keep the deaths from going beyond the Braison Family members—with Stefanie being his greatest concern in that respect, as someone who had inadvertently been touched by Mia and Jasmine. In this instance, he saw that as a negative that a killer might see fit to use against Stefanie.

MASON SAT AT his desk while Hopper sat in front of the picture window, staring out at the meadow.

With all the information, statements, photographs and whatever else he had been able to keep as a cold case reminder of what had eluded him as a police detective taking up much of his desk space and some of the floor—Mason went through it all once more, hoping to find the proverbial needle in a haystack.

Sipping black coffee, he bit back on the frustrations at seemingly going around in circles. Just as had been the case twenty years ago. *Maybe I wasn't meant to ever fill in the blanks*, Mason surmised. Could be that some things in life were better left in the past.

He didn't believe that to be the case in this instance. Especially when the past and present had merged as though time had stood still. If Lynda's death was related in any way to the recent cult-related deaths, Mason sincerely believed it was incumbent upon him to lend his son a helping hand. And put his own mind at ease for the bargain.

As Mason went through the main suspects in Lynda's murder, he focused primarily on Wendell Braison, who'd had her under his thumb and in his bed as part of the cult manipulation and seemed more than capable of taking Lynda out if she crossed him. Or wanted out, if this went against his wishes.

But Braison was clever enough to keep from being boxed into a corner. They couldn't lay a finger on him in terms of an arrest and conviction.

Mason took another look at his son, Kenneth Braison. He was supposed to have been in Boise when Lynda was poisoned to death. But what if he had doubled back to commit the deed? Wendell would have done anything to shield his son from trouble—including paying off as many people as he needed to cover for him.

Studying the material, Mason wasn't feeling it about Kenneth being the culprit in Lynda's death, for whatever reason. Which didn't mean he wasn't responsible for the recent deaths of his followers in the Braison Family.

Mason turned to another suspect, Roger Pennock. A forty-nine-year-old professor, he was seen flirting with Lynda at Harriette's Café, where she worked part-time as a waitress, the day before her death. He was cleared after it was determined that he was in the hospital being treated for a peptic ulcer during Lynda's estimated time of death.

Similarly, Howard Henesy, a thirty-six-year-old homeless veteran, who was found lurking near Reston Hills Park just after midnight on Founder's Day in the vicinity of where Lynda's body was found, was dropped as a suspect when it was discovered that he'd solicited the services of a local prostitute—the two spending more than an hour together smoking marijuana and having sex, around the time of Lynda's death.

Mason sipped his coffee and sighed, nearly ready to call it quits on what was starting to look like a futile attempt at unlocking the past, when he came across another name that barely registered.

Sidney Sedwick.

Mason saw that Sedwick was forty-two at the time and worked as a gardener for Stuart Reston, whom Mason had done some off-duty security work for himself from time to time for extra pay outside of police work. Looking deeper at his notes, he noted that Sedwick had been seen with Lynda in his Ford F-150 pickup days before she was killed. He claimed he was only giving her a lift as a friend.

Sedwick's solid alibi for Lynda's death was that he was working with other volunteers all night on Founder's Day preparations. Many vouched for him. Moreover, Stuart Reston backed Sedwick as a hard worker with not a bad bone in his body. Given Stuart's stature in the town that bore his family's surname, this carried a lot of weight in looking elsewhere beyond Sedwick—who had no criminal record—for a killer.

But now Mason found himself revisiting the former gardener as a possible suspect in Lynda's death. Was his relationship with Lynda truly only platonic in nature? Or was there something more to it, such as sexual, at a time when Sedwick was divorced and lived alone?

As Hopper got up and made his way over to him, Mason couldn't help but think that, as a gardener, Sidney Sedwick may have had access to the poisonous rodenticide and insecticide, thallium sulfate, that Lynda died from. Though the tasteless, odorless and colorless pesticide had been banned for decades at the time in the United States, it was still available and accessible in some other countries.

Could Sedwick have gotten his hands on some and used

it on Lynda? Moreover, could he have graduated from thallium sulfate to fentanyl…and picked up where he left off in lethal poisonings of women in Reston Hills?

Mason chewed on these disturbing thoughts.

CAMPBELL SAT ON a mesh-back side chair in Chief Gloria Schecter's office as he briefed her on the latest—and no less disturbing—death to hit Reston Hills Park.

"This might be the work of a serial killer—possibly spanning two decades," he told her, bothered by the prospect.

Seated at her desk, Gloria's eyes widened behind her glasses. "Go on…"

Campbell sighed. "According to the autopsy findings, Jasmine Roxburgh's death was caused by acute fentanyl intoxication—or a lethal overdose of fentanyl combined with carfentanil—the same as Mia O'Dell. Both were found in the park naked—which, in and of itself is highly suspicious, even if they were under some delusional state from the effects of the fentanyl poisoning. The fact that they were members of the Braison Family—much like Lynda Boxleitner, who, as you know, had no clothes on when she died at the same location twenty years ago, albeit from thallium sulfate poisoning—suggests that the deaths are linked to the cult either by association or by someone who has it out for the followers…"

"Hmm…" Gloria pursed her lips. "If it's true that we're dealing with a poisonous serial killer, then it would effectively exonerate Wendell Braison in the unsolved death of Boxleitner," she threw out. "Am I right?"

Campbell considered this for a beat. "Yeah, that would seem to be the case—assuming we're talking about the same killer of all three women…" He paused. "It's still possible that Braison killed Lynda Boxleitner and someone else—perhaps Kenneth Braison—has taken up the cause, ritual, retaliation or whatever in using fentanyl to kill Jasmine Roxburgh and Mia O'Dell. We're not ruling anything out at the moment," he emphasized.

"Nor should you." Gloria leaned forward and said, "Keep digging and see what you unearth. If these are serial homicides—especially two decades in the making—we may need to bring the FBI in on this investigation. Given our somewhat limited resources, any help would always be welcome."

Maybe not always, Campbell thought, knowing the penchant the Bureau had to want to take the lead in any investigation they were involved in. Still, he wasn't so territorial that he would turn his back on their assistance, if offered. But first, he wanted more clarity as to whether he was onto something about the serial killer angle. Or if it was possible that Mia's and Jasmine's deaths were simply fatal drug overdoses that had landed them in the park—with the nudity merely a reflection of their affiliation with the Braison Family and being comfortable with no clothes on for the freedom it gave them.

IN HER STUDIO, Stefanie led the way in a Yin yoga class, which focused on stretching exercises, as part of the mind-body routines she offered. The attendees, including two men, seemed all in with her instructions and were following her lead nicely. Bella was there in her designer yoga wear, flashing a brilliant smile, and had no trouble keeping up.

Stefanie sucked in a measured breath. Frankly, she welcomed taking her attention away from the Braison Family and the mysterious deaths of their two followers. At the same time, she wanted Campbell to figure it all out and—if he could prove that Kenneth Braison or anyone else was at the center of the fatal poisonings—put the mystery to rest. And presumably prevent any other cult members from dying due to a drug overdose.

She returned her thoughts to the yoga class, feeling good about having brought her skills and knowledge on this and tai chi to Reston Hills. Maybe she could talk Campbell into attending one class or the other, even if he obviously needed no help whatsoever in the fitness department—in or out of bed. It would still give them another opportunity to bond in her world, as a measure of spending time together for whatever the future might bring. Beyond that, she imagined that he would even enjoy the classes, which were designed to be fun as much as healthy exercising. It was also something that would give Campbell a probably much-needed breather of his own from the tricky world of law enforcement and the challenges that undoubtedly came with the territory.

Chapter Fifteen

"I may have a lead on my cold case—or actually yours now..." Mason said over the phone.

Campbell, who was still at his desk, responded attentively, "Okay, what do you have?"

Without elaborating, his father said flatly, "Can you meet me at Sedwick's Greenhouse and Nursery on Bledton Road in Wally Ridge?"

"Yeah, sure," Campbell told him. "I can be there in about twenty minutes."

"See you then."

Campbell heard the phone disconnect. He finished up some paperwork and headed out of the building, stepping into the sunshine, while more than curious as to where this was headed. Not too surprisingly, his father had taken an active interest in the unofficial reopening of the Lynda Boxleitner homicide.

Had he made a breakthrough?

Campbell was just as keen to solve the decades-old murder. Especially if it was connected to the two current drug-related deaths he was investigating. After getting into his SUV, he sent Stefanie a quick text to say that he was thinking about her—and often. A return text came back from her, stating the same was true from her end. It brought a smile to his face as he realized how good it felt to have someone like her that enjoyed his company and wanted more of it.

He drove off to the rural town in Eckerslin County—about halfway between Reston Hills and Fallon's Creek. Spotting his father's Land Rover Range Rover in the parking lot of Sedwick's Greenhouse and Nursery, Campbell parked alongside him.

After climbing into the passenger side of his father's luxury SUV, he said, "Hey."

"Hey." Mason, wearing his cowboy hat, turned to face Campbell. "I've been going through my old files, hoping to find something...anything that might catch my eye..." He drew a breath. "Something did click. I came across info on one of the original suspects in Lynda's murder... His name's Sidney Sedwick—"

Campbell strained his mind to recall the name through his own perusal of the cold case files. He seemed to remember that Sedwick was barely mentioned, with the focus being almost entirely on Wendell Braison.

"I remember the name Sidney Sedwick," Campbell said, leaving it at that for now.

"Sedwick was employed at the time as a gardener by Stuart Reston," Mason pointed out, piquing Campbell's interest with the mention of Bella Reston's late father. "A witness reported seeing Lynda riding with Sedwick in his Ford F-150 pickup just days before her body was found in the park."

"Hmm..." Campbell muttered thoughtfully. "Where was Sedwick—or where was he supposed to be—when she was killed?"

"According to witnesses, he spent the entire night before

Founder's Day into the early morning hours working on preparations for the event, apparently giving him no time to poison Lynda. Beyond that, Stuart came to Sedwick's defense—insisting that he was a stand-up guy, incapable of doing anyone harm."

Campbell eyed his father. "What made you think—or reconsider—otherwise?"

Mason ran a hand across his mouth. "Well, although Sedwick came back clean in a criminal background check, the fact that he was a gardener and may have been able to get his hands on the pesticide used to fatally poison Lynda just stuck out with me this time around."

"What about his alibi?" Campbell asked as he weighed this.

"Yeah, there is that," Mason admitted. "But from my own volunteering for past Founder's Day planning, I know firsthand that it can be chaotic. People come and go without anyone truly being the wiser—but would swear that someone never left their sight."

Campbell cocked a brow. "So, you think that Sedwick could have slipped away, poisoned Lynda, dumped her in Reston Hills Park and returned to the Founder's Day preparations unnoticed?"

"Maybe." Mason sighed. "Guess I'd like to hear what Sedwick has to say about it twenty years later—if he'll talk to us… I did some digging, made some phone calls and learned that he now owns this greenhouse and nursery."

Campbell nodded. "Well, let's go see if we can find him."

"Okay."

They walked inside the greenhouse and, after asking to see Sidney Sedwick, were directed toward the perennials department. A medium-sized man in his early sixties with a silver Viking haircut and a Balbo beard was getting his hands dirty on some shrubs when they approached him.

Flashing his badge, Campbell took the initial lead. "I'm Detective Sawyer, Reston Hills Police Department."

Mason said evenly in a throwback, "I'm Detective Sawyer, too, and his father. Are you Sidney Sedwick?"

His shoulders slouched and his brown eyes narrowed while responding, "Yeah, that's me."

"We've spoken before," Mason told him matter-of-factly. "Twenty years ago…about the murder of Lynda Boxleitner—"

Sidney nodded. "I remember. How could I not?"

Campbell told him straightforwardly, "The case has been reopened… We'd like to ask you a few questions about it…" Even then, he was sizing up the suspect, wondering if he could be responsible as well for the deaths of Jasmine and Mia. "Is there somewhere we can talk?"

Sidney took a breath and replied, "Yeah—my office…"

They followed him back through the greenhouse and into a small windowless office with a standing desk workstation, wooden square table and two leather chairs.

Mason peered at the suspect and asked point-blank, "Is there something you'd like to get off your chest after all these years? Did you kill Lynda Boxleitner?"

Sidney stared at the question for a long moment. He sighed, then said levelly, "No, I did not kill Lynda… Had an alibi. And I could never have done that—"

"But she was in your truck days before her death," Mason said tersely.

Sidney freely admitted, "Yeah, I gave her a lift…"

Campbell sensed that he was holding back, prompting him to ask, "Do you know who could have poisoned her to death?"

Before he could respond, Mason put forth stridently, "As a gardener, you might have had knowledge of and access to thallium sulfate—the banned pesticide someone used to fatally poison Lynda. Maybe you chose to use it on her, for whatever reason…?" Mason glared at him and said, "Maybe you're at it again?"

Sidney's head snapped back as if he had been punched. He paused, then said thoughtfully, "There are some things I need to get off my chest. I've wanted to for a long time. Guess I was just waiting for you to show up—" he eyed Mason "—to say what should have been said twenty years ago…"

Campbell exchanged a curious glance with his father, both wondering, no doubt, if Sidney Sedwick was about to have second thoughts and confess to the murder of Lynda Boxleitner, for starters…

Sidney sucked in a deep breath, jutted his chin and said, "I was able to obtain some thallium sulfate from abroad… But not for myself. I got it for Stuart Reston."

"Stuart—" Mason lifted a brow with surprise. "What are you saying?"

"I'm saying that Mr. Reston asked me to order it…said he thought the pesticide might be more effective in dealing with a pest problem that was getting out of control on the property than what we were using."

Campbell contemplated this, then asked the obvious question, "Did Stuart Reston know Lynda Boxleitner?"

"Yeah, he knew her," Sidney said without hesitating.

"How well did he know her?" Mason asked pointedly.

"They were having an affair." Sidney's voice rose an octave. "Mr. Reston was sleeping with Lynda right under the nose of his wife, Eloise Reston, and their daughter, Bella. Or maybe not so much. You see, Mr. Reston often had me pick up and drive Lynda to various meeting places behind Mrs. Reston's and Bella's back. Sometimes he and Lynda even got together at my cottage. But from what I'd heard, Lynda wanted more than what he was offering her in their arrangement—I don't know, maybe to become the next Mrs. Reston—to keep her from letting the whole world know about their illicit affair. Mr. Reston, with too much to lose in this town, would have none of it."

Campbell narrowed his eyes as he digested this. "Are you saying that it was Reston who killed her—his lover?"

Sidney licked his lips and responded, "He never came right out and confessed to it—though I asked him if he used the thallium sulfate to kill her—but sidestepped it, saying it was better if I didn't know. He paid me to keep quiet, which I did. Knowing it was in my best interests not to cross him, I've stayed silent till this day…"

Mason cast him a firm look. "If you're leveling with us, you really believe neither Eloise nor Bella had a clue that Stuart was fooling around with Lynda…?"

"I never got that impression," Sidney claimed, "from when I was around them—which wasn't very often. I think that, being as clever as he was, Mr. Reston was able to pull the wool over their eyes about this."

Campbell took a step closer and asked pensively, "Do you recall how Reston felt about Lynda being a member of the Braison Family?"

"Yeah, I remember. He wasn't that thrilled about it, but it was her life." Sidney pulled on his beard. "Mr. Reston didn't care much for the cult—believing they were simply brainwashing gullible followers. Including Lynda. I guess he was happy to have her whenever he could—which wasn't as often as he would have liked, given his other obligations."

Mason set his jaw. "Since Stuart Reston is no longer around to defend himself from your insinuation and you admit to being the one to illegally bring thallium sulfate into this country, why should we believe Reston used the poison to kill Lynda—and not you—the so-called alibi notwithstanding...?"

Sidney sucked in a deep breath and answered unwaveringly, "Because this has been eating away at me for the past two decades and I gain nothing from lying. I liked Lynda, even if I didn't really know her all that well. She didn't deserve to end up like she did at the park that Founder's Day." His mouth tightened. "If Mr. Reston didn't poison her, he had the means to get someone else to do his dirty work. But it wasn't me."

Campbell looked at his father and Mason held his gaze, both contemplative in that unexpected moment of revelation.

HE FOLLOWED HIS father's SUV to Harriette's Café, which Mason had introduced Campbell to as a boy when his father was still on the force. They needed to talk about what Sidney Sedwick had confessed to. Or more precisely what he hadn't taken ownership of. He had pointed the finger squarely at Bella's father, Stuart Reston, as the person responsible for Lynda Boxleitner's death.

In Campbell's mind, this implication completely upended the belief that Wendell Braison had murdered Lynda. Whether she was romantically involved with him too was immaterial. Given Sedwick's role in supplying Reston with the thallium sulfate—in combination with his alleged infidelity with Lynda and possible blackmail on her part—it wasn't too much of a stretch to think that Reston, with much to lose in his marriage and position in society, might have chosen a deadly way out of his dilemma. And used Sidney Sedwick to achieve his goals.

Wonder how Dad is feeling about this sudden twist in a cold case? Campbell asked himself. He also couldn't help but wonder if Bella had ever suspected that her father was cheating on her mother. If so, there was no indication that she had ever held it against him, typically speaking of Stuart Reston in glowing terms—similar to her grandfather, Malcolm Reston, and great-grandfather, Arthur Reston. Or maybe she simply chose to judge her father for the good contributions he'd made to Reston Hills and not the bad.

Campbell pulled into the parking lot and caught up to his dad as they went inside the café.

They took a seat at the counter, and Sarah Huffstetler quickly came over to fill their coffee mugs. "Hey, handsome," she said with a big smile to Campbell.

He blushed. "Hey, Sarah."

She turned to Mason and said, "And another handsome gentleman, too."

"My father," Campbell told her proudly.

"Hey," Mason said, a small grin playing on his lips.

"Hi there." Sally put a hand on her hip, studying them. "I can see the resemblance."

"Not surprised." Campbell smiled at her, then waited for her to leave them alone.

Mason watched as she walked away, then eyed his son. "Is there something you want to tell me?"

"Yeah, since you ask—I am seeing someone," Campbell took the opportunity to reveal. "Only it's not Sarah."

Mason lifted a brow. "Oh?"

Campbell tasted the coffee. "Her name's Stefanie. She's a yoga and tai chi instructor in town." *And so much more*, he thought. "We met on Founder's Day."

"Uh-huh," Mason muttered thoughtfully, putting the coffee cup to his lips. "The same day that Mia O'Dell's body was discovered?"

"Stefanie was the one who found her on the trail in the park," Campbell noted. "We've been in each other's lives ever since."

His father nodded. "Good to hear. Hope this one works out."

"Me too." Campbell smiled when thinking about Stefanie. "I have a feeling she's the real deal."

Mason grinned. "Look forward to meeting her."

"You will," Campbell promised. He drank coffee and turned his thoughts to the visit with Stuart Reston's former gardener. "What do you make of what Sidney Sedwick had to say? Are you buying any of it?"

"I have to admit, Sedwick's bombshell sort of came out of left field." Mason rested an arm on the counter. "I went to the greenhouse hoping to extract a confession out of him, two decades removed—not have Sedwick claim that it was Stuart Reston who used poison to kill Lynda, after having an affair with her." Mason sipped his coffee. "When I did some work for Stuart, he seemed to be a bona fide family man who loved his wife. But looks can always be deceiving. Especially if Stuart wanted to present a false picture for obvious reasons. Lynda wasn't the same person I dated in high school at that stage. But she was still nice looking and she brought something to the table that might have enticed Stuart enough to go after her."

Campbell finished his coffee and asked probingly, "So, where does this leave Wendell Braison as a suspect in Lynda's murder?"

Mason considered this while closing his eyes for a moment, before regarding him and replying candidly, "It turns what I thought I knew about the man upside down. And turns my thoughts on Stuart right side up. Or, in other words, I'm starting to believe I had it all wrong that Braison killed Lynda—with Stuart Reston now taking up that position as a killer..."

Campbell was of the same view on Reston topping the list of suspects, though Sidney Sedwick's word alone wouldn't be enough to close the books on Lynda Boxleitner's murder.

Nor did it tell Campbell who was responsible for supplying Mia O'Dell and Jasmine Roxburgh with deadly fentanyl in what amounted to serial murder, through one deliberate action or another.

THAT NIGHT, IN HER bed with Campbell, Stefanie was still reeling after being told about the suspicions that Bella's father, Stuart Reston, had poisoned Lynda Boxleitner, his alleged lover. Stuart's former gardener was apparently credible enough that both Campbell and his father, Mason Sawyer, were sold on the notion enough that Wendell Braison was no longer at the top of the list of suspects in Lynda's murder.

Stefanie wondered where this left Kenneth Braison as a suspect in being the mastermind—if not actual culprit—of the drug-induced deaths of Jasmine and Mia. Were the cold case and current cases now thought to be unrelated?

"Do you think that Bella could've known her father was having an affair with Lynda—if, in fact, he was?" Campbell asked curiously as Stefanie rested her head on his firm chest.

She lifted her chin musingly. "Probably not. I think most cheating parents go to great lengths to keep it a secret," she told him. "Especially from their children, who would then be put in a rather awkward position as to whether or not to reveal this to the other parent."

"Maybe best if she didn't know—which would have meant knocking Stuart Reston off whatever pedestal she had him on." Campbell sighed. "Unfortunately, the cat may need to be let out of the bag—no disrespect to your wonderful cat, Curlie," he quipped. "If we get anything else concrete on the Boxleitner homicide that can tie it directly to Stuart Reston, it will have to made public—the town's namesake or not."

"I understand," Stefanie said acceptingly. She just wondered if Bella would. "So, do you still feel that the Braison Family is behind Jasmine's and Mia's deaths?"

With his arm wrapped around her, Campbell waited a beat and responded, "That's still open for consideration—but, as of now, there's reason enough to believe that someone within the cult's orbit is involved in the fatal fentanyl poisonings. Question is who—and to what degree? If not Kenneth Braison, then another cult member…" Campbell ran a hand along her bare shoulder. "Beyond that, it's not far reaching to think that they could have a serial killer in their midst—if not outside of the Family—on a deadly mission of targeting followers—"

"Hmm," Stefanie murmured reflectively while taking comfort being in Campbell's much-needed company. She thought about Mia and Jasmine and who could be next if an unidentified killer was roaming free to poison Braison Family members one by one.

Chapter Sixteen

The next day, Campbell sat inside his Chevy Tahoe in the police department lot. He was looking at his laptop, requesting a video chat with FBI Special Agent Rudi Villanueva, based in the Bureau's resident agency in Boise. She happened to be a criminal profiler who specialized in serial killers, whom he had worked with in joint task force investigations when he was with the Boise Police Department.

When Rudi accepted the call, her heart-shaped face appeared on the screen. In her late thirties, she was green-eyed and had blond hair in a whisper pixie. "Hey, Sawyer," she said cheerfully.

Campbell grinned. "Good morning, Rudi."

"How's life treating you in Reston Hills?"

Great on the romance front, he thought, but that wasn't the purpose of his call. So he responded frankly, "Not as well as I'd like these days…"

"Oh?" Her eyes widened. "What's up?"

Campbell told her about the two fentanyl-mixed-with-carfentanil fatalities connected to a cult, including the victims both found in the nude, with no indication of being sexually assaulted. Though it appeared as if the deaths were unrelated to the two decades old murder of Lynda Boxleitner, it seemed worth throwing it into the mix, given the notable similarities.

"I'm wondering if the overdoses, coming so close to one another at the same park, could be something more than the supplying of fentanyl and its analog as a drug-induced homicide," Campbell put out. "Such as the deliberate actions of a serial killer operating inside or outside of the Braison Family cult—possibly for years…?"

Rudi contemplated the info he'd shared with her for a minute or two, digesting it as her profiler side kicked into gear, before responding coolly, "Aside from the realities of the fentanyl epidemic and its devastating impact on communities across the country, these scenarios you've laid out are certainly thought-provoking." She drew a breath. "So, without having more time to delve into the deaths and their characteristics, with respect to fatal ODs, there does seem to be some symmetry between the two recent deaths and the death twenty years ago—which isn't to say they are directly related or orchestrated by the same person. That being said, the cult angle is interesting."

"Okay," Campbell said after hanging on her every word. "How much so?"

"Well, by its very nature, a cult is typically associated with a religious group of sorts that indoctrinates its followers to buying in to whatever philosophy they're selling—usually going against the grain of mainstream society and, at times, drifting into questionable or aberrant behavior." Rudi sighed. "Anyway, based on what you've told me, the way I see it, there are likely two strong possibilities here relative to serial murder… The first is that the two recent drug-related deaths are ritualistic killings by the cult in a ceremonial method of maintaining control over their followers—which, if true, would still qualify as serial homicides."

She ran a hand through her hair and continued, "The second, and probably most likely possibility, is that someone today—either within the Braison Family or not— was influenced by the Founder's Day homicide from twenty years ago. So there is a copycat killer deliberately mimicking it or pretending it's the same killer to perhaps throw you off from the real agenda, while substituting the thallium sulfate for the more accessible fentanyl to carry out the killings."

Campbell peered at the screen and stated, if hearing her words correctly, "So, the unsub—if there is one—is probably reenacting the murder of cult member Lynda Boxleitner as a smokescreen to perpetrate the modern-day cult-related killings of Mia O'Dell and Jasmine Roxburgh with another motive in mind?"

"That's where I would go with this and what you need to figure out," Rudi suggested. "Of course, there's always the possibility—slim as it might be—that a cold case killer has lay in wait for two decades, till the opportunity came to resume Braison Family members."

"Hmm..." Campbell weighed that angle. His current belief was that Stuart Reston had likely been the one to use thallium sulfate to kill his lover, Lynda Boxleitner. Thus, there was little reason to think that someone else—perhaps who had been incarcerated for another crime or otherwise prevented from acting out—had chosen to target followers of Kenneth Braison. Campbell preferred to believe that a killer was motivated to kill based on present circumstances and not past ones. "We'll see where this goes," he said. "Appreciate your thoughts."

Rudi smiled. "Always happy to help whenever I can." She paused. "Good luck with your investigation."

"Thanks." Campbell ended the video chat. He certainly wasn't counting on luck to solve this, but he was happy to accept it nevertheless. He closed the lid to the laptop and went inside the building.

"STUART RESTON?" GLORIA'S MOUTH stayed open in shock, as she stood in the conference room, which had a curved big-screen monitor, a rectangular wooden meeting table and leather chairs with wheels.

"Yeah, looks like he could have killed Lynda Boxleitner," Campbell reiterated, standing beside her, after giving the chief and Georgina, along with other detectives sitting around the table—including one from the Cold Case Unit—the rundown on what he and his father had gotten out of Reston's former gardener, Sidney Sedwick. "If Sedwick is to be believed—and his argument was pretty persuasive, I must admit—he got his hands on some thallium sulfate at the request of Reston, who used it to poison Boxleitner, his lover—presumably to keep their tryst from being exposed, as she may have threatened to do."

Gloria sighed. "Reston wasn't even on our radar as a suspect, which I'm sure Mason told you," she said, her voice rising an octave.

"He did," Campbell acknowledged, hoping his dad wouldn't be blamed for missing the boat here. "Guess Reston's prominent position in town and even apparently having an alibi of being with his wife, Eloise Reston, at the time Lynda Boxleitner was killed was more than enough to keep him from being looked at strongly as a suspect. And Sedwick had an alibi as well that held up." Campbell suddenly felt the need to defend his father's original investigation. "Whereas Wendell Braison—whom Lynda was also linked to romantically and as a member of the Braison

Family cult—was a more likely person of interest in her death, given the manner in which she died and other circumstantial evidence that pointed in Braison's direction."

Gloria nodded and said thoughtfully, "Sedwick's accusations, serious as they are, against a deceased Stuart Reston—in which Sedwick admits to being complicit in obtaining the poison used to kill Boxleitner—may not be enough to reopen the investigation formally. But it does give us good reason to take the onus off Wendell Braison, with the long-held belief that he had gotten away with murder."

"I agree," Campbell said, even if he wasn't quite ready to say the same for Kenneth Braison, who was still a suspect in the current investigation.

Ulrich González, the slim thirtysomething, brown-eyed cold case detective, whose black hair was in a military-style undercut, looked at him and then the chief before saying, "I'd be happy to do some more digging into this if you like."

Campbell took the liberty of replying unenthusiastically, "Knock yourself out." He knew that it would ultimately be Gloria's call and doubted she would want to prioritize this ahead of other cold cases that had more to work with at this point in time. She didn't disappoint him in dissuading Ulrich from this.

Georgina leaned forward at the table and asked for further clarification, "With the Lynda Boxleitner murder moving in a different direction, where does that leave us in connecting it to the OD deaths of Jasmine Roxburgh and Mia O'Dell?"

"Glad you asked," Campbell told her with a slight grin. "I think the Boxleitner death inspired a copycat to use a currently available poison to kill O'Dell and Roxburgh in a manner that links all three deaths to the Braison Family." He sighed. "The degree of that linkage and whether or not it amounts to a serial killer at large in Reston Hills remains to be seen."

THAT AFTERNOON, CAMPBELL AND GEORGINA, along with armed detectives from the Reston Hills Police Department's Narcotics Unit, a SWAT team, K-9 unit's dual-purpose drug-detection canines, and US Drug Enforcement Administration special agents, converged on a ranch house on Quakely Road. Based on evidence that strongly suggested that the fentanyl powder mixed with the potent synthetic opioid fentanyl analog, carfentanil had come from a known purported local drug dealer named Luther Valdez, a search warrant was issued for his Reston Hills residence.

Valdez, fifty-six, had served a dozen years in federal prison for various drug-trafficking offenses. Now Campbell wondered if he was up to his old tricks, supplying the deadly drugs that killed Mia and Jasmine. Just as important was, if true, whether or not Valdez had sold the fentanyl directly to the victims. Or to someone else, who had chosen to commit serial murder.

Campbell noted that there were two vehicles parked on the property—a black Mitsubishi Outlander SUV that was registered to Valdez, and a red Honda Pilot Sport SUV. The assumption was that the occupants of the house were armed, so they would act accordingly in executing the warrant.

Wearing a ballistic vest beneath his blazer, Campbell made contact with Georgina, also with a vest on, then the rest of the team, before giving the go-ahead for the raid to proceed.

Within moments, they had stormed the house. It had

little in the way of furnishings—mostly traditional—with hardwood flooring. The citrusy scent of marijuana permeated the air as they were confronted by a Rottweiler guard dog. The K-9 unit was able to effectively deal with the threat by subduing the animal and safely removing it from the premises.

They detained, without further resistance, the sole occupant—a medium built, short male with textured brown hair in a mullet cut, a scruffy beard and dark eyes—who identified himself as Luther Valdez.

After presenting him with the warrant, the search of the residence ensued. Confiscated were illegal narcotics—including fentanyl pills in multiple colors, fentanyl powder and liquid, methamphetamine, heroin, and cocaine—and oxycodone, a painkiller. Also seized were illegal firearms and ammunition.

Valdez was taken into custody to face charges.

IN AN INTERROGATION ROOM, Campbell got the first crack at the suspect, before the Feds would ultimately take possession of him, seeing that a number of suspected serious drug-related violations of federal law had been made by Luther Valdez.

Sitting in a wooden chair across a metal table from the suspect, Campbell glanced at the video camera that was recording the interview, then back at Valdez, and said to him in a deep tone of voice, "It looks like you had quite an operation going there." And obviously had not learned any lessons from his previous stint behind bars.

Valdez scratched his beard and muttered, "Yeah, I guess."

"Uh, this means you're in a lot of trouble," Campbell told him mockingly, in case he didn't get that. "Drug trafficking happens to be a serious crime in this state—and the country."

Valdez rolled his eyes. "So why am I here?"

"You're here because I'd like to help you, if you'll help me—" Campbell said, watching his reaction.

"How's that?" he asked suspiciously.

Campbell dodged the question. He pushed two pictures in front of his face and said solemnly, "Since Founder's Day, these two women have OD'd on fentanyl mixed with carfentanil… I have good reason to believe that the drugs came from you. The question is, did you sell or give it to them directly? Or did you sell it to someone else?" He considered that it was a leap of faith that they had zeroed in on the right drug trafficker. Now he only needed him to bite the bait.

Valdez studied the two faces of the dead women, taken after the fact for maximum effect on the results of drug overdoses. He jutted his chin and said tonelessly, "I've never seen either of them before."

Campbell wasn't sure he bought that, and pressed him. "Your drugs killed them," he said flatly. "If you didn't hand them a death sentence directly, then someone else did. Who did you sell the fentanyl powder laced with carfentanil to on or around Founder's Day?"

Valdez set his jaw. "What's in it for me?"

I was afraid he'd ask that, Campbell told himself. He responded straightforwardly, "If you're legit, I can put in a good word for you when your case moves forward. Could make the difference in how you fare at the end of the day. Now, I need a name." He wondered if Kenneth Braison's name would pop out of his mouth.

After a moment or two of contemplation, Valdez leaned

toward him and said, "I sold the fentanyl to Juan Barrientos—"

"Barrientos?" Campbell hoisted a brow, glancing at the video camera.

"Yeah. We go back a ways. Juan said he needed it to help keep some people in line with that cult he belongs to..." Valdez rubbed his nose. "I only sold him the drug. How he chose to use it wasn't my call."

"You can't get off that easily," Campbell told him unsympathetically, as Valdez was just as culpable in knowing that fentanyl could be deadly. But right now, the onus was on Barrientos. Had he taken it upon himself to drug the women for one reason or another? Or had he acted on behalf of Kenneth Braison as a means to control his followers—whatever the costs? "When exactly did this drug transaction take place?" Campbell demanded of the drug trafficker.

"A day before Founder's Day," Valdez answered without runup. "Said he needed some of the stuff in a hurry."

Campbell sighed thoughtfully. If this was the real deal, Barrientos would be held accountable for his decision to perpetrate drug-induced homicides on Mia and Jasmine. As would the man who sold him the deadly drug. "We'll check out your story," he told him keenly. "And go from there..."

Valdez seemed content to let this play out, undoubtedly hoping it would work in his favor to one degree or another when he was handed over to federal authorities.

Fifteen minutes later, Campbell was at his desk, going over the claims by Valdez with Georgina, who was at her own desk.

"If Valdez is telling the truth about Barrientos, there's our smoking gun," Campbell said matter-of-factly, "with respect to linking Mia O'Dell and Jasmine Roxburgh's fatal ODs. The big question is what does Kenneth Braison know and how long has he known it?"

"Yeah, both need to be answered, sooner rather than later," Georgina said, staring at her laptop. "Valdez, the creep that he is, has basically pointed the finger at the Braison Family itself and their involvement through Barrientos in Roxburgh and O'Dell's deaths."

Campbell lowered his chin. "Now we need to make the case for this."

"I think I found something that backs Valdez up on his claim of selling the fentanyl to Barrientos—if only by connotation in Mia's fatal OD..." Georgina said. "Come take a look..."

Campbell got up and walked over to her desk. "What are we looking at?" he asked, watching the video over her shoulder.

"It's surveillance video we obtained from a security camera not far from where Mia O'Dell was last seen alive," she responded. "There's Mia..."

"I see her." Campbell stared at the small screen, waiting for more.

"Watch as the blue Volvo XC60 SUV pulls up alongside Mia," Georgina said anxiously. "She looks inside, says something, then gets into the passenger seat before the SUV drives off—toward the direction of Reston Hills Park."

Since he couldn't make out the driver of the vehicle, Campbell said, "Can you back that up and zoom in on the license plate?"

Georgina did so for his benefit while saying excitedly, "I'm already two steps ahead. I checked out the plate."

She drew a breath. "The SUV's registered to Juan Barrientos—"

"We've got him," Campbell told her, feeling that the pieces had fallen into place that Barrientos had, in fact, lured Mia into his vehicle and gotten her to ingest the powdered fentanyl—before or after he took her to the park to leave her to die. The pattern fits as well in the death of Jasmine Roxburgh. Now they only needed to get him into custody and see just how far up the Braison Family chain this went.

Chapter Seventeen

Stefanie was a little surprised to see the door opened by Bella, after having come to expect that task to be done by her dependable, and seemingly always present, housekeeper, Nadine Marinkovich.

Bella grinned attractively. "Hey."

"Hey," Stefanie said, smiling back as she walked inside, paying her friend a planned visit just to chill out. "Where's Nadine?"

"I gave her the day off," Bella explained, as if feeling guilty for not doing so sooner. "Nadine works way too hard, cleaning up after me and my guests—present company excluded," she added with a laugh. "You're too much of a neat freak!"

Stefanie chuckled. "We are who we are," she said, taking ownership of what she assumed was a compliment.

"So true." Bella flashed her teeth. "Anyway, let's go sit in the den. I made herbal tea."

"Okay." Stefanie glanced toward the incredible kitchen with its luxury appliances, waterfall island and quartz countertops.

They got past the great room and formal dining room before entering the den. It was spacious, with white-wood paneling, interlocking hardwood flooring, a vaulted ceiling, two matching upholstered swivel armchairs and a corduroy modular sectional.

Bella sat on the sectional sofa and waited for Stefanie to sit beside her, which she did. She handed Stefanie a cup of herbal tea from a bamboo serving tray on a farmhouse coffee table, and then picked up the other cup for herself.

"So, how's your day been?" Bella asked casually.

Stefanie sipped the tea, thoughtful. "Same old, same old."

"Anything new on the dual investigations?"

"Not really," Stefanie told her. *Should I mention anything about the allegations leveled at her father, that he was having an affair with Lynda Boxleitner, only to poison her to death?* she wondered before deciding it wasn't her place to do so.

Stefanie suspected that Bella, being as devoted as she was to her family, would deny any unproven insinuations against her father. The fact that he was now deceased made it highly unlikely that the truth would ever come out, one way or the other, in spite of his former gardener's accusations regarding the affair and Stuart's use of the toxic thallium sulfate to silence Lynda forever.

Stefanie tasted the tea. "Have you heard anything?" she asked nonchalantly.

"Nothing comes to mind," Bella said, putting the cup of tea to her glossed lips.

"Guess we'll just have to wait and see how things turn out," Stefanie suggested, knowing that whatever came out about Stuart Reston, Bella would just have to deal with it and, hopefully, get past it.

"Right." Bella sat her teacup down and watched as Stefanie sipped more. "Is the tea as good as I think it is?"

"Yes, excellent," Stefanie replied with a smile, tasting the blend of elderflower, chamomile and lemon.

Bella grinned. "Glad you like it." She waited a beat before taking a breath and saying evenly, "There's something I have to tell you, Stefanie... I've been wanting to talk about this with someone for the longest time, but it never quite seemed like the right time. Till now..."

"Okay." Stefanie regarded her, curious as to what was weighing on her friend's mind. "You've got my full attention."

"Thanks." Bella lifted her cup, took a sip and put it back on the tray. "Where do I begin?"

"Anywhere you're comfortable with," Stefanie prodded, and sipped the tea again before setting it down.

"All right. Here goes..." Bella sat back, thoughtful. "My father had an affair with Lynda Boxleitner—"

Stefanie raised an eyebrow. "Really?" she asked innocently.

"It was apparently during a time that he and my mother were going through a rough patch," Bella suggested. "Lynda threw herself at him, and my father, being vulnerable at he was, took the bait." Bella's eyes narrowed. "She threatened to reveal their dirty little secret to the world—starting with my mother... Panicking over what that might do to her—and everything else my father stood for—he killed Lynda..."

"What?" Stefanie's eyes shot wide at this blunt admission. Had Bella known about this all along?

"I know, I was floored when first learning about it," Bella told her, a catch to her tone of voice. "More tea?" she asked, as if evading the difficult subject matter.

"I'm good," Stefanie said, then picked up the cup to sip a bit more of it for effect. "Go on..." she urged her.

"Okay." Bella nodded. "Anyway, my dad made the confession in a journal that he kept. I'd known about the journal for years, but never gave much thought as to what was in it. Not till after he passed away. He confessed to poisoning Lynda with the thallium sulfate that Sidney Sedwick hooked him up with—then made an effort to blame her death on Wendell Braison, knowing that Lynda was a follower of the Braison Family at the time and their controversial lifestyle."

"Wow," was all Stefanie could say at the moment. "So, you found the journal?"

"If only that were true." Bella's face contorted. "Then everything might have turned out differently." She sighed, meditative. "As it is, this all only came to light when I discovered that Mia O'Dell, my father's former housekeeper, had stolen the journal. She intended to blackmail me for a considerable amount to get the journal back. Or else, she planned to hand it over to the police as a two decades old confession to murder. Neither were particularly good choices for me to chew on and swallow—or spit out…"

Stefanie batted her lashes. "So what did you do, Bella?"

"The only thing I could do," she answered boldly, flashing her eyes at Stefanie. "I killed her!" She sighed. "Or participated in killing her with some able-bodied help—"

"What?" Stefanie tried to digest what she had just heard while absentmindedly taking another sip of the tea. Who helped her? "Please tell me you didn't go that far?"

"I had no choice," Bella insisted. "Okay, my dad was a bastard. But he was *still* my father. I wasn't about to allow a money grabber to put the squeeze on me—or else!"

"There's always a choice." Stefanie's mouth hung open with disbelief. "How could you?"

"It wasn't that difficult, truly." Bella's voice grew dark.

"I had my family's legacy to think about. And since most people bought into the notion that Lynda Boxleitner's death was directly attributable to her involvement with the Braison Family, I wanted to keep it that way. As Mia also happened to be a member of the cult, it made sense to connect her death to them as well—make it appear that both women were poisoned by someone within the cult—albeit twenty years apart. Fentanyl was much easier to come by these days, especially if you knew where to get it."

Stefanie batted her lashes. "Did you know where to get fentanyl?"

"Not exactly." Bella wrinkled her nose. "Fortunately, the person I aligned myself with did."

"Who?" She locked eyes with her, while pondering who would help her kill someone. "Is it Kenneth Braison?" Stefanie found that hard to fathom, considering everything else she had just heard. But Bella seemed to have no trouble getting what—or whom—she wanted, so anything was possible.

"Actually, it's Juan Barrientos," Bella told her proudly.

"Juan?" Stefanie looked at her with shock. "And you?"

Bella laughed. "It's not what you think. Not really. Yes, we hooked up a couple of times and that's it. This was all it took to have him wrapped around my little finger," she said satisfyingly, lifting up her pinkie to make her point. "It's primarily a business arrangement. He's helped me take care of some problems…and he's got his own agenda. So there you have it."

Stefanie was beginning to feel a little queasy, but thought it must have been an unsettled stomach with what she'd just been told. She peered at Bella and asked pointblank, "So you and Juan poisoned Jasmine, too?"

Bella sighed. "She asked way too many questions and

became a liability. Beyond that, Jasmine's death was another way to point the finger at the Braison Family as being responsible for poisonous deaths across two generations—"

"This is crazy," Stefanie said, unable to keep the thought to herself. "You'll never get away with it…"

"Don't be too sure about that," Bella boasted confidently. "Everything's going according to plan—"

What's that supposed to mean? Stefanie wondered. How could Bella truly believe she would be able to keep her deadly secrets? "If you're expecting me to keep this to myself—I can't do that. Campbell needs to know what you and Juan have been doing…"

Bella chuckled. "I'm afraid he won't find out from you, Stefanie… You see, unfortunately, you've become a liability, too. If only you hadn't fortuitously come upon Mia on Founder's Day, you and I could have maintained a wonderful and lasting friendship. But you did find her—and in the process, came into Campbell's orbit—putting a real damper on our camaraderie. I knew it was only a matter of time before it would come to an end. That time is now…"

As if on cue, Stefanie found herself feeling even sicker, shaky and starting to perspire. She leveled her eyes at Bella and demanded, "What have you done to me?" The answer came to her before a response came from her unexpected new adversary.

Fluttering her lashes, Bella answered cruelly, "I took the liberty of spicing your herbal tea with enough fentanyl laced with carfentanil powder—and even some fentanyl liquid put in for good measure—so you'd die from an overdose. Like Mia and Jasmine—as well as Lynda from back in the day—you'll show up naked in Reston Hills Park as another victim of the Braison Family…"

Stefanie tried to get to her feet, intent upon leaving the house, but fell back onto the sectional as dizziness overcame her. She tried to remove the cell phone from her jeans, but Bella beat her to the punch, grabbing it first.

"Sorry, can't let you warn Campbell," she hissed. "It would ruin everything…"

Just then, Stefanie heard a door slam shut and footsteps coming their way. Moments later, she watched as Juan Barrientos entered the den.

Bella narrowed her eyes at him. "What took you so long?"

"Had to be creative in getting out of the compound without too many questions being asked," he explained. "Sorry."

Bella's nostrils flared. "Anyway, you're here now."

Juan regarded Stefanie and asked, "She give you any problems?"

"None that I couldn't handle," Bella responded succinctly.

Stefanie, who found herself even struggling to speak, forced out words anyhow. "Ca-Campbell is ne-never going to buy that I OD'd on fentanyl—no matter h-how you try to frame it," she stammered.

Bella laughed and bragged, "I can be very persuasive when I want to be with Juan's help. He'll plant some of your clothing—even your cell phone—and fentanyl powder and liquid at Kenneth Braison's ranch house…and I'll insist that it be thoroughly searched. When the evidence is found, Kenneth will be arrested for your murder and, undoubtedly, Mia's and Jasmine's, too. I'll get what I want in protecting my family's legacy and Juan will assume the leadership role in the Braison Family. It's a win-win. But not for you, Stefanie, I'm sorry to say."

"I don't think you are!" Stefanie spat out, furrowing her brow while peering at Bella. "Neither of you!"

She glared at Juan, who grinned at her maliciously and said, "You're right—not sorry at all. It is what it is." He gazed at Bella. "Let's get this over with."

"Okay," she uttered unfeelingly.

Stefanie, her heart racing wildly, life flashing before her eyes, tried getting to her feet again as the effects of the poison given to her spread like cancer throughout her entire body. But before she could even contemplate her next move, in what seemed to be a truly hopeless situation—one in which Campbell was likely none the wiser and, as such, unable to come to her aid in time—Stefanie passed out.

CAMPBELL STILL FELT UNSETTLED, even after they got Judge Ellen Ramiscal to sign a warrant for Juan Barrientos. They had more than enough probable cause to believe that he had purchased the deadly fentanyl mixed with carfentanil— from drug dealer Luther Valdez—that ended up inside of Mia O'Dell and Jasmine Roxburgh, killing them both. Moreover, Mia was seen getting into Barrientos's Volvo XC60 SUV, shortly before her estimated time of death.

The man killed her, intentional or not, Campbell told himself as he headed toward the Braison Family property. That meant that he had to have given Jasmine the lethal drug combo, too. So was this the work of a serial killer who was intentionally getting rid of cult members who had become expendable? Or did Barrientos have another purpose in mind for the OD poisonings made to resemble the fatal poisoning of Lynda Boxleitner?

Was he acting alone? Or in concert with another member of the Braison Family, if not Kenneth Braison?

Somehow, it didn't figure that Kenneth would direct the execution of two of his likely faithful followers—going against his declaration of a drug-free, peaceful environment—by causing two of them to overdose to death on fentanyl. That would be bad for the business of trying to keep current members and recruit new ones, if they stood a good chance of dying by joining the cult. Why jeopardize what Braison might have thought was a good thing going by throwing caution to the wind?

Campbell sat on that thought for a moment, before rejecting the notion that Kenneth was in on this. Much less, condoning it. No, the greater likelihood was that Barrientos was operating outside of Kenneth's knowledge.

Just like his father, Wendell Braison, Campbell had a feeling that Kenneth Braison was getting a raw deal where it concerned the poisoning of Braison Family devotees, other controversies of the cult notwithstanding.

But what am I missing? Campbell asked himself as he pulled onto South Petriss Road, nearing the Braison Family ranch. Something told him that there was an element or two that had yet to be fully fleshed out in hitting the mark in the investigation.

Unless they could pinpoint this soon, other followers of the Family could still be in danger. Or someone from the outside, such as Stefanie—who had taken an interest in the cult for altruistic reasons after being indirectly connected to the deaths of two members. Campbell felt comfort knowing that she was at least in a safe space at the moment, spending time with Bella.

He drove up to the gate, alongside another detective's vehicle, while ready to track down Juan Barrientos and bring him in for questioning.

Chapter Eighteen

Campbell and Detective Xander Wilde, a forty-three-year-old African American who was tall and muscular with a shaved head, entered the Braison Family compound. Apart from their Glock 19 pistols, they were armed with an arrest warrant for Juan Barrientos. Backup officers were on standby.

"Think there will be any resistance?" Xander asked, his brown eyes gazing at the property, its members seemingly going about their business nonchalantly.

"Shouldn't be, if they know what's good for them." Though he didn't dismiss the notion altogether, Campbell didn't believe that Kenneth Braison was looking for a fight. Especially when it appeared that Barrientos's wrongdoing was more of a solo effort than representing the Family, per se. "Let's find Barrientos."

With no luck and no cooperation, they wound up running into Kenneth outside his ranch house. He was in the company of a tall, slender and attractive twentysomething female with long raven hair in a U-shaped cut and big hazel eyes.

Kenneth peered disapprovingly at Campbell. "Detective Sawyer..."

Without beating around the bush, Campbell said tersely, "This is Detective Wilde. We have a warrant for Juan Barrientos's arrest. Where is he?"

"He's not here." Kenneth narrowed his eyes. "What's this all about?"

Xander responded with an edge to his tone. "We believe that Barrientos bought the fentanyl in powdered and liquid form, that Mia O'Dell and Jasmine Roxburgh OD'd on, from a known drug dealer."

"What?" Kenneth's jaw dropped. "There must be some mistake—"

"It's no mistake!" Campbell's forehead creased. "Apart from Barrientos being identified by the drug dealer, we also have him on surveillance video picking up Mia not far from Kieke's Nightclub shortly before she ended up dead from the lethal fentanyl concoction."

Kenneth set his jaw. "How could Juan betray my trust like this?" he asked in disbelief. "And do such harm to members of the Braison Family? Why…?"

"You'll have to ask him that," Campbell said, sensing that the cult leader wasn't the wiser to what his likely ambitious right-hand man was up to. "Now, where can we find Barrientos?"

"He's out doing some personal business. I never asked what that was…"

"Maybe you should have," Xander spoke harshly. "Could be that he's buying more drugs to poison your followers."

Kenneth bristled at the suggestion. "You're right," he muttered. "I thought Juan had my back—our backs… Looks like I totally misjudged his intentions as a disloyal member of the Family…"

"Apparently so." Campbell wondered how the cult leader could have missed the mark there. He favored him musingly. This seemed as good a time as any to come clean with him on another matter. "Speaking of misjudging—regarding the cold case homicide of Lynda Boxleitner, your father, Wendell Braison, is no longer considered a person of interest."

Kenneth's brow shot up. "Since when?"

"Since new info surfaced and the case and culprit pointed in an entirely different direction," Campbell said sincerely. He wished Braison's son hadn't been forced to carry the burden of his father's possible guilt through the years, but he now had the opportunity to move past it. While facing new demons, what with the current investigation tying a member of the Braison Family to two poisonous deaths.

"I see," Kenneth said, then added bitterly, "Better late than never."

"Yeah." Campbell glanced at Xander, then looked at the young woman beside Kenneth, who eyed him back.

She uttered tentatively with a British accent, "My name's Siobhan Froggatt. There's something I need to say—"

"I'm listening," Campbell told her, watching Kenneth's uneasy—and perhaps possessive—reaction before turning back to her face.

Siobhan tucked some loose strands of hair behind an ear and said, "If what you say about Juan giving Jasmine and Mia deadly drugs is true, it makes me concerned about Lois Ohashi, the Family member he shares a cabin with…" She took a breath, venturing a glance at Kenneth. "Lois told me in confidence that she took a look at Juan's cell phone while he was sleeping and discovered through text messages that he was seeing someone on the outside… Maybe Juan will try to poison Lois so he can be with the other woman—"

Campbell didn't discount her fears about what Barrientos was capable of. Fixing his eyes on Siobhan, he asked thoughtfully, "Did Lois happen to get the name of this woman Barrientos is involved with?"

Siobhan regarded Kenneth, as if for permission to answer and he nodded with approval and maybe curiosity, before she responded confidently, "Bella Reston."

BELLA AND BARRIENTOS? Campbell thought with shock after having already returned to his SUV, where he was riding solo. He never saw that coming. Apparently, neither did Kenneth Braison, based upon his negative reaction. How did those two come to be romantically involved, when Campbell thought that she and golfer Russell Kercheval were an item? And just what else were Bella and Juan up to? Or had been?

More disturbing to Campbell at the moment was that Stefanie had texted him earlier to say that she was going to pay Bella a visit. Now he was having trouble reaching Stefanie by phone. Was there a legitimate reason for this? Would Bella—and her latest lover—actually try to harm Stefanie?

While the search was underway for Juan Barrientos and his blue Volvo XC60 SUV, with a BOLO alert out for him and his vehicle, Campbell was about to head over to Bella's house, when his cell phone rang. He took it out of his blazer and saw that it was Georgina.

Her voice was anxious as she said, "We just got a bead on Barrientos's SUV. An automated license plate reader picked up his vehicle on Hepmore Avenue, headed toward Reston Hills Park. There appears to be at least two people inside the vehicle—"

That news caused Campbell's heart to skip a beat. He

drew a deep breath and said, "Turns out that Juan Barrientos is involved in a romantic relationship with Bella Reston."

"Seriously?" Georgina voiced in surprise.

"Yeah, his Braison Family girlfriend read his texts and discovered it."

"Do you think Bella is a party to the deadly drug overdoses?" Georgina asked. "Or could she too become a victim of Barrientos?"

Campbell considered the two possibilities. Having known Bella, she didn't at all strike him as the victim type. At least not where it concerned drug abuse. Or being conned by Juan Barrientos. It seemed more likely that she would be calling the shots in their relationship. That included wanting Mia and Jasmine dead for some bizarre reason that had to be about Bella's father, Stuart Reston, his former lover, Lynda Boxleitner, and the opportunistic entanglements involving the Braison Family.

After a long moment, Campbell replied with conviction, "I think that Bella and Barrientos are in this together. Right down to obtaining the fentanyl mixed with carfentanil—and poisoning Mia and Jasmine. I also fear that they may have abducted Stefanie, drugged her, and are taking her to the park to leave her for dead like the others." He sighed. "I need all available units—along with a SWAT team, crisis negotiator and EMS—to get to Reston Hills Park immediately, which is where I'm headed right now..."

"You've got it," Georgina said tensely.

"On the chance that Stefanie is being kept at Bella's house or was able to return home, get the same personnel to both places—just in case..."

"Okay. I'm close to Bella's house, so I'll pop over there myself and take a look, while waiting for backup."

"All right."

Campbell disconnected. He pressed down on the accelerator, knowing that every second could be a matter of life and death. He didn't even want to think about his world without Stefanie being in it for years to come. But how could he not? Hadn't Mia and Jasmine been the victims of fatal fentanyl poisonings in the park? Could Stefanie possibly avoid their fate?

Yes, if at all possible, in any way, shape, or form, he told himself. How else could he get to tell Stefanie how much he loved her? And wanted to build a life with her—and have a family with as many children as she wanted?

Campbell put on even more speed, determined to stop Barrientos from carrying out another death as, undoubtedly, part of Bella's agenda.

STEFANIE FELT WOOZY, sweaty and had trouble breathing as she sat in the back seat of the Volvo, with Juan Barrientos holding her down forcefully and Bella behind the wheel. She was driving them to Reston Hills Park, where they planned to dump her as another fatal overdose victim—and blame it entirely on Kenneth Braison and his Family by association.

At some point—probably after she passed out at Bella's house—they removed Stefanie's clothes, so that she was now totally naked and oddly cold in the warm summer-evening temperature. Just like Mia and Jasmine had been forced to endure, humiliation and all.

How long would it take for the authorities—Campbell, especially—to find her body? How would he react to seeing her dead from fentanyl poisoning? Would he accept that Kenneth was responsible for it—ending the life she had hoped to have with Campbell and the children they would produce together—with Bella and Juan getting away with another murder scot-free?

Can I do anything at this point to prevent the inevitable? Stefanie wondered, knowing how weak she felt, while aching all over like living a nightmare. If she could only breathe freely again, before she took her last breath.

Maybe she could find the strength to use her tai chi self-defense skills to fight back.

Or at least die trying to live.

When the SUV drove into the park, Bella found a place to park, then said to Juan in a hardened tone, "Get her out!"

"Okay," he muttered obediently.

Stefanie felt herself being pulled from the car roughly. Then she heard Bella direct him to take her toward the trail—not far from where Stefanie found Mia. Wouldn't it be ironic if they both ran out of life at the same spot, leaving someone else to find Stefanie's corpse.

I can't let that happen...have to do something, her mind told her. As Juan half dragged, half carried her, when Stefanie was on her wobbly legs as he took a quick breather and let down his guard—it was her one and probably only opening to survive her ordeal—so she went for it.

Feeling she was too weak to attempt a joint lock against Juan—knowing that failure would only result in a counter move on his part that would probably be the painful end of her—instead, Stefanie hoped she could hurt him just enough, and maybe Bella, too, to get away from them. Till help arrived.

She used a tai chi technique with her hands to strike him at the bridge of his nose as hard as she could—maybe breaking it—followed in quick succession by a solid blow into his groin. As Juan yelled an expletive, then made an eerie groaning sound, and Bella looked confused, Stefanie took advantage of this to punch her once to the side of the head with enough force to cause Bella to lose her balance and nearly fall, wailing from the discomfort.

As her abductors were sulking, Stefanie tried to make a run for it. She didn't get very far, as her legs were like rubber. And lead weights, all at once.

"Stop her, you idiot!" Bella blared nevertheless, then warned, "But not with the gun! It has to be the fentanyl if we're going to get away with this!"

Stefanie recalled seeing the firearm that he'd pulled briefly from his jacket pocket at Bella's house—meant to intimidate her into cooperating with this diabolical scheme. She tried to move her feet away from them. But they were able to easily close the distance and grab her. Then Juan, angered by the pain she inflicted upon him, slammed a fist into her jaw.

Between that and the effects of the fentanyl poisoning beginning to take full effect, Stefanie fell flat on her face. She went out like a light, while sure she had seen the last of what was once a bright future—one she'd hoped to share with Campbell.

Now none of that seemed possible, now that it appeared as though Bella and Juan had won the battle—with Stefanie's death being their prize.

CAMPBELL SPOTTED JUAN'S SUV parked haphazardly in the lot. Checking it, he saw no signs of Stefanie. Or, for that matter, Juan Barrientos or Bella Reston. So where were they? And was Stefanie with them—and still alive?

He was left to hope for the best as Campbell locked eyes with Xander Wilde, both detectives converging on the location, holding their firearms and flashlights.

"This place should be swarming with cops shortly," Xander said, as if to make Campbell feel better.

But he didn't. Not till knowing that Stefanie was safe. Wherever she happened to be at the moment.

"Until then," he told Xander, "why don't we split up and see if we come across Barrientos or Bella Reston—"

Xander nodded. "Okay."

Campbell headed into the park in search of Stefanie—who was the best thing to ever happen to him. It certainly felt that way, how she'd managed to warm his heart in ways he never thought possible. Now he only needed to convey that to her. If given the chance.

He heard the sounds of voices up ahead. They were coming his way.

Shining his flashlight in that direction, Campbell saw Bella and Barrientos. But not Stefanie.

The two suspects froze when they laid eyes on him.

Pointing the light beam at Barrientos, Campbell said doggedly, "Juan Barrientos, I have a warrant for your arrest on suspicion of causing two drug-induced homicides. Put your hands up—"

Barrientos hesitated. Then abruptly, he pulled a handgun from his jacket and aimed it at him. Before Barrientos ever had a chance to pull the trigger, Campbell shot him once in the chest.

Barrientos went down as the gun flew from his hand. Bella made a move to try to grab it, but Xander, who had shown up at the scene, his own gun pointing at her, spoke in a commanding tone of voice, "I wouldn't try that if I were you—"

Thinking better of ignoring his advice, Bella stayed where she was and Xander quickly came up to her and handcuffed Bella, without resistance.

Campbell, grateful for Xander's teamwork, kept his weapon aimed at Barrientos, who was seriously injured, but still conscious and groaning. The flashlight shone on Barrientos's firearm, which looked to Campbell like a Sig Sauer 10mm pistol. He kicked it farther from Barrientos's reach—for the CSI Unit to take possession of as evidence of the suspect's clear intent to shoot him.

Campbell peered at Barrientos and asked him demandingly, "Where is she—Stefanie Nguyen?"

Barrientos moaned, then responded defiantly, "You tell me."

Campbell took that as an admission that she was in the park. He handcuffed the suspect and stepped toward Bella, who was being held firmly by Xander. "Bella, where's Stefanie?" Campbell demanded.

She glared at him with a snicker and answered coldly, "It's too late for her…"

Campbell wondered how she could go from friend to foe almost in the blink of an eye where it concerned Stefanie. He was sure Bella would put it all out on the table, now that the jig was up.

"Like hell it is," Campbell retorted, not wanting to believe this—against the odds that Stefanie was still alive.

Bella hissed, "Believe it or not, you can't save them all, Campbell—any more than your father could—not even your precious Stefanie…"

Campbell flinched at the venom in Bella's voice, like a cobra. "Stay with them till help arrives," he told Xander. "I'm going to look for Stefanie."

"All right." Xander looked at him. "Find her."

Campbell headed farther into the woods near the river, cutting through the darkness with his flashlight. It occurred to him that he was getting dangerously close to where Mia O'Dell's body was located—by Stefanie. This sent chills down his spine at the thought of the woman he'd fallen in love with suffering the same fate.

When he neared the trail, Campbell spotted the naked figure lying on the ground, motionless. Stefanie. He rushed toward her as his heart sank in seeing her so vulnerable—likely the victim of fentanyl mixed with carfentanil poisoning—and possibly dead.

Campbell put the flashlight in his tactical holster. "Stefanie," he uttered her name in desperation, hoping for a response, while checking for a pulse.

There was one. She was still alive.

Not wanting to waste even one second waiting for paramedics, Campbell removed his blazer to cover Stefanie up as much as possible and then lifted her limp body to carry her back to his SUV or a waiting EMS vehicle.

"I've got you, darling," he uttered mawkishly while getting nothing in return. "Don't you die on me." *I won't let you*, Campbell thought. He prayed that he could keep his word to her and Stefanie would pull through. So that they could get the opportunity to have a wonderful life together, and then some.

Chapter Nineteen

Stefanie was groggy and disoriented, with a sore jaw after being hit, and thirsty, as she opened her eyes—surprised to see that she was still alive. She focused on the attractive oval face of a slender thirtysomething female with a blond balayage A-line haircut and blue eyes behind rectangle glasses standing over her in what Stefanie determined was a hospital bed—and obviously not the morgue.

The woman smiled and said softly. "You're awake…"

"Yes, it appears so," Stefanie quipped, thankfully, noting she was wearing a hospital gown and no longer naked.

"I'm Dr. Hennessy," she told her, wearing a white lab coat. "You were brought into the ER after overdosing on fentanyl."

"I remember all too well." Stefanie made a face, not taking her eyes off the doctor. "So, how did I manage to survive?" She recalled Mia and Jasmine not being so lucky.

"Well, fortunately, paramedics were able to quickly administer naloxone to reverse in time the effects of the fentanyl poisoning or opioid overdose." Dr. Hennessy glanced at a chart and back, smiling. "Aside from some bruising on your face and body and a mild concussion—all of which should heal—your vital signs are all normal. I'd say you can expect a full recovery."

Stefanie nodded, counting her blessings. "Thank you, Doctor."

"Actually, I'm not the one you should be thanking..." she insisted, and averted her eyes to the other side of the bed.

Stefanie followed suit and gazed at Campbell's handsome face. He grinned at her, but she could see the strain in his features, despite his best efforts to hide it.

"Campbell..." she uttered weakly.

The doctor said coolly, "I'll leave you two alone—"

After she left the room, Campbell moved closer. "Thought I'd lost you for a minute there," he admitted caringly.

Honestly, I thought that, too, Stefanie told herself, against her best wishes. More importantly, she feared she'd lost him forever once the fentanyl and its deadly effects kicked in. She forced a smile. "Afraid you can't get rid of me that easily."

Campbell chuckled. "That's good to know. Especially when I wasn't at all prepared for that to happen anytime soon."

"Neither was I." Stefanie swallowed into her dry throat and coughed. He handed her a cup of water, which, after sitting up, she happily drank. "So, how did you find me...?" *And save my life*, she thought, sensing that Campbell had come to her rescue. In spite of Bella and Juan's plans to the contrary.

He sighed. "We were able to establish that it was Juan Barrientos who—in cahoots with his lover outside of the Braison Family, Bella Reston—gave Mia and Jasmine the deadly combo of fentanyl mixed with carfentanil. A license plate reader spotted Barrientos's SUV headed toward Reston Hills Park. Something told me that he and Bella—whom you were visiting—had planned to kill you as well with a drug overdose…and, I suppose, sail off into the sunset afterward—if you could call getting away with murder that…" Campbell rolled fingers through his hair. "When Barrientos resisted arrest, he was shot. But he'll live. And so will Bella, whether she wants to or not…"

Stefanie was pleased to know that her onetime friend, as well as Juan Barrientos, would face justice for what they had done. "I'm glad they were caught," she said, gazing up at him. "Who knows what else they were capable of."

"Right," he agreed, a contemplative expression crossing his face. "Getting back to how I managed to locate you in the park… With no time to waste, I suppose I just let my instincts guide me…till I came upon you on the trail. You were unconscious, but had a strong enough will for survival that you were able to escape the fate that Bella and Barrientos had in mind—"

Stefanie pondered her brush with death—focusing on Bella's role, in particular, and her dark family legacy. "Bella admitted to conspiring with Juan to kill Mia O'Dell, after Mia tried to blackmail her. This came about when Mia discovered from Stuart Reston's journal—which she stole—that he poisoned to death his lover, Lynda Boxleitner, to prevent Lynda from making public their affair after he refused to leave his wife, Eloise Reston, for her. Mia, who was struggling to make ends meet, in spite of her involvement with the Braison Family, hoped to cash in on her knowledge."

Campbell frowned and said matter-of-factly, "But Bella, wanting to protect her family heritage, rejected this—choosing to kill Mia instead…"

Stefanie nodded. "Bella wasn't about to allow Mia to ruin everything her family stood for. Using the Braison Family angle, Bella tried to tie Mia's fatal poisoning to the poisoning death of Lynda Boxleitner—to make it seem that both were orchestrated by the father-son cult leaders, Wendell and Kenneth Braison. Jasmine was poisoned with fentanyl after she asked too many questions and Bella panicked that the truth might come out. Also, it didn't hurt if another drug-induced death could be connected to the Braison Family to further try and influence the investigation."

Campbell took a breath, meeting her eyes. "Why did Bella want you dead, too?" Before Stefanie could answer, he said intuitively, "Let me guess... Bella felt further threatened by your interest in the investigation and how that might come back on her?"

"Yes, something like that," she told him. "Apparently, Bella became paranoid by my talking to Jasmine and any type of rippling effect that might expose her. Then there was also her determination to make the Braison Family wrongfully culpable for past and present sins in the poisonings. She hoped to use my death to set up Kenneth Braison—short of tattooing his initials on my arm—by planting evidence at his house and making sure it was found. All to protect her family's good name. Though just how good it is, is questionable."

"Yeah, quite." Campbell rolled his eyes. "And what would Barrientos get for his trouble?"

"Control of the Braison Family and all that comes with being the cult's leader," Stefanie told him.

"I thought as much, when trying to piece it all together." Campbell ran hand across his jawline. "But they failed to achieve their goals, with both now in custody and facing years behind bars."

"Good." Stefanie adjusted herself in the bed and looked up at him, while thinking about them and their own future prospects. "So, when will I be released?"

"As far as I'm aware, the process is already in the works for you to be discharged," Campbell answered equably. He sat on the side of the bed, and held one of her hands affectionately. "But before they let you out of here, there's something I've been dying to say to you…"

"Oh?" She met his gaze, interest piqued. "What might that be?"

"Just that I've fallen in love with you, Stefanie Nguyen," he expressed soulfully.

Stefanie beamed. "Is that so?"

"Yeah, definitely so." He kissed her hand. "When I feared that I might never have gotten the opportunity to say that—had Bella and Barrientos gotten their way—I promised myself that I wouldn't allow myself to miss the chance again as soon as it presented itself to express my true feelings in living color. And any other way to say I love you, Stefanie."

She blushed, squeezing his fingers. "Well, I'm in love with you, too, Campbell," she cadenced.

He grinned crookedly. "Really?"

"Yes, really." Stefanie was filled with happiness. "I also feared that I might have lost that window to tell you how I felt," she said tearfully "But now that the window has reopened, I won't wait for it to nearly shut again before putting my heart on the line, forever and a day." She drew a breath and fixed his eyes. "I do love you and always will—whatever our destiny is…"

Campbell's face lit up with raw emotion. "In that case, we can't go wrong, as I'm with you all the way!"

He leaned over and gave her a hard kiss on the mouth that Stefanie embraced for all the strength she could muster. In time, she hoped to be able to show him just how much she cared for him through long, tender kisses and otherwise. But for now, this was more than enough for her to hang onto and relish to her heart's content, while knowing that Campbell felt the same way, through and through.

THE NEXT MORNING, in Harriette's Café, Campbell sat with Gloria at a table, going over the case and its unexpected twists and turns. He knew she had more than a passing interest, given her time with the department, dating back to the murder of Lynda Boxleitner. And how that managed to work its way to the present drug-related homicides.

While nibbling on a Danish pastry, Gloria batted her lashes and said, as if still trying to come to terms with it, "Bella Reston and Juan Barrientos…who would have thunk it?"

"True." Campbell bit into a cinnamon roll, then took a sip of his coffee. "I guess power and privilege—not necessarily in that order—makes for strange bedfellows."

"I suppose." She tasted her green tea. "The important thing is that you figured out many of the sordid details and stopped them from adding another victim to the madness."

"Yeah." He took a breath. The thought that he had come so close to losing Stefanie made Campbell almost nauseous. Being deprived of expressing his love and receiving the same in return was almost too much to bear. But they had come out on the other end, stronger than ever. In spite of Bella's and Barrientos's efforts to the contrary.

"Now we just need to put them away for good. Or at least for the better part of the life they have left."

"That would be nice," Gloria agreed before taking another bite of the Danish. "But you can be sure that Bella Reston—at least—will have the best lawyers that money can buy to try and worm her way out of this."

"I expect as much," Campbell acknowledged. "But money can only go so far."

"You're right. But in this instance, as far as her admission to Stefanie that Mia O'Dell was killed because of blackmail regarding Stuart Reston's confession in a journal to murdering Lynda Boxleitner—it's Stefanie's word against Bella's, who would surely deny having ever said such. It would never hold up in court on that basis alone." Gloria sipped her tea and sat back. "I'm guessing that the journal in question was found by Bella or Barrientos and destroyed."

"That's always a possibility," Campbell allowed musingly. "But since Bella is strongly invested in the Reston family history, I suspect that she would have wanted to hold on to her father's journal—even if damaging to him and the Reston legacy—to preserve it from one generation to the next. Especially if Bella, so full of herself, believed that she would succeed in keeping the onus for Boxleitner's murder entirely on Wendell Braison—by adding some new homicides to the mix to further protect the family's place in this town—and it would never come back to haunt her. Meaning that she likely still has Reston's journal in her possession."

Gloria nodded. "You make a good point." She ate another piece of Danish. "I hope you can find it and use it as evidence to help make the case."

"Me too." Campbell liked his chances. But there was

more to it than that. "Beyond finally giving Lynda Boxleitner the peace in death that she deserves after all these years, Bella has more serious concerns for her attorneys to deal with. She's on the hook—along with Juan Barrientos—for the lethal fentanyl poisonings of Mia O'Dell and Jasmine Roxburgh. And the attempted murder of Stefanie Nguyen. No amount of dirty family money will be enough to worm her way out of that hole."

"I agree," Gloria said, tilting her face. "Bella Reston will get what she deserves, as will Juan Barrientos. Maybe then, this town—and even the Braison Family—can get back to some semblance of normalcy and move forward."

"That's the hope," Campbell said, sipping his coffee contemplatively. He particularly liked the part about moving forward—which is exactly what he hoped to do with Stefanie, now that they had gotten past life and death issues that, for a moment or two, had left things between them hanging in the balance.

IN SEPTEMBER, STEFANIE WENT with Campbell to visit his father and ride horses. It was just her second time ever getting on a horse. The first was a month earlier when they visited the ranch and she and Campbell went on a trail ride on Appaloosas. Though a bit sore, she truly loved the experience, as the horse was gentle and it gave her an opportunity to spread her wings in further bonding—not only with Campbell, but with Mason and his lovely partner, Sally. They made her feel welcome, as though part of the family.

Stefanie relished this, eager to have the same type of strong connection she once had with her own mother and father, whom she missed more than she could say, though feeling they were always angels on her shoulders. Just as

Edward was, in wanting her to be happy in life. Which she was, knowing how precious each day could be, when it so easily could be taken away.

Campbell was just as thrilled that she had warmed to his father—and she was delighted to see that the two men had put aside any differences they may have had through the years and were forging stronger ties themselves.

In Stefanie's mind, knowing that a cold case and current case between father and son had merged into one and been closed, more or less, made their relationship that much stronger.

It seemed as if Bella, on the advice of expensive lawyers, had cut a deal in confessing to her part in the deaths of Mia O'Dell and Jasmine Roxburgh. *And the intent to kill me with the same fentanyl poisoning*, Stefanie thought as her horse trotted across the meadow. As a result, instead of spending the rest of her life behind bars, Bella would still have the opportunity to one day go free. But would still pay a very high price for the bad decisions she made. Her family legacy—thanks in part to Stuart Reston's journal and the testimony of his former gardener, Sidney Sedwick—was now in tatters and likely never to be fully repaired as the town's namesake.

Juan Barrientos didn't get off nearly as easily. With his case transferred to federal jurisdiction and a solid case against him for serious drug-related offenses, including two drug-induced homicides—and the willingness of drug trafficker Luther Valdez to testify against him—Juan confessed. Even with that, he would not see the light of day again with a sentence of life imprisonment.

Stefanie found solace in that, knowing Juan had tried to kill her and would never get that opportunity again. In spite of him having been used by Bella to achieve her own objectives—with frequent phone calls and spicy text messages to Juan that were produced as evidence to illustrate the romantic nature of their relationship—it was Juan who acquired the deadly fentanyl and carfentanil from Valdez that nearly sent Stefanie to an early grave. *How can I not hold him responsible to a slightly higher degree?* she asked herself, as a part of her wanted to believe that in an alternate reality, she and Bella could have truly ended up as real friends.

"Are you all right?" Campbell asked in earnest, riding alongside her.

Stefanie gazed at him, looking every bit the cowboy with his cowboy hat on and clothing to match. She flashed a genuine, loving smile and answered, "Better than ever! Race you back?"

He laughed. "You're on."

She chuckled as her horse trotted off ahead of him, pretty sure he would catch her. As surely as he had captured her heart. And she had captured his.

Epilogue

Founder's Day was gorgeous, in terms of the perfect June temperature and not a cloud in the baby blue sky to be spotted. The annual celebration didn't miss a beat as the locals and visitors alike gathered in Reston Hills Park, following a big parade down Hepmore Avenue, where floats, dignitaries, marching bands, riders, walkers, students and onlookers came together to make it the best parade ever in town.

Stefanie and Campbell were joined by Mason and Sally as they moved about by the river, where many of the carnival rides had been set up for children and adults to enjoy, while viewing the boats out in the water that were taking advantage of ideal conditions.

"I can't believe it's been a year since I found Mia's body," Stefanie said, sharing a bag of walnuts and pistachios with Campbell. She hated to be on a momentary down note, but was sure that the anniversary of the tragedy—as well as one from twenty-one years earlier—did not go unnoticed by him. Or Mason, for that matter.

"Yeah, I know," Campbell muttered, a slice of remorse in his voice. "It was definitely a day to forget for most of us in town—as if anyone ever could," he said truthfully.

Mason looked at him and said earnestly, "We all had to endure a rough patch, son—spanning more than two decades—but we've dealt with it and come out stronger, each and every one of us."

Campbell nodded. "True. It's brought us closer together, Dad, and for that, I'm forever grateful."

Mason grinned, tapping his shoulder. "I feel the same."

"Me too." Sally smiled, holding Mason's hand. "Absolutely, I know that we're stronger because of it," she told him, "and I wouldn't want it any other way."

"Neither would I," he voiced affectionately.

Campbell turned to Stefanie and said candidly, "For me, even with all that went down—including seeing Bella and Juan held accountable for their crimes—the silver lining was meeting you, Stefanie. One thing might never have happened without the other. Can't imagine you not being in my life now."

"Me neither." She blushed, pushing past the misfortune that befell Mia O'Dell and Jasmine Roxburgh, in favor of a perhaps once-in-a-lifetime opportunity to get to know him on a deep level that grew deeper over time. "The good thing is, you don't have to imagine that. I'm not going anywhere."

"Actually, there is somewhere I'd like you to go—with me," Campbell said, gazing down at her intently.

"Oh?" She met his blue eyes curiously. "Where would you like to go?" Perhaps back to his place for some afternoon delight? Or hers for the same?

"The Ferris wheel," he told her bluntly.

She raised a brow in surprise. "The Ferris wheel?"

"Yeah. Haven't been on one of those since I was a kid." Campbell flashed her a grin askew. "Guess you bring out the kid in me. So what do you say?"

"Go on," Mason prodded her lightheartedly. "Live dangerously—just a little."

Sally chuckled. "I say go for it, Stefanie. We'll go, too, if it makes you feel more comfortable."

Stefanie laughed. "That won't be necessary." She knew she would be more than comfortable being on the Ferris wheel with Campbell by her side. "Let's do it," she told him enthusiastically.

"Okay." He grinned, taking her hand. "Come with me."

CAMPBELL WAS ON pins and needles as he led Stefanie onto the Ferris wheel. Sitting next to her, he went through the usual chitchat as the carnival ride began to go up, stopping slowly but surely, for everyone to experience life at the top. It offered a great view of the Founder's Day festivities and the activities taking place on the Beeks River.

He thought briefly about the last year that seemed to whiz by in some ways. Not so much others. It had seen a cold case and present time case merge together just enough to put both to rest and imprison the perpetrators that were still alive. A disgraced Stuart Reston escaped justice. But he had managed to taint the Reston name, as had Bella—which would never be the same again. Fortunately, Arthur Reston—the town's founder—was not being held accountable for the sins of his descendants. Meaning Reston Hills would live on for future generations who only wanted to make a good life for themselves like those in other small towns across the country.

Campbell turned his thoughts to the gorgeous woman beside him and how she had managed to overcome her brush with death as a survivor, who showed him the love he'd never experience before and wanted to hang onto for the rest of his life.

With that in mind, knowing how strongly he felt for her, Campbell waited for the Ferris wheel to come to a stop at the very top. He turned to Stefanie and said tenderly, "I love you, Stefanie Nguyen, which I've probably told you more times than you care to hear for nearly a year now... But the only way I can do the actions-speak-louder-than words thing is to give you this—" He pulled a small box out of his plaid sport coat and opened it to reveal an oval-cut diamond engagement ring in 14k yellow gold. Having already given his father a heads-up on his intentions, Campbell hoped she was ready to give marriage a second chance at happiness. He asked her smoothly, "Will you marry me, Stefanie—and make the happiest man in the world—which has far greater reach than Reston Hills alone?"

"Yes, and a thousand more yesses!" Stefanie cried out joyously and kissed him solidly on the mouth. "I will marry you, Campbell Sawyer—which will make me by far the happiest woman in the world today, Reston Hills notwithstanding!"

"Marvelous!" His voice rose a couple of octaves with emotion. "Music to my ears."

She eagerly held out her ring finger for him to place the engagement ring on, and he did so, for a perfect fit.

"I love it," Stefanie said exuberantly. "Almost as much as I love you, my darling!"

"That deep love works both ways," Campbell told her affectionately. "And so much more!"

"Always nice to hear those words," she expressed.

"Then I'll keep them coming and coming," he promised, cupped her cheeks and kissed Stefanie passionately, hardly aware that the Ferris wheel had started to move again.

* * * * *

DANGEROUS GAME

SANDRA OWENS

This book is dedicated to the awesome book lovers in my reader group, Sandra's Rowdies. Rowdies, y'all rock! Thank you for your love, your support, and for the crazy fun we have each day.

Prologue

Cooper Devlin wasn't supposed to be kidnapped. Wrong place, wrong time had never been more evident than when he found himself bound and gagged in the back of a van next to Grayson, a boy he'd just met at spring break in Florida.

What followed were two weeks locked up in a room with Grayson Montana and Liam O'Rourke, both boys with fathers richer than anything Cooper could begin to imagine. From the best they could determine, Grayson and Cooper were being held until their fathers paid the ransom demand.

What did it mean for him that not only did his father rarely have more than pocket change, but if the men demanded a ransom for his release, his father would laugh in their faces and then find the nearest bar to see if he could talk someone into buying him a beer.

He knew both boys were worried about him. Grayson had even begged their kidnappers to pass a message from him to his father. The message being to ask his father to pay the ransom for Cooper so he would be freed with them. Grayson swore his father would do it. Whether the kidnappers passed that message on, they didn't know.

Liam told the kidnappers to give his father that same message but later admitted that he doubted his father would fork over any money he didn't have to. Sounded to Cooper like Grayson had the better father.

He'd like to believe that Grayson's father would get the message and would pay his ransom. If he did, Cooper would spend his life paying the man back. It was a big *if*, and he just didn't see it happening. Why would anyone hand over a fortune for someone he'd never met? Cooper kept his fear to himself, but his chest was heavy and his stomach sick with dread that he wasn't going to walk out of this room alive.

The kidnappers were ripping his dreams right out from under his feet. He had a full scholarship to Vanderbilt University in Nashville, a school with one of the top-ranked baseball programs. Cooper's goal, his dream, was to pitch for his home-state Atlanta Braves.

He was supposed to meet the Vanderbilt coach this week, a meeting he would miss and couldn't call to cancel. The coach was going to think Cooper had blown him off, never considering the possibility that he'd been kidnapped.

The kidnappers were stealing his chance to escape the hell that was his homelife. Even worse, he'd worked hard so that he'd be able to get his sister away from their father and into a life where he'd see her smile again. They had stolen that, too. He missed her sweet smile, her laughter.

He wasn't even supposed to be in Florida. It had been a last-minute thing, an impulsive decision to tag along with two of his teammates when they decided they wanted to go to spring break. He was only supposed to be gone for two days, and he tried not to think about his sister being alone with their father for two weeks without him there to protect her from the old man's rages. If he was alone, he'd curl up in a ball and cry, but he refused to cry in front of his two new friends.

"I don't understand why they haven't released us yet," Grayson said. "My dad would've paid the ransom the minute they contacted him." His gaze fell on Cooper. "As long as they passed my message on, he'll pay it for you, too. I promise."

"It's okay if he doesn't." It really wasn't, but he'd learned early in life not to expect good things to happen.

"Maybe my dad called the police, and now any chance of getting out of here has gone to shit," Liam said. "I wouldn't put it past him."

Cooper didn't know what to think. It seemed like Grayson and Liam had very different fathers, and he felt like he had more in common with Liam. In his wildest imagination, he couldn't conceive of having a father like Grayson's. The man sounded almost too perfect, like he couldn't possibly be real.

He liked both boys and wished he'd met them under different circumstances. The three of them had grown close since being thrown in this room together, but desperation hung heavy in the air between them. There was no laughter, no teasing, no telling bad jokes like there would have been if they'd become friends outside this room that was their prison.

They were huddled in the corner of the room, as far away from the bucket that was their bathroom as they could get. Their jailers weren't so good at emptying it. There wasn't any furniture, no pallets to sleep on, not even a thin blanket, and no pillows to rest their heads on, but worst of all, no privacy. They were fed once a day, two peanut butter and jelly sandwiches and a bottle of water each. When...*if* he got out of here alive, he was never eating another peanut butter and jelly sandwich. And if they were released, he was going to take the longest shower ever.

Out of boredom, they'd played Never Have I Ever, Twenty Questions and Truth or Dare, although it was hard to dare anyone to do anything in what was essentially a jail cell. There probably wasn't much they didn't know about each other now. He'd even opened up and told his new friends about his homelife, something he never shared with others.

"I'm worried about my sister," he said. "She's going to think I ran away and left her to face our father alone." Emmie often begged for both of them to run away, but as much as he was tempted, they were too young to be out on their own. They'd probably end up living on the streets, and he'd never allow that to happen to his sister. He had a plan, and in the end, he'd be able to take her away and give her the life she deserved. If he could survive this and make things right with the Vanderbilt coach, that was.

"I'm going to ask a big favor," he said. "If I don't make it out of here and you both do, will you try to get my sister away from our father? I don't know, maybe call someone and report him? I'll give you a list of things about him that should work to make that happen. Without me there to take care of her, Emmie would be better off in foster care." He hated that it might come to that, but it would be best.

Grayson pressed his shoulder against Cooper's. "You have my promise, but man, don't talk like that. You're leaving with us."

"If the unthinkable happens, and they free us and not you, we'll come back for you," Liam said. "We'll bring an army if we have to."

"Thank you." He managed to get the two words past the rock lodged in this throat. For as long as he could remember, he'd had to go it alone, and now here were two boys who promised to have his back. It was the first time in his life he didn't feel so alone.

Both boys held up their fists, and he bumped each of theirs with his. "The only good thing about this is I met—"

"Freeze, asshole!"

The loud, commanding voice filled the air, and Cooper froze, even though he wasn't the asshole in question. He hoped not, anyway. That wasn't the voice of one of their kidnappers. He exchanged glances with Grayson and Liam, who appeared as startled and wary as he did.

"Do you think it's the police?" he whispered. It was almost too much to hope they were being rescued.

"He didn't say he was the police. Don't they have to identify themselves?" Liam said.

When a shot rang out, the three of them flattened themselves on the floor. Cooper dared to hope. "I think we're being rescued."

A body hit the wall outside their room, and the sounds of grunts filled the air.

"They're fighting," Grayson said.

Liam glanced at the closed doors. "Hope whoever it is beats the shit out of those assholes."

Cooper couldn't agree more. The fight didn't last long before it went silent, and that silence was ominous. Who was out there? Were they good guys? Who had won the fight? The door eased open, and he held his breath.

A man dressed in all black, including a black face mask, and holding a revolver down by his side stepped inside. His gaze roamed over each of them. "Time to go home, boys."

"Who are you?" Liam said.

A second man stepped up behind the first. "Your angels."

The first one glanced back. "I ain't no angel, Bear."

Bear—who was about the size of a grizzly—laughed. "True that." Bear stepped around the first man. "I'm Deacon, and my friend here is Sam, but he prefers you to call him Hollywood."

Sam growled and stomped out of the room as Deacon pulled off his mask. "Hollywood gets a bit touchy if you call him Hollywood." He grinned. "Which is why we go out of our way to do it. Any of you need medical care?" At the shake of their heads, he said, "Good. You boys ready to go home?"

All three of them jumped up, and as one, shouted, "Yes!"

"Thought so. Which one of you is Grayson?"

Grayson raised his hand. "Me."

"Your dad sent us to find you. Looks like you have some friends here, so we'll take them, too."

Cooper's legs almost buckled under him that he wasn't going to be left behind.

"Are you SEALs?" Grayson asked.

The question seemed odd to Cooper until he remembered Grayson had said his father had been a SEAL, which he and Liam thought was cool.

"Yes, but civilians now," Deacon said.

Grayson grinned. "Right. Once a SEAL, always a SEAL."

"Right on." Deacon raised a fist for Grayson to bump.

As much as they wanted to leave immediately, they had to give statements to the police first. While that was happening, they were checked out by two paramedics who'd arrived with the officers.

The two kidnappers were hauled off in handcuffs, and after the police and EMTs were gone, Deacon said, "Other than you boys could use a couple of cheeseburgers, fries and a big milkshake, sounds like you're good to go."

They did in fact make a stop for cheeseburgers, fries and milkshakes—the best meal Cooper had ever had in his life—and then they were put on a private plane. Deacon and Sam accompanied them to Myrtle Beach, to Grayson's house.

Cooper had driven by rich people's houses, but he'd never been in one. He'd never met a rich man either. Both were more than he knew how to process. As soon as they walked through the door, a man held out his arms and Grayson flew into them.

"Son," the man said. "Thank God you're home and safe."

Cooper couldn't imagine such a greeting from his father, and he tried not to be envious. He tore his gaze away from the father-son reunion and took in the room. It was a big house, but the surprise was that the interior wasn't what he was expecting. The living room was warm and inviting. He could imagine hanging out with Grayson, kicking back on the brown leather sofa and watching a ball game on that huge TV mounted to the wall above the fireplace.

"My dad will probably put me on dishwasher duty for a year for missing work," Liam said. "Getting kidnapped won't be an acceptable excuse."

Cooper glanced at his new friend. There was envy in Liam's eyes that matched his own as they stood by, waiting for Grayson's father to let go of his son.

"Let's promise we'll stay in touch, you, Grayson and me," Cooper said.

"Absolutely."

Grayson must have heard them because he turned to them and said, "Brothers for life."

A promise was made and kept.

Chapter One

"Good evening, friends. This is Kendra Hartley with another episode of *Find This Child*. Our child tonight is McKenzie Haywood. Six years ago, on a hot, summer day, thirteen-year-old McKenzie disappeared in broad daylight on her way to the corner store to buy a Dove bar, her favorite ice cream. McKenzie had the permission of her mother to walk the one block to the convenience store, something she'd done many times before."

Kendall Hart wrapped up her podcast an hour later and leaned back in her chair. She'd given her listeners all the facts of the cold case, and soon, probably even tonight, she'd start getting questions and suggestions in her podcast pen name Kendra Hartley's dedicated email account. She was too tired to read them tonight, and she still had tomorrow's lesson plan to do.

She shut down her equipment, turned off the baby cam and left the small closet she'd made into a sound booth. She'd been doing her once-a-month podcasts for three years, beginning a year after Olivia was born. In those three years, two of her cases had been solved thanks to input from her listeners. Even though delving into the lives of the missing children depressed her, that two child predators were behind bars because of her podcasts was all the motivation she needed to continue. And maybe, one day, her kidnapper would be caught.

Kendall shuddered, thinking of how terrified her seven-year-old self had been when that man had snatched her right out of her front yard in broad daylight. That was the downside of doing these podcasts. They always brought back the memories and the questions that haunted her. Were any of these children still alive? Was her kidnapper out there, still taking children?

Her guilt was that she hadn't been able to describe the man or his car well enough to help the police find him. If he was still kidnapping little girls, it was partly her fault. If only she'd been able to describe his face or knew cars well enough to tell the police what he looked like and what he drove.

All she knew was that he had a scarf wrapped around his face and a beanie on his head—which wasn't strange as it was winter and snowing—and that his eyes were brown and his car was white. She'd been so excited that it was snowing, and her mother had let her go outside to build a snowman with the promise that she not leave the yard. She hadn't. Even in her front yard, she hadn't been safe. Shaking off the memories, she left the sound booth, closing the door behind her.

After a stop in the kitchen to put a pod in the coffee maker, she went to her daughter's room. Olivia was a restless sleeper, and as she did every night, she'd kicked off the covers. Kendall pulled them back over her, then kissed her little girl's cheek. "Sweet dreams, baby."

She stood over Olivia's bed and stared at her daughter. Even at four—almost five—years old, Livie was rebelling at the tight reins Kendall had on her. As much as she tried to loosen those reins, she just couldn't make herself do it. Evil was out there, and she'd be damned if it touched her baby girl. If she was overprotective of her child, she had a right to be. No one knew better than her how fast a child could disappear.

There was a lesson plan to work on, and the sooner she got it done, the sooner she could go to bed, so she returned to the kitchen to get her cup of coffee. The dining room table was her workspace, and she settled down and got to work.

MONDAY MORNING, KENDALL STOOD at the door to her second-grade classroom, greeting each child by name and telling them the question of the day. They couldn't answer yet, but they had the morning to think about it. Today's question was, "What is something you wish you knew how to do?" She loved the daily questions because often their answers were hilarious.

Once all her little people were seated, she started their five minutes to talk to each other about their weekend, something they did every Monday. Letting them chat among themselves seemed to settle them down after being away from class for two days.

By the time the final bell rang, she considered the day a success. There had only been one argument between two of her kids and only one set of tears when Carly fell down at recess and skinned her knee.

The best answer to their Monday question was Blane's. "I wish I knew how to be invisible so my mom can't see me when I give my broccoli to Max. He's my dog and he'll eat anything, even gross broccoli. And, if I was invisible, I wouldn't have to wear clothes 'cause no one could see me." He gave her a big grin.

Blane was her most creative student, and she liked to think he'd be a famous novelist one day. By four o'clock, all her kids had been picked up or were safely on the bus, and she returned to her classroom to gather her things.

At four fifty, she was home after picking up Olivia from her preschool.

"You know what, Mommy?" Olivia asked as she sat at the counter, waiting for her after-school snack.

"What's that, sweetie?" Kendall slid the plate with three cheddar cheese slices and grapes across the counter to Olivia.

"Ford's not my boyfriend anymore."

"He's not? Why's that?" Ford had been her daughter's boyfriend for three days now.

"Well." She sighed as she rested her chin on her hand. "He likes Macy better."

Oh, the drama of young love. Kendall chuckled softly, shaking her head at the fickleness of four-year-olds. "Well, that's all right, sweetheart. It's okay to not always have a boyfriend. You can have another boyfriend when you're twenty-five."

Her daughter's eyes widened. "But I'll have white hair when I'm twenty-five." She scrunched her nose. "And wrinkles."

Kendall resisted the urge to go find a mirror and check for gray hair and crow's feet. "Why don't you finish your snack and not worry about boyfriends. Okay?"

"Then I can go outside and play?"

"No. You know you can't go outside without me."

"I won't leave the yard. Please, Mommy." She pressed her hands together as if in prayer.

"No, sweetie." They went through this most nights, Olivia wanting to go outside and play by herself. The answer was always the same, but her daughter was persistent. It was an impossible request for Kendall to agree to. "Tell you what. If you don't mind if dinner's a little late, we'll play outside for a few minutes."

"Yes!" Olivia clapped her hands.

"Just give me a few minutes to change."

"Hurry, Mommy."

Later that night, after Olivia was in bed and asleep, Kendall settled at the dining room table to search for her next podcast child. She was scrolling down the links in the search engine when an article caught her attention. She clicked on the link. It was a feature on three men who'd started a company called The Phoenix Three, their mission to rescue children who'd been kidnapped or had run away. She started reading the article and was impressed with their success.

Midway through the piece, there was a photo of the three men, and her gaze roamed over their faces. She gasped at seeing the man on the right. "Dear God," she murmured as she pressed her hand over her pounding heart. It was him, Olivia's father. The man whose name she'd never known. And now she knew.

"Cooper Devlin," she said, testing his name on her lips. She would have told him he was a father if she'd known who he was and how to find him. She'd always wished she could thank him for her bright, beautiful daughter.

She closed her eyes and thought of him and that night. On the eighteenth anniversary of her kidnapping, a date that always sent her into a funk, she'd impulsively stopped at The Tipsy Turtle, a bar near her apartment that served good food. It was either that or go home, heat up a microwaveable dinner and be depressed by herself.

The man who took a seat at the bar next to her bought her second glass of wine. "Thank you," she said.

"You're welcome," he replied with a smile.

He was pretty hot. His hair was cut military style, and his dark coffee eyes were warm and kind. They talked about everything and nothing as they ate their dinners. Later, when he stood and held out his hand, she slipped hers in his and left with him.

It was at her insistence that they did not trade names. All she knew about him was that he was a soldier on bereavement leave, and he was returning to base the next morning. That was perfect. She'd never have to see him again. He'd made love to her as if she were something precious. She had never felt more alive and wanted than in his arms that night, a stark contrast to the painful memories that usually haunted her on this anniversary. He'd made her forget, and he'd left her with a precious gift.

Her eyes stung with tears as she opened them. She had to tell him he had a daughter. But how? And what kind of man was he? What would it mean for Olivia? Oh, God. What if he tried to take her baby girl away from her? Should she call him or tell him in person? She didn't know.

A week. She'd give herself a week to decide when and how to tell him.

KENDALL GLANCED AT the clock on the wall. One more hour before she could send all her kiddos home. She'd been uneasy all week, and at times had felt like she was being watched. She chalked it up to stress and nerves because of the decision she had to make. Her time was up, and she still hadn't decided how to tell Cooper Devlin about Olivia.

She hadn't had a decent night's sleep since seeing his

photo in the article. Maybe she didn't have to tell him, then she wouldn't have to worry that he'd try to take Olivia away from her. What he didn't know wouldn't hurt him, right? No, she had to tell him. It was the right thing to do.

"Time's up," she said to her class. "Close your journal and set your pencils down." Most of her students loved writing in their journals, especially Blane, who always had to be told twice to put down his pencil. "Blane, time's up."

He loudly sighed as he dropped his pencil to the desk. "I wasn't finished, Ms. Hart."

"You can finish it—"

The door to her classroom opened, and Rebecca King, their principal, walked in followed by Susana Weaver, the school's secretary. "Ms. Hart, I need to see you for a few minutes. Susana's going to sit with your class."

"Okay." What was up? Both women had serious expressions.

"Bring your purse," Rebecca said when Kendall stepped toward her.

Now she was nervous. She opened her desk drawer and grabbed her purse. "What's going on, Rebecca?" she asked when they were in the hallway.

"We'll talk in my office."

Kendall tried to think of something she'd done that necessitated a trip to the principal's office. She drew a blank. When they entered Rebecca's office, a man wearing black pants and a white button-down stood looking out the window. He turned, and her gaze went to the gun and badge on his belt.

"Kendall, this is Detective Rossi." After introducing the officer, Rebecca stepped back.

Please, God, no. But she knew. Oh, God, she knew what he was going to say. Her worst nightmare had come true.

Her heart hammered in her chest so hard that it hurt, and her vision blurred.

"Ms. Hart," he said, his eyes filled with sympathy. "There's no easy way to say this. Your daughter's missing."

Kendall fainted.

Chapter Two

Cooper Devlin was the odd man out. He should be used to that. Had thought he was. Growing up in a home that made the word *dysfunctional* sound like playtime, he'd learned at an early age not to expect anything. Not a smile or kind word from those who were supposed to love him. His childhood had been a blur of neglect, punctuated by moments of violence that had left both physical and emotional scars.

He'd found a home, though. His Phoenix Three brothers had become the family he never thought he'd have. They were the ones who'd shown him what loyalty truly meant, who taught him that love didn't have to come with conditions and fists. Grayson and Liam weren't his blood brothers. He didn't have one of those. But they were his brothers all the same.

Now Grayson was married to Harlow, and Liam and Quinn were expecting a baby and engaged to be married. He was happy for his brothers, he really was. But would they still have room for him, the odd man out? Maybe he wasn't used to that after all because here he was, in a rented apartment, feeling sorry for himself while hiding from the sweet grandmother next door who wanted him to come over tonight and meet her granddaughter.

"Get over yourself," he muttered. Ruby, his rescue dog, lifted her head from where she was curled up next to him on the couch. "Didn't mean you, girl." He really did need to start looking for a place to buy like he kept saying he was going to do. A house with a yard for Ruby to play in.

He was supposed to be at Grayson's for an afternoon at the beach and then a cookout. He was procrastinating. The cookout was to celebrate Liam's and Quinn's engagement. Not that he could just not go. That would require explaining, and he didn't want to rain on their parade with his poor-me story. Tomorrow, he'd be over it. He always got over it.

He sighed as he stuck his wallet in his pocket, and as soon as he picked up his keys, Ruby raced to the door, tail wagging. She loved riding in his truck, and she loved when that truck took them to Grayson's, where she could play with her best friend, Einstein, a very talkative cat.

Now all they had to do was sneak past Mrs. Seagrave's apartment. Not an easy task as he was sure she had her ear to the door listening for his footsteps. Turned out to be his lucky night, and he and Ruby were able to sneak past.

As he was getting in his truck, his phone chimed, the ringtone telling him it was a Phoenix Three call forwarded to him since he was on duty tonight.

"The Phoenix Three. Cooper Devlin speaking."

"Thank God, it's you. My name's Kendall Hart, and I have to talk to you. Tonight."

He heard the panic in her voice. "I have somewhere I have to be right now, Miss Hart. Can you tell me what this is about?"

"Not over the phone, but it's urgent. Please. Oh, God, please."

She was crying now. "I really do need to be somewhere. I assume you're in Myrtle Beach. I can meet you in three hours." This would give him an excuse to leave right after dinner.

"You don't understand. We can't wait. She's been missing since this afternoon."

"Who's missing?"

There was a long pause, and then, "Your daughter."

"Ma'am... Ms. Hart, I don't have a daughter. I can tell you're upset, and I'll do what I can to help you. When did you—"

"She's yours, Cooper. Olivia's the result of our night together. You were home on leave, and we met at The Tipsy Turtle. Please tell me you remember."

The phone slipped out of his hand, falling to the floor of his truck. Remember? Hell, yes. He'd never forgotten that night and the woman who wouldn't give him her name. "I have a daughter?" Ruby, sensing his distress, whined as she tried to lick his face.

He reached down and picked up his cell phone. "Ms. Hart... Kendall." Surely, it was okay to use her first name considering they'd spent an entire night in each other's arms. "I remember." He couldn't wrap his mind around learning he had a daughter. "Where are you and what do you know?" And what's my daughter's name? What does she look like? Is she happy? A thousand questions crammed their way into his mind.

"I still live in Decatur, not far from where we met."

"Do you have someone with you? A husband or boyfriend?" He didn't like the thought of her being alone right now.

"No, it's just my daughter and me."

The relief that there wasn't a man in her life surprised him. He hadn't seen her in five years, had no claim on her, but he'd thought of her often, regretted that she was only one unforgettable night in his life. "This is your cell phone number we're talking on?"

"Yes. Please, Cooper. You find missing children. You have to help me find Olivia."

His daughter's name was Olivia. It didn't occur to him that he might not be Olivia's father. The woman he'd spent a night with wouldn't lie about something like that. "Do you have a pen handy?"

"Yes."

"Take down this number. It's my personal cell." After giving her his number, he said, "Text me your address. I'm going to find the fastest way to get to you that I can. I'll call you when I have the details."

"Okay. Thank you. Thank you so much."

He started his truck while he talked to her. "Have you contacted the police?"

"Yes, they're aware, but they don't have much to go on. I'm so afraid."

He hated hearing the quaver in her voice. "Listen to me, Kendall. We're going to find her."

"Please hurry."

"I'll call you back shortly." He dropped his phone into the cupholder. It was normally a fifteen-minute drive to Grayson's. He made it in nine.

His friends would be on the deck, so he bypassed the front door and jogged to the back. Ruby thought this was a new game and bounced around ahead of him. "I need you to find me a charter that can take me to Atlanta," he said, stopping in front of Grayson. "Tonight. Now."

Without asking questions, Grayson picked up his phone from the table and scrolled through his contacts. That was what he loved about his brothers. They knew if he needed a plane immediately, there was a damn good reason for it. He paced while Grayson talked to someone.

"What airport?" Grayson asked.

"Decatur."

"Your plane takes off from Beach Aviation in forty-five minutes."

He glanced at his watch. It would take him at least twenty minutes or more, depending on traffic, to get to the airport. "Thanks."

"What's going on?" Liam asked.

"My daughter's missing. Gotta go."

"Whoa. Stop," Grayson said.

He was halfway down the steps, and he turned. "What?" Four pairs of eyes stared at him as if he'd lost his mind.

"How come you never told us you have a daughter?" Harlow asked.

"Because I didn't know until tonight." He glanced at Ruby, who was sitting by the door waiting to be let in so she could play with Grayson and Harlow's son and their cat. "Can you keep Ruby for me?"

"Of course." Harlow got up and let Ruby into the house.

Quinn, Liam's fiancée said, "Your daughter's missing?"

"Yes."

"You can spare five minutes to tell us what's going on," Grayson said.

Liam nodded. "And you know we'll give you any help you need."

He blew out a breath. "I got a phone call tonight." He told his friends how he'd met Kendall and what she'd said on the call. "So, that's it. Now, I have to go."

"I'll have a car waiting for you in Decatur," Grayson said. "As soon as you get a handle on what's happening and you need us there, call. Anything you need, we'll get for you."

"Thanks." He hadn't thought past getting on the plane and getting to Kendall. "I'll keep you in the know."

He always kept a go bag in his truck, so he didn't have to return home and pack. Two hours and thirty-three minutes after Kendall called, he turned into the driveway of the house his GPS took him to. There was a police car parked on the street, and it appeared every light in the house was on.

The sun was low in the sky, and it was going to be dark soon. The thought of his little girl somewhere in the dark, probably crying and begging for her mother... No, now was not the time for the rage building inside him that someone would take an innocent child. His child. More than ever in his life, he needed a clear head, and for that to happen, he had to stay calm so he could think clearly.

As he walked toward the front door, he noted that the house was small but well kept. Flower beds gave color to the landscape, and the scent of what he thought might be lavender filled the air. This was where the woman he'd thought of often lived with the baby they'd made, and for five years, he hadn't known he was a father.

Whom should he be mad at over that? Kendall for refusing to give him her name? Himself for not insisting? Maybe he shouldn't be mad at all as neither one of them even considered they would make a baby that night, but the regret for not being here for Kendall was heavy.

A pink bicycle with training wheels leaned against the wall of the house, and he paused. His daughter rode that little bike. *His daughter.* He was still having trouble wrapping his head around that. He touched the handlebar, smiling at the pink tassels. What was she like, his little girl?

He moved on to the front door. There was a knocker in the shape of a heart, which he assumed was a play on Kendall's last name of Hart. Before even walking inside, he had the sense of a home filled with love.

The door swung open before he could lift the knocker, and Kendall stood there, her eyes red-rimmed and puffy but she was as beautiful as he remembered. Acting on instinct, he wrapped his arms around her in a hug. "I'm here," he softly said. She melted into his embrace, and nothing had ever felt so right as holding this woman in his arms.

"Who's that?" a man said.

Refusing to let go of Kendall, he pulled her to his side as he met the gaze of the man in a police officer's uniform. "I'm Olivia's father."

The officer's eyes narrowed as he called someone on his phone. "The father's here. What do you want me to do with him?"

Do with him? Still keeping Kendall by his side, he walked them past the officer and down a hallway. "Where can we talk?"

Chapter Three

He was here! Kendall took his hand and pulled him to the closest room and closed the door. "You came."

"Of course I did." His gaze roamed around the room. "This is Olivia's room?"

"Yes." She'd never expected to see him again, much less have him in her home, in Livie's room. It was surreal to have him standing in front of her, but if he could find Livie, she'd owe this man, a stranger to her now, more than she could ever repay.

He smiled as he took in Livie's room. "She likes pink."

"It's her favorite color, but we don't have time to talk about that. We have to find her."

"We will." He took her hand, clasping it between both of his. "I promise. What do you know? How did she disappear?"

His touch calmed her, and the why of that was something she'd think about later. When she had her little girl back. There was something she had to say before she answered his questions. "I need you to know that you are Livie's father. I would have told you I was pregnant if I knew how to find you. I swear on that."

"I believe you, but how did you find me?"

"The article about The Phoenix Three. I recognized you in the photo. After I saw it, I was going to call you and tell you about Livie. Then this happened before I could. Thank you for believing me."

"We'll do DNA testing later so it's official, but for now that doesn't matter. What does matter is finding our daughter."

"Thank you." He'd said *our daughter*, and he had no idea how much that meant to her. She'd been afraid that he wouldn't believe her, and the relief that he was here and trusting her was so great that the tears she'd been holding back since he'd arrived streamed down her face. "I'm sorry." She swiped at her cheeks.

"Hey, hey." He pulled her in for another hug. "You don't need to be sorry. I feel like crying, too."

She could feel his strength as he held her, and that gave her hope that this man could find her daughter. That and his expertise at finding lost children. For the first time since Livie went missing, she had hope that she'd have her little girl home soon.

"Tell me what you know."

"Not much, and that scares me. I had an early evening adult reading class to teach, which I do every Tuesday night. Amanda, Livie's babysitter, picks her up from preschool on Tuesdays and stays with her here until I get home." She squeezed her eyes shut, trying not to imagine a stranger taking her baby.

"Where was Livie taken? From here?"

"No, at the grocery store. This has always been my greatest fear, that someone would kidnap her, and now it's happened."

"Why would that be your greatest fear? Has someone

been bothering you? Stalking you? Paying too much attention to Olivia and it made you suspicious?"

"No, nothing like that. I was kidnapped when I was seven, so it's always been a fear of mine." She saw the shock on his face at hearing that, but she couldn't talk about that time in her life right now. "That's a conversation for another day. Amanda doesn't know what happened. She was putting Livie in her car seat when someone hit her from behind. When she woke up, she was on the floor of her car and Livie was... She was gone." She swiped at her eyes. "I thought I was done crying. I keep thinking of her out there somewhere with a stranger. Scared and begging for me."

"Where is Amanda now?"

"Home. She has a mild concussion, but she doesn't know anything."

"She might not think she does, but I still want to talk to her. Does the grocery store have video of the parking lot?"

"Yes, the police have it."

"I want to see it."

The door opened, and a frowning Detective Rossi strode in. Kendall frowned right back at him. This was her home. Did he think he had the right to just walk in without knocking? She was already growing unhappy with him for shutting her out of his investigation.

He'd stopped to see her earlier after she'd called him to ask if he had any leads. He'd patted her hand and told her that he couldn't share any details with her. When she'd protested, telling him she was Livie's mother and had a right to know, he'd had the gall to say, "You just need to stop questioning me and let me do my job, Ms. Hart."

"Is this the father?" he said as he narrowed his eyes at Cooper.

"I am."

"He is," she confirmed.

"Where were you this afternoon between three thirty and four?"

"He didn't take—"

"It's okay," Cooper said. "He has to ask me that." He put his arm around her. "I was in Myrtle Beach when Kendall called me to tell me our daughter was missing. I can give you proof of that."

The detective's gaze shifted to her. "You didn't tell me the father was in the picture."

"I would imagine all she was thinking about was finding Livie." Cooper smiled at her.

"You didn't ask," she said. Taking a clue from Cooper, she didn't offer that she'd only recently learned who Livie's father was.

"So, you two are together?"

Kendall didn't like the detective's suspicious tone, but she wasn't sure how to answer.

"It's complicated," Cooper said. "But our *complicated* doesn't have anything to do with our daughter being missing. I'd like an update on what you know so far."

"You need to leave the investigation to the police, Mr...."

Oh, she hadn't introduced them. "This is Cooper Devlin. Cooper, Detective Rossi."

Cooper held out his hand, and, she thought, the detective reluctantly shook his hand. "Sorry we're meeting under this circumstance, Detective. I'd like to see the video from the grocery store."

"This is police business, Mr. Devlin. You need to leave this to us."

"No, this is a daughter missing. Our daughter. We have a right to know what you do."

"Cooper finds missing children," Kendall said. "He's good at it."

"Kendall's right. My team and I are one of the best at finding missing children. We have resources you probably only dream about. We can work together, Detective, or I'll go it alone. Don't care either way, but I will find my daughter with or without you."

"I don't appreciate your attitude," the detective said. "You interfere with my investigation, I'll throw you in a cell."

"You can try."

"Stop it." Kendall stepped between the two men before they decided fighting it out was the thing to do. "This isn't helping." She glared at the detective. "Why wouldn't you want the help of someone who specializes in finding missing children? Go look up The Phoenix Three, then come tell me you don't want to utilize his expertise." She turned to Cooper. "This isn't helping."

His smile and his eyes turned soft. "You're right. But I won't stand by and do nothing."

"Of course not, but the two of you fighting isn't going to find Livie."

The detective made a phone call. "It's me. Check out an outfit called The Phoenix Three, then call me back." He slipped his phone back in his pocket. "You have a card?"

Cooper took one from his wallet and handed it to the detective. "My cell phone is the second number. I want to see the video from the grocery store."

Detective Rossi stuck the card in his shirt pocket. "When I hear back with a report on you and your company, I'll call you." He nodded at her as he walked out.

"What now?" she said. "I don't think I can handle just waiting around for something to happen."

"Me either. If Olivia should find a way to call you, will it be on your landline or your cell phone? Does she even know your number?"

"Yes, I made her memorize it, and I don't have a landline, so it will be my cell."

"Good. That means you don't have to stay here and wait by the phone. Do you think your babysitter is up to talking to us?"

"I'll call her now." She was prepared to fight to be involved in finding her daughter, so it was a relief that he was including her. While she talked to Amanda, he roamed around the room, touching Livie's things, picking some up, then carefully setting them back down.

"I missed so much of her life," he said when she finished her phone call. He gently trailed a finger down a doll's face. "Her first smile, first word, seeing her take her first steps."

He sounded so sad, and her heart broke for him. All those things he'd missed, she'd been right there, sharing it all with their daughter. "I have her baby book and videos you can watch."

"Thank you, I'd love that. Is your babysitter up to seeing us?"

"Yes. We can go over now."

"Good. Let's go."

She expected to find the officer still in her living room, but he'd apparently left with Detective Rossi. Cooper took her keys from her when she fumbled with locking the door. They took his rental since she was wrecked and had no business behind the wheel of a car.

Amanda only lived ten minutes away, and for the first

five minutes of the drive, they each were lost in their own thoughts and didn't talk. Her thoughts swirled around Cooper missing almost five years of Livie's life.

She glanced at him, struck again by how beautiful he was. She didn't think men liked to be thought of as beautiful, but facts were facts, and he was. Livie had his chocolate brown eyes and full lips. She didn't have his sun-streaked chestnut hair that women paid top dollar for, which was too bad. Livie had her black hair, but it was only fair that her daughter had something from her.

Five years ago, he'd been a hot soldier with haunted eyes on the barstool next to her. He'd helped her put aside the dark places in her mind—on an anniversary she wished to God she didn't have—without asking questions. She hadn't asked what put the haunt in his eyes. They'd needed each other that night for reasons they hadn't shared, never imagining they'd see each other again.

Now, he was the father of her child, a man who'd dropped everything to come to her the minute she'd called him. She was filled with regrets. Not because they'd met and spent an amazing night together, but because she hadn't let him tell her his name.

"I'm sorry," she said.

He glanced at her with those dark eyes she'd once gotten lost in and probably could again if she wasn't careful. "For what?"

"That I didn't let you tell me your name. That you missed so much of Livie's life."

Surprising her, he reached over the console and took her hand. "You couldn't know you'd get pregnant. We used a condom. Guess it failed." He softly smiled. "I'm weirdly okay with that."

"What if we can't find her?" She'd been doing missing

children podcasts for several years now, and she knew all too well that some children disappeared into thin air, never to be seen again. What if Livie was one of those children? "I'm sorry," she said when tears fell down her cheeks again. She turned her face toward the window.

"Hey, you have absolutely nothing to be sorry about." He squeezed her hand. "Look at me, Kendall."

"Do I have to?"

"You don't have to do anything you don't want to, but I want you to look in my eyes and believe that I'll do everything in my power to find our daughter."

"I believe you." And she truly did. It seemed like there was so much more they needed to say, but she honestly couldn't handle any more confessions or sorrys. "Turn right at the next street. Amanda's house is the second one on your right."

"Give me a quick summary of her."

"Amanda's in her late fifties, widowed, is financially okay, and her two children live out of state, one in Orlando and one in Chicago. They only come home at Christmas. I met her at my book club. When she learned that I was looking for someone to pick Livie up on Tuesdays and stay with her until I get home from my adult reading class, she wanted to do it. Said she was lonely. Livie adores her."

"Then she played no part in—"

"Oh, no way. Why would you even think that?"

He stopped the car in Amanda's driveway. "Because every possibility has to be considered. I've had cases where the last person I thought would harm or take a child was the guilty party. You say Amanda had no part in Livie's disappearance, then I believe you. I trust you to know in whose hands you put our daughter, Kendall." He opened his door. "Let's go talk to her."

"Please be nice to her. She's very upset about this and blames herself."

"I promise to be gentle with her. Does she know who I am?"

"No."

"Let's leave it that way for now. Just tell her I'm an investigator you've brought into this."

Did he want to keep it secret that Livie was his daughter?

Chapter Four

Cooper trusted Kendall's instincts to an extent, but he'd decide for himself how trustworthy his daughter's babysitter was. As he'd told her, he'd learned to be suspicious of everyone until he was satisfied they were innocent.

Only a few seconds passed after Kendall rang the doorbell when the door opened to reveal a tiny woman with short gray hair whose eyes were red and puffy from crying. She held out her arms, and Kendall walked into them, and the two women sobbed as they held each other.

Cooper eased around them and walked to the middle of the living room. The room was tidy, everything in its place and not a speck of dust that he could see. An afghan and a pillow were on the sofa and a half cup of tea on the coffee table. Next to the cup was a box of tissues.

"Cooper, this is Amanda Eckerd, Livie's babysitter. Amanda, Cooper Devlin. Cooper is with The Phoenix Three. They specialize in finding children."

Amanda grabbed his hand. "Please, you have to find our precious girl."

"I won't rest until she's back home with her mother." He led her to the sofa. "Can we sit and talk for a few minutes?"

"Yes. I'll do anything I can to help you find her." She pulled a tissue from the box and wiped her eyes.

"I appreciate that," he said. Kendall sat next to her and put her arm around Amanda. She also grabbed a tissue. He took a seat on the chair facing them. He'd already decided that the woman wasn't involved in taking Olivia. Her tears were real. "I know you've told the police what happened, but I'd like to hear it from you myself."

A shudder traveled through her body. "I should've stopped him from taking her." She leaned against Kendall. "I'm so sorry."

"It's not your fault," Kendall said. "No one blames you."

"Kendall's right, no one blames you, Amanda. Talk me through what happened." He hoped she'd remember something that would give him a lead.

She blew out a breath. "Okay. Livie wanted mini meat loafs for dinner."

"Amanda makes these miniature meat loafs with cheddar cheese inside, and Livie loves them," Kendall said.

"She does," Amanda said with a soft smile on her face. "That was all she talked about after I picked her up from preschool. That and would I make double fudge brownies for dessert."

He made a mental note that his daughter loved brownies. So did he, and the idea of them eating the decadent treat together sent an unexpected longing through him to create memories with her.

"We went to the grocery store on the way to Kendall's to get what I needed to make her dinner."

"How long were you in the store?"

She stared up at the ceiling, thinking, then lowered her gaze to his. "Fifteen, twenty minutes."

"Did you notice anyone paying attention to you? To Olivia?"

"No… Wait, maybe. I'm not sure. The police didn't ask that question, so I hadn't thought about it before, but there was a man."

"Tell me about him."

"It's probably nothing. We were in the cake aisle getting the brownie mix when he came by. Livie was trying to decide between the salted caramel and the chewy fudge. He chuckled as he leaned down and whispered loud enough for me to hear, 'Tell your grandma to get you both.' I rolled my eyes at him, like thanks for that. He was still chuckling when he walked away."

Probably was an innocent encounter, but twelve years in special ops and a few years' experience in tracking down missing children had his antennae twitching.

"What did he look like?"

"I didn't pay close attention. He had on a ball cap, wore glasses and had what my husband called a beer belly, a big one. That's all I can really tell you about him."

"Was he short, tall, have a scent?"

She closed her eyes. "He was average height, not short, not tall. And he smelled like cigarette smoke." She opened her eyes. "I'd forgotten about that."

"Eye and hair color? Any tattoos?"

"He never turned his face to me, so I didn't see his eyes. He had on a ball cap, but brown hair was sticking out the bottom of the cap. He had on a blue, long-sleeved button-up shirt, so if he did have tattoos, I couldn't see them." She frowned. "The police never asked if anyone talked to me or Livie inside the store. It seems like they should have."

Yes, they should have. "You did good, Amanda. Did you see him again after that?"

"No. Livie decided on the chewy fudge, and after paying for our groceries, we pushed the cart to my car." A soft smile crossed her face. "Livie likes to help me push the cart. After putting the bags of groceries in the back, we returned the cart to the... I don't know what you call it, but the place you leave empty carts in the parking lot. Then I was buckling her into her car seat, and that's the last thing I remember." Tears filled her eyes. "I'm sorry."

"She woke up on the floor of her car," Kendall said. "The police think whoever took Livie pushed her into the car after hitting her on the head, then closed the door so no one would see her."

"From the time I was buckling Livie in, to the time I woke up, about five minutes passed. I called the police as soon as I realized Livie was gone."

Plenty of time for the kidnapper to disappear with Olivia. "Thank you for talking to us. You've been very helpful."

"I hope so." Amanda clasped her hands as if in prayer. "Please, find her."

"That's the plan." He stood. "We'll leave you to return to your rest. If you think of anything else, please call Kendall."

"I will."

The two women hugged again, and when they let each other go, he got a hug from Amanda.

"Still think she might be involved?" Kendall asked when they were back in the car.

"No, but I do have a bad feeling about the man who talked to Olivia in the grocery store."

"Why? It could have just been an innocent remark."

"Entirely possible, but in today's world, where people

are more suspicious of strangers, men don't tend to talk to little girls they don't know."

"I close my eyes, and I can almost hear her crying, begging for me."

He reached over the console, took her hand and squeezed. It was the best comfort he could give her as there was nothing he could say to dispute what she feared was probably true. His phone chimed as he was backing out of Amanda's driveway, and he stopped. "It's one of my teammates," he said when Grayson's name appeared on the screen.

"Hey. I'm in the car with Kendall. What you got for me?"

"Just got off the phone with one of Decatur's finest. He was doing a background check on you."

"Yeah, the detective on the case is territorial and isn't happy having me on the scene."

"Bet that didn't go over well with you."

"Affirmative. I asked to see the video from the grocery store, and he finally agreed if I and The Phoenix Three checked out."

"I managed to impress him, and you're good to go."

"Thanks, brother."

"Let me know if there's anything we can do from here."

"I will." He disconnected, then dropped his phone in the cupholder. His stomach growled, reminding him that he'd missed Grayson and Harlow's cookout. "You have dinner?"

She shook her head. "Not hungry."

"Well, I am. Where's a good place to grab a bite?"

Although it was small, the first smile he'd seen on her appeared. "The Tipsy Turtle."

"Ah, the scene of the crime." He returned her smile. "I think I remember how to get there. Let me know if I take a wrong turn."

He only took one wrong turn, and after they were seated at a booth this time, he glanced at the bar where they'd sat that night. "Brings back memories, being here. Good ones."

"My memories that night weren't so great," she murmured.

He didn't know what to say to that. He'd thought they'd had something special for two people who didn't know each other.

She blinked and her cheeks pinkened. "I didn't mean that like it sounded. I have wonderful memories of you and our time together. Before you sat down next to me, I... Well, that night was the anniversary of my kidnapping, and it was always a hard day for me." Her eyes locked on his. "You helped me forget, and for that, I was grateful."

"I wish I'd known then. I would've been gentler with you."

She shook her head. "I didn't want gentler. I needed what you gave me, and the best thing that came from that night was Livie. After I had her, those anniversaries aren't as difficult anymore, so thank you for that."

"I still wish I had known." He couldn't know for sure, but he thought he would have tried harder to get her to tell him her name.

"Can we not talk about this anymore?"

"Sure." But he hoped she would eventually share that part of her life with him. He picked up the menu and scanned it. "What are you having?"

"I'm not hungry."

"You need to eat something, Kendall, even if it's a bowl of soup and a little bread. You're no good to Olivia if you end up making yourself sick." He picked up the menu again. "How about a bowl of vegetable soup?"

"I don't know if I can eat."

"At least try." The waiter came to their table, and he ordered a melted ham and cheese on sourdough with a side salad, along with a bowl of the soup, and asked for some bread.

When they were alone again, he said, "Tell me about Olivia."

She opened her purse and took out her phone. "Here's a picture of her. She has your eyes and mouth."

He took her phone and saw his daughter for the first time. Something cracked open in his chest as he traced the outline of Olivia's face in the photograph, feeling a surge of love and protectiveness wash over him. "She's beautiful," he whispered, his voice choked with emotion.

"I'll forward it to you."

"Thank you." A few seconds later, a text notification alert sounded. If you'd told him yesterday that he'd have a photo of his daughter on his phone, he would've laughed in disbelief. He really was shocked by how okay he was with that.

"Will you... Will you want to be a part of her life now?"

He met her gaze, wanting her to see the truth in his eyes. "Yes. I want to be there for her. I want to make up for all the lost time and be a father to her."

She tore little strips from her napkin. "Do you blame me for someone taking her? Are you going to try to take her away from me?"

"Hey, now." He reached across the table and pulled the napkin she was shredding from her hands. "No, I'm not going to take her away from you. I'll never do that. And no one blames you for what happened, okay? I want to be in my daughter's life, but how we manage that will be a decision we make together. After we have her back with you."

"I'm sorry. You're being amazing about everything, and here I'm worried about what you might do." She raised tear-filled eyes to his. "What if we don't find her?"

"Kendall, listen to me. We're going to find her even if we have to tear this county apart or the state of Georgia if it comes to that."

The waiter came to their table with their dinner. "Eat some," he said when she just sat, staring at the soup. He buttered a slice of the corn bread the waiter had brought with the soup and slid the plate across to her. "Please, eat a little."

She looked exhausted, not just physically, but mentally, too. Even with red, puffy eyes and the lines of tension, she was as beautiful as he remembered. Her black hair had been halfway down her waist when he'd met her, but now it was shoulder length. Framed by that black hair, her baby blue eyes were a startling contrast. Over the years, he'd dreamed of kissing those full lips. He'd never forgotten her, had always regretted not getting her name and contact information.

Now, he was sitting across from her in the same place he'd met her. Was it fate? Destiny? He'd never been a believer in such things, but he found he was open to the possibility that there was such a thing as destiny. That they were meant to find each other again. He only wished that it hadn't taken Olivia being kidnapped for him to find Kendall again.

"Eat," he said, putting a touch of command into his voice. He dug into his sandwich, pleased when she picked up her spoon and started on her soup. Not wanting to distract her from eating, he kept quiet. He didn't think she even realized she'd finished the bowl of soup and half of the corn bread.

His phone chimed as the waiter was handing him the check. It was a Decatur area code. "Cooper Devlin here," he said as he handed the waiter his credit card.

"This is Detective Rossi. You can come to the station tomorrow and see the video."

"Excellent. We'll be there in the morning."

"You're bringing Ms. Hart? You think it's a good idea for her to see it?"

He lifted his gaze to Kendall's. "It's her choice, but I doubt she'll let me leave without her."

"Be here at nine." With that, the detective disconnected.

"We're to be at the police station at nine, but if you don't want to watch the video, no one would blame you."

She shook her head, determination shining in her eyes. "I need to see it."

"Thought you'd say that." He signed the receipt, then put his credit card in his wallet. "You ready to go? I'd like to see Olivia's baby book." What he didn't tell her was that as soon as he'd seen the photo of his little girl, he'd been an instant goner, and the thought of his daughter crying, begging for her mother made him want to tear the town apart with his bare hands until he found her.

There was no fear inside him that he'd be anything like his father. No fear that he'd treat Olivia the way their father had treated him and Emmie. If anything, from a young age, he'd stepped up and been a father to his sister in a way his father had never been. Emmie had taught him what little girls needed, and now, he would thank her for that. As soon as they had Olivia back, he'd call his sister and tell her she was an aunt.

Was she ever going to be surprised.

Chapter Five

While Cooper turned the pages of Olivia's baby book, Kendall couldn't take her eyes off him. It wasn't just because he was gorgeous to look at. He so was, but it was more that the emotion in his eyes and the soft expression on his face as he took his time to absorb each memory captured in the book tugged at her heart. His brows furrowed slightly at the sight of Olivia's first steps, then on the next page, a small chuckle escaped him as he read about her first word.

"*Mine*?" He glanced up at her. "I always thought *Mama* was a baby's first word."

"She said that when I tried to take a cookie that was a slobbery mess away from her."

"That's my girl." He went back to paging through the baby book. There was so much tenderness in his touch as he traced the outlines of tiny footprints and handprints left on the pages. He glanced up and caught her staring at him, a soft smile playing on his lips that made her stomach flutter. "She's lucky to have you as her mom."

"I think it's more like I'm the lucky one. I need her back, Cooper." Tears swelled in her eyes again as she thought of her little girl out there somewhere in the dark, wondering why her mommy didn't come get her.

He closed the book and set it on the coffee table. "I think you need a hug. Come here."

She hesitated a moment. Although they'd once been as intimate as possible, he was a stranger. Was it weird to want the hug he was offering, one she really needed?

Maybe so, but he was Livie's father, and she thought he might need a hug as much as she did. She scooted over and Cooper tucked her against his side. She'd known he was a nice man from their one night together. That night, he'd been a lot of things; sweet, considerate, and had confirmed her consent even after they were in his hotel room, where it had to be obvious she was agreeable with being there.

He'd shown her he was a man who could be trusted, and that meant everything when it came to her little girl. The way he'd stared at the photos of Olivia in her baby book and the album she'd brought out, she was sure he was already in love with the daughter he'd not yet met. Unless he was an amazing actor, Livie was going to have a wonderful father.

"Tell me about Olivia... Livie. Is it all right if I use her nickname?"

See, considerate. "Of course. It's Olivia if she's in trouble."

"And is she in trouble a lot?"

"No. She's actually pretty well behaved, but she does have her moments. She can be impatient when she wants something. She laughs a lot. Thinks the silliest things are funny."

"Like what?"

"Silly jokes, kid movies like the *Minions*... She'll laugh hysterically at them."

"Well, the *Minions* are funny."

She rolled her eyes. "I'll wait to hear you say that again after you watched them ad nauseam. She really wants a dog, but we're gone all day, so it's just not feasible."

"I have a dog. Maybe the two of you can visit me sometimes and she can play with Ruby."

"She'd love that." What was Livie doing right now? Was whoever had taken her at least taking care of her? Feeding her? "I feel like we should be out looking for her."

"If we had any idea where to search, believe me, we'd be doing that." He twirled a lock of her hair around his fingers, something she didn't think he realized he was doing.

"Why were you in the bar that night?" She'd felt back then that he'd been a bit sad, and she'd always wondered when she thought of him if she was right.

"I told you I was home on leave, right? I seem to remember that I did."

"Yes, but you didn't say why."

"I was home to bury my father."

"Oh, I'm sorry. I did think you seemed sad that night."

"Don't be sorry. If I appeared sad, it was because I was worried about my sister. This will sound harsh, but he's not missed. Not by me or Emmie. He was mean, miserable and a drunk. But he was my father, and someone had to make arrangements for him. Emmie and I agreed to have him cremated. We didn't want him buried somewhere that we would feel obligated to visit. I also had to meet with a Realtor that week to put his house up for sale."

"Does your sister live here?"

"No, Emmie... Her name's actually Emilia, but when she was little, she couldn't say that, and she called herself Emmie. It stuck. She lives in Boston with her husband. She's finally happy."

She wondered what the story was with his sister and her finally being happy, but when he didn't offer more, she didn't ask.

"Tell me about you," he said. "What do you do?"

"I'm a second-grade teacher, and I also have a monthly podcast that averages a thousand downloads."

"Is that good?"

"It puts me in the top ten percent for podcasts."

"Impressive. What is your podcast about?"

"Cold-case children's kidnappings, but I don't want to talk about that right now." She'd have to explain why she did the podcasts, and she just wasn't up to reliving that part of her life tonight.

"Okay, but I'd like to hear more about it when you're ready. As for your full-time job, I can see you as a teacher, a good one."

"I love teaching children." He'd taken her mind off her missing daughter for a while, but she needed to be alone now. She leaned away from him. "It's getting late. You can sleep in my bed."

"The couch is fine. I don't want to kick you out of your bed."

"I'm sleeping in Livie's bed. I know it's silly, but I feel closer to her in her room. I'd sleep there even if you weren't here." Or not sleeping at all.

"Okay, then."

After getting him settled, she went to Livie's room, where she curled up with her daughter's stuffed animals and cried herself to sleep.

"Are you sure you want to watch this?" Detective Rossi said the next morning when she and Cooper arrived at the police station.

"Yes." It was going to be hard, but she had to. Had to know everything about what had happened to Livie.

"Come with me, then."

As they followed him, Cooper put his hand on her back,

and his touch gave her the confidence that she could do this. The detective pulled up a second chair and had her and Cooper sit at his desk in front of his monitor. She sucked in a breath as Detective Rossi clicked Play to show them the video.

Cooper reached for her hand as the video began to play, and again, his touch gave her the strength to watch. At seeing Amanda and Livie pushing the cart to the car, she wanted to yell at them to go back in the store.

This was the first time Cooper was seeing his daughter on film, and Kendall glanced at him. His eyes were glued to the monitor, and there was a small smile on his face as he watched Livie chattering away while Amanda loaded the groceries.

A white van was parked next to Amanda's car, and even knowing what was going to happen, Kendall gasped when a man got out of the van and then came around the other side and eased the sliding door open. Amanda had her back to him as she helped Livie into her car seat. The man glanced around, then he hit Amanda on the back of the head with his balled-up fist. As she began to fall to the ground, he pushed her onto the floor of the car.

Confused and scared, Livie started crying. The man moved swiftly, grabbing Livie and shoving her into the van. He shut the back door of Amanda's car, then jumped into the van, sliding the door closed behind him.

As she watched the van speed away, Kendall burst into tears.

"I told you she didn't need to see this," Detective Rossi said.

Ignoring Rossi, Cooper turned his chair to face her and took her hands in his. "Listen to me, Kendall. We're going to find her."

"Promise?" She lifted her gaze to his, searching for the assurance she needed from him.

"You have my word." Keeping her hands in his, he glanced up at the detective. "What do you know so far?"

"We're looking for a fat man driving a white van with an unreadable license plate. That's about it right now. The video's too grainy to see his face clearly, but we're running it through our facial recognition program in the hopes we can get a match. I'm not too hopeful."

"Did you see how fast he moved? He's not fat. He's wearing padding. Watch it again and see how thin his face is. Also, if he was that heavy, he should have a double chin. It's unfortunate the video probably isn't distinct enough for facial recognition to make a match. I think when you do find the van that he's already ditched, you'll probably find that it's stolen."

"How do you know all that?" she asked.

"It's what I do, and I'm good."

All she could think was thank God she'd called him.

"I want to watch it again, but I think maybe you'd rather not?"

She pushed away from the desk. "I can't."

"We have a break room if you want to wait in there," Detective Rossi said. "There's coffee if you want some. Not that I recommend it. There's also a coffee shop next door."

"I'll wait in the break room."

"Down the hall, second door on the left."

Cooper touched her arm. "I'll come get you as soon as we're done here."

"Take as long as you need. All that's important is finding Livie."

Nothing else mattered. Not a damn thing.

Chapter Six

"You shouldn't have brought her here," Rossi said. "She didn't need to see that."

"It was her choice, and she said she needed to see it. She's stronger than you seem to think."

"She cried. I don't call that strong."

"That's our daughter on that video. I almost cried myself. Crying when your heart is being ripped out of your chest has no bearing on how strong a person is." Cooper backed the video up to where Amanda and Livie were coming out of the store. "Have you had any reports of a stolen van?" he asked when he finished watching the video for a second time.

"We have a BOLO out. It's unfortunate the camera didn't pick up the license plate, but there was a dent above the rear tire and the left taillight was broken, so that's helpful."

"I noticed that." He tapped the screen. "I'm betting this is the man who talked to Olivia in the grocery store, so you need to get that video from them. We might be able to get a better description of him." Amanda had said he wore glasses, but he didn't have any on when he took Livie.

"How do you know that?"

"Amanda Eckerd told me."

"She didn't tell me that."

"You didn't ask the right questions." He wasn't trying to antagonize the detective, but he was losing patience with the man. If Kendall hadn't called him, she would be dealing with this alone, and he didn't even want to think how much harder this would have been for her.

"She should have told me about the man."

Maybe so, but Amanda hadn't realized the encounter might be important. "It would be too traumatizing for Ms. Eckerd to watch this video, but let's make a photo of the man to show her. See if it triggers anything else she can remember about him."

"We can do that. I'll run by her house this afternoon."

It was encouraging that the detective no longer resented Cooper's involvement. "You contact the FBI?"

"I plan to do that. I held off, hoping we'd find Olivia by now."

Cooper was glad he hadn't brought them in yet. If they didn't find Livie in the next two days, he would personally call Sean Danvers, an FBI friend to The Phoenix Three. Until then, he preferred not to have the interference of another law agency. He wasn't bound by rules, and unlike the police and FBI, he'd break every damn one if necessary to find his daughter.

"Don't contact them yet. The assistant FBI director is a friend. I'll call him if we don't find her today." He stood. "Call me when you get the video from inside the store."

He found Kendall sitting at a table in the break room, staring at her phone. Her cheeks were wet with tears, and he glanced at the phone's screen, his breath catching at seeing the photo of Livie wearing a Braves shirt and ball cap. She stood in front of the Braves' stadium with a big smile on her face and holding hands with an older man.

"Who is that she's with?"

"My father. He's a huge Braves fan, has season tickets and takes her with him to the weekend games. She's loves baseball and the Braves."

He dropped into the chair next to Kendall. "I played baseball all through high school. My coach said I was good enough to go pro one day. My dream was to play for the Braves." That his daughter was a baseball fan and loved the team he'd dreamed of playing for was...just wow. They had something in common they could bond over.

"Maybe she inherited her love of baseball from you. Livie says she's going to be a catcher for the Braves when she grows up."

He chuckled at that. "She likes to catch balls?" He loved the idea that he might have passed on something he loved to his daughter.

"Yes. She even has a little glove. She loves hitting them, too. Says she's going to hit a home run in every game when she plays for the Braves." She swiped to the next photo, then held the screen up to him.

"That's about the cutest thing I've ever seen." It was a picture of Livie wearing her Braves shirt and ball cap, a glove on her hand, ready to catch a ball.

"I was sick one weekend last year, and Dad had already planned to go to a game. He decided to take Livie with him so I could rest." She smiled. "When she got back home, all she could talk about for days was baseball, corn dogs and ice cream cones. It's the only time she gets to eat junk like that, so I think she fell in love with the food first, then the game."

"A girl after my own heart." She really was. Baseball

and food. Two of the most important things in life. He'd grown up never having enough to eat, and because of that, as an adult, he made sure his refrigerator and pantry were well stocked. "I need to learn how to make corn dogs."

She laughed. "Livie's going to like you, Cooper."

God, he hoped so. "You ready to get out of here?"

"Yes."

Detective Rossi stopped them in the hallway. "The van was found early this morning by a patrol officer, and it was stolen. It was towed to the police lot and the crime lab is going over it now."

"Where was it found?"

Rossi sighed. "Why don't the two of you go home. I'll call you when we know something."

And here he'd thought they'd turned a corner. Guess not. "Detective, I feel like we've already had this conversation, but I'm going to say it again. I'm either working with you or without you, but I'm not going home and sitting on my ass while my daughter is missing. Just not happening. I'm not an amateur investigator, and if I were you, I'd want all the help available to me. So, I ask again, where was the van found?"

"Not far from here." Rossi gave him the location.

"Thank you," he said as he put the address in his phone's GPS. "I'll be sure to let you know immediately if I find anything useful and would appreciate the same from you." He put his hand on Kendall's back. "Let's go."

"Thank you," she said as soon as they were out of the building.

"For?"

"Not letting him push us aside. I'm not feeling very hopeful right now that Livie's a priority with the police."

"Livie isn't his only case, so she won't get a hundred

percent of his attention. I'm sure he's doing the best he can." He wasn't really sure of that, but she didn't need more to worry about.

"I just feel so much better with you here. You give me hope that we'll find her."

He opened the passenger door for her. "We are going to find her, Kendall." He'd found children no one thought could be found, children whom he wanted the best for but who weren't his child. Now that it was his child who was missing… He would go to hell and back to find her.

Kendall didn't seem to want to talk, so the drive to the location where the van was found was in silence. He stole a glance at her. Damn, she was pretty with those blue eyes and her ink black hair.

He'd gone into The Tipsy Turtle after making arrangements for his father's cremation. Emmie hadn't wanted any part of the process. She'd said, "Good riddance. He made our life hell, and he can rot in hell. That's all I have to say about the man." Truer words had never been spoken, but someone had to see to the old man's farewell to this life, and that someone had been him.

That night, his last on leave, after returning to his hotel room, he'd sat on the edge of the bed as memories of life as Rex Devlin's son haunted his mind. Ghost memories that refused to be banished. The beatings he took to protect Emmie, the nights trying to fall asleep when hunger felt like it was eating his stomach inside out, the bullying at school because he was considered white trash simply because of his clothes. There was never money to buy clothes since his father considered jobs he could actually get beneath him. So what if his children were hungry and wore rags. What money he could scrounge up went for beer and cigarettes.

Baseball had saved him. If not for falling in love with the game, being damn good at it and the coaches who'd mentored him, Cooper figured he'd probably be dead or in prison. His kidnapping and meeting Grayson and Liam had changed the direction of his life, though. Where he'd thought baseball would be his salvation, turned out it had been those two men and the Army.

He'd kept in touch with Grayson and Liam after they were rescued, and one night in their text messages, the idea to make their life's work saving children had sprouted. From that idea, The Phoenix Three had been born. They'd each joined a different branch of the military to get the skills they'd need to make the dream of rescuing children a success.

He'd put distance between him and his father as soon as he turned eighteen. Before leaving for the Army, he'd arranged for Emmie to live with a teacher who'd always been nice to the two of them. Then, he'd dared his father to go near Emmie. That scene had been ugly, but Cooper had grown and was bigger than his father. He'd thrown every threat he could think of at his father if he didn't forget he had a daughter. The old man must have believed him, because he had left her alone.

Unable to sit on that bed in that room with the ghost of his father and his cruel words, he'd gone out, walking into the first bar he'd come to. That turned out to be The Tipsy Turtle, where he'd met a beautiful woman who'd silenced his father's voice. They'd also made a baby, and with that came major changes he was willingly going to embrace. He fully intended to be a part of his little girl's life.

"You look deep in thought," Kendall said.

"I guess I was." He wasn't going to get into a conversation about his father, but he'd admit to the only good part of this thoughts. "I was remembering the night I met you."

"Yeah?"

"Best night of my life, Kendall. Even better than I believed now that I know we created a beautiful daughter." He couldn't wait to meet his little girl. He just needed to find her.

"I haven't had any regrets about that night, not even when I found out I was pregnant. What if..." She shuddered.

"Don't. Don't even think it. We're going to find her, and she's going to be okay." He prayed to God that was true.

The GPS led them to a small apartment building in a not-great part of town. There was a police car parked in one of the spaces. He stopped next to it. "Stay here a minute." He got out and approached the car. The officer was writing something, a report probably. At seeing Cooper coming at him, the officer set his paperwork aside, his expression growing alert. Cooper kept his hands visible, and his own expression relaxed.

It was warm already, and the driver's side window was down. "Good morning," Cooper said, stopping a few feet from the car.

"Can I help you?"

"Yes. I'm Cooper Devlin, and I'm working with Detective Rossi from your special crimes unit. He gave me this location where a stolen van was found."

"Okay."

He heard the suspicion in the officer's voice. "You can call him if you want to confirm that. All I want to know is, where was the van found?" He glanced around. "Which parking space?"

"Guess there's no harm in telling you. It's the space on the other side of my car."

"Thanks." Cooper walked to the middle of the space and looked around. There was a cigarette butt near where the driver's door would be. Amanda had said the man in the grocery store smelled like smoke. The kidnapper could have dropped it, and the police should have bagged that for evidence.

He returned to the officer. "Our witness said the kidnapper smelled like cigarettes, and there's a butt the man might have dropped. I need you to bag it and see that Detective Rossi gets it." He gave the officer credit for not arguing with him.

Kendall opened her door after the officer drove away, and he walked over to her. "Let's look around. Maybe we'll spy a camera or find someone who might have seen something."

They hit pay dirt at the second apartment they came to, and he eyed the angle of the camera. If it was a working one, it should have the van on their feed. As they were walking up to the door, two tween boys carrying skateboards came out of the apartment two doors down.

Cooper headed for them. Both had spiked hair, one with brown hair and one a blond, leather bands on their wrists, oversize shirts and baggy pants. "Dudes, sick boards."

Grinning, they both held their boards up for his inspection, and one of the boys said, "They're—"

"Santa Cruz boards." He hid his grin when both their eyes widened. He'd had a case with a teen boy who was an avid skateboarder. He'd run away, intending to go to a competition where his idol was going to be. After catching up with him, Cooper had concluded that the boy was going to keep running away until he met his idol. He'd taken the boy to the competition, spent time with him and had learned more than he ever wanted to know about skateboards.

"Yeah, man," the other boy said. "They're the best."

"Totally." Kendall had walked up, and she was staring at him as if he were a green man from outer space. He winked at her before turning his attention back to the boys. "Listen, there was a van parked here earlier. Either of you see the man who drove it?"

"I did," the blond said. "Dude parked it, took his little girl out and they got in a car."

Next to him, Kendall gasped. He shook his head, signaling her not to say anything. "When was this?"

"Yesterday afternoon."

"What kind of car did he get into?"

The brown-haired boy frowned. "Why you asking all these questions? You a cop?"

"No, but the man kidnapped that little girl, and—"

"For real?" the blond asked.

"Yes, and that little girl is our daughter. We'd appreciate anything you can tell us."

"Please," Kendall said.

"It was a white sedan, maybe a Nissan," the blond said. "Never saw the van or the car before, so I don't think he lives here. Never seen him before yesterday."

"What did the man look like?"

The boy shrugged. "Fat. That's all I remember. Didn't really pay attention."

"Every little bit helps, so thanks. The police are going to want to talk to you. They need to know what you told me."

"Oh, man, I don't want to talk to the cops."

Kendall put her hand on the boy's arm. "Do you have a sister?"

"Yeah. Two of them. They're always getting into my stuff."

"What if someone took one of your sisters, and what if I saw who did it? Would you want me to tell the police what I saw?"

The boy kicked at the grass. "I guess."

"So you're good with me giving the detective assigned to the case your name?" Cooper asked.

"Yeah."

He got the boy's name, phone number and address. After they left, he called Detective Rossi and passed the information on.

"I was headed out there to knock on doors this afternoon," Rossi said. "Guess you saved me some time."

"There's a camera under the eaves of the apartment right in front of where the van was parked. We're going to see if it's working."

"Wait for me. I'm headed that way now."

He didn't want to wait, but it was probably better to have a police officer with them to view the video if there was one. No reason they couldn't see if anyone was home. No one answered the doorbell. He called Rossi back, told him that he and Kendall were leaving and asked the detective to call him if there was a video. It would be great if the camera caught a tag number, but he'd be surprised if it did.

"What can we do now?" Kendall asked after they were back in the car.

"Let's get some lunch and talk about that."

"I'm not—"

"Hungry. I know, but I am." He'd get her to eat something.

"I don't know how you can think about food when our daughter's missing."

They were coming up to a grocery store, and he turned the car into the parking lot. After stopping and turning off the ignition, he shifted to face her. "One thing I learned growing up and in the military is that you eat when you can because you don't know when you might get a chance to do it again. Food is fuel, and without fuel, you won't have the energy to keep going. You need to stay strong for Livie, and that means taking care of yourself, too."

"What do you mean you learned that growing up?"

"That's a story for another day. So, lunch?"

"Okay."

"What sounds good?"

Her phone chimed, and she fished it from her purse. "It's Amy, my neighbor." She answered, then listened, then gasped. "We'll be there in fifteen minutes." She dropped the phone onto her lap. "Oh, God."

Chapter Seven

Kendall was afraid to believe it, but Amy wouldn't lie to her or play that kind of joke on her. "We need to go home."

"Talk to me. What happened?"

She thought she might pass out and sucked in air.

"Kendall. What's wrong?"

"Wrong? Nothing. Nothing at all. Amy found Livie sitting in the yard."

"Is she okay? Does she know how Livie got there?"

"No, she was just sitting in the yard, crying. Can you go any faster?"

"Yes."

Breaking all the speed limits, he got them home in eight minutes. As soon as he stopped the car in her driveway, she jumped out and raced to Amy's house with Cooper right behind her. She didn't bother knocking, and when she made it into Amy's living room, she almost fell to her knees at seeing her daughter safe on Amy's lap.

"Mommy!" Livie cried at seeing her.

"Oh, baby." She rushed to take Livie in her arms, and Livie wrapped her arms and legs around Kendall like a spider monkey. She glanced at Cooper, who'd come up behind

Livie. He met her gaze, and there was so much longing in his eyes. There was also relief that their daughter was safe.

"Mommy, where were you?"

"I'm right here, sweetie. Are you okay?"

Cooper eased around until he was in Livie's view. "Do you hurt anywhere, Livie?"

Livie buried her face against Kendall's neck. "Don't let the bad man take me."

"Oh, baby, he's not a bad man. This is Cooper, Mommy's friend. He helped me look for you."

Livie shook her head, refusing to look at Cooper. "Make him go away."

"I'm sorry," Kendall said to Cooper. "She's traumatized right now."

He backed away until he was out of Livie's sight. "I understand. She just needs the comfort and safety of her mother right now."

"There's a note pinned to her shirt," Amy said. "I didn't touch it."

Kendall pulled Livie away from her neck and leaned away. Yes, there was a note on her shirt. It was folded in half, so she couldn't read it. A bad feeling traveled through her.

"Don't touch it," Cooper said. He turned to Amy. "Do you have any rubber gloves or dish gloves?"

"Who are you?" Amy asked.

He glanced at Kendall before answering, and she nodded, giving him permission to tell Amy he was Livie's father.

"Can we go find some gloves where we can talk without little ears nearby?"

"Ah, sure. In the kitchen."

Kendall couldn't hear their conversation, but she could

imagine Amy's surprise when she learned who Cooper was. All she'd told her friend was that Livie's father wasn't in the picture. While they talked, she moved to the sofa, sitting with Livie in her lap.

"Do you hurt anywhere?"

"No, Mommy."

Although relieved she seemed to be physically all right, they'd need to have her checked by a doctor.

Cooper returned carrying yellow gloves and a baggie. He stopped a few feet from Livie. "I don't want to scare her, but we need to get the note off her."

"Why don't I do it?"

"Probably better."

Livie looked back at him when he handed Kendall the gloves. "Mommy, make the man go away."

Cooper backed up, and Kendall felt sad for him. He'd been excited to meet his daughter, but Livie didn't want anything to do with him. She'd never reacted like this around men, and Kendall didn't want to think about what the past twenty-four hours had been like for her. They were going to have to ask her, though. Maybe not tonight when she obviously still wasn't feeling safe.

"That's Cooper, sweetie, and he's Mommy's friend. He's a very nice man." She pulled the gloves on. "Hold still a minute, and let me take this note off you, okay?"

"The bad man put it on me."

"Well, the bad man isn't here, and he's not coming back." She wanted to cry, to yell, to pound on something. How dare the bad man scare her little girl. But she couldn't break down in front of Livie. She had to make her daughter believe she was safe now.

Cooper held open the baggie, and she dropped the note

in. What did it say? She almost didn't want to know. Whatever words were on it, they wouldn't be good.

Tears welled in her daughter's eyes. "He said he's coming back. I don't want him to, Mommy. Don't let him take me again."

"I won't, I promise." She met Cooper's gaze. Was he going to leave now that Livie was back? Would he stay for a while if she asked him to? Livie would be safer with him here. His face was unreadable. Was that his soldier face, the mask he wore when walking into danger?

"Can I do anything?" Amy asked.

Livie started crying. "I want to go home."

"Okay, baby." As she stood, Livie tightened her grip on Kendall's neck.

Cooper touched Amy's arm. "There's really nothing you can do but thank you for taking care of her until we got here."

"Of course."

Propping Livie up with one arm, Kendall gave her friend a hug. "I'm so glad you were home and found her. Thank you."

"If you see a stranger hanging around or anything out of the norm, call the police," Cooper told Amy.

"Believe me, I'll be watching."

When they arrived home, Kendall handed Cooper her purse. "My keys are in the side pocket."

He got them out, and when he unlocked the door and followed them in, Livie cried harder. "The man can't come in, Mommy. No mans!"

"Remember I told you Cooper's Mommy's friend? He's big and strong and won't let the bad man take you away again."

"Livie, I promise I won't let the bad man take you," Cooper said softly.

She hiccupped as she peered around Kendall to look at Cooper. "Okay, Mommy. He can stay with us." She buried her face into Kendall's neck again.

"I'm going to give her a bath and get her in her pajamas."

"You can't. I know you don't want to hear this, but she needs to be checked by a doctor before you bathe her."

Kendall squeezed her eyes shut. He was right, but she hated that she couldn't wash the twenty-four hours and whatever had happened in that time off her daughter.

"Do you have a doctor you can call now?"

"Yes." God, she hated having to put Livie through an exam.

"We'll need to call Rossi, but I'd rather get this taken care of first, and I'd also like you to see if she'll tell you what happened before Rossi knows she's back."

"Okay." She leaned away so she could see Livie. "Sweetie, Mommy needs to make a phone call. Will you sit on the couch for a few minutes while I go do that?"

"No, Mommy!" She pushed her face back against Kendall's neck.

Kendall sighed. "I don't want to explain things where she can listen. I'll call, tell Dr. Townsend who you are, then you can go in the other room and talk to her."

"Okay." He glanced at the baggie he still held. "Do you have rubber gloves? We need to see what this says."

"Under the sink." She wished she never had to know what was on that note. While he was in the kitchen, she pressed her face against Livie's. "Are you thirsty or hungry, sweetie?"

"Can I have ice cream?"

Tonight, she could have anything she wanted. "Yes. We'll all have some." Maybe she'd get comfortable with Cooper if he ate ice cream with them. She stood and carried Livie to the barstool. "You're going to have to sit here while Mommy makes our ice cream."

Livie tightened her hold and shook her head.

"I'll make us some ice cream," Cooper said.

He'd put on the gloves and had taken the note out of the baggie. She stared at it for a few seconds, then nodded and returned to the living room. She could see him from the couch, and his lips thinned as he read the note. He glanced up at her, and there was fury in his eyes. Her stomach rolled, and she swallowed hard, afraid she was going to be sick.

"What does it say?"

He shook his head as his gaze fell on Livie. "Later. Right now, let's get something into her stomach, then you can call the doctor."

She managed to get Livie to sit on the couch to eat her bowl of ice cream, and she didn't freak out when Cooper sat at the other end from them. When they finished, Cooper took their bowls to the sink, rinsed them, then put them in the dishwasher.

When he returned, he sat on the sofa next to her. "We should bag up the clothes she's wearing and give them to the police. It's quite possible his DNA is on them," he quietly said.

"I hate this." What had happened to Livie while she was with the man? Livie lowered her head to Kendall's lap and closed her eyes.

"I know," Cooper said. "I'm not going to call Rossi until the doctor has checked her out. He'll show up, demanding to talk to her, and she's not ready for that."

"Thank you. Can I tell you how much I hate thinking of a strange man having his hands on her?"

"Yeah, makes me want to hunt him down and show him just how much we hate what he did. Can I get your phone out of your purse so you can call the doctor? You can change her clothes while I do that."

"Sure. Can you get her pajamas from the top drawer of her dresser?"

"Of course."

Thankfully, Livie didn't wake up while her clothes were changed. Kendall had never in her life known such rage. She'd never thought she'd want to physically hurt another person, but she would gladly go with Cooper to hunt the man down who'd traumatized her little girl.

After getting Livie's pajamas on her, Kendall called the doctor. "Hi, Patty," she said when Dr. Townsend's receptionist answered. "This is Kendall Hart. It's urgent that I talk to the doctor as soon as possible."

"Is Olivia sick?"

"No, I just have to talk to Dr. Townsend about a private matter, and it really is urgent."

"Okay. She's with a patient, but she's almost finished. I'll give her the message as soon as she comes out."

"Thank you." She glanced down at Livie to see she was still soundly asleep.

Cooper had returned to his end of the couch, and his gaze was on Livie. "Our daughter's beautiful, Kendall."

She liked that he hadn't hesitated claiming Livie as his. "What did you tell Amy?"

"I wasn't sure how much you wanted her to know, so I only told her that I'm Livie's father, and that it was your story to share. What did you tell her about Livie's father?"

"Only that he wasn't in the picture. She'll have questions, for sure."

"I wish…" He shook his head.

"What? You wish what?"

Chapter Eight

Cooper wished... Well, he wished a lot of things. Mostly, that his little girl wasn't afraid of him. He got why. He was a man, and right now, men were scary monsters to her. Just because he understood didn't mean it didn't still hurt.

She'd fallen asleep with her head on her mother's lap, and it was his first chance to really look at her. He hadn't before because scary man here, so he'd kept his distance. Now, he was able to take her in, to search for characteristics she'd gotten from him. Her hair was dark like her mother's, but Kendall was right. Livie had his mouth and eyes.

A little progress had been made when she'd let him eat ice cream with them as long as he stayed at the end of the couch.

"You wish what, Cooper?"

That he could have a do-over the night they were together and tell her his name and how to find him. "That I could take away the last twenty-four hours for her."

"Yeah, me, too." She gently combed her fingers through Livie's hair. "What did the note say?"

When her phone chimed, he said, "Let's save that for later, after Livie sees the doctor." He didn't want to tell her what the note said. It was going to upset her, even scare her, but he was going to have to. He picked her phone up from the coffee table and handed it to her.

"Dr. Townsend, thanks for calling me back." She explained the situation, then said, "Thank you. See you soon." She set the phone on the couch next to her. "She said to come in now."

"I'll drive." Livie woke up long enough to refuse to sit in her car seat. When she started sobbing, he said, "Sit in the back with her and hold her. I'll drive carefully."

Following Kendall's instructions, twenty minutes later, they were at the doctor's office. Livie was taken right in. He went in the room with them for a few minutes because he wanted to meet his daughter's doctor. A crying Livie clung to Kendall, begging to go home. He wished she wasn't afraid of him so he could wrap his arms around her and Kendall, who also had tears in her eyes.

Once he'd spent a few minutes with Dr. Townsend and liked her and her gentleness with Livie, he left the room. While he waited, he walked outside and called Detective Rossi. The detective wasn't happy that Cooper refused to bring Livie to the police station immediately.

"We're not bringing her to the station at all. You can come by tomorrow and talk to her, but she's traumatized and afraid of men now, so I don't know what you'll be able to get out of her. Not to mention that she's a four-year-old and won't even know some of the answers you want."

He disconnected with the unhappy detective, but he wasn't going to back down on his refusal to bring Livie to the police station. Tomorrow, before Rossi showed up, he'd guide Kendall on questions to ask Livie. Doing it that way would more likely give them some information over an interrogation by the police.

Kendall and Livie still weren't out when he returned to the waiting room, and unable to sit, he paced until he realized his tension was getting the attention of those in the room. He went outside again and called Grayson.

"Talk to me," Grayson said on answering.

"We have Livie back."

"Great news. Is she okay?"

"No. She's afraid the bad man's going to come back for her." He brought his friend and teammate up to date, including what the note said. "The man's playing games with Kendall, and I'm taking him seriously."

"Agreed. Why don't you bring them here where you have backup, and we can make a plan to find the bastard."

"I was thinking the same. It will be a few days before I can do that. We have to deal with the police here. Also, Livie needs a few days at home where she feels safe." Although, she wasn't safe there, especially if he returned home, leaving them unprotected. That was not going to happen. He'd just have to convince Kendall that it was a good idea to go to Myrtle Beach for a while.

"Send me a copy of the note. I'll have Sean give it to one of his profilers. Maybe they can get a read on the man."

"Good idea. I'll do that when we get back to Kendall's house." Sean had helped them on several of their cases, most recently when Liam's fiancée had been kidnapped.

Kendall came out, carrying Livie. "Gotta go. I'll let you know our plans." He walked ahead of them to the car and opened the back door. He wanted to ask how it went, if Livie really was physically all right, but it wasn't a question to ask in front of Livie. It about killed him that his daughter's cheeks were wet with tears. "You need to make any stops on the way home?"

"Yes. Dr. Townsend called in a prescription for a mild

children's sedative in case she has trouble sleeping tonight."

At the pharmacy, he had them stay in the car with the doors locked while he picked up the prescription. He didn't like leaving them, but Livie had fallen asleep again, and Kendall didn't want to wake her.

Back in the car, he leaned around the headrest so he could see them. Now that Livie was asleep, he could ask the question that was burning in his mind. "Did the doctor do a physical exam?"

"Yes, and there's thankfully no sign of physical abuse... of any kind."

Thank God.

COOPER SAT ON his end of the couch as Kendall read Livie a story. She had given Livie a bath, and then they'd gotten her to eat a few chicken nuggets and apple sauce. One thing was different from this afternoon. Livie was sneaking peeks at him, more out of curiosity than fear. Progress. After she'd done that for a while, he started making funny faces at her. The first time he did it, her eyes widened, but she didn't shy away. The second time, her lips twitched. The third time, she giggled.

The sound was so surprising that both he and Kendall glanced at each other in surprise. That little giggle was music to his ears. And that smile from Kendall was a beautiful thing to see. It was a simple, sweet moment, but it felt like a turning point for all of them.

Kendall hadn't gotten halfway through the story when Livie fell asleep again. "Don't think you're going to need the sedatives," he whispered.

"Good. I didn't really want to give her one. Maybe she'll sleep through the night. I need to put her to bed."

While she was doing that, he went to the kitchen and took out the note from the drawer he'd put it in. With the rubber gloves on, he snapped a picture and sent it to Grayson. He put the note back in the baggie, then back into the drawer.

The note was disturbing. His sense was that the man had been stalking Kendall for a while. That he was playing a game where he was the hunter, and she was the prey. He had no doubt the man already had the opportunity to take her, but he wanted her scared.

What the man didn't know was that the men of The Phoenix Three were experts at playing those kinds of games, and they played to win. He had a family now to protect, which made this game personal. He wasn't going to be the loser.

"You want a drink?" Kendall asked when she returned.

"I'd love one, whatever you have on hand."

"The cabinet above the fridge. My secret stash."

He reached up and opened the door. "Ah, a minibar." There was a bottle of vodka and a bottle of tequila and a Kahlúa. He grabbed the vodka. "What's your poison?"

"A vodka and cranberry."

"I'll have the same." He got the cranberry out of the refrigerator. "How strong do you want it?"

"Not very."

He made their drinks, handed her the lightweight one, then followed her to the living room. As soon as they were seated, she asked the question he didn't want to answer.

"What did the note say?"

Rather than respond, he found the photo he'd taken, then handed her his phone. As she read the note, color drained from her face. He leaned toward her and read the message again.

Dearest Kendall, your little girl is such a beautiful child. I thought about keeping her, but she's not the prize I want. It was fun, though, being able to steal her away from you. To let you worry. You, with all your sad podcast stories. Now you understand how those families felt when their child went missing, so think of it as me doing you a favor. You're welcome.

I'll be seeing you, love. Soon.
A devoted fan.

"What does he mean, he'll see me soon?"

"He's playing games, Kendall. It's all about having the power for him. He wants you scared and looking over your shoulder."

"Well, he's succeeded."

"And he knows that. I'd like you to think about coming to Myrtle Beach for a little while."

"What?" She handed him back his phone. "I have a job here that I can't afford to just not show up for."

"The Phoenix Three will cover your expenses, so that's not a worry. I'm sure if you explain the situation to the school principal he'll agree to a leave of absence."

"She, and I'm not a charity case. My kids need me."

"Livie needs you more."

She frowned. "That's not fair."

"Isn't it? And what about Livie? Are you going to be able to send her off to preschool knowing this man is out there, probably watching both of you? As for being a charity case, that's not even close to true. We have a fund that's only used for situations like this." That was true, but he'd cover her bills and expenses. That would be a drop in the bucket compared with the child support he should have been paying for the past almost five years. Something they'd talk about once she and Livie were safe.

"Think about it. Are you going to be able to let Livie out of your sight while danger is still out there?"

She shuddered. "No," she whispered. "I don't even know who to watch out for."

"Exactly." He shifted closer and took her hand. "I'm going to find this man, but until I do, you're not safe. Neither is Livie. I want to get you both away until it is safe for you to be home. In Myrtle Beach, you'll have the protection of not only me, but my Phoenix Three brothers. We're good at what we do, Kendall, and we will end this."

"Livie won't be happy leaving her home."

"Maybe not at first, but I think she'll come around, especially once she meets Ruby." He'd bet Ruby and Livie would become best friends.

"Who's Ruby?"

"My dog. She's gentle and loving and will be good for Livie. Come to Myrtle Beach. Let me keep you safe."

"Why can't you stay here?"

He'd considered it, and he would if she refused to come home with him. But if they stayed here, he wouldn't be able to let them out of his sight. At home, he had a support system, a group of people who'd have their backs. He'd be freer to investigate. An added bonus, Harlow and Quinn would adopt Kendall and Livie.

"I think it will be good for you both to get away from here for a while. Another reason, I'm going to find this man, but if we stay here, I won't be free to do that because my support system isn't here. In Myrtle Beach, I'll have a team to help me protect you and Livie. Will you come home with me?"

Chapter Nine

Kendall was torn. Cooper was right. It would be impossible to be separated from Livie while the man who'd taken her was out there. The thought that he'd been watching them sent a chill snaking down her spine. He'd proved that he could steal a child without a trace, and knowing he was out there, watching, waiting... Was he watching the house right now? Cooper was right. She couldn't stay here.

"Okay, we'll go home with you."

He squeezed her hand. "Thank you."

"When do you want to leave?"

"As soon as we can, but we have to deal with the police tomorrow, and you need to arrange for a leave of absence. When those things are done, we'll go. Two or three days."

"I'll talk to my principal tomorrow. I wish Livie didn't have to talk to the police."

"Yeah, me, too. I spoke to Rossi while you and Livie were with the doctor. He demanded that we immediately bring her to the police department. I refused. Told him she was too upset right now. I also told him if he wanted to talk to her, that he'd have to do it here."

"Thank you. She would've had a meltdown if we had to take her there."

"We do need to ask her questions, see how much she can tell us. I think it would be better for you to do that in the morning before Rossi comes over."

"You're right. I just hate this."

"I know. We're going to be busy tomorrow. Why don't you call it a night?"

"Probably a good idea. I'm sleeping with Livie, so you can have my bed again."

"Are you sure? The couch is fine. Trust me, I've slept in much worse places."

"Even if you weren't here, I'd sleep with her tonight."

"All right."

She leaned over and kissed his cheek. "Thank you for being here, Cooper. I don't know how I could have gotten through this without you."

"There's no place I'd rather be."

Later, as she lay beside Livie, she thought about the man sleeping in her bed. That he was in her life again was something of a miracle. If she hadn't seen that article with his picture, she would have been alone through the horror of the past two days.

He'd dropped everything to come as soon as she'd called him. Instead of questioning that Livie was his as she thought many men would, Cooper had trusted her. Although she'd only known him for that one night, she had sensed his inherent goodness. That wasn't even taking into consideration that the man was yummy. Gorgeous face. Hot body. Full lips that knew how to kiss. And his smile. That was the thing she'd loved best about him. When he smiled, his eyes did, too.

Now that he knew about Livie, he'd be in their life, maybe on a regular basis. She hadn't dated much since finding out she was pregnant. The few times she had, she'd compared the men with Cooper, and they'd come up lacking. Now she was going to be seeing the man who'd rocked her world one night, a man she'd never forgotten, and how was she supposed to ignore these fluttery feelings she got whenever he was near, and especially when he touched her.

Did he have a wife or girlfriend? He must not if he was taking her home with him, but what if he did? And if he didn't, how was a man like him unattached? She shifted slightly, careful not to disturb Livie. With a sigh, she closed her eyes, willing sleep to come.

It took a while, but she finally dozed off. It was still dark when screaming penetrated her sleep. Heart pounding, she shot up in bed. Livie was thrashing and crying. She gathered her daughter in her arms.

"Shh, baby. It's okay. Mommy's here. You're safe."

"What happened?"

Cooper's voice coming out of the dark startled her, and she yelped.

"It's me," he quietly said. "Is she okay?"

"Nightmare." Livie quieted as Kendall rocked her. "She didn't wake up, so maybe she won't remember it in the morning."

He stepped out of the room, and the hall light came on, then he returned. There was enough light now to see him, and all right, then. He wore sleep pants that rode low on his waist and no shirt. His short hair was mussed…bed hair. Sexy. She had the urge to smooth it down. He eased down next to her, and she also resisted the urge to lean against him and soak up his warmth.

"Can I touch her?"

There was longing in his voice. Livie's rejection had hurt him, but he'd understood the reason for it and hadn't blamed Livie. She nodded, giving him permission. This would be his first time touching his daughter, and wonder lit his face as he gently trailed the tips of his fingers over Livie's cheeks.

"She's so soft."

"I'm sorry you missed so much of her life."

His eyes lifted from Livie's face to hers. "Me, too, but no one's to blame. We never considered that we'd create a baby that night. I've thought about you a lot over the years, always regretted not finding out your name."

Her heart did that fluttery thing at hearing he'd thought about her. "Me, too. Thought about you, that is." There was that smile that kicked up her heartbeat.

"I like hearing that. I better go before I decide kissing you is a good idea." He left as silently as he'd arrived.

"Wish you'd kissed me," she whispered.

She fell asleep reliving the time he had kissed her.

THANKFULLY, LIVIE WASN'T as clingy as she had been the day before. The aroma of coffee drifted into Livie's room as Kendall got her daughter dressed. Anticipation at seeing Cooper this morning had her smiling. She carried Livie into her room so she could get dressed. If she took a little extra time with her hair and choosing an outfit, it didn't mean anything.

It was probably better to prepare Livie for Cooper still being here. She sat on the edge of the bed and turned the TV off.

"I was watching that, Mommy."

"Well, I need you to listen to me for a minute. You remember my friend Cooper?" Livie nodded. "He's going to spend the day with us."

She shook her head. "No bad mans."

"Cooper's a good man. He helped me find you. He wants to be your friend, too."

"Does he like to play?"

"I'm sure he does." He'd love to play with his daughter.

"He's a good man?"

"A very good one. I promise. Come on, let's go see him."

Livie held her hand as they walked to the kitchen, and when they reached it and found Cooper standing at the stove, she hid behind Kendall's leg. "Livie, can you say good morning to our friend?" A little head shook against her leg.

"Someone's shy this morning." He peeked around Kendall. "Guess Livie doesn't want any pancakes with chocolate chips in them."

"I want pancakes," Livie said, peeking back at him.

Kendall poured herself a cup of coffee. "You're cooking us breakfast?" A man had never made her breakfast, not even her father, who loved her to the moon and back.

"Is that okay? I found the pancake mix and a bag of chocolate chips, so I thought it might be something she liked."

"Her favorite breakfast. I only make pancakes on the weekend or special days."

"Well, today's a special day, so pancakes it is." He squatted in front of Livie, who was still peeking around Kendall's leg at him. "Good morning, Livie. I wonder how many pancakes you can eat. Just one?"

Livie shook her head and held up four fingers.

"That's how many I can eat, too."

"Really?" Livie said.

Cooper grinned. "Yes, really."

"She can eat two."

"On a normal day sure, but this is a special day, right, Livie?"

Livie nodded.

He smiled at his daughter. "Then four it is." He stood, leaned close to her and said, "I'll make her small ones."

"Okay." He smelled like minty soap and something spicy, and she wanted to press her nose against his neck and breathe him in.

"What do you want to drink, Livie?" he asked.

Livie mumbled something. Before Kendall could tell him she wanted orange juice, he said to Livie, "Can you tell me that again, just a little louder? You see, I'm way up here." He held up a hand near the top of his head. "That's a long way up, isn't it?"

Livie nodded, and Kendall marveled at the fascination in her...*their* daughter's eyes. It was a big difference from yesterday's fear of all men.

"So, tell me again what you want to drink so I can hear you, okay?"

"Orange juice."

"Now that's funny, because I want orange juice, too."

Livie's eyes widened. "You do?"

"Yep." He pointed at himself and then her. "Same, same."

"Same, same," she parroted as she pointed at herself and then him.

"That's right."

He was winning Livie over faster than Kendall thought possible, and if that made her happy, she could only imagine how it made him feel. Normally, she and Livie ate at the kitchen island, but she only had two barstools, so she pushed her classroom papers and laptop to the end and set the seldom-used-for-eating table.

"Mommy." Livie tugged on the hem of her blouse.

"What honey?"

"Is the man going to eat with us?" she whispered.

"He is."

"Okay."

Well, that was a surprise. Livie needed a booster seat to sit at the table, and Kendall put it in a chair. After getting her settled in it, she said, "His name is Cooper, okay?" They were going to have to tell her that Cooper was her father, but not today. Maybe when they were in Myrtle Beach, after Livie got to know him.

"Pancakes are ready," Cooper called.

She helped him take the plates and their orange juice to the table. "This looks great, Cooper." He'd also cooked bacon. "Let me pour that for you, sweetie." She took the syrup from Livie before she could drown her pancakes.

"I want—" she gave Cooper a shy smile "—you to do it."

"Say, 'Please pour my syrup for me, Cooper.' Then he'll do it for you."

"Please, will you do it, Cooper?" Livie said, then giggled.

"It would be my pleasure, Princess. Say when."

"When," Kendall said when there was enough. "She'll have her pancakes swimming in syrup if you let her."

"Mommy, Cooper said I'm a princess."

"Of course you are," Cooper said. "Did your mommy not know that?"

Kendall ate her pancakes as she listened to father and daughter get sillier by the minute. It wasn't long before they were trading riddles, one of Livie's favorite things.

"What's black, white and blue?" Livie asked. "A zebra," she yelled before Cooper could answer.

Cooper chuckled. "Good one. I've got one for you. What do you call a cat that likes to swim?"

Livie scrunched her eyebrows, then shrugged. "I give up."

"A catfish."

Livie laughed. "I like that one. My turn. What do you call a fairy that doesn't like to take a bath?" Again, she answered her own question. "A stinkerbell."

"That's the best one yet," Cooper said.

"Okay you two, eat your pancakes."

Cooper winked. "Yes, ma'am."

"Yes, ma'am," Livie parroted and tried to wink.

"Detective Rossi will be here in an hour," Cooper said after breakfast and the kitchen was cleaned up. "We need to get Livie prepared for that."

"Can we just run away instead?"

Chapter Ten

Cooper would give anything to be able to run away and not have to question Livie about the bad man, but it was unavoidable. "I think it would be best if you asked the questions. I've made a list of some I know the police will ask."

"I hate this." She went to the living room, where Livie was watching a movie with talking fish.

He was going to have to brush up on kid movies.

Livie grinned at seeing them. "Are you going to watch *Nemo* with me?"

"No, honey, we want to talk to you a minute." Kendall sat next to her, then turned off the movie.

No longer banished to the end of the couch, he settled on the other side of his daughter. He took out his phone, went to the list of questions he'd made, then handed his phone to Kendall. He held up her phone that he'd picked up from the kitchen island. "I'm going to record this."

"Okay." She scanned the screen, closed her eyes for a second and took a deep breath. "We need to talk to you about the man who took—"

"No, Mommy! No talk about bad man." She put her hands over her ears.

Cooper gently pulled a hand from her ear. "Princesses

are brave, right?" The look of suspicion she aimed his way wasn't encouraging. "You're a very brave princess. You can do this. We just need you to answer a few questions for Mommy. You like baseball, right?"

"I love baseball."

"So do I. After you tell us what happened, a policeman is coming to talk to you. Then after he leaves, you know what?"

"What?"

"You and I will go outside and play some baseball. I'm a very good baseball player, and I can teach you how to be a good baseball player, too."

"Really?"

"Yes, really. So, can you be a brave princess and answer some questions for Mommy?" This little girl owned his heart, had him wrapped around her finger, and there was no place he'd rather be. He couldn't wait to tell her he was her father. Would she be happy about that? Would she call him Daddy?

"Okay." She looked at her mother. "You can ask me questions 'cause I'm a brave princess."

Kendall smiled, first at Livie, then at him, and he wanted to wrap both these girls in a protective shield and fiercely guard them so that nothing bad ever happened to them again. He would protect them with his life if it came to that. He held her phone out to her so she could face activate it, then he set it to Record.

"Very brave," Kendall said. "Here's the first question. Can you tell us what the man looked like?"

"He was fat."

"Very good. What color were his eyes?"

Livie stared up at the ceiling. "Um. Black." She lowered her gaze to Kendall. "His eyes scared me."

"Why was that?"

"They were..." Her gaze went to the ceiling again. "Crazy eyes."

Cooper was surprised that at almost five years old, she could comprehend crazy eyes. She was answering the questions, so he stayed quiet, afraid if he spoke, she might clam up.

"He was stinky, too," Livie said.

"Stinky how?"

"He smelled like Mikey."

"Like cigarettes?"

"Yes!"

Who the devil was Mikey?

"Mikey mows our yard, and he does smell like smoke," Kendall said. She glanced at the phone. "Did the man say anything to you?"

"He told me I was pretty like my mama. He said we would all be a family one day. What did he mean?"

Like hell. His jaw ticked in anger, and it took every ounce of his control to swallow the growl that threatened to escape. Anger was in Kendall's eyes, too.

"I don't know, sweetie. Did he say anything else?"

"He yelled at me when I cried and told him I wanted my mommy."

Kendall cleared her throat. "Did he hurt you at all?"

"He said he would spank me if I didn't stop crying. I tried to stop, Mommy, but I didn't. He got mad and put me in a room. I was glad when he closed the door. I got on the bed and got under the covers where he couldn't see me."

Cooper shared a glance with Kendall, and he knew they both were raging inside.

She eyed the phone again. "Is there anything else you can remember that you want to tell me about the man?"

"No. I don't want to talk about the bad man anymore."

"That's enough," Cooper said.

Kendall blew out a breath. "Thank you. I don't think I could keep going without breaking something."

"You did really good, Livie," he said. "You really are a brave princess."

Livie grinned. "I really was." She patted his arm. "Cooper, can we play baseball now?"

"Yes, we can. Your mommy told me you have a glove."

"I do. You wanna see it?"

"Yes. Get it and your ball, okay?"

She clapped her hands. "Yay!" She ran to her room.

"Detective Rossi should be here any minute," Kendall said. "What should I tell him?"

"That Livie won't talk to him, but that you have a recording he can listen to."

"What if he insists on talking to her?"

"Bring him outside if he won't take no for an answer. I need to speak with him anyway." He glanced down the hallway to make sure Livie wasn't on her way back. She wasn't, and he traced her bottom lip with his thumb. "I fell asleep last night thinking about how much I wanted to kiss you."

"Funny, I fell asleep thinking the same thing."

He'd thought she might still be attracted to him. "Maybe instead of just thinking about it, we should—"

"I'm ready, Cooper," Livie yelled as she ran down the hallway.

"We'll finish this conversation later," he said.

She smiled. "I'd like that."

"Hoped you would." He turned to Livie. "All right, Princess, let's see what kind of ballplayer you are."

"I'm the best!" She had a glove on her hand, a softball in the other and a pint-sized bat.

"Let me carry your bat for you." At Livie's age, Emmie had been all about dolls. He thought it was crazy cool that his daughter was all about baseball. After handing him the bat, she skipped to the back door, and he followed.

Outside, he grinned when he saw the miniature baseball field. There was a home plate and three bases in the far corner of the yard. Where in a normal baseball field there were ninety feet between bases, he estimated that there were only fifteen feet between bases.

"This is cool, Livie. Did your mommy do this for you?"

"No, Papaw did." She took the bat from him, then handed him the ball. "I'm the batter, so you pitch to me."

"Yes, ma'am."

"No, you say, 'Yes, Princess.'"

"My apologies, Princess." She was adorable, and she was his. How about that. He took his place on a spot bare of grass where he thought her Papaw stood to pitch to her. It was only about ten feet from her batter's box.

If things had gone as he'd planned before he'd been kidnapped, she could have watched him pitch for the Braves. Although if that had happened, there probably wouldn't be an adorable princess in his life.

"You ready, slugger?"

"What's a slugger?"

"A ballplayer who is really good hitting a ball."

She grinned. "I'm a slugger princess."

"Yes, you are." He'd never believed in insta love, but he'd been wrong because he already loved this little girl. "Ready?"

"Play ball," she yelled.

He slow-pitched the ball underhanded, right across the plate. She swung and missed. "Strike one."

"That didn't count. I was just practicing."

"Of course. I forgot the batter has to practice first." He'd watched where she swung the bat, and he put the next ball in that small space. Her bat connected with the ball, and the ball rolled along the grass toward him. She dropped the bat and took off for first base. He guessed that he was supposed to pick it up and race her to the base, so he did, but slowly, getting there a few steps behind her.

"Safe!" she yelled.

He wanted to laugh. She was something else. "Yes, you are. Now what, slugger?"

She put her little hands on her hips. "Well, we don't have more people, so I bat again."

"I see. When do I get to bat?"

"When you get me out, but that's hard 'cause I'm too good."

"You sure are." She jogged back to home base and picked up her bat. With a little help from him pitching the ball where he knew she could hit it, she didn't strike out. He slowed down on trying to get her out even more when she did hit it and twice, she reached second base. Each time she reached a base, she beamed with pride, and damn, was he ever proud of his little girl. He couldn't remember when he'd had this much fun.

It had been a long time since he'd played baseball, and now he wondered why. Well, he knew why. It had been a dream that had been stolen from him, and it had hurt to even watch a game on TV. But he was over that now. His life was a good one, better than he'd thought possible back then. He should join a local amateur league if there was one in Myrtle Beach, and he bet Livie would love T-ball.

She was old enough to join. He'd look into that when all this was over.

The back door opened, and Kendall came out with Detective Rossi. At seeing him, Livie hid behind Cooper. "Is he a bad man?" she whispered.

"No, honey, he's a policeman."

She didn't come out from behind him, though, and his protectiveness came out in full force. Rossi had a job to do, and he understood that, but Livie had been traumatized enough.

"Detective," Cooper said.

He nodded as he tried to see around Cooper. "She seems to be doing okay."

"That's where you're wrong."

"All right, I guess you'd know better than me since you haven't let me talk to her."

Livie wrapped her arms around his leg as if afraid she'd be snatched away, and Cooper wanted to pick her up and take her away. Instead, he said, "Kendall, why don't you take Livie inside and let me talk to the detective."

"I need to talk to her, Devlin."

"No." He squatted down in front of his daughter. "Go inside with Mommy, okay?"

Her gaze darted over his shoulder to the detective, and fear was in her eyes. "Okay." She took off running for the house.

After she and Kendall were inside, he faced Rossi. "If she was willing to talk to you, I'd have no problem with that. But she's afraid of you because you're a man, and all she'll do is cry if I make her sit down with you. That's why Kendall and I went ahead and questioned her. To get you the answers you need. What's on that recording is all she can tell us."

"I can have one of my female detectives talk to her."

"Again, no. She's been through enough. Yesterday, she was close to a meltdown. Like children are inclined to do, she's already bouncing back. If you try to send her back to that nightmare, the progress she's made will be lost. I won't allow my daughter to be more traumatized than she already is." It was amazing how easily he was claiming Livie as his.

"I don't like it."

"Don't care. Have you talked to those boys that saw Livie's kidnapper yet?"

"Yes. They don't know any more than what they told you yesterday. And before you ask, the camera you told me about isn't a working one. It's just for show."

"Damn, I was hoping you might get a license plate number. I do have something for you. There was a note pinned to Livie's shirt. We didn't touch it, so maybe there are prints on it." Not that he thought they'd get that lucky.

The man looked tired, and no doubt like most detectives, he was overworked. Now that Livie was back home and safe, she was no longer a high priority on Rossi's list. Cooper got that, but the man who took her was still out there, and if you believed his note, he wasn't going away. Cooper believed him. The reason he was taking Kendall and Livie to a safer place.

"You should know that I'm taking them back to Myrtle Beach with me for a while."

"Not acceptable. Kendall did good on getting her to answer the questions, but I still need to talk to Olivia."

"Is Livie under arrest?"

"That's a ridiculous question."

"Yes or no?"

"Of course not."

"Then she's free to go to Myrtle Beach. We're leaving in the morning." He took a card out of his wallet, handing it to the detective. "Those are the numbers you can reach me at any time of the day or night. If The Phoenix Three can assist you in any way, all you have to do is ask."

The girls weren't in sight when he brought Rossi in to give him the note. He was sure the police would do what they could to find the man who'd kidnapped Livie, but The Phoenix Three had the time and resources the police didn't. He and his brothers would do their own investigating.

Chapter Eleven

Kendall had thought Livie would have a meltdown when they told her that she'd be leaving home, where she felt safe. When they'd said they were going to Myrtle Beach, all she'd heard was the word *beach*. The only thing she wanted to know was could she take her glove, ball and bat. The icing on the cake had been when Cooper had told her he had a dog she could play with.

The plane that had brought Cooper to Decatur had flown them to Myrtle Beach, and Livie, never having flown before, thought the whole thing was grand fun. Cooper's truck was at the airport, and he'd loaded them up, and now, they were minutes from his house.

Was she doing the right thing letting him talk her into coming home with him? She barely knew him. Yes, she liked him. A lot. But was it smart just taking off like this with him? When she'd told Rebecca her plans after asking for a leave for a few weeks, her boss had agreed it was a good idea to remove herself from the unknown danger. Rebecca also said she'd find a replacement for the adult reading class, thus removing any objections Kendall could think of for not going.

What if she and Livie got on Cooper's nerves? He had

been great with Livie so far, but he wasn't used to a rambunctious four-year-old. And what about this chemistry that still existed between them? She wasn't looking for a relationship, and with a daughter, she didn't do flings... Well, she might make an exception where Cooper was concerned. Before him, she hadn't done one-night stands either.

If something did happen between them, she wouldn't have to worry about Livie getting attached to a man who would disappear from her life. Cooper said he planned to be a part of Livie's life, and Kendall believed he meant that, so even if she and Cooper didn't have a future, he'd always be here for his daughter.

"Some deep thinking going on over there," Cooper said. "Anything bothering you?"

You are. Why do you have to be so hot? She glanced behind her to see Livie was asleep. "I'm a little worried that Livie's going to get on your nerves. She has a lot of energy and wants to be entertained all the time."

He turned into an apartment complex and came to a stop in a numbered parking space. He turned the key, shutting down the engine, then shifted to face her. "That's not something you need to worry about. That little girl already owns my heart, Kendall. She's a joy to be around, and I plan to spend every minute I can with her. Come on. Let's get her inside, and I'll come back for your suitcases."

Instead of taking Livie out of the car seat, he carried her in it so that she didn't wake up. They took the elevator to the second floor of a three-floor building.

"It's not much," Cooper said as he held the car seat with one arm and unlocked the door with his free hand. "I'm renting until I decide where I want to buy. I'm thinking a house with a yard for Ruby." He grinned. "And now a yard I can put a baseball field in for Livie when she visits."

Warmth filled her that he was including Livie in his life. "She'd love that."

They stepped inside his apartment, and he flicked on the light. "The furniture's pretty basic and came with the rental."

"Stop apologizing." He was right, though. The door opened right into the living room, and there was a brown leather couch, a matching chair, one side table and a coffee table. It was one big room, and a round dining table that sat four was the only other furniture. All of it screamed "I'm cheap rental furniture."

"There are twin beds in the guest room."

She followed him into the room. "This will work fine for us."

"I'll go get your luggage so we can put her to bed." He set the car seat on one of the beds. "Be right back."

While he was gone, she got Livie out of the car seat. Her daughter was a heavy sleeper and did nothing more than mumble when Kendall removed her clothes. When Cooper returned with their suitcases, she found Livie's pajamas and got her into them.

Cooper touched her arm. "Come out when you're done, and we'll talk a little."

"Okay."

He pressed his lips to Livie's forehead. "Sweet dreams, Princess."

After he left, she sighed. Livie had won the daddy lottery. She'd recently started asking about her father. Who was he? Why didn't he come see her? Kendall knew it was because now that she was in preschool, she was seeing other children had fathers and she didn't understand why she didn't have one.

"Your daddy would be here if he could," she'd finally said after avoiding answering a few times. "He's in the Army, and he lives in a faraway land." That was really all she had known about him, and for now, it seemed to satisfy Livie.

Before Cooper had appeared in their lives, she'd worried about what she would tell Livie when she got older, and that answer wasn't good enough. Well, that was one good thing that came out of this. She wouldn't have to admit to her daughter that she had no idea who or where her father was.

She pulled the covers up under Livie's chin, kissed her baby girl on the same spot Cooper had and, leaving the door open, she joined Cooper. He sat on his rental couch, and a glass of wine and a beer were on the coffee table.

"Which one's for me?" she asked as she settled next him but not touching.

She'd like to touch him, though. She'd gone out with a few men since that night with Cooper, and that was her trying to feel wanted again. Sadly, the men hadn't made her feel wanted the way Cooper had in just one night. After that, she'd decided she didn't need a man in her life. She had Livie, a good job and a home she'd bought without help from her father. Life was good, and she hadn't felt like she was missing anything. Now, she did.

"The wine's yours." He picked it up and offered it to her.

"I'd rather have that beer."

He grinned as he stood. "I knew I liked you."

A minute later, her wine had disappeared, replaced with a bottle of beer. "Thanks."

"I'm surprised Livie didn't wake up when you changed her into her pajamas."

"Once she's out, you could have a loud party in her room, and she'd sleep right through it."

"She's amazing, Kendall. You've done a wonderful job with her."

"That means a lot that you'd say that." It really did. She kicked off her sandals, pulled her legs up under her and shifted so that she was facing him. "She's pretty easygoing as long as she's not bored, then I'm sometimes ready to give her away."

He chuckled. "I'll help you keep her entertained while she's here. You mentioned that she's close to her grandfather. I'm surprised he wasn't by your side as soon as you told him she'd been kidnapped."

"If he'd been home, believe me, he would have been. He's on an Alaskan cruise with his lady friend. I didn't want to worry him when he was so far away and couldn't do anything. If we hadn't found her when we did, I would have gotten a message to him. He would've come straight home." She noticed a basket full of dog toys. "Where's… Ruby, is it?"

"Yes. She's at Grayson and Harlow's. I'll get her in the morning. She loves kids and will be excited to see one in her house." He picked at the label on his bottle. "Has there been anyone special in your life since we were together?"

"No. Between Livie and teaching, there wasn't much time for me. You?"

"No. I wasn't really looking while I was still in the Army. I was gone too much to have any kind of successful relationship."

"You're out now, so…"

He smiled. "Maybe I was waiting for you."

Oh, he shouldn't say things like that. Her silly heart was doing ridiculous somersaults.

"There are things we need to talk about, I know there are, but all I can think about is kissing you." His gaze fell to her lips. "Do you taste as sweet as I remember?"

She stretched her legs out and tapped his thigh with her foot. "Would you like an answer to that question?" From the moment he'd sat down next to her at The Tipsy Turtle bar, and she'd looked into those warm chocolate eyes, there had been chemistry. There still was.

"I would very much like an answer." He put his hands around her ankles and pulled her to him, then took her bottle and set it on the coffee table with his.

She stared into his eyes again and the five years between then and now disappeared. And when his lips brushed over hers as light as a feather, goose bumps prickled across her skin. He brought his hands up, cradling her face, and deepened the kiss. Her eyes slid closed, and all she felt was his mouth possessively on hers and the stroke of his thumbs over her cheeks. It had been this way that night. Nothing existed but him and his touch, his scent, his heat.

He lifted his head and smiled. "Sweeter than I remembered. If you only knew how many times I wished I could kiss you again."

Same. She traced her fingers along his jawline, feeling the roughness of his stubble beneath her touch. She wanted to ask him where they went from here. Aside from her one night with him that she thought would never be repeated because she'd never see him again, she wasn't one who could have an affair with an expiration date. Which would be the case for them.

She lived in a different state, had a good job and, most importantly, was a mother. If she was single, different story, but she wasn't. He was Livie's father, and she wanted him in Livie's life, but a relationship between the two of them would be complicated. Maybe too complicated.

"More deep thinking going on there." He tapped her forehead. "Talk to me."

"I—"

Livie screamed, then began crying. "Mommy!"

Chapter Twelve

Cooper's heart dropped to his stomach when Livie screamed. The anguish and fear in her voice tore at him. He followed Kendall as she ran to the room. Livie was sitting up in the middle of the bed crying her little heart out. He flipped the light switch on.

"Sweetheart," Kendall said, scooping Livie up.

Livie wrapped her arms and legs around Kendall. "Mommy, the bad man came."

"Oh, honey, it was just a dream. The bad man isn't here."

"He was!"

Cooper wasn't sure if he'd make it worse by approaching her, but he couldn't stand back while his little girl was hurting and afraid. He eased up next to Kendall. "Livie, I promise the bad man isn't here. I wouldn't let him come here, and I'm way bigger and stronger than he is."

She lifted water-filled eyes to his. "You promise?"

Just go and slay me, little girl. That she trusted him to keep her safe humbled him. He tapped his chest. "With all my heart, I promise."

"Let's get you back to bed," Kendall said.

"You stay, Mommy."

"I will, but I need to put on my jammies, okay?"

Livie shook her head. "No. You stay."

"What if I stay with you while your mommy puts on her jammies?" Had he ever before now said the word *jammies*? Pretty sure he hadn't. What other words would he learn to use because of his daughter? He couldn't wait to find out.

"Cooper will stay with you while I change, okay? I'll only be a few minutes."

Livie looked from Kendall to him, and he had the feeling she was judging his ability to keep her safe. Then, surprising him—and Kendall by the expression on her face—Livie held out her arms to him. It was a momentous moment, and he was overwhelmed by the trust she put in him and the deep-seated protectiveness he already had for his child.

Kendall pulled some clothes from her suitcase, and after she left the room, he sat on the edge of the bed with Livie wrapped around him. It was the first time he held his little girl, and he swallowed against the lump in his throat as he gently rocked her.

"Did you know that princesses have magic powers?"

She leaned her head back so she could see him. "I'm a princess."

"Yes, you are. What are your magic powers?"

"I can run fast. And...and I..." She lifted her eyes to the ceiling.

"Hit home runs?"

"Yes!"

"That's a very good magic power to have."

"Can we play baseball?"

"Not tonight, but sure, we will tomorrow."

"I brought my bat and ball. And my glove."

"Yes, you did."

Kendall returned, and when she sat next to them, Livie

didn't try to go to her, which made him absurdly happy. It seemed she'd forgotten her nightmare and was, unfortunately, wide awake.

"We need to get under the covers and go to sleep," Kendall said.

He lifted Livie and set her on the bed. "I'll leave you two now."

"No, Cooper," Livie said, tears welling in her eyes again. "You stay, too. The bad man might come back."

How was he supposed to walk away and make his little girl cry?

"I can sleep in Livie's bed if you want the other one," Kendall said.

"We'll have a family sleep-in. I just need to change into my jammies, too."

"Don't go, Cooper," Livie said when he reached the door.

"I'll be back in a few minutes." In less than five minutes, he returned, wearing sleep pants and a T-shirt. Kendall and Livie were under the covers, and Kendall was reading Livie a story.

"You're back!" Livie said, grinning at seeing him. "You can get in bed with us. Mommy can read you a story, too."

His gaze shot to Kendall. Amusement lit her eyes, and when she didn't seem inclined to help him out, he shifted his eyes back to Livie. "I'm too big to fit in your bed with you and Mommy, but I'll be right next to you in this bed." Once he was settled in a bed that his feet dangled over the end, he said, "Okay, Mommy. Read me and Livie a story."

She chuckled, then began to read again, something about a unicorn named Uni that wanted to find a little girl to have for a friend.

"I'll be her friend," Livie said. She looked across her bed to Cooper. "You're a boy, but you can be her friend, too."

"Do you think she'll like me?"

Livie gave an adamant nod. "I'll tell her you're nice and you're strong, so if anybody scares her, you'll save her."

His little girl tickled him. "I will."

After Kendall finished reading the book, she slipped out of bed, turned off the light and returned to bed. "Time to go to sleep, sweetie."

"Good night, Princess."

"Good night, Cooper. Sleep tight." She giggled. "How do you sleep tight, Mommy?"

"It just means to have a good sleep. Now hush and close your eyes."

Cooper rolled onto his back. His bed would be more comfortable, but a family sleep-in beat comfort any day. He wasn't used to going to bed this early, and his thoughts drifted to how drastically his life had changed since Kendall's phone call.

Tomorrow morning, he would introduce his daughter to his friends, and he couldn't wait to be the proud father. As for Kendall, he wanted to see where this chemistry between them could go. He liked her, wanted her in his bed, wanted a chance with her. At least, a chance to see if he could be more than just her baby daddy. He chuckled at the thought that he was a baby daddy.

"Can't sleep?" Kendall whispered.

"A lot on my mind," he whispered back. He rolled onto his side to face her. It was too dark to see her other than a dim outline but whispering to each other in the dark felt intimate. "You can't sleep either?"

"No. Same reason."

They could talk for a while, get to know each other

better. He wanted to know more about when she was kidnapped as a little girl, but that might bring up too many dark memories for her. She'd already said the anniversaries of her kidnapping were hard for her, and the reason she was out the night he'd met her. He thought of another thing he wanted to know.

"Tell me about your podcasts."

"I don't remember what I've already told you about them. My head was messed up with Livie missing."

"You only said they were about cold-case children kidnappings."

"Well, I do one the first Monday of every month. I feature one cold case of a missing child. I've been doing them for three years, and two of the cases I've featured have been solved thanks to my listeners."

"That's great, Kendall. I'm curious, though, how does that work?"

"I have a dedicated email that I give out at the end of each podcast. Anyone who knows something or has a suggestion or picks up on a clue the police missed can email me. I pass any of those emails on to a retired homicide detective. I've never met Ray, but he's pretty awesome in that he investigates on his own time."

"Because of you, you said two cases were solved. That's amazing."

"It's because of my listeners and Ray that the families finally got closure."

"I'd say it's because of you, your listeners and Ray, so give yourself some credit, too. You said you were kidnapped when you were seven." It was bizarre that they'd both been kidnapped, and now Livie. "Will you tell me about it?"

She was quiet for so long that he thought she wasn't

going to answer. Maybe if he shared his own story, she'd feel more comfortable sharing hers.

"When I was a senior in high school, I went to spring break in Florida. Funny thing. I was accidently kidnapped."

"What?" She'd exclaimed that, and she glanced at Livie before lifting onto her elbow. "How do you get accidently kidnapped?"

He told her the story. "And that's how I met Gray and Liam and why my life took a direction entirely different from what I'd planned."

"Wow," she said. "That's... Just wow." Still facing him, she dropped her head back down on her pillow. "What had you planned?"

"My dream was to play professional baseball, hopefully for the Atlanta Braves. I had a full baseball scholarship to Vanderbilt in Nashville."

"You must have been good to get a full scholarship."

"That's one thing I can't be humble about. I was damn good."

She chuckled. "Do you regret the way things turned out?"

"Not for a minute. Gray and Liam are my brothers, and as much as I would have been happy playing ball, I fully believe I wouldn't have the satisfaction I get from rescuing children." He grinned. "Besides, if my life had gone the way I'd planned, I wouldn't have met you."

"And we wouldn't have Livie," she whispered.

"Now that I know about her, I can't imagine a world without her in it. Has it occurred to you that if you hadn't been kidnapped, you wouldn't have been at The Tipsy Turtle that particular night?"

"And we wouldn't have our daughter. I never thought about it like that."

"So as awful as that time in our lives was, something incredibly amazing happened because of those events. We had a baby."

"Yeah, we did."

"Tell me what happened to you, Kens."

Chapter Thirteen

*K*ens. She liked that. Or maybe she only liked it because he was the one giving her that nickname. Coming from him, it made her feel special.

"So, I guess it's my turn." She hated talking about that time in her life. No one could understand how frightened she'd been and how it had changed her and her family. Cooper had been kidnapped, though, so if anyone could understand it would be him.

"The man snatched me right out of my front yard where I should have been safe, you know?"

"You should have been. Obviously, you were found. How and how long did he have you?"

"I got away that night."

"You saved yourself?"

"I did. He drove for a long time, and when it got dark, I guess I fell asleep. When the car stopped moving, I woke up but pretended I was still asleep. When he got out of the car, I opened my eyes and saw we were at a motel. I could read well enough by then to understand what the sign said. It was the Pearl Motel, and the sign said they rented rooms by the hour. At the time, I didn't understand what that signified."

"Hell, Kendall."

"I know. I try hard not to think about what he might have done to me in one of those rooms. I guess he thought I was fast asleep and wouldn't wake up for the few minutes he was getting a room. As soon as he walked into the office, I got out of the car and started running. I didn't know where I was, and I don't know how long I ran before I saw a gas station. There was an older woman working there, and she called the police."

"He didn't come after you, try to find you?"

"If he did, I never saw him."

"Did he touch you? Do anything to you?"

This was the part that still sometimes gave her nightmares. "While I was in the car, he put his hand on my leg, told me I was a pretty girl and that I was going to be a good friend to his sister. I didn't know what all that meant." She shuddered just remembering that long-ago day.

"I told him I wanted my mother, and he told me that my mother gave me to him because she didn't want me anymore. I didn't really believe him, but a part of me wondered if it was true. If she wanted me, she wouldn't have let him take me, right?"

"It's easy for predators to play mind games with a child. Children tend to believe what adults tell them. Did they catch him?"

"No. By the time the police went to the motel, he was long gone. The clerk claimed he didn't pay attention to what the man looked like, and there weren't security cameras everywhere like there is now. I couldn't give them a good description, and I didn't know what kind of car he drove other than it was white. What if he abducted other girls because I couldn't tell the police what he looked like? I think about that a lot." Tears gathered in her eyes, and she squeezed them shut. She would not cry.

"That's why you do the podcasts, because you feel like it's your fault he's still out there somewhere."

"Yes," she whispered as tears she hoped he couldn't see fell down her cheeks.

"All the blame falls on the man who took you. All of it. You were seven years old, Kendall, and terrified. Even adults often can't give accurate descriptions of a suspect. That you had the courage and bravery to escape like you did is amazing in itself. So instead of thinking anything about that time was your fault, think instead of the courage that little girl had and the good that grown-up girl is doing now."

Was it that easy? "To this day, I sometimes look over my shoulder, watching for him to come take me back. Except I don't think I'd recognize him even if he stood in front of me."

"I think if you were to see him again, you'd sense something was off. Always trust your instincts. I'm guessing your parents were overly protective of you once you were back home."

"They were never the same, especially my mother. Mom was as afraid as I was that he'd come back, and except for school, and until the day she died, I wasn't allowed to be out of her sight. I added feeling suffocated to the fear that was always with me. We moved to a gated community where it would be harder for someone to get me."

"Come here, Kendall."

"There?"

"Yes. I need to hold you."

When was the last time someone had held her? It was an offer she couldn't refuse, didn't want to. She checked to make sure Livie was still asleep, then she eased out of bed. He held the covers up for her to slide under. Once she was in the bed, he dropped the covers over her.

"Turn on your side, facing away from me," he said. "Good. Now snuggle your back against me."

Oh, she was liking this.

"Go to sleep now." He wrapped his arm around her waist and rested his palm on her stomach.

She was safe, Livie was safe and peace and contentment settled inside her. "Thank you for this, for being here," she whispered. For making her feel safe.

"There's no place I'd rather be than here." He pressed a gentle kiss to the nape of her neck in response.

She smiled. He'd said that before, and she liked hearing it. The steady rise and fall of his chest against her back was a comforting rhythm, lulling her to sleep.

WHEN SHE AWOKE, it was to find Livie in bed with her and Cooper gone. How had she slept through Livie joining her and Cooper leaving? That had been the best sleep she'd had in a long time, and she was tempted to go right back to sleep. What time was it? She glanced at the clock on the night table. Whoa, it was 9:17.

She slipped out of bed. She'd get Livie up after she got dressed. She slipped on a sundress and sandals, then made a quick trip to the bathroom. Where was Cooper? She heard his voice but couldn't make out what he was saying. Whom was he talking to?

"We have company, so you're going to need to behave," he said. "You're going to love Livie, and she's going to love you."

No one answered him. Curious, Kendall followed the sound of his voice, finding him in the kitchen, but she didn't see anyone else. "Who were you talking to?"

His gaze had been on the floor, and the kitchen island kept her from seeing what he was looking at. He lifted his eyes to hers and smiled. "Good morning."

"I can't believe I slept so late. Why didn't you wake me up?" She walked around the island, stopping when she saw the trembling dog glued to Cooper's leg. Because of its multicolored fur, it was the oddest-looking creature she'd ever seen. It wasn't a pretty dog except for the big, soft brown eyes. Those were pretty. "This must be Ruby."

"Yes, Gray dropped her off this morning. She's shy, but once she learns that you won't hurt her, she'll be your friend."

"Ah, sweet girl, do I scare you?" She dropped to her knees a few feet away from Ruby, then glanced up at Cooper. "Was she mistreated?"

"I don't know her story, but from the way she reacts to sudden movements, I'm sure she was. There was a chain around her neck, and she was dragging about three feet of it when she jumped into my car. Shortly after, a man with mean eyes came looking for her. I hid her and brought her home with me."

"You poor girl." Kendall held out her hand and Ruby stretched her nose to sniff her fingers. "I hope you know how lucky you are to have found Cooper." She looked up at him and smiled. "From the way she's glued to you, I think she does know."

"Ready for some coffee?" he said.

"Yes, please."

Livie ran into the kitchen. "Mommy, I lost you."

"You'll never lose me. You ready for breakfast?"

"I'm hungry." Her eyes grew wide. "Doggie!"

Kendall pulled her back when she headed for the dog. "Easy, okay? This is Ruby, and she's shy. We have to be gentle with her. Here, I'll show you. Hold your hand out like this." She showed Livie how to let Ruby smell her fingers.

"Well, look at that," Cooper said.

Ruby was licking Livie's hand, something she'd not done to Kendall. Ruby inched closer to Livie, then rolled over on her back.

Cooper chuckled. "She wants you to rub her belly." He lifted his gaze to Kendall. "It seems she likes children. She loves playing with Gray's son, Tyler."

She stood, leaving Ruby and Livie to make friends. "How old is Tyler?"

"Six, almost seven, I think. He's a good kid, and he'll be nice to Livie. We'll head over there after breakfast. If Livie's okay with it, we'll leave her with Harlow and Tyler while we go to my office. Gray and Liam want to sit down with us and debrief."

She glanced down at Livie, who was now stretched out next to Ruby. "Are you sure she'll be safe there?"

"Absolutely. Harlow will keep her in the house, and they have a first-rate alarm system. We won't be at the office long, but Livie would be bored if we take her there with us. She can take Ruby with her."

"Okay. If Ruby's there, too, I'm sure Livie won't have a problem with staying with them."

"Great. Let's eat so we can head over."

TOO FASCINATED WITH her new friends Ruby and Tyler, Livie hadn't glanced back once when Kendall left with Cooper. Kendall had liked Harlow, Grayson's wife, a lot, and their home on the beach was beautiful. She hadn't wanted to leave herself.

She was at The Phoenix Three now, and she wasn't sure

what she'd expected, but she was impressed. The three-story building was rough-hewn brown brick, the windows mirror tinted so you couldn't see in, and the landscaping around the building was perfectly manicured hedges and colorful flowers.

A young security guard nodded as she and Cooper entered the building. "Good morning, ma'am, Mr. Devlin."

Cooper nodded back. "Morning, Josh."

They rode the elevator to the third-floor lobby where a professionally dressed, middle-aged woman sat behind a high counter. Above her head was the company's name in large chrome letters.

"Veronica, this is Kendall Hart," Cooper said. "Kendall, this is the woman who keeps us organized."

Kendall smiled. "I bet that's a job in itself."

"You don't know the half of it." Veronica grinned at Cooper. "And this one is the worst of the lot."

"Hey, now. Don't forget I sign your paychecks."

The fondness between them was obvious. "It's nice to meet you, Veronica."

"And I you." She shifted her gaze to Cooper. "Grayson's in his office, and Liam's on the way."

"Thanks."

"Veronica seems nice," she said after they went through the door into interior offices.

"She is. She was a part of a case Gray was working a while back. Her daughter was murdered, and she was alone without any family. We offered her a job as our receptionist. One of the best decisions we've ever made. She really does keep us organized."

"That's sad that her daughter was killed."

"Yes, it is. Harlow's ex-husband is in prison now, for among other things, being behind the murder. Even though she had nothing to do with it, Harlow felt guilty about that, which was primarily the reason Gray wanted to offer Veronica the job. Turned out to be a win for us."

"And for her, I imagine. Gives her a purpose. I'm guessing she mothers you three."

He chuckled. "That she does. In here."

"This is your office?"

"Yes."

"Nice." She walked to the window and looked out. "I can see the ocean." Their building was higher than the ones between them and the water, giving him a nice view.

"It's a four-minute walk to the beach. There's a good restaurant right on the sand we can have lunch at."

"That would be nice."

"Morning, people."

She turned from the window to see an extremely handsome man smiling at her.

"You must be Kendall," he said. "I'm Grayson, or Gray. Either works."

"I am Kendall." He'd already left when they stopped at his house to drop off Livie and Ruby. "I met Harlow this morning, and I must say, she's lovely."

"Yes, she is. I just got off the phone with her. She said to tell you that your daughter and my son are besties already."

"Thanks. I was worried about leaving Livie after what she's been though, so it's good to know she's having a good time."

Another man walked in. His black hair and striking blue eyes made for a mighty fine-looking man. Where did they grow these guys? Her gaze swept across the men, and although the newcomer was the hottest of the three, it was Cooper who made her heart flutter.

"You must be Kendall," he said with a warm smile.

"I am."

"Kendall, this is Liam O'Rourke," Cooper said. "We're your team."

"I have a team?"

Chapter Fourteen

Cooper smiled at the surprise in Kendall's eyes. "You certainly do."

"Why don't you give Kendall a quick tour," Grayson said. "We'll meet you in the conference room in ten."

"Can do." His phone chimed, and he smiled when he eyed the screen. "It's my sister." He put his phone to his ear. "Hey, unless the sky's falling, I can't talk right now, but I need to tell you something. You going to be around tonight?"

"Yes. Can you give me a hint?"

"Nope. Talk tonight." He disconnected before she could ask more questions.

"You're going to tell her about Livie?" Kendall asked.

"And you. Come on, let's take that tour." The war room always impressed everyone, so he took her there first.

"Cool," she said when he put his palm on the black box next to the door and the click of the lock rescinding sounded.

"This room is where we plan missions."

"Wow," she said as her gaze took in the room.

It was pretty cool. In the middle of the room was a conference table that would seat ten with monitors in front of each seat. The top half of one wall was a flat screen that was connected to the three high-tech computers placed on the three desks along the wall. They could project any location in the world onto the screen.

She walked to the whiteboard in the back of the room. "Who are all these children?"

"They're kids we've rescued." There weren't any names attached to the photos, but he and his brothers knew every child's name. "Most of them have been reunited with their families."

"What about the ones who weren't?"

"Those are in foster homes, but we keep tabs on them, make sure they're okay and being treated right."

She turned to him, and her eyes were watery. "Incredible what you guys do. You find them alive. Mine are all dead."

He moved until he was in front of her. "But you help give their families closure." He trailed his thumb over her cheek, catching a tear. "That's important, too."

"I know. I just wish I could do more, you know?"

"Yeah, I do. What's your feeling on guns?"

"My dad gave me shooting lessons when I turned seventeen. I do own a gun, but it's in a locked case high on a shelf in my closet. Why?"

"Your answer depended on whether I showed you another room before we go meet Gray and Liam." He took her hand. "Come with me." At the door to their weapons room, he put his hand on the security reader. When the lock disengaged, he opened the door, then stepped back, letting her enter first.

"Whoa," she said.

He followed her into the room. The walls were filled with guns of all kinds, smoke bombs, night vision goggles, bulletproof vests and more. Some were weapons they'd collected during their time in the military, but most were items they'd added after starting The Phoenix Three. They seldom had to make use of any of the weapons in this room, but they occasionally had.

She picked up a pair of night vision goggles. "I've always wondered what it looked like with these on."

"Put it on." He flipped the on button, activating the battery.

"This is weird." She turned to him and grinned. "You're green." She removed them and placed them back on the hook. "I think they'd take some getting used to."

"It doesn't take long."

"What's next on the tour?"

"It's time to sit down with my brothers."

She glanced up at him, surprise on her face. "Oh, I didn't realize you were brothers."

"We're not blood brothers, but brothers all the same."

"I love that."

"When you're held in a room for two weeks with two other boys, you bond. I hated the kidnapping part, but that event brought Gray and Liam into my life, and I'll never regret that."

"The Phoenix Three. The three of you from the ashes."

He smiled, liking that she got it. "That's right. Here's the conference room where we're meeting." He opened the door, allowing her to walk in first. Without waiting to be told, she took a seat across from Grayson and Liam, and he sat next to her.

"What the three of you have created here is pretty incredible," she said. "My favorite thing was the board with pictures of all the children you've saved."

"We couldn't have done it without each other," Liam said.

Grayson nodded. "He's right. Each of those children has a story, a life that we were able to hopefully help change for the better."

"Amen to that," Cooper said. He swiveled his chair toward Kendall. "Ready to talk about why we're here?"

"I wish there wasn't a reason for it, but since there is, yes."

He wished the same. When they found who had taken Livie and was now threatening Kendall, Grayson and Liam were going to have to hold him back from doing serious damage to the man.

"I'm going to put the note that was pinned to Livie up on the screen," Grayson said. "There are some clues in it." He glanced at Kendall. "Is that okay with you?"

When she visibly swallowed as she nodded, Cooper wanted to pull her onto his lap, wrap his arms around her and make all of this go away. Cooper read the note again when it appeared on the screen.

Dearest Kendall, your little girl is such a beautiful child. I thought about keeping her, but she's not the prize I want. It was fun, though, being able to steal her away from you. To let you worry. You, with all your sad podcast stories. Now you understand how those families felt when their child went missing, so think of it as me doing you a favor. You're welcome.

I'll be seeing you, love. Soon.
A devoted fan.

The note ignited a rage inside him. He'd had to kill when in the military, but he'd never liked that he had to. Now, though? There was a man out there he could kill and still sleep at night. "He listens to her podcasts and is obsessed with her."

Grayson nodded. "Yes, and there's something else. We have to consider the possibility that Livie isn't the first child he's taken. We've sent the email to an FBI profiler but haven't heard back yet."

Kendall gasped. "Oh, God. You think he's done this before?"

"After Coop sent us a copy of the note, Gray and I agreed it was likely," Liam said. "I did some research, and there are five unsolved child kidnappings within a two-hundred-mile radius of Decatur. I've been listening to some of your podcasts, and you did one on Lacy Alexander. Remember her? Six years old, taken from her bed in the middle of the night three years ago?"

"Yes. The parents were suspects until her body was found in a shallow grave in the woods." Her eyes widened. "There was a note pinned to her shirt. Just like Livie. What the note said wasn't released to the public, but apparently it was enough to clear the parents. Her abductor was never caught, which is why I did a podcast on her."

Grayson picked up his pen and wrote something on a notepad. "I'll see if the police will tell me what it said."

"I only went back ten years, so there could be more," Liam said.

Kendall sat back in her chair. "His note to me says he'll see me soon. I can't live my life jumping at every shadow. What can I do?"

"What can *we* do?" Cooper said. "First, you and Livie aren't going to be left alone until the man is behind bars." He'd worked with his brothers long enough to know what they were thinking, and it took only a glance at both of them to see them look from him to Kendall, to know they had the same thought as him.

He wished there was another way, but they needed to

draw the man threatening Kendall in, set a trap. "How often do you do a podcast?" he asked her.

"Once a month. I record it and then air it on the first Monday of every month. Why?"

"Three weeks before the next one, then. Would you be willing to record one using a script from us?"

"If you think it will help, absolutely. I'll do anything to help you find him."

"Do your listeners communicate with you?" Cooper asked.

"Yes. I have a special email... Oh, his note is addressed to Kendall, and he says he's a devoted fan." Her gaze lifted to the screen again. "I should have picked up on that the first time I read it, but at the time, all I could think about was having Livie safely home and taking care of her. I podcast under a pen name, Kendra Hartley. I'm cautious about giving out my identity. He says he's a devoted fan, but the note's addressed to Kendall."

"We picked up on that," Cooper said.

She pushed away from the table. "I have to go."

Chapter Fifteen

Cooper caught Kendall's hand, stopping her. "Go where?"

"To get Livie. What if he followed us? What if he's here? He could be watching her right now."

"He's not." He tugged her back down to her seat. "Unless he had a plane ready to take off when we did, he didn't follow us. He doesn't know where you and Livie are. He doesn't know about me or The Phoenix Three. You're safe. Livie's safe, and that's the way it's going to stay."

She blew out a breath. "Right, we flew."

Grayson pushed his phone across the table. "Here, Kendall. Talk to Harlow. Let her tell you that Livie's safe, then talk to Livie."

"Thank you." She took the phone, glanced at Cooper, then put it on speaker. "So you can hear."

He could kiss her for that, for knowing he'd want to talk to his daughter, too.

She held the phone between them. "Hi, Harlow. Sorry to bother you. Is Livie behaving?"

"You're not bothering me. She sure is, and she's a sweetheart. At the moment, she and Tyler are sitting on the floor, teaching Ruby to roll over. They've been having a great time."

He smiled at hearing the kids laughing in the background. "Can we talk to Livie a moment?" Hearing their daughter's voice would ease Kendall's mind.

"Sure. Livie, come here a minute and talk to your mom and Cooper."

"Mommy, me and Tyler teached Ruby a trick."

"Did you? You'll have to show us when Cooper and I get there."

"Cooper's coming, too?"

He loved that she sounded excited to see him. "Hi, Princess. Yes, your mommy and I will see you in a little while." He didn't want to be Cooper to her. He wanted her to call him Daddy. He'd ask Kendall tonight when they could tell her.

"Tyler told me a joke. Wanna hear?"

"I sure do."

"Okay. Why did the banana go to the doctor?"

"I don't know." He was the king of riddles and dad jokes—most of which he'd taught Tyler—and knew the answer, but he wasn't going to steal his little girl's fun.

"'Cause he wasn't peeling well." She giggled.

He and Kendall both laughed. "That was a good one, Princess."

"I know. I got more."

"And I want to hear them, but why don't you save them for when I see you. Okay?"

She loudly sighed. "What if I forget them? Can you come now, so I still member?"

He shared a smile with Kendall. Their daughter was the cutest thing. Across the table from him, his brothers chuckled.

"We'll be there soon," Kendall said. "You have fun with Tyler and be good for Harlow, okay?"

"Okay, Mommy. Bye."

"She's adorable," Harlow said, coming back on the conversation. "I was where you are not that long ago, worried about my son. To set your minds at ease, all the doors and windows are locked, and the alarm is on. Grayson's phone is set to get a notification if something should happen, but it won't."

"Thank you," Kendall said.

She handed Grayson his phone, the panic in her eyes gone. "Sorry, I just freaked out after realizing he knows my real name."

"Understandable." That disturbed him, too. How long had the man been stalking her, because that was what was happening here. They needed to find this man before he made good on his threat that he'd see Kendall soon. "Do you save the emails you get from your listeners?"

"Yes. Do you think he's written others to me?"

"I do."

"As do I," Grayson said.

She stared at her hands resting on the table. "I can't tell you how much that creeps me out. I do the podcast because I hope to give some families closure. This man, whoever he is, is playing some kind of sick game. He's tainting what I do. Not to mention the more I'm learning about him, the more he scares me."

Cooper put his hand over hers. "We'll find him, but to do that, we're going to have to do a deep dive in your emails and your podcasts. We need to read the emails."

"They're all in a file in my laptop. I can send the folder to each of you when I get back to Cooper's."

"Let's do that, then we'll get back together and share our thoughts after reading them," Liam said. "I'll be involved on this along with Gray and Coop, but my fiancée's due to have our baby in three weeks, so I'll mostly be working from home."

"Oh, congratulations. First child?"

Liam nodded. "Yeah, and I'm driving her crazy apparently." He grinned. "She says she's pregnant, not helpless."

"Do you know what you're having?" Kendall asked.

"A girl. Erin Fiona O'Rourke."

From the moment Liam and Quinn had found out they were having a baby, they'd been excited, and Liam had shared the experience. He'd showed them her first sonogram when they'd found out it was a girl, their excitement when the baby started kicking, his middle-of-the-night trips to the store to get Quinn's weird cravings.

Not for the first time, Cooper wished he'd known Kendall was pregnant, wished he'd been there from the beginning for his daughter...and for Kendall. What foods had she craved? Had she had morning sickness? She'd gone through her pregnancy alone, no one to take care of her, no one to go out in the middle of the night to get her pickles or whatever she was craving.

"Let's collect our daughter, go home and laugh at Livie's jokes." Other than sending the file to them, Kendall needed an afternoon of not thinking about any of this. Tomorrow, after they'd read the emails, they would get down to business and plan how to catch this bastard.

"That sounds wonderful," she said.

"What do you call a bear with no teeth?" Livie said.

"I give up." Another one he'd taught Tyler. He was sitting on the couch, and Livie was leaning on his leg. Kendall was on the opposite end of the couch with her feet tucked up under her and smiling at both of them. Ruby was next to Livie, staring at Livie as if hanging on her every word. It was a perfect family afternoon. He wanted it to be real.

"A gummy bear." She scrunched her brows together. "What's a gummy?"

Cooper opened his mouth and tapped his finger against his gums. "Those are gums, so if the bear doesn't have teeth, all he has are gums, so he's gummy."

"Why doesn't the bear have teeth?"

"I'm not sure. Maybe he ate too much candy, and they all fell out."

She pondered that for a moment, then, "Why did he eat too much candy?"

Kendall laughed. "Welcome to the world of four-and five-year-olds where their favorite word is *why*."

He winked before turning his attention back to Livie. "Maybe while his mommy was asleep, the bear was a bad boy and ate all the candy that he was supposed to share with his brothers and sisters."

"That's silly."

He tapped her nose. "You're silly."

She giggled. "I'm not silly, you are."

"Both of you are," Kendall said. "Come up here. Cooper and I want to talk to you about something."

His gaze shot to hers, and when she nodded, his heart pounded. They were going to tell Livie he was her father. What if she didn't want him to be her father?

Kendall took both Livie's hands in hers. "Do you remember when you asked where your daddy was, and why he didn't come to see you?"

Livie nodded. "My daddy lives far away."

"That's right, he did. But what if I told you your daddy is here now."

Livie's eyes grew big. "He is?"

"Yes, in fact, he's sitting right next to you. Honey, Cooper's your daddy."

His heart was going to pound itself right out of his chest as he waited to see Livie's reaction.

She turned those big eyes toward him. "You're my daddy?"

"Yes, Princess, and I've been wanting to meet you for a long time." If he'd known about her, that would be true. "Are you happy?"

She threw her arms out wide. "So happy!" She jumped up and wrapped her little arms around his neck. "My daddy."

After hugging him, she smacked him on the cheek, then got off him. "Daddy, watch." She made a circle with her hand and Ruby immediately rolled over.

Daddy. That was the sweetest word he'd ever heard. "That's awesome."

His eyes locked on Kendall's. There were tears in hers... and damn it, his, too. His heart swelled with a love he never thought possible. For this little girl, and for her mother who'd raised their beautiful daughter alone for almost five years. "Thank you," he mouthed.

Kendall swiped at the tears on her cheeks, and he reached out his hand. She put hers in his, and he gently squeezed it in gratitude that she'd found him, had accepted him as Livie's father and that she was letting him into their lives. Where they went from here had a question mark, but he had hopes for a future with them.

Was he in love with his daughter's mother? He thought he was, but if not, he was headed that way. Everything he'd learned about her since they'd reunited he liked. She was both kind and beautiful. Although it was restrained on both their parts because of having to deal with an evil man who was intent on harming Kendall, there was crazy chemistry between them.

The night he'd spent with her had been one of the most amazing nights he'd spent with a woman, and when she was in his bed again—because that was going to happen—he didn't for one minute doubt they'd light the sheets on fire.

He wanted to know everything about her. Her hopes and fears, her dreams and all the little quirks that made her who she was. Yes, he wanted her in his bed, but the feelings growing inside him went far beyond the sexual side of their relationship.

She had been through so much and had done it alone. He was in awe of her. She deserved a special night, and he wanted to be the one to give it to her.

"What's your idea of a perfect evening?" he asked.

Chapter Sixteen

Kendall, her hand still being held by Cooper, had never thought about that question. She was a mother with a young child and with no one to share the good and the bad. Not that there was anything bad about having her daughter, but some days were exhausting, both mentally and physically. There was no one else to feed Livie dinner, give her a bath, to get her child who never wanted to go to sleep to actually go to sleep.

Her father did take Livie on occasion, but he had his own life and a girlfriend, so she rarely asked him to babysit. He did like to take Livie to a Braves game sometimes, and she enjoyed those few hours when the house was quiet. She mostly spent those times catching up on either lesson plans for her second-grade class or working on her next podcast. Even though she had pushed self-care and adult fun to the side, she had no regrets.

What was her idea of a perfect evening?

"I guess playing with Livie or—"

"No. No. Something that's just for you. Something special."

"Mommy plays with me. You can play with me, too, Daddy."

Oh, that soft smile on Cooper's face at hearing Livie call him Daddy was about the sweetest thing she'd ever seen.

"We're going to play together a lot, Princess."

"Now, Daddy?"

"Why don't you play with Ruby for a few minutes and let me talk to Mommy, okay?"

"Okay, but don't talk long."

"I won't."

After Livie was on the floor with a pile of dog toys next to her and Ruby excited to have her new friend playing with her, Cooper chuckled as he watched them for a minute. Then he turned that intent focus on her that he was so good at. "Think of what your perfect adult evening would be."

"Ah, an adult evening." She glanced at Livie to see that she and Ruby had moved farther away, and Livie wasn't paying attention to them. "I have no idea what those are like, so I guess I'll have to use my imagination. I love Livie to death, but one night of not being a mommy would be wonderful." She closed her eyes and smiled. "I'd put on some soft music and start my evening with a glass of wine and maybe some cheese and fancy crackers."

"Are you alone in this adult evening?"

She opened her eyes, her gaze locking on his. "No. There's a man I've thought a lot about over the years with me. We have adult conversation, something lacking in my life as I spend my days with seven-and eight-year-olds and my evenings with a four-year-old."

"I'm liking this adult evening of yours so far. Then what happens?"

"We have dinner by candlelight."

"What are we eating?"

"We?" She grinned. "You think you're the man in my special evening?"

"I'm hoping."

"I guess we'll have to see. As for what we're eating, this man who might or might not be you, maybe Tuscan chicken pasta paired with a glass of pinot grigio. I had that once at a restaurant and it was delicious. Honestly, anything I don't have to cook that isn't chicken nuggets or mac and cheese."

"What's for dessert?"

"Oh, that's an easy one. Pistachio ice cream and chocolate shortbread cookies."

"I want a cookie," Livie said, jumping up from the floor.

Cooper grinned. "Little ears."

She laughed. "That's something you'll have to get used to."

"I can see that." He shifted his gaze to Livie. "Princess, if you'll wait five minutes, I'll give you two cookies."

"Is five minutes a long time, Daddy? I don't think I can wait a long time."

"Not a long time at all. Look, Ruby has her tug toy in her mouth and wants you to play with her some more." That did the trick, and he turned back to Kendall. "What comes after that romantic dinner?"

"I guess that depends on my dinner date."

He grinned. "I think your dinner date might have some ideas you'd like."

"Yeah? Like what?"

"Maybe you'll find out sometime." He stood. "Right now, I have a princess to make happy."

Kendall couldn't shake the feeling of curiosity that Cooper had ignited in her. Why had he asked all those questions? As she watched him play with Livie and Ruby, a smile tugged at the corners of her lips. The two of them had taken to each other as if they had known each other for years, not mere days. The way he interacted with Livie, so patient and kind, warmed her heart in a way she hadn't felt in a long time. What would it be like to have him a part of her and Livie's life permanently?

They kept dinner simple, grilled cheese and canned tomato soup. She and Cooper worked together to grill the sandwiches and heat the soup. His kitchen was small, and it seemed he took every opportunity to brush against her, to touch her. Each time he did, her heart did a funny fluttering thing.

After dinner, they settled down on the living room couch, with their daughter snuggled between them, and watched *Frozen*, Livie's favorite Disney movie. When Cooper told her he'd never seen the movie, Livie was stunned.

"It's the bestest movie ever, Daddy. Why did you never watch it?"

"Because I was waiting until I could watch it with you, Princess."

From Livie's big smile, that answer pleased her. "We can watch it now, right, Mommy?"

So, *Frozen* it was. Livie made it halfway through the movie before she began to drift off to sleep.

"Should I carry her to bed?" he asked.

"Bath first. She played hard today, and she's stinky."

"How dare you call my daughter stinky." He sniffed Livie's neck, then wrinkled his nose. "Even if she is."

"You're a good daddy, Cooper."

He glanced down at Livie before lifting his eyes to hers. "I'm planning to be."

Chapter Seventeen

While Kendall gave Livie a bath, Cooper sat on the couch with his laptop open. After jotting down Kendall's dream for an adult evening so he wouldn't forget anything, he read the emails sent to Kendra Hartley. Most seemed harmless, but he'd forwarded a few so far to a separate file he'd created. Grayson and Liam were also reading them tonight, and tomorrow, they'd compare notes.

"Livie wants to know if her daddy will read her a bedtime story," Kendall said, poking her head around the hallway wall.

As if he could refuse his princess. "Absolutely." He set his laptop on the coffee table. He'd read Emmie bedtime stories countless times when his sister was a little girl and it was left up to him to get her to bed. *Thank you, Emmie, for training me on how to make bedtime stories fun.*

"What are we reading?" he said as he sat on the edge of the bed. Ruby had followed him into the bedroom, and she curled up on the floor at his feet.

Livie thrust a thin book at him. "This one, Daddy."

"*Attack of the Underwear Dragon*? Sounds...uh, fun." Children's books sure had changed since he'd read bedtime stories to Emmie some twenty years ago. And since when did dragons start wearing underwear? Turned out it was a cute story that Livie knew by heart and interrupted his reading to tell the story herself. He loved every minute of it.

"Read me another one, Daddy."

Kendall, who'd been lying on the other bed listening to them, sat up. "No more tonight. It's time to go to sleep." She came to Livie and kissed her cheek. "Sweet dreams, precious girl."

He leaned over and kissed Livie's forehead. "See you in the morning, Princess."

"Can Ruby stay with me? She'll bite the bad man if he comes."

"She sure can, but I promise you, I won't let the bad man come here."

"Okay. I love you, Mommy. I love you, Daddy."

This girl. "I love you, too." He'd only known her for a few days, and she already had him wrapped around her little finger. He'd plugged in a night-light earlier so the room wouldn't be so dark in the hopes that would help her sleep without a nightmare.

As soon as he'd turned to leave, Ruby jumped on the bed, curling up next to Livie. He should probably tell the dog to get off the bed, but Livie already had her arm around Ruby, and having the dog with her probably made her feel safer, so he let Ruby stay where she was. He followed Kendall out of the room, leaving the door open so he could hear her if she cried out.

"I promised my sister I'd call her tonight, so I'm going to do that," he said.

"Okay, I'm going to jump in the shower while you talk to her."

"Emmie can wait if you need help showering." He waggled his eyebrows.

She laughed. "Tempting, but you promised to call her. She's probably sitting by the phone, waiting for it to ring."

"You're no fun," he grumbled. He called her as he walked to the living room.

"Finally," she said on answering. "I've been trying to guess all day what you wanted to tell me."

"And what did you guess?"

"That you met someone. Did you? What's her name?"

He grinned, imagining her shock when he told her. "I did meet someone. Her name is Olivia, but I call her Livie."

"I knew it. Is she pretty? What am I saying? Of course she is."

"She's beautiful, actually."

"What does she do?"

"She goes to school."

"You mean like college?"

"No, like kindergarten…or maybe preschool. I'm not sure. Considering she's my daughter, I need to know these things." He chuckled at the silence on the other end. He wished he could see her face right now.

"Cooper? What are you saying exactly?"

"Exactly what you heard. Livie is my daughter. She's almost five and is the cutest, funniest and sweetest thing in the world."

There was more silence, and then, "You have a daughter? How come you never told me?"

"Because I didn't know myself until a few days ago." He told her the story from the night he first met Kendall up to now.

"Wow, this is all unbelievable. In my wildest guesses of what you were going to tell me, this wasn't even on the radar. You've had your world turned upside down. Are you okay with this, with having a daughter?"

"Emmie, I'm so okay with it that I want to shout it to the world."

"And Kendall, what are your feelings on her?"

"That I'm in love with her, but she's not ready to hear that yet. She does have feelings for me, that much I know, but right now, she's scared for both Livie and herself. When she feels they're both safe again, I'll—"

"Romance her. That's what you need to do."

"I plan to." Emmie had always believed in love and happy endings, even when growing up in the misery that was their homelife. She'd found it with her husband. John loved her deeply and treated her like a princess. Cooper had liked him from their first meeting and was thankful she had someone like him in her life.

"When can I meet them?"

"Soon. When all this is over, I'll bring them to Boston." He hoped Kendall wanted to explore this thing between them enough to meet his sister. "When we hang up, I'll send you a picture of them."

He'd taken one today that he loved. When they'd returned to Grayson's to pick up Livie, she'd begged them to let her go down to the beach so she could touch the water. The photo was of Kendall, Livie and Ruby at the water's edge, his two girls laughing at Ruby being silly.

"I can't believe I'm an aunt."

"Aunt Emmie has a nice ring to it." He heard the shower shut off. "Gotta go, though."

"Okay. Congratulations, *Dad*. Send me that picture. Love you."

"Love you, too, Emmie."

He sent the photo to her, then set his phone on the coffee table. They'd come a long way, he and his sister, and there'd been many times when he'd worried about their futures. Emmie had found her happily-ever-after with John, and he could only hope he'd finally found his.

Kendall appeared, carrying her laptop.

She sat close enough that he could smell her vanilla scent. "How about a glass of wine?" he said before he decided it was a good idea to run his nose over her skin, inhaling her scent.

"I'd love one."

"Go relax. I'll pour." When he returned to the living room, she had her laptop open. He set one of the wineglasses on the end table near her, then sat close to her but not touching. What was she reading and why was it making her frown?

"Cooper." She turned her laptop so he could see the screen. "This is really weird. It's a response to my last podcast. It's signed the same way the note penned on Livie's shirt was."

He read the email.

Hello, Kendra... I have to wonder, though. Is Kendra really your name or is it just your on-air persona? Your last podcast on McKenzie Haywood was touching. You have a way of bringing these children to life. Almost as if you've experienced something similar. Have you?

Here's something to consider. What if instead of suffering, these children you cry your tears over were given a better life? What if they're little angels now, existing in a place so beautiful that we here on earth can't begin to imagine the pinnacle of their joy? A place where there is no suffering, no hunger, no tears. Nothing on earth could compare to that, don't you think?

I would love to hear you talk about that possibility in your next podcast.
A devoted fan

"Send that to me, then Grayson and Liam."

"It has to be him, don't you think?" she said after forwarding it to the three of them.

"Yeah, I think so."

She frowned as she read it again. "Except here, he's just hinting that he thinks my real name might not be Kendra. The note penned to Livie was to me, Kendall." She lifted her eyes to his. "So, maybe it's not the same person."

"Or he's playing games with you. Do you remember other emails signed the same way?" If he were a betting man, his money would be on yes, it was from their subject.

"Honestly, I don't pay attention to how they're signed. What I'm always hoping for is good ideas from my listeners that will help solve the case. Occasionally, my listeners pick up on clues the police missed."

"What about an email with the wording similar to this?"

"No, I'd definitely remember if I'd gotten anything like this one. It gives me the creeps."

It did him, too. "It's getting late. We have another busy day tomorrow. Why don't you get some rest?"

"Are you calling it a night?"

"Not yet. I want to finish reading these emails." He needed to see if there were any more that raised suspicion.

"I am tired, but I don't know if I can sleep after reading that."

"How about I give you something else to think about?"

"Like what?"

He set his laptop aside. "Like this." He leaned toward her, and when his mouth was an inch from hers, he asked for permission. "Yes?"

In answer, she put her hands on his cheeks and touched her lips to his. "Yes," she whispered against his mouth.

He spread his fingers along the back of her neck and

softly groaned when her tongue teased the seam of his mouth. He opened for her and stroked his tongue over hers. In that moment, as they tasted and explored, nothing else on earth mattered except the two of them. He was an addict, craving the taste of her, the feel of her, the scent of her. He kept one hand on her neck, holding her close, and the other, he put on her waist.

Bed. Now. Great idea.

No, not tonight. Before he could give in to his inner caveman and carry her to his lair, he forced himself to pull away. He had plans, a special evening to give her, and he still had the details to work out.

She blinked as if coming out of a daze, and desire shimmered in those blue eyes. If she didn't go now, all his good intentions to make being together again special would be tossed out the window. "Go to bed, Kendall."

"Did I do something wrong?"

"Never. I'm hanging on to my control by a thread." He took her hand, turned it over and dropped a kiss to her palm. "This is going to happen between us, but not tonight. Go."

"Humph." She pranced away with a teasing sway of her hips.

"Minx," he muttered with a chuckle. He glanced down at his crotch. "Down boy. Not happening tonight." *Boy* was not at all happy.

He was going to be up for however long it took to read all the emails that had been sent to Kendra Hartley and decided to make a cup of coffee. He'd just sat back down when his phone chimed, Grayson's name on the screen.

"I've been expecting your call," he said on answering. "You read the one Kendall sent you tonight, right?"

"Yeah. It's him, and it's troubling. I forwarded it on to

the profiler. Hopefully, we'll get something back from her soon."

"Agree on the troubling," Cooper said. "He's taunting her, telling her that he knows her real name."

"Yes, and I'd bet everything I own that this is the same bastard who took Livie."

Cooper agreed. What if Kendall hadn't called him? He didn't even want to think of her and Livie unprotected while an overworked detective tried to identify Livie's kidnapper. He made a mental note to call Rossi tomorrow, find out if he'd learned anything.

"I think the person who wrote that email is a very disturbed man," Grayson said.

"My question at this point, does she do a podcast and talk about the missing children being in a better place? That if anyone thinks that, they're wrong, or something like that? The aim to goad him into keeping him communicating with her." He wished to God there was a better way, and they didn't have to ask her to respond to the man.

"It's something to consider, and she did agree to do it, but first, I think she should answer his email. Open a line of communication with him. Of course, we'll draft the response to him for her. We can discuss that when we meet tomorrow."

"Okay, but if she doesn't want to answer him or do the podcast, I won't force her."

"Agreed. It's her decision."

"I have a favor to ask. How would you feel about Livie and Ruby spending the night at your house tomorrow?"

"We'd love to have them. Tyler will be excited. Any particular reason?"

"Kendall's stressed out and scared. I'd like to give her

an evening away from worrying about what's going to happen. A night just for her."

"Say no more."

"Thanks, brother."

"No thanks necessary. Talk tomorrow."

Now to plan for her adult evening without spoiling the surprise.

Chapter Eighteen

"Tyler wants to have a slumber party with Livie and Ruby tonight," Cooper said.

Kendall glanced at him over the rim of her coffee cup. "When did that come up?" She wasn't sure about Livie being away from her overnight. What if she had a nightmare?

"When I talked to Grayson last night. I think it would be good for her. She loves playing with him, and she'll have Ruby with her."

Livie and Ruby had quickly become besties, the dog not letting her new friend out of her sight. "I'm not sure Livie's ready to be away from us. What if she has a nightmare?"

"Believe me, Harlow and Grayson will be right there for her if that happens."

"I don't know." She would be safe with the Montanas, Kendall knew that, but what if something happened and she wasn't there?

He set his coffee cup on the kitchen counter and came to where she sat on a barstool. "She couldn't be in safer hands, Kendall. I think it would be good for her to have a night of fun with another child. If she cries to come home, we'll go get her."

"Okay, I guess, but only if she wants to."

"Let's go ask her."

She followed him into the living room, where Livie watched cartoons with Ruby's head on her lap. She sat next to them, and Cooper sat on the other side of Livie.

"Mommy and Daddy, are you coming to watch cartoons with me?"

"Actually, we want to ask you a question," Kendall said. "Would you and Ruby like to spend the night with Tyler? Have a pajama party?"

"I get to wear my pajamas at Tyler's house?"

"Yes."

"Does Ruby have to?"

"Ruby doesn't have any pajamas," Kendall said.

"Why?"

Cooper grinned at her over Livie's head. "Because, Princess, they don't make pajamas for a dog."

"Why? She likes pajamas. She told me that."

"I didn't know Ruby could talk," Cooper said.

"She only talks to me."

"Then you're very special," Kendall said. "Do you want to spend the night at Tyler's?"

"Yes!"

That settled, she stood. "What's the plan for today?" she asked Cooper.

"We'll have lunch here, then drop Livie at Tyler's on our way to Phoenix Three. I have a few errands to run, and while I'm out, I'll pick up something for lunch. Subs or burgers? There's also a great noodle bar nearby that does takeout."

"Livie loves dumplings, so that would be good. Dumplings works for me, too."

"Noodle bar it is." He kissed Livie's cheek. "Back soon, Princess."

While he was gone, Kendall got dressed, then got Livie dressed. She packed pajamas, clean underwear and an outfit for her to put on in the morning.

Tonight, she'd be alone with Cooper. She'd been disappointed last night when he'd sent her to bed. He'd said that something would happen between them. Would that be tonight? Did she want something to happen?

"If you're agreeable, we'd like you to do a podcast scripted by us," Cooper said. "We want him to communicate with you in the hope that he'll give us some clues as to who he is. Also, would you be willing to let us write a response to his email to send to him?"

They were back in The Phoenix Three's conference room. "I'm willing to do anything you think will help us find this man." She wanted her life back.

"What do you need to do a podcast?" Grayson asked.

"Preferably, my home studio, but I can do it from here with the right equipment."

"Write down what you need," Cooper said.

"I was able to learn what the note pinned to Lacy Alexander said." Grayson brought the note up on the wall screen.

Tears burned her eyes as she read the words.

"Don't be sad. This beautiful child is an angel now."

"It sounds like what he wrote in the email to me." How could he think Lacy's parents shouldn't be sad?

"Although it's close," Cooper said, "the words aren't exact to what he wrote to you. There's not enough there to positively say they're both the same man."

"But you think it is?"

Cooper nodded. "I do."

"Anything else we want to talk about today?" Grayson asked.

Cooper raised his hand.

"Are we in grade school now?" Grayson grinned as he winked at her. "The boy's adorable, yeah?"

She thought so.

"You just wish you had my charm, brother," Cooper said.

The guys had a great relationship, and she was a little envious. From the day Livie was born, she'd cocooned them in a bubble meant to keep them safe. Her fears had kept her from having the kind of bonds these three men had. As she sat here, listening to Cooper and Grayson razz each other, she wished she could have a do-over for the past five years.

Sure, she had friends, mostly other teachers, but those relationships were superficial. She sat with them at lunch, talked with them a little before school or after, but she never opened up to them. Never shared her dreams and fears with them, never did fun things with them.

The only person in her life who truly knew her was her father. He was a great father and grandfather, but he had his own life. They did try to have dinner together once a week.

When this was over and she had her life back, she was going to make changes. She was going to work on her relationships with the people in her life, start accepting the invitations to do things with those superficial friends. She was going to ease up on Livie, stop controlling her every minute out of fear. Well, that one was going to be hard, but Livie was already pushing at the limits Kendall tried to put on her. She needed to find a compromise that they both could live with.

"Where's Liam?" Cooper said.

"At the doctor's with Quinn."

"Everything okay?"

Grayson nodded. "It's a routine checkup."

"Okay, good." Cooper touched her hand. "Ready to go?"

"Sure." She stood. "Thanks, Grayson, for taking the time to deal with my situation and for hosting tonight's pajama party."

"No thanks necessary, and Tyler's thrilled to have Livie and Ruby spend the night." He waved her away. "Go enjoy your evening."

Cooper's gaze flicked to Grayson, and they both smiled as if they knew something she didn't. What was that about?

"How's a nice bubble bath sound?" Cooper asked as soon as they were back at his apartment.

"I'd never refuse a bubble bath, but now?"

"Why not? Take a little time for yourself. I have a few things I need to do for about an hour. When you get out, put on something soft and comfortable."

She stared at his retreating back as he headed toward the kitchen. He was up to something, but it had been a long time since she'd indulged in a bath, so she did as he suggested. When the water cooled, she stepped out. It had actually been a pleasant hour. She had a soft jazz playlist on her phone, and she'd almost fallen asleep while luxuriating in the warm scented water and listening to the music.

Now, she was more relaxed than she'd been in... She couldn't remember when. Before Livie was born, she knew that much. After drying off, she slipped into the pale blue jersey sundress she'd brought. The back was open, so the only thing she wore under it was panties. A few swipes of mascara on her lashes, a bit of blush on her cheeks and cherry-flavored lip gloss, and she was ready to go find Cooper. She found him in the kitchen.

He pulled a barstool away from the counter. "Sit here."

Bluesy music played softly from the speakers, and at least a dozen candles were spread out on the counters. In front of where he wanted her to sit was a glass of wine and a plate of assorted cheeses, fancy crackers and grapes. She stilled and her heart fluttered madly at seeing the warmth in his eyes and the soft smile on his face.

He performed a perfect bow. "Your adult evening awaits you, my lady."

What could she do but curtsey? "Thank you, kind sir." Already charmed beyond measure, she eased onto the stool. "Something smells awesome." She had no idea what the food was, but the aroma of spices and garlic had her mouth watering.

"That's dinner." He picked up a glass of wine she hadn't noticed and came around the counter, taking a seat next to her. "To a beautiful evening with a beautiful woman," he said as he held up his glass.

"Thank you for this." She touched her glass to his before taking a sip of the wine, savoring the fruity flavor of the pinot grigio on her tongue. The dim lighting in the kitchen cast a cozy glow over everything, making it seem as if they were in their own little world.

"If I kissed you now, would you taste like apples and spices?"

"You could kiss me and see." *Please kiss me.*

He set down his glass and leaned in, his lips a whisper away from hers, his breath warm on her skin. She couldn't move, barely breathed, waiting to feel his mouth on hers. Finally, he closed the distance between them. His lips were soft against hers, and the taste of wine lingering on them blended with the sweetness of her own. It was as if a spark ignited a flame, filling her with a warmth that spread to every corner of her being.

Lost in this little world of theirs, she didn't know how long they kissed. Probably only minutes, but if you told her it was days, she would smile dreamily and murmur in agreement. No man had ever kissed her so tenderly, yet so passionately.

When he pulled away, she opened her eyes to find him gazing at her intently, his eyes dark with desire and need. For her. She reached out to touch his face, tracing the line of his jaw with her fingertips. "I never knew adult evenings could be so...."

"Sexy with the hottest man you've ever known?"

He waggled his eyebrows, making her laugh. "Well, I was going to say *enchanting*, but sure, let's go with that." He was adorable. She picked up a grape and held it out. When he caught her fingers between his lips, looking at her with so much heat that she thought she might melt, she couldn't stop the moan bubbling up from her throat.

A wicked smile tilted his lips as he sucked the grape from her fingers. "Something you should know about me, Kens."

Kens. She really liked him calling her that. "What's that?"

"Just this. In order for a mission to be successful, one must plan down to the last detail. I'm a great planner because the end game is always for success. I have a very detailed plan for tonight, and it's taking all my willpower to stick to the plan and not toss you over my shoulder and carry you to my bed."

Pfff. Who needed a plan anyway?

"But I'm not going to do that."

Well, that was disappointing.

"You want to know why?"

She nodded.

"Because tonight is for you." He danced his fingertips

across her shoulders, nothing more than a feathery touch, but she felt that touch down to her very core. "If we successfully stick to my plan, the reward will be amazing. And I want you to have some *amazing* in your life." He picked up her glass and handed it to her. "Let's enjoy our wine and get to know each other a little better. Okay?"

"Okay," she said, the only word she was capable of after that, and yes, a thousand times yes, she wanted that *amazing* he was promising.

They fed each other cheeses and grapes, sipped their wine, and their conversation flowed effortlessly, weaving between topics both lighthearted and profound. He told her about his baseball coach, a man who'd mentored him, helped him to see that if he worked for it, he could make something of his life. She learned that he was a reader, his preferred genre thrillers, espionage and military histories. She loved it when he admitted he secretly read military romances. His favorite color was red, and his favorite TV show was *Yellowstone*.

"I'm sorry, but those are the most unhappy people ever. I tried watching it after everyone raved about the show, but I just can't deal with them. And that Beth woman. She's over the top." She rolled her eyes.

He chuckled. "She is something else." He refilled their wineglasses, then pushed to his feet and picked up the almost empty appetizer plate. "Step two of my plan commencing."

"Can I help?"

"No, you may not." He dropped a kiss on the corner of her eye. "Tonight is for you. Move over to the dining room table." He grinned. "Please."

He'd listened to her when she'd told him her imagined perfect night, and he couldn't know what that meant to her.

Chapter Nineteen

Cooper had prepared the Tuscan chicken pasta while Kendall was in the bath, and he pulled the fancy casserole dish he'd bought this morning out of the oven.

"Whatever that is, it smells amazing," she said.

He set the dish in front of her. "Tuscan chicken pasta, made especially for the lady."

"Really? You made me one of my favorite meals?"

"Yes, really. Enjoy." He'd taste-tested it earlier and thought it was pretty good. Because he wanted to watch her face when she ate his meal, he took a seat across from her.

She took a bite, then her eyes slid closed. "This is so good."

"As good as the one you had at the restaurant?"

"Might be even better. Are you trying to win me over with your cooking skills?"

"Is it working?" Whatever worked, he'd do. He'd never clicked with a woman the way he did her, and he'd never wanted a woman the way he did her.

Mischief danced in those incredible blue eyes of hers. "Oh, I don't know. Maybe I should hold out for a few more amazing meals before answering that."

"Ah, the lady is going to make me work for her admiration." He leaned toward her and whispered, "Just so you know, I never give up when I want something."

"I'm counting on it."

He almost got up to go kiss her then, and he was sure she wanted him to, but not yet. "Finish your dinner. The chef worked damn hard cheffing your dinner."

"Maybe I'll personally thank the chef."

"The chef thinks that's a great idea."

"I'm sure he does."

"Ready for dessert?" he said after they finished the meal.

She patted her stomach. "I'm not sure there's room in here for another bite."

"Not even for pistachio ice cream and chocolate shortbread cookies?"

"You remembered everything I said."

He tapped his head. "My brain is a sponge. If you're full, maybe we can save dessert for a little later."

"And what shall we do in the meantime?"

"I have some ideas about that." He shifted his chair away from the table. "Come here."

She moved to stand between his legs. "Now what?"

"Now, you put your arms around my neck, and I wrap mine around your waist." He smiled when she did as instructed. "Do you want me to kiss you?"

"Thought you'd never ask."

"Sit on my leg." After she did, he slowly lowered his mouth to hers. As he kissed her, her hands drifted up to tangle in his hair, and she leaned into him until her breasts were pressed against his chest. Her dress was open in the back, almost down to her waist, and as he trailed his fingers down her spine, he realized she wasn't wearing a bra. He liked this dress. Very much.

He broke the kiss and put his mouth next to her ear. "I

want you, Kendall." She had to feel his erection pressed against her thigh, had to feel just how much he wanted her.

"I want you, too."

That was all he needed to know. "Bed. Now." He stood with her in his arms, grinning when she giggled.

"I've never been carried before." She wrapped her arms around his neck. "It's very sexy."

He'd show her sexy. When he reached his bed, he let her legs drop, and as she slid down his body, he captured her mouth again. She responded to the kiss with a hunger to match his own, and in a frenzy, they tore at each other's clothes. The air around them filled with the sounds of their heavy breaths and the scent of their arousal.

When his shirt was tossed aside, her gaze roamed over his chest. "Oh, my," she whispered. She danced her fingers over his abs, pushed her fingers into his skin, testing the firmness of his muscles, then over and up as if she was mapping his body. "I've never touched a body as magnificent as this."

"It's yours to touch whenever and however you wish." He and his brothers worked hard at keeping in shape, and at this moment, he was never gladder for that.

"So, it's okay if I do this?" She flicked his nipple with her fingernail.

He groaned. "Oh, yeah. Do it again." She did, and pure pleasure shot down to his groin. Her dress was pooled at her feet, and he leaned back, wanting to see her. His gaze slid down to the white bikini panties, the only thing she wore now. "You're beautiful." Her breasts were a little larger and her hips a bit wider than they'd been the first time they'd been together. Before, she'd had the body of a girl, but now, she was all woman, and sexy as hell.

"I've had a baby, so I'm not—"

"Do not finish that sentence. You're ten times sexier than you were back then."

"I have stretch marks."

She did, and he traced one of the barely visible white lines. "Because you had our baby, and each mark is a testament to your courage to go it alone and the love you had for that baby growing inside you." He traced another line. "Your beauty is stunning, Kendall. Thank you for being the mother of my child…our child."

"There was never any question that I wouldn't have her."

"And for that you have my eternal gratitude." He wanted to tell her that he was falling for her, but he was afraid that would scare her away. He'd just have to show her that his feelings for her already ran deep. "If you knew how badly I want you, you'd probably run away."

A small smile played on her lips. "The last time a man wanted me that badly was five years ago. I was sure that kind of intense intimacy would never happen again, so I fiercely guarded my memories of that night." She fumbled with the button of his jeans. "I want these off."

"Don't know if I'm up to the pressure of living up to those memories if they were that good," he teased.

She lifted her eyes to his. "One hopes you're up to the challenge."

"Trust me, baby, I'm up." He glanced down at the tent in his pants. "Way up."

"So I see." She got his jeans unsnapped, then went to work on his zipper. She grinned triumphantly as she finally undid his jeans, pulling them down along with his boxer briefs. He stepped out of them, his erection standing at full attention, and she reached out and touched him. Her fingers wrapped around him, stroking gently as she looked up at him with eyes darkened with desire.

He was so turned on that it wasn't going to take much to send him over the edge. He took her hand away. "I'm about to embarrass myself. You can play with me all you want later." He lifted her up and gently laid her down on his bed, then stretched out next to her on his side. "I get to play with you first."

His hands traced the curves of her body, exploring every inch of her skin that he could reach. He found her nipples hard and erect, and he gently caressed them with his fingertips before taking one into his mouth. She moaned softly, her fingers running through his hair as he kissed and licked at her sensitive flesh. He'd thought he remembered everything about their night together, but he'd forgotten how responsive she was.

He moved farther down her body, his hands sliding over her hips and thighs as he kissed his way down to her stomach, then to the top of her panties. "These are pretty," he said as he slid his finger just inside the waistband. "But they need to go."

She lifted onto her elbows and looked down at herself. "Take them off."

"Happy to." His gaze never left hers as he slowly slid them down her legs. When they were finally gone, he ran his hands up and down the length of her thighs, tracing the soft skin with his fingertips.

"Cooper."

"Yeah?"

"Do something. Anything."

He chuckled. "Impatient little thing." He could feel her tremble slightly under his touch, and he rubbed his nose over her skin below her belly button. The scent of her arousal filled the air, driving him toward the edge of his control.

With his tongue, he began to explore, licking and tasting every inch of her sex. Her taste sent waves of pleasure through him, and she made sexy little noises with each flick of his tongue. Her breaths grew shallower, each one a small gasp that spurred him on. He wanted…needed to hear his name on her lips.

Her hands gripped his hair. "I need…"

"What, Kendall? What do you need?"

"To come. Please."

He lifted his face a few inches. "Say my name, and I'll make it happen."

"Cooper. Cooper. Cooper." She pushed on his head in an effort to get his mouth back on her.

He blew on her clit, then as he sucked on it, he slid a finger inside her, and then a second one. She was drenched, and her core muscles clenched around his fingers. Her breaths were coming faster now, her moans growing louder and more desperate.

"Please, Cooper."

"Come for me, baby." He curled a finger, teasing that most sensitive spot inside her, and his efforts were rewarded when her hips bucked, and she gasped.

He grunted in pure male satisfaction when her body tensed, and she cried out his name again. He wrapped his arms around her waist and pressed his face against her stomach, holding her as her body shuddered through her climax. A fierce sense of possessiveness and protectiveness swelled inside him. He never wanted to let her go.

Once her breaths had calmed, he crawled up her body. Staring into her eyes, he cupped his hand over her sex, and said, "Just so you know. I licked it, so it's mine."

She stared back at him for a moment before a big grin appeared on her face. "I want to play that game, too."

He sure as hell wasn't going to say no to that.

Chapter Twenty

Kendall listened to the soft, even breaths from the man asleep beside her. She'd never dreamed Cooper would come back into her life, never dared to hope for it. Yet, here she was, in his bed. He'd made love to her as if she were the most special woman in the world.

With the warmth of his body next to hers, she closed her eyes and tried to sleep, but it was impossible. Her mind was full of thoughts of him. He'd said he wanted to be in Livie's life, and she was beyond happy for that, but what about her? Did he want her or was this just a temporary thing between them?

Her life was in Decatur and his here in Myrtle Beach. He was deeply entrenched in The Phoenix Three, so he wouldn't want to move. And he shouldn't. He and his two friends were doing great things by rescuing and saving children. What they did was something that was close to her heart.

Was she willing to move to Myrtle Beach? She liked it here, liked his friends... Well, she'd yet to meet Liam's wife, but she didn't doubt she'd like Quinn. Her job, her father, her life was in Decatur. That was all true, but if Cooper was willing to commit to a relationship, she'd seriously consider moving. Livie would love to live near or with her daddy.

Her mind was all over the place, and she wasn't going to fall asleep. She eased out of bed, slipped on her panties, then stole the T-shirt he'd been wearing earlier. It smelled like him, and she inhaled deeply, savoring the spicy scent of him. She quietly padded out of the room.

It was too late to call and see how Livie was doing, but Harlow would have called if there was a problem, so she wasn't going to worry. She was too sated and happy to worry anyway. They'd left all the dirty dishes on the dining room table when Cooper had carried her to his bed, and she set about cleaning up the dishes and kitchen.

She was loading the last plate in the dishwasher when she sensed she was being watched, and she glanced over her shoulder to see Cooper leaning against the wall, his gaze on her. "I didn't mean to wake you." He wore only his boxer briefs, and his hair was tousled from sleep. The man was absurdly sexy. She wanted to drag him right back to bed.

He prowled toward her. "You didn't. I reached for you, and you weren't there."

She smiled at how grumpy he sounded.

He stopped behind her and wrapped his arms around her chest. "Couldn't sleep?"

The feel of his body aligned along the back of hers sent a shiver down her spine. She leaned back into his embrace, loving the warmth and strength of his body. "I was just finishing up here. Didn't want to leave a mess for tomorrow."

He pressed a kiss to the nape of her neck. "This mess could've waited until morning." His hands moved gently down her arms, sending tingles of warmth through her.

"I can think of a much better way to spend our time than cleaning up the kitchen."

She turned in his arms. "Yeah? Like what?"

"Like an encore performance of earlier."

Yes, please. She slipped her hand in his. "Lead the way."

THE NEXT MORNING, it was her turn to wake up to find Cooper gone. She found him sitting at the kitchen counter, a cup of coffee next to him, and his laptop open. She hadn't taken two steps—silent ones because she was barefoot—when he turned on the barstool and smiled at her.

"Good morning, beautiful. There's K-Cups if you want coffee."

"I didn't make any sound. How did you even know I was here?" She padded to the coffeepot.

"For one, I grew up in a house where it paid to be alert to a change in the air. Second, the military trained me to sense when there were eyes on me. Awareness was a matter of life or death. Bring your cup over here."

"Did you like being in the Army?" She poured a cup, then sat on the barstool next to his.

"There were things I liked about it and things I didn't. I learned much that is invaluable to what I do now, so it was worth every minute of my time in the military." He turned the laptop's screen toward her. "Gray, Liam and I have been working on a response this morning for you to send to our bad man."

"Bad man. Good name for him." She read the words on the monitor.

Devoted fan,
Do you think you're God? I ask because only God has the right to decide when a soul leaves this earth. Do you

have feelings? Compassion? Regret for a young life taken too soon? Do you even give a thought to the heartbreak of the families who lost a precious child? Or are you a cold-blooded bastard who thinks he can justify these crimes by pretty words? Well, your words are ugly, and you disgust me.

What you claim is a beautiful thing is sickening to me. I will not be discussing anything you said on my next podcast. In fact, fuck off.
Kendra Hartley

They couldn't be serious. "No, we can't send him this. It's going to make him furious."

"We want him angry. Angry people make mistakes, and we'll be waiting for that to happen."

"I don't know. This scares me, like we're poking a monster."

He pushed the laptop away from her, then shifted on the barstool to face her. "That's exactly what we're doing." He took her hands in his. "Monsters like him want attention. They want control. He won't be able to ignore this email and won't be able to help himself from responding. We want him communicating with us."

"What if he comes after me? Or God forbid, Livie?"

"He's not going to come near you or Livie. We won't allow that to happen. I promise."

She believed him. "Okay. When do you want me to send this?"

"Now if you're willing." When she hesitated, he said, "If you want to think about it, take the time to do that."

She didn't want any contact with the bad man, but if the guys believed this would draw him out so they could catch him, she'd do it. "Here goes nothing." She hit Send.

"I'm proud of you, Kens." He cupped her cheeks and kissed her.

Her nerves were like live wires, snapping wildly. The dangerous game they were playing made her want to crawl into bed and pull the covers over her head. But his kiss calmed her. As if he knew that, he deepened the kiss. Too soon, though, he leaned back and studied her.

"You okay?"

"Scared, but yeah, I'm good." Only because she knew there were three formidable men at her back.

"Ready to go get our daughter?"

"Definitely. She's never been away from me overnight."

"Gray invited us to have breakfast with them. Thirty minutes enough time for you to get ready?"

"Make it twenty."

He grinned. "That's my girl."

"MOMMY!" LIVIE RAN to her with her arms in the air as soon as they stepped inside Grayson's house.

"Good morning, sweetie." She kneeled and hugged her little girl. "Did you have fun?"

"Yes! So much fun." Livie's eyes lit up at seeing her father. "Daddy!" She pushed away to get to Cooper.

Kendall wasn't used to sharing Livie, and for a brief second, she resented Cooper for taking Livie away from her. Then she rolled her eyes at herself because that was silly, and her resentment faded as fast as it had come.

Cooper scooped Livie up. "Hey, Princess. Mommy and Daddy missed you, but I'm glad you had a good time."

"I have a joke, Daddy. Tyler told it to me."

"Yeah? Let's hear it."

"What has legs but can't walk?"

"I give up. What?"

"A chair. That's so funny."

Cooper laughed. "It sure is. Ah, here's Ruby." He set Livie down and scratched Ruby's head. "Was Ruby a good dog?"

Livie wrapped her arms around Ruby's neck, giving the dog a big hug. "She was so good, Daddy. I was, too."

Kendall's heart was a gooey mess watching Cooper with Livie and how he looked at their daughter with nothing but love in his eyes. And when he glanced up at her with a smile that felt like it was meant just for her, she finally understood when a book heroine claimed to melt into a puddle at the hero's feet, because she was seconds from doing just that.

"Good morning, Kendall," Harlow said, coming into the room.

"Morning. Hope Livie was good for you."

"She's been a perfect guest. Come in the kitchen and meet Quinn." She turned to Cooper. "The boys are on the deck. Tyler's out there, too."

"Great." He picked up Livie. "Let's go outside." Ruby followed them out.

"He's really good with her," Harlow said.

"It was love at first sight for them both. Livie's so happy to have a daddy, and he's been amazing with her."

"Cooper has a big heart and a lot of love to give," Harlow said.

She was seeing that. She'd truly hit the jackpot on a baby daddy. When they walked into the kitchen, a woman who looked like she was due any second was standing at the counter eating cake. The funny thing about that was that she was digging her fork into the entire chocolate cake.

The woman—Quinn, she assumed—narrowed her eyes at seeing Kendall, pulled the decimated cake closer to her and said, "Mine."

Kendall wasn't sure how to respond until the woman burst into laughter. "You should see your face. Like who's the crazy lady?"

Harlow shook her head but had an amused smile on her face. "Behave, Quinn. Kendall, this is Quinn, who's due just about any day now and really is a bit crazy right now."

Kendall chuckled. "Been there, so I totally get it. Nice to finally meet you, Quinn. I've met your other half, and his eyes get all soft when he talks about you."

"Although I know that's true, right now, he's a little afraid of me. If I don't get this bowling ball out of me soon, I might murder the man in his sleep who put it there, and he knows it." She forked up another large bite of cake. "Just kidding." She grinned evilly. "Probably."

"Livie was two days late, and I was miserable and snarling at anyone who came near me."

"Tyler was the best boy," Harlow said. "He arrived a week early."

Quinn scowled at Harlow. "I hate you."

"No, you don't. Put that cake away. Breakfast is ready."

Grayson and Harlow's home was on the beach, and as they ate breakfast on the deck on a perfect late spring morning, Kendall thought she might like living on the beach someday. Did that mean she wanted to move to Myrtle Beach? She peered up at the man next to her...the seriously hot man who happened to be her baby daddy. Maybe.

Chapter Twenty-One

What was that secretive smile on Kendall's face for? Cooper would sure like to know. She'd fit in with his chosen family as if she'd known them all her life. Because there were only six chairs around the table, Tyler sat on Grayson's lap, sharing his breakfast, and Livie was on his.

This was the life he wanted. Kendall by his side, his daughter giggling when he made funny faces at her and his brothers and their wives close by. He just had to make it happen.

"SHE'S OUT FOR the night," Kendall said as they both stood by Livie's bed, watching their daughter sleep.

"Not surprised. She played hard today." They'd spent the day on the beach, and, of course, that had included a baseball game with everyone but Quinn playing. His chest had swelled with pride that Livie had outplayed Tyler. He'd also been impressed that Tyler hadn't minded at all like a lot of boys would have. Tyler's thing was surfing, though, and he was extremely good at it, especially considering he wasn't quite seven years old.

"She wants to learn to surf now," Kendall said. "I don't know about that."

"Maybe I'll learn with her." Grayson and Tyler surfed every chance they got. He'd never had the desire to, but it would be cool to be able to surf with his daughter.

Kendall rolled her eyes. "What am I going to do with you two?"

"I know what you can do with me." That made her smile. "Want me to tell you?"

"Pretty sure I can guess." She winked at him before walking out of the room.

He followed her out, his gaze on the sexiest ass he'd ever seen. She still wore the shorts she'd put on this morning, and he had a vision of having those long legs wrapped around him.

She glanced over her shoulder at him. "Like what you see?"

"Busted," he muttered, unable to hold back a grin. "But I sure do." He moved up next to her, bumping his shoulder against hers.

"I have sand in places where sand doesn't belong," she said. "I think a shower is in order."

"We could save water and shower together."

"Now that's a brilliant idea." She walked into his bedroom, pulled her T-shirt over her head and handed it to him.

"That's what I'm talking about." He took his off and dropped both shirts on the floor, then reached back and shut the door, locking it. "What's next?"

She unbuttoned her shorts and pulled down the zipper. She stepped out of them, letting them puddle at her feet.

"I like this game." He pushed his board shorts down over his hips, dropping them to the floor.

"Thought you might."

And he really liked her. "Go start the shower. I'll be there in a sec." He detoured to his bedroom and got a condom out of the nightstand. By the time he made it to the bathroom, she was stepping into the shower. After removing his boxer briefs, he followed her in, dropped the condom on the small shelf and wrapped his arms around her waist.

She leaned back against him. "I've never showered with a man before."

"You have no idea how much I love hearing that." Warm water cascaded over them as he trailed kisses over her shoulder. She turned in his arms and lifted her face, inviting him to kiss her, so he did. Steam filled the shower as their hands roamed over each other, fingers tangling in wet hair and caressing slippery skin.

Raw desire for this woman, the likes of which he'd never experienced, roared through him and all that mattered was her. It wasn't just desire or lust; it was something more profound, more meaningful. It was a connection unlike anything he had ever known before.

She looked into his eyes with a mixture of trust and longing that almost brought him to his knees. "You want this, baby?" He trailed his lips down her neck to the swell of her breasts.

"More than anything."

"I like that answer." After sheathing himself with the condom, he took her hands and pinned them to the tile wall with his hand. With the other, he wrapped his fingers around her neck in a gentle hold.

He slowly slid inside her, and with his eyes locked on hers, he made love to her. *Made love.* The two words were foreign to him until her. Had sex before? Yes. Enjoyed it? Always. But this—the way they fit, like they were made for each other, like this was where he was meant to be—this was powerful.

Her breath hitched and she arched against him, meeting

his thrusts with her own. He let go of her hands, and she wrapped her arms around his neck and pulled his mouth to hers. The sound of the water drumming on their skin and the steady rhythm of their bodies against one another was a symphony playing just for them. His heart pounded in sync with hers, and her moans mixed with his.

Their bodies slid against each other, skin slick from the water, and when her muscles clenched around him, he knew she was close. A fire burned in him, and with each trust, it flamed brighter.

"Oh, God, Cooper." She arched against him. "Harder."

He obliged, and when she stepped over the edge, he stepped with her. Gasping for breath along with her, he put his hand on her chest, over her heart and felt it pound against his palm. "You're beautiful when you come, Kens. You know I'm going to want to see that look on your face again and again."

"I'm all for that, stud."

He snorted. "Stud?"

"If the shoe fits, and all that." She brushed her thumb over his bottom lip. "And believe me, it fits perfectly." She winked, then left him standing in the shower. She wrapped a towel around herself and walked out of the bathroom.

He shook his head as he chuckled. "Witchy woman," he muttered. She'd sure cast a spell over him. He turned off the water, stepped out, disposed of the condom and then grabbed a towel.

After drying off, he wrapped the towel around his waist, then he shaved. He was slapping aftershave on his face when she called to him. The urgency in her voice had him rushing to her. "What?" He found her standing next to his bed, reading something on her phone. Wordlessly, she handed it to him.

Kendra, you disappoint me. I thought you of all people would understand, but you don't. Not yet anyway. You will soon, I promise.
Still your devoted fan

The bastard was both taunting her and threatening her, but they wanted him communicating with her, so he took a deep breath to calm the rage inside him.

"What does he mean that I'll understand soon?"

That he was coming after her, and damned if he was going to let that happen. "It means he's planning something, a way to make you a believer."

"He scares me."

"I'm not going to let anything happen to you or Livie." He set her phone on the night table, then wrapped his arms around her and held her close. "I'm not saying to ignore the potential threat. You need to be alert and aware of your surroundings, but until we catch this man, I'll be your shadow."

"Have I told you how glad I am that I got up the nerve to call you?"

"And I'm damn glad you did."

"I want my mommy!"

"She's having a nightmare," Kendall said. She pulled away and headed to Livie's room.

He followed her and was halfway down the hall when he realized he only had a towel wrapped around him. He detoured to his bedroom, pulled on sweat bottoms and a T-shirt, then went to comfort his daughter.

Chapter Twenty-Two

Ruby was stretched out across Livie's body, nuzzling her neck. Kendall eased down on the bed. Ruby looked at her and whined as if to say, "Do something." Livie cried out again, and Kendall scooped her little girl into her arms and gently rocked her. Slowly, Livie's sobs quieted, her breathing evening out.

"Did she wake up?" Cooper said as he dropped his knees to the floor next to her.

Kendall glanced at him. "No. I hope that means she won't remember having a nightmare. Ruby was trying to comfort her."

He scratched under the dog's chin. "Good girl."

She could swear that Ruby smiled. "You know, she might make a good therapy dog. She seemed to understand Livie needed comforting. Do you think she's an empath?"

"I wouldn't be surprised. I'm sure she was abused by her previous owner, so she can probably sense when someone's hurting." He leaned down and kissed Livie's forehead. "Have sweet dreams, not nightmares, Princess."

Kendall eased Livie back into the bed, then pulled the cover over her. Leaving Ruby to guard her, they left the room. "I was hoping her nightmares were done."

"I think if she has another one, we should have her talk to someone. A therapist that specializes in working with children."

"Not a bad idea." When they reached the living room, he sat on the sofa, then pulled her onto his lap. "We need to talk about that email."

"Do we have to?"

"Just that we need to send it to Gray and Liam tonight. We'll talk about how to respond tomorrow."

"Okay. Be right back." She returned to his bedroom and picked her phone up from the night table. Back in the living room, she forwarded the email to Grayson and Liam. "There. Done. I don't want to talk about this or even think about it anymore tonight. I'd much rather talk about kissing you."

He grinned. "My mouth is yours to do with as you please."

Oh, she pleased.

THE NEXT MORNING, Cooper's phone chimed while they were eating breakfast. "It's Gray." He glanced at Livie. "I'll take it in the other room."

Livie frowned at Cooper's retreating back. "Daddy didn't eat his breakfast."

"He has to talk to Grayson for a minute. He'll finish eating when he comes back."

"Can I go play with Tyler?"

"Not today. You don't want to wear out your welcome."

Livie's brows scrunched together. "What does that mean, Mommy? How can you wear a welcome outside?"

Kendall chuckled. She loved the minds of children. "It means you don't want Tyler to get tired of you always being at his house."

"I don't want Tyler to get tired of me."

"Exactly. So, you can visit him on another day."

"What'd I miss?" Cooper said, returning to the table.

Livie started crying.

"Hey now, what are those tears for, Princess?" He lifted her out of her chair and onto his lap. "Talk to me, sweetheart."

"I don't want you to get tired of me always being at your house, Daddy."

"Why would you think that? I'll never get tired of you being at my house or anywhere I am." He lifted his eyes to Kendall, his expression confused.

"She wanted to go play with Tyler, and I told her she didn't want to wear out her welcome. She asked what that meant, and I told her that it meant she didn't want Tyler to get tired of her."

He gave her an amused smile over Livie's head, then said, "Look at me, Princess." When Livie did, he brushed the tears on her cheeks away with his thumbs. "It's not the same thing as always being at Tyler's house. I'm your daddy. Daddies never get tired of their little girls. Never, ever. You can be at my house as much as you and your mommy want to be here. And when you go back home, I'll come see you sometimes at your house. I hope you won't get tired of me."

Livie's eyes widened. "No, Daddy. I'm not tired of you." She threw her arms around his neck. "I love you, Daddy."

"And I love you, my beautiful girl. Let's finish our breakfast, then how about we go do some batting practice?"

"Yes!" Livie screamed.

If it was possible for a heart to melt, Kendall's would have on the spot. It wasn't the first time she'd thought how amazing it was that Livie had won the Daddy Lottery. Where did that leave her, though? Was there a chance of a future with him? Or did he only want a fling? She couldn't bring herself to ask because his answers might not be ones she wanted to hear.

"Okay, Princess," Cooper said. "You need to get dressed so we can go hit some balls."

"I want to wear my Braves shirt, Mommy."

"Okay, let's go find it."

Batting practice turned out to be at a sports complex, and Kendall settled on a bench to watch Cooper coach Livie on hitting balls. She knew Livie was good at hitting balls for her age, but with Cooper's coaching, she was getting even better. A group of tween boys had gathered to watch her.

"She's better than you, Stephen," one of them said.

"Nuh-uh. No girl's better than me."

Kendall smiled as they wandered off, still arguing who hit a ball the best, Stephen or Livie. When she'd found out she was having a girl, she'd never imagined her daughter would be a tomboy and love baseball.

"You bat now, Daddy," Livie said, stepping out of the batter's cage.

Cooper had said he played ball in high school and before his kidnapping had wanted to one day play for the Braves. That had to mean he was good, and Kendall watched with interest as he tested a few bats before selecting one.

He proved how good he was as he hit every ball the machine threw at him, all of them bouncing off the net. Some of those would've been home runs in a ballpark. She was impressed.

"Daddy! You're the best! You should play for the Braves, and I could come watch you," Livie exclaimed, excitement in her voice. She raced to the cage wires. "Mommy, did you see Daddy bat? He's so good."

"I did, and he is." She lifted her eyes to his, and the grin on his face widened.

"Guess I still got it," he said.

He sure did have it, in spades. And she didn't mean just his batting skills. Everything about him called to something deep inside her. It wasn't just his hotness—because he was definitely that—but his innate goodness. She was falling for him, and that scared her. She'd never had a broken heart before, but with him, it could happen.

He scooped Livie up and planted a kiss on her cheek. "Did you have fun?"

"So much fun, Daddy."

"Think we should go for some ice cream now?"

"Yes!"

"SHE'S DOWN FOR the night," Kendall said. She sat on the couch next to Cooper and picked up the glass of wine he had ready for her. "She had a great time today. Thank you for that."

"Hey, I had as much fun today as she did. It's been a long time since I've been in a batting cage. I'm going to do it more often."

"You should. You're really good at it. Do you regret not going for a baseball career?"

"There have been times I've wondered if I would have made it into the pros, but no, I don't for a minute regret the way things turned out."

"That's good, then." She finished the last of her wine, then set the glass aside. "So, am I going to respond to the creep's last email? Not that I want to talk about it, but I feel like there's a black thundercloud hanging over my head as long as he's out there somewhere. I didn't want to ask while Livie was with us, but did Grayson have any news this morning when you talked to him?"

He took her hand and tugged her next to him. "Yes, and we'll talk about that in the morning. For tonight, let's pretend he doesn't exist, and we're just a normal woman and man who are getting to know each other while we date."

She snuggled closer and rested her head on his shoulder. "Is that what we're doing? Dating?"

He leaned over and brushed his lips over hers. "If that's what you want."

"I'd like that."

"Good. Should we make out like teenagers in heat?"

She laughed. "I don't think I was ever in heat... Well, there was that one night in Atlanta about five years ago. I might have been then."

He stood, pulling her up with him. "Let's go see if we can recreate that night."

"You think you can? I mean, you were a lot younger back then."

He stopped, stared hard at her for a moment, then grinned as he picked her up and tossed her over his shoulder. "Trust me, baby, I'm up to the task."

"Put me down, you beast." She giggled when he lightly spanked her bottom.

"I'll show you a beast."

And he did. Quite awesomely, in fact.

"THIS IS THE response we want you to send to our bad guy," Cooper said.

She so didn't want a bad guy. They were back in the conference room at The Phoenix Three. Livie was spending the morning with Tyler again, and she'd been both excited about seeing him and worried that she was going to wear out her welcome.

Sometimes the things you said to your child could come back to bite you. It had taken both her and Cooper to convince her that Tyler wasn't going to get tired of her. They were lucky that Tyler was out of school for the week for spring break, and that he liked playing with Livie.

The monitor in front of her came to life, and she read the response the guys had crafted.

Do you think I care that you're disappointed? What I do care about is that I told you to fuck off but here you are again, bothering me with your stupid threats. I have no intention of seeing you soon, so goodbye.

"I guess we really are trying to make him angry." Her gaze traveled from Liam to Grayson before landing on Cooper. She trusted him, all three of them actually, but she was far outside her comfort level. "What do you expect him to do after he gets this?"

"The whole point of your responses to him is to make him so angry he makes a mistake that will lead us to him," Cooper said.

Grayson tapped a finger on the table. "We've traced his emails back to computers in three different libraries. One in Decatur, one in downtown Atlanta and one in Marietta. Right now, he's a faceless, nameless entity hiding behind the protection of public computers. He thinks he's invisible. He's not, and we'll know who he is soon enough."

"Libraries have cameras. Can—"

"We're on it," Cooper said. "We have someone going to those libraries and viewing the security feeds during the time the emails were sent."

"Someone? Shouldn't we send this information to Detective Rossi?"

Liam shook his head. "No. Our bad guy might be watching for the police to show up at the libraries. He might have someone he's paying to let him know if anyone starts asking to see the security videos. We don't want to alert him that we're bearing down on him. Our man knows how to investigate this without alerting anyone as to what he's doing."

And that was why they were so good at what they did. She never would have thought of any of those things. "Okay. Let's do this. Can I just hit Send on this?"

Cooper placed his hand over hers to stop her from hitting Send. "We don't know how computer savvy he is. You need to do it from your laptop since that's what you've been communicating with him on."

"I didn't bring it with me."

"We'll do it when we get home," Cooper said.

"Okay." She was happy to delay baiting the monster.

Grayson picked up a sheet of paper. "I got a reply from the FBI profiler this morning. She apologizes for not having the time to delve deep on our man, but she gave us a brief sketch of him." His gaze focused on the paper as he read. "He's between forty and fifty-five years of age, average height and appearance, lives alone and is a professional of some sort. Maybe an attorney or business owner." He dropped the page to the table. "In other words, could be just about anyone."

"How do they do that?" Kendall asked. "Take a few facts and come up with things that more often than not are correct." Profilers were beyond her scope of understanding.

"It's not really that mysterious," Cooper said. "They

have strong analytical skills, an understanding of criminal behavior and human minds for a start. Some of it, though, is..." He leaned over and loudly whispered in her ear, "woo-woo."

Grayson laughed. "All true."

She wished the profiler could have woo-wooed the monster's name right out of the air.

Chapter Twenty-Three

"I got a joke," Livie said. "Tyler told me it."

Cooper set his fork down and gave his attention to his daughter. "Hit me with it."

She frowned. "I don't want to hit you."

He chuckled. "That just means tell it to me." He needed to learn to think how what he said would be interpreted by a child.

"Oh. Okay. What has hands but doesn't clap?"

A clock. "I give up. What?"

"A clock." She giggled. "Get it?"

"That's a good one, Princess."

"I know. Can we play baseball after dinner?"

He glanced at Kendall with raised brows. She nodded, and he said, "Sure, but you have to eat your peas."

She glared at the peas as if they had personally offended her. "Do I have to?"

"If you want to play baseball you do."

With a loud, drawn-out sigh, she ate her peas, and when she was done, Kendall sent them out while she cleaned up the kitchen. He took Livie to the yard behind his apartment building. They'd been playing for twenty minutes when Kendall came outside. He took one look at her and knew something was wrong.

He handed the ball he was about to pitch to Livie. "Hold this a minute. I need to talk to Mommy." He jogged to Kendall. "What happened?"

"My alarm service just called. My alarm is going off. They're calling the police."

"Call Rossi. Tell him you want him to go to your house, then call you as soon as he knows if there's a problem."

"Daddy, come back."

"Just a minute, Princess." He put his hand on Kendall's shoulder. "I'll pitch a few more balls to her and then we'll come in. Go make that call."

"Okay. It's probably a false alarm."

He wasn't so sure about that. She'd sent the email this morning, and now her alarm had been triggered. He didn't believe in coincidences. He played with Livie for five more minutes, then brought an unhappy girl inside. Kendall was sitting on the sofa, staring at her phone as if she could will it to ring. "Were you able to get a hold of him?"

She set the phone on the coffee table. "Yes. He's heading over now."

"Good." He put his hand on Livie's head. "Time for the princess to have a bath."

Kendall stood. "I'll do it."

"You need to listen for him to call back. I'll get her in the tub if that's okay with you." He wanted to get Livie bathed and in bed so he could concentrate on Kendall. He didn't like it when she was upset.

"It's okay with me. Livie, Daddy's going to help you take a bath, okay?" She sat back down and picked up her phone.

"I don't want a bath. I want to play with Ruby."

"You must not be a princess, then."

She put her little hands on her hips and scowled at him. "I am a princess, Daddy."

"I don't know. Princesses like taking baths because then they smell good. If you want to be stinky, you can't be a princess."

She took a moment to think about that before saying, "I want a bath so I smell good."

"That's my girl." Another lesson he learned about kids. They fought you on taking a bath, but once they were in the tub it was fun and games and they didn't want to get out. He finally got her bathed, in her pajamas and in bed. Of course, she had to have story time. As soon as her eyes closed and he knew she was asleep, he went to Kendall.

"Nothing yet?" he said.

She shook her head. "That's not a good sign, is it?"

Probably not. "Let's wait to hear from Rossi before thinking the worst." He wanted to find the man stalking her and who'd kidnapped Livie, have him arrested, and then she'd be free of the fear hanging over her. After that happened, he only hoped she'd still want him in her life.

"It's hard not to think the worst when—" Her phone chimed, Rossi's name coming up on the screen. She picked it up, then put it on speaker before answering. "This is Kendall. Cooper is with me, and you're on speaker."

"Detective Rossi here. Where are you?"

"Myrtle Beach. Is everything okay at my house?"

"No, there was a break-in, Kendall. Some things of yours were destroyed. I need you to come here to see if anything was taken."

"Damn. When is this going to stop?"

Cooper put his hand on her leg reassuring her he was here for her. "How did he get in?" She had a doorbell camera, but he doubted they'd be so lucky to have the person's face on camera.

"Through a window in her daughter's bedroom. He

probably thought the window wouldn't be alarmed, but fortunately, it was."

Kendall gasped. "What if we'd been there?"

"You weren't," Cooper said, and squeezed her leg before asking Rossi his next question. "How long did it take the police to get there?"

"Seven minutes."

"Time to search through her things and do the damage." She'd never feel safe there again. Maybe that would help convince her to stay in Myrtle Beach with him.

"I really do need you to come back, Kendall," Rossi said. "When can you be here?"

"We'll be there tomorrow, early afternoon," he said. It was about a six-hour drive, one he hoped he could spare Livie.

"Call me when you get close, and I'll meet you here."

"Will do." After Kendall disconnected the call, he pulled his own phone from his pocket. "I need to call Gray, tell him what's going on. Would you have a problem with Livie staying with him and Harlow while we're gone? I don't think this is a trip she needs to be on."

"If they're okay with that, yes." She buried her face in her hands. "He was in my house, Cooper. In Livie's room."

Her words were muffled because of her hands over her mouth, but he heard the despair in them. As for him, he was enraged. Her home, her safe place, had been violated.

She dropped her hands to her lap. "I don't know if I can ever live there again."

"Let's not think about that tonight, okay? I need to call Gray. Why don't you pack what you'll need to take and what Livie will need for a few days?"

Before she could walk away, he caught her hand and pulled her to him. "I know you're upset and scared, and you have every right to be. But hear me on this, Kendall.

You're not alone. I'm right here and I'll be by your side until this is over." And if he had his way, still by her side after it was over. "I'll keep you safe."

She rested her head on his chest. "I know."

"Good." He pressed his lips to the top of her head. "Now go pack while I call Gray. We'll get an early start in the morning."

WHEN THEY ARRIVED at Kendall's house, Rossi was parked in the driveway, waiting for them. Crime tape crisscrossed her front door. Cooper glanced over at her. Her gaze was on that door, and her eyes reminded him of those soldiers who'd seen too much and were checking out. The thousand-yard stare, they called it.

"Kens." He waited for her to look at him. When she just kept staring at her door, he said her name again, louder this time, with command in his voice.

Her head jerked, and she threw him an irritated glance. "What?"

"Just this." He leaned across the console and kissed her. "He's not in there. He's not in control. He's not worth your fear. He doesn't deserve it. Don't give it to him."

She rapidly blinked as if coming out of a trance, then she nodded, her hand reaching for his and, when finding it, holding on as if her life depended on her connection to him. "I won't give it to him," she whispered.

"That's my girl."

Resolve hardened her eyes. "Let's do this."

He exited the car, and by the time he reached her side, she was out and marching toward the detective. Cooper stayed a few steps behind her. This was her show, and she needed to feel in control. But he'd be right here next to her, ready to support her in whatever way she needed.

She stopped in front of Rossi. "Is it really bad?" Her gaze went to her house. "In there?"

"I'm afraid it is, but there's something I want to warn you about before you go in."

Cooper stepped close enough to Kendall that she'd feel his presence at her back. *I've got your six, baby,* he thought. He didn't like the wariness in Rossi's eyes.

"What is it?" Kendall said.

"There's a single rose on your bed along with a note. It says, 'You can't hide from me forever, Kendall.' We'll take it for evidence, but I thought you should see it before we did."

When she shuddered, he took her hand and squeezed. "He's playing games, Kens, trying to mess with your head. I know it's not easy, but don't let him."

"You're right. It's not easy."

"Ready to go in?" Rossi asked.

She eyed her house again, and Cooper thought she was debating the answer to that question, that she'd just as soon get in his truck and leave. He put his hand on her back, wishing he could send her courage through his fingertips.

"Yes." She straightened her shoulders and lifted her chin. "I am."

He was proud of her.

Rossi led the way, and when he reached the door, he tore the crime scene tape off. "We didn't have a key, so we left the door unlocked. If you have a spare you can give me, we can lock up when we leave."

"I have one inside."

Rossi went in first, then stood back to let them enter.

"Oh, God," she said.

The place was destroyed. Furniture was overturned, books and pictures in frames were all over the floor. This was done by someone in a rage. He must have thought she'd be here and was furious when she wasn't. He'd come here last night intending to...do what? Take her away? Do something to her in her own house? And what about Livie? Was he going to take her, too?

"He was gone when patrol got here?" he asked.

Rossi nodded. "There wasn't anyone in the house."

"And you said it took seven minutes for them to arrive?"

"Yes."

The man had been busy in that seven minutes. "Is it a silent alarm?"

Kendall shook her head. "No. It's loud. If it ever went off, especially if I was asleep, I wanted to know."

"So, he stayed and did all this even with it blaring." Ballsy. He glanced at Rossi. "He stayed until he saw patrol pull into the driveway, then he left the way he came. Did any of the neighbors see anyone suspicious? An unknown car parked where it shouldn't be?"

"No. We canvassed the neighborhood. No one saw anything. We asked everyone we interviewed to check their Ring cameras, see if it caught a person running through their yard. So far, no one's reported back that they have something for us."

"That's unfortunate." He'd take a walk around her backyard before they left. He didn't have to ask if she wanted to stay here tonight. There was no way she'd be able to sleep here. They'd have to find a nearby hotel.

Kendall let go of his hand and headed down the hallway. Already warned about what waited for her on her bed, he followed her. She stopped just inside her bedroom and stared at her bed. Standing behind her, he put his hands on her shoulders, and she leaned back against him.

"It looks obscene," she whispered.

He agreed. It was something a lover would do, and from

the right man, it would please a woman. But this… Her sheets and comforter were white, the red rose the only color on the bed. The bed wasn't messed up, which was also disturbing as he couldn't say that about the rest of the room. Drawers were pulled out, and her clothes, including her underwear, were all over the floor.

She turned and walked out of the room. He met Rossi's eyes, and the anger in them matched what he knew was in his. The man who'd done this was a sick bastard, and they needed to find him fast.

Her next stop was Livie's room, and strangely, not a thing was out of place that he could see. Had the police arrived before he could get to this room, or had he not felt the need to destroy Livie's room?

"I can't stay here," she said, her voice trembling.

"No, you can't. We'll check into a hotel. Do you need anything before we go?"

She shook her head. "I don't want to touch anything he has."

"Okay."

"My studio." She went to a closed door and opened it.

He peeked in. It was a guest room, also undisturbed. She crossed the room and opened another door. He looked inside. He hadn't seen her studio when he'd been here, and he was impressed with what she'd done with a small closet. Soundproof foam covered the walls, and on a small desk was a computer, microphone and a few other pieces of equipment. He smiled at seeing the baby monitor.

"He didn't mess with any of my equipment," she said. "That's one small favor."

Probably because he ran out of time to find it. "Let's get that spare key for Rossi and get out of here."

"Gladly."

Chapter Twenty-Four

Kendall took the spare key from the hook in the pantry. As she was handing it to the detective, Cooper frowned.

"Let me see it," he said. He studied one side, then the other. "Did you try to make a copy of this?"

"No, why?"

His expression darkened as he handed it to the detective. "Do you see what I see?"

Detective Rossi did his own study of the key. "Wax."

Cooper nodded.

She was confused. "What does that mean?"

"He pressed this key into wax so he can have a copy made." He took the key back from the detective and showed her the tiny bit of wax on the edge. "We need to change your locks, which I planned to do anyway for better ones."

She felt so violated. What she wanted to do was scream, then cry. Instead, determined not to let the fear and anger consume her, she took a deep breath. "Can we get them changed today?"

"I'll do it," Cooper said. "We just need to go buy what I need."

"Wish I'd noticed that before all three of us handled it," Rossi said. "If his fingerprints were on it, they're smeared now." He put the key back on the hook. "Guess I won't need this after all. Make sure to give me a spare to the new locks. My CSI team needs to get back in here. Until you get back from the store, I'll have a patrol officer park in your driveway."

"I appreciate that." Even with the locks changed, she didn't know if she could ever live here again. The thing that bothered her the most was the sight of her panties and bras scattered around in her bedroom. Had he taken any? She shuddered at the thought of her underwear in his hands.

"Let's take a walk around the backyard," Cooper said. "Then we can go buy some locks."

Rossi followed them outside, and the two of them trailed behind Cooper as he made a sweep of her yard. At their first meeting, the two men had been like dogs marking their territory. Growly and suspicious. Now, it appeared that they respected each other, and that the detective accepted Cooper's experience and skills.

"He stood here and watched the house," Cooper said, stopping behind a large azalea bush.

That was it. She was having all the plants taken out so there was nothing to hide behind. The area he was showing them had been mulched, and it was obvious that someone had shuffled their feet while standing on the wood chips.

Detective Rossi stepped next to Cooper and eyed the ground. "I'll have my people look at this, see if they can get a shoe size."

From there, Cooper circled the perimeter of the yard but didn't find any other evidence of the man's presence. He took her hand. "Let's go buy some new locks."

"I CAN'T GO back to my house," Kendall said. "Not today." She'd have to return to clean up the mess after the police said she could go back in, but she couldn't face it now.

Cooper glanced at her before returning his gaze to the road. "I won't leave you alone. Not even in a hotel."

She'd noticed that he'd kept an eye on his rearview mirror. "Do you think he's following us?"

"No, we're not being followed right now. I understand you not wanting to be there, but I need to know you're safe."

"I'll visit my father while you change the locks. You can drop me off there."

"He's home now?"

"Probably. He got home from his cruise yesterday. I'll call him." After talking to him and confirming he was home, she said, "He's there. I need to tell him what's going on anyway. You can meet him when you come back to get me. Turn left at the next light."

He grinned. "Meet the parent, huh?"

"And I should probably warn you. He's never liked any boy I've brought home." That wasn't true, but it was fun to tease him, and she could use some fun right now.

"So, the bar is high." He made a funny face. "Will I have to have you home by midnight when we go on a date?"

"My curfew was eleven. If I wasn't home by then, he'd come looking for me."

"For real?"

"Yep. Because of my kidnapping, my parents were overly protective. Mom more than Dad, actually. Take a right at the stop sign. It's the white house with the blue shutters in the middle of the cul-de-sac."

"Didn't you tell me that you lived in a gated community?"

"We did, but after I left home, he downsized."

"Does he live alone?"

"Yes, but his lady friend spends a lot of time here. Just drop me off. You can meet him when you come back."

"I figure about three hours by the time I go to the store, then to your house and get the locks changed."

"That's fine." When she opened the door to get out, he slipped his fingers around her arm, stopping her.

"Do me a favor and don't go anywhere else, okay?"

"I won't."

"Good. Now give me a kiss to hold me over until I see you again."

The kiss was brief, but even so, the spark was there. After she pulled away, he gave her that smile that could break hearts the world over. She traced her thumb along his bottom lip. "See you soon."

"Count on it."

She unlocked the door with her key, then glanced back and waved. Always in protection mode, he waited to leave until she was safely inside her father's house. She found her dad in the kitchen, stirring something on the stove. "What smells good?" She walked to him and gave him a kiss on the cheek.

"Chicken and dumplings."

"Yum. My favorite."

He grinned. "I know. I was about to call you, see if you and Livie wanted to come to dinner."

"You know I can't resist your dumplings. Did you have a good time on your cruise?"

"We did. You should do that someday. Alaska is pretty awesome. I'll show you pictures later."

"Is it okay if my friend joins us for dinner?"

"Friend?" He set the ladle on the paper towel he had on the counter, turned down the burner to simmer, then leaned back. "Stacy coming over?"

Stacy was another teacher she was friends with who sometimes joined them for one of her dad's meals. "No, this is a guy friend."

His brows went up. "A man?" He peered around her. "Where's Livie?"

"I have a lot to tell you. Make yourself a cup of coffee, and I'll make a cup of tea, then we'll talk."

He took two cups from a cabinet. "Sounds serious."

"You could say that." He was going to go ballistic when she told him about Livie's kidnapping, that Livie's father was back in the picture and that she had a stalker. Because he'd been gone, she hadn't told him any of that yet.

After they settled at the kitchen table, her gaze followed the steam rising from her cup. She wished she didn't have to tell him any of what had happened this week. None of it was good...well, except for Livie having her father in her life.

Before she was halfway through telling her story, a storm was brewing in his eyes, and his expression darkened with each detail she shared. She gave him credit for not interrupting her until she finished. "So, that's pretty much it."

He sat back in his chair, the silence between them thick as she waited for him to speak. "You and Livie are moving in with me," he finally said.

"No, Dad. Cooper and his friends are experienced at this kind of thing. We're safe with them...with Cooper."

"You don't know this man, Kendall. How do you know you can trust him?"

"He's Livie's father. She loves him already, and he would die for her. That I do know."

"I'll make up my own mind about that. Why isn't he here now?"

"Because he's at my house installing new locks. Actually, I wouldn't be surprised if he's also putting up cameras around the house." He hadn't said he was going to do that, but she'd bet money that he was.

"If you refuse to stay here, I'm coming to Myrtle Beach with you."

She loved her father beyond measure, but he could be stubborn and opinionated. The guys didn't need him interfering in this mess she'd found herself in, and he would want to be right in the middle of it. She also wanted time with Cooper, to see if maybe there was something between them, maybe even a future for them. With her father there, she wouldn't have that chance.

"No, Dad." At seeing the hurt in his eyes, she reached for his hand. "I understand you're worried, but we need to let The Phoenix Three do their job. This is what they do, and they're very good at it."

He sighed heavily. "And I'm supposed to just sit back and do nothing?"

"I don't know. Why don't you talk to Cooper about that? He might be open to having you help in some way." She felt kind of bad that she was handing over the job of telling her father to stay out of this, but he was more likely to listen to Cooper over her.

"He's here now," she said when the doorbell chimed. This was going to be interesting.

"Good timing." Her dad headed to the stove. "I'll plate our dinner while you get the door."

"That didn't take lo…" Her smile faltered at seeing it was a stranger at the door and not Cooper. So stupid. Why had she just assumed it was Cooper at the door? "Can I help you?" There was something about the man's eyes that raised the hair on her neck, and she tried to slam the door.

He put his foot inside, blocking her from closing it. "Hello, Kendall." He brought up his arm and pointed a gun at her. "You have two choices, my dear one. Come quietly with me right now, or I come inside and shoot your father."

It was him, Livie's kidnapper. But those eyes were ones that haunted her childhood memories, eyes she'd had nightmares about. "You," she whispered.

He smiled. "Yes, me. I wondered if you'd remember, and it pleases me that you do. So, tell me. Does your father get to live another day?" He peered around her, looking into the house. "Or not?"

Her mind wanted to shut down, go blank, crawl under the covers and hide. Her body wanted to faint. Her stomach took a sickening roll, and she thought she was going to be sick. Her seven-year-old self wanted her mommy. She remembered crying for her mother and the bad man—this bad man—laughing. She was paralyzed, unable to think, talk or move.

"Kendall?" her dad called. "Bring your man in so I can give him a hard time."

She heard the humor in her father's voice, and if she didn't do something, she'd never hear him tease her again. The thought that this evil man standing in front of her would shoot her father woke her up, freed her limbs to move.

There was no choice to be made here. She stepped outside and closed the door behind her.

Chapter Twenty-Five

Cooper's phone chimed as he finished installing the last outside camera. Kendall thought he was only replacing her locks with better ones, and he hadn't told her any different because he didn't want to argue with her when she said it wasn't necessary. Not much she could say once it was done.

He pulled his phone out, and seeing it was Grayson, he said, "Whatcha got?"

"The name of Kendall's stalker."

"Wasn't expecting that so soon. Great news. Who is he?"

"Chadwick Manning Schroder the Third."

"That's a mouthful. How'd you find him?" He gathered up his tools.

"Henderson went to each of the libraries he used to send her the emails, and using the date and times on them, he found the same man at each one. The libraries had better video than we got from the grocery store. He ran the man's picture through his facial ID program and got a hit. Schroder was arrested in California when he was nineteen on a charge of peeking while loitering. In simpler terms, he was a peeping Tom. His family's wealthy and got him a top-notch attorney. Schroder got a slap on the wrist and a warning that if he continued with the behavior, he would get jail time."

Henderson was a private eye friend of theirs based in Atlanta. "How old is Schroder now, and is he married?"

"Forty-six. Never been married."

Their profiler had gotten that much right. "And no other arrests?" He knew that many serial killers got their start as peeping Toms as a teen before escalating to their deadlier crimes.

"No, which tells us that he's been very careful since then. Where are you?"

"At Kendall's. Just finished installing new locks and outside cameras. I need to drop off a key to the detective on the case to the new locks, then I'll go pick her up at her dad's house." He locked up behind him and headed for his truck. "Where does Schroder live?"

"Atlanta. Get this. He's a juvenile court judge."

"You're kidding. How is that possible if he has a record?"

"Good question. He comes from an influential family, so I'd guess they had connections or something like that."

"I'm not liking this, Gray. He could have been using his position of authority to prey on children no one cares about."

"The thought occurred to me. Listen, I'm on my way there. Liam wants to come, too, but Quinn's due any time, and—"

"No, he needs to stay with her, and I'd rather he be close to Livie. Make sure she stays safe."

"He will. Where are you staying tonight?"

"Kendall says she can't stay in her house. It's so messed up, she couldn't even if she wanted to. She feels so violated that I don't know if she will ever be able to live there again. I booked us a hotel room."

"Understandable. Harlow said the same thing about Pressley's house."

"No surprise there considering what she went through with her ex-husband. I'm texting you the hotel info now so you can book a room. Call me when you get here."

Knowing the man's name and who he was created a sense of urgency he couldn't shake. After dropping off the key to Rossi, he went straight to Kendall's father's house. When he pulled into the driveway, an older man was standing on the steps, a puzzled look on his face.

Cooper exited the car and walked to him. "Mr. Hart?" When the man nodded, Cooper said, "I'm Cooper Devlin. Is Kendall inside?"

"That wasn't you at the door?"

"When?"

"Five minutes ago? She said it was you."

"Sir, I just got here." Every instinct, every bad vibe he'd ever had screamed at him in voices so loud he almost covered his ears. Chadwick Manning Schroder the Third had gotten to her.

He'd promised to keep her safe, and he'd failed.

"Someone came to the door. She thought it was you. I was in the kitchen plating dinner, and she went to let you in. Was it him?" The man wilted before Cooper's eyes. "He took her, didn't he?"

It was only because of his special ops training that he managed to keep it together. He pushed aside the man in love with her and brought out that man who stayed calm under enemy fire, the one who'd gone after the bad guys with single-minded focus.

"Do you have a Ring camera, Mr. Hart?"

"It's Frank, and yes, I do. Kendall made me get one."

"Good. Let's look at it." He felt as if he were separate

from himself. As if he were looking down on the soldier calmly taking the right steps, not the man hovering above who had never felt such fear in his life. What if he couldn't find her?

He followed Frank inside, to the kitchen. "Is that your phone?" he asked, pointing to the one on the island.

"No, that's Kendall's."

Damn. So much for tracking her.

"My phone's right here." Frank picked it up from the counter and brought up the camera video.

They both watched as a man rang the doorbell, then the man lifting a gun after Kendall opened the door.

"Oh, God," her father cried.

There wasn't sound, so Cooper read the man's lips as best he could before they walked out of sight of the camera. "Damn," he muttered. The camera wasn't angled toward the driveway, so he couldn't see the make of the man's car. When the video finished, he called Grayson. "He has her, Gray."

"How?"

"Came to her father's house, and she opened the door, thinking it was me. He pointed a gun at her. There wasn't any sound, but I was able to read his lips enough to understand that he threatened her father if she didn't leave with him."

"And she did what any of us would've done with that threat. She went."

"I need Schroder's address."

"I'll bring it with me."

"Give me the damn address, Gray."

"No. You need to stand down until I get there. You know it."

"We need to call the police," her father said.

Cooper shook his head. "No."

"Who's that? Her father?"

"Yeah. How fast can you get here?" It was going to kill him to wait, but his brother was right. Going in half-cocked meant mission failure nine times out of ten.

"The plane is ready to go as soon as I get there, so two hours max."

"I'll wait, but only that long." It was going to be two hours of torture. "Text me Schroder's address so I can put it in my GPS."

"Sending it to you now. I'll call Jules from the plane and have him start searching for any other properties Schroder owns or leases."

"Good." Jules was a hacker they used in extreme cases, and if there ever was one, this was it. "I'll be at the airport waiting for you." He disconnected.

"Why aren't we calling the police?" Frank asked.

"Because my partner and I are not only the best at what we do, but we're not bound by the restrictions the police have. They'll need a warrant unless they actually see Kendall in his house, which they won't. He'll have her hidden. I don't care what laws I have to break to rescue her. If she's not at the house where he lives, which she probably isn't, we have resources who my partner already has searching for any properties he owns or rents."

"But you are going to find her, right?"

"Frank, if I have to, I'll tear the town apart with my bare hands until I find her. I mean to bring my daughter's mother home." Unharmed he prayed.

"About that—"

"Yes, we need to talk about that, but right now, the priority is planning this mission." His phone pinged with an incoming text. "That's the text with Schroder's home address. I'm going out to my truck to put it in my GPS, then grab my laptop. Back in a minute. Stay by the phone in case she manages to call."

Outside, he put his hands on the roof of his truck and dropped his chin to his chest. Every mission he'd ever planned had been meticulously prepared, and during his time in the military, all but two had been successful. Not one of them had been personal. This one was, but he had to take his emotions out of it and bring back the skilled operative he once was. The cold, calculating soldier.

Kendall's life depended on him making the right decisions. Failure was not an option.

He wasn't a churchgoing man, but he believed in God. He'd always said a short prayer before each mission. Tonight, his prayer was longer. When he lifted his head, he looked up at the sky. *I'll find you, Kendall. I promise.*

Once he was back inside, he sat at the dining room table, opened his laptop and brought up several satellite images of Schroder's house and the surrounding streets. "Do you know this area?" he asked.

Frank had taken a seat next to him and leaned over to view the screen. "Sandy Springs. Yeah, it's a nice suburb of Atlanta. It's about thirty minutes from here."

Cooper's phone chimed, and he glanced at the screen. "It's my partner, Grayson." He put it on speaker. "Gray, I'm here with Frank, Kendall's father, and you're on speaker. That okay?" He wanted to include the man as much as possible. If it was his daughter, he'd insist on it.

"Sure. Hello, Frank. Listen, Jules just sent me another address for a cabin Schroder owns outside of Cleveland, Georgia. It's actually not in his name, but an LLC owns it. Jules traced the LLC back to Schroder."

"That's in the mountains," Frank said. "About an hour and a half from here."

"So, he's hiding that cabin's his. My gut says that's where he's taking her. He took Kendall only thirty minutes ago, so he'll have another hour before he gets there."

"It's a long way to go only to find she isn't there," Grayson said. "We just took off, so I expect to land in an hour and a half."

"Here's what I'm going to do. I have time to go to Schroder's Sandy Springs house before you land. If it's unoccupied, then it has to be the cabin, and we'll go there. If it is occupied, I'll come get you and we'll go back to his house."

"I'm good with that as long as you wait for me so you have backup before acting."

"Roger that." And he would as long as he didn't find Kendall in imminent danger. If he did, all bets were off. Grayson knew that because he would go in without backup if Harlow's life depended on it.

"I'm coming with you," Frank said after Cooper disconnected.

"No, you aren't." He put his hand on the older man's shoulder. "Grayson and I are highly trained operatives. You're not. Not to offend you, but you'd be in the way, one more person to worry about. Besides, you need to stay here in case she manages to escape and make it back home. She's brave and resourceful, and that's a possibility." He doubted that would happen, but Frank needed a purpose.

"You'll find her?"

"I will, and, Frank, I don't make promises I can't keep."

Frank nodded, apparently satisfied. "I'm not sure what your intentions are toward my daughter, but I think you're a good man."

"Thank you for that. I try to be." Now was not the time

to talk about his intentions, but he fully expected to be asking her father for her hand in marriage one day. Soon. Was that still a thing, asking the father for permission to marry his daughter? If not, he'd still be doing it if for no other reason than the gratitude on Frank's face.

He picked up his phone. "What's your number?" As Frank gave it to him, he entered it into his contacts, then texted Frank. "There, you have mine now. If you hear from her, call me immediately." He stood. "And whatever you have cooking on that stove smells good, so save some for me and Kendall, okay?"

"It's chicken and dumplings, her favorite."

"Been a long time since I've had that. I'll call you as soon as I have her back and safe."

"Cooper, thank you."

"No thanks necessary. I'm doing this for me as much as I am for you." He didn't tell Frank he was in love with Kendall. She needed to be the first one to hear that from him. He picked up his laptop. "I'm expecting to find Schroder's Sandy Springs house empty, which means he's taken her to his cabin, so it's going to be a few hours before you can expect to hear anything."

"I won't lie, son. Those are going to be a hard few hours."

Son. It was said with affection, something he'd never gotten from his own father. He wasn't going to let this man—his hopefully future father-in-law—down.

He'd checked them into the hotel before going to buy the locks, and he stopped there first to change into black pants and shirt. He had a gun in a secret compartment in his truck, but he took his Glock 19 from the safe in their hotel room, slipped the holster through his belt loop, then pulled the hem of his T-shirt over the Glock, hiding it. Grayson would bring additional weapons, coms and night goggles.

"Let's go hunting," he muttered as he closed his hotel room door, leaving the Do Not Disturb sign on the handle.

As he'd willed himself to do, he'd brought out his operative persona, the cold and calculating specialized soldier. So far, it had worked, but the thirty-minute drive to Schroder's house gave the man in love with Kendall too much time to think.

When had he known he was in love with her? He'd been falling for her. That he knew. But in love? He'd known it the second he'd watched Schroder pull a gun on her and the possibility of never seeing her again had stared him in the face. He couldn't lose her. Livie couldn't lose her.

No emotions, soldier. You have a job to do.

Right. The most important job of his life. He banished that man who was too afraid of losing her. He couldn't think like that. For the rest of the drive to Schroder's house, he visualized the ways the mission could go down in the same way athletes visualized winning.

The sun was setting when he arrived at his destination, and he slowly drove by the house. It was a classic red-brick two-story home befitting a judge. Well-kept lawn with heavy landscaping. That was good, easy to hide if he could get close to the house. Getting close might be a problem. This was the kind of neighborhood where the residents would be suspicious of a man dressed in all black sneaking around. He'd just have to make sure he wasn't seen. The good news, the homes here were on what he estimated to be one-acre lots, so no real close neighbors.

The house was completely dark except for a light over the front door. Cooper was positive Schroder wasn't here, but he had to confirm that. The question was, where to leave his truck? He circled the block. There was a ballpark one street over and a game was going on. He pulled into the parking lot and stopped at the back between a van and an SUV.

He sat and studied the other cars, the area around him and the people watching the game. No one was paying attention to him. The sun had set and there were lights on the field and in the parking lot, but none back where he was. He took his lock-pick kit and a penlight from his middle console.

All he could do was hope that luck was with him as he exited the truck and quietly closed the door, locking it. It took him five minutes to reach Schroder's house, and he was pretty sure he wasn't seen as he slipped behind some bushes. To be certain, he took a minute to scan the houses across the street to make sure no one was watching from a window. Satisfied he was in the clear, he made his way to the back of the house. Although it surprised him, he was thankful there weren't any motion lights.

There was a screened-in porch and the door to it wasn't latched. French doors led to the inside, and it took him two minutes to pick the lock. He had another piece of luck when there wasn't a deadbolt. And surprisingly, no alarm went off. If one had, he would have had to walk away. Inside, he shined his penlight, careful to keep it away from any windows. The man was a neat freak, the bed perfectly made, not a thing out of place. As much as he wanted to search for any evidence that would help in convicting Schroder, he didn't have the time.

Five minutes was all he gave himself before leaving, locking the French doors again. He returned to his truck and headed to the airport to pick up Grayson.

Chapter Twenty-Six

"If you open that door and try to jump out, I'll shoot you. Then I'll go back to your father's house and shoot him." The man tapped the barrel of the gun in his hand against his leg, reminding her that he had it.

Kendall dropped her hand down to her lap. They were coming up to a traffic light, and she'd hoped he wasn't paying attention. Her hope was that the light would turn red. If it did, she planned to jump out. She'd escaped from him once. She could again. She had to believe that.

"Who are you?"

"You can call me John."

That wasn't his name. She could tell by the way he smirked. Refusing to talk to him anymore, she stared out the window. Maybe she could catch the attention of someone next to them and mouth the word *Help*.

Her father would have called the police by now, so they would be looking for her. Why hadn't she given him Cooper's number? Had he returned to the house? If so, he'd know she was gone, and he wouldn't stop until he found her. She took more comfort from that than knowing the police would be searching for her.

Unfortunately, her dad hadn't seen her leave, so he

didn't know what kind of car she was in. Where were they going? How would Cooper even know where to look for her? He didn't know who this man was.

About twenty minutes after he'd taken her, he turned into a grocery store parking lot and stopped in a space next to a white van. Surely, he didn't mean to buy groceries.

"You try to get out, I'll shoot you. You try to call for help, I'll shoot you."

Would he, though? People would see him. They'd call the police. Should she try to get out and run?

"And then I'll go shoot your father."

That was the one threat that had her staying in the car when he got out. He walked around the hood, keeping his eyes on her the entire time. When he reached her side of the car, he walked past her. What was he doing? The moment she decided to look back and find out, her door opened.

"Out."

As much as she wanted out of this car, the fear of the unknown had her frozen where she sat. She had a really bad feeling about this. When she didn't move, he jerked her arm, pulling her out. Before she could get her bearings, she was shoved into the open door of the van he'd parked next to. This had to be a different one from the van he'd put Livie in since the police had that vehicle now. Did he just go around stealing white vans?

Bad things happened in the backs of nondescript white vans, and panic seized her. She fought back, tried to kick away from him, tried to bite the hands holding her down. When her teeth bit into the skin on his wrist, he slapped her.

"Damn it." He wrapped his fingers around her hand, holding it down to the floor, and she felt cold metal circle her wrist. She fought harder, and he laughed as the click of the handcuff sounded. "Just have to wipe my fingerprints from the car, and then we'll be on our way."

The van's sliding door closed, and she turned on her side. She was handcuffed to an iron hook secured to the floor. She yanked on it, but there wasn't the slightest give to the hook. How was she going to get away? And where was he taking her? Why hadn't she kept her phone in her pocket instead of leaving it at her dad's? The man hadn't searched her, so she could be calling the police…or Cooper. Wouldn't they have been able to track her phone?

The driver's door opened, and the man got behind the wheel. "Ready for your adventure, sweet Kendall?"

Adventure? By the cheerfulness in his voice, you'd think they were off to Disney World. She refused to answer him. It was dark in the back, and all she could see was a bit of the windshield over the top of the seats. Nothing but black sky. She didn't know where they were going, or what he had planned for her.

She was scared. Petrified. Had she been this afraid the first time he'd kidnapped her? She didn't think so. She'd been too young to know and understand the things an evil man could do to a young girl, but she was a woman now, and she knew. Oh, God, she knew. She hated the tears that burned her eyes and fell down her cheeks. If she was going to survive this, she had to be strong. She had to use her mind.

It seemed like he drove for hours, too long to be left with her dark thoughts. As much as she tried not to think of all the research she'd done for her podcasts, the evil she'd learned people were capable of, she couldn't stop those images from flowing through her mind like a horror movie reel.

She didn't know what he'd intended to do with her when he'd taken her years ago, and she didn't know what he intended now. If she knew, she could plan for whatever was coming. The brave part of her thought that. The frightened part preferred to stay ignorant.

When the road changed from a smooth highway to an obviously bumpy dirt road, she tensed. About five minutes later, the van stopped. Wherever he was taking her, they had arrived. How long had they traveled? Two hours, give or take. How would Cooper even find her?

He leaned around his seat. "You just be patient. I'll come back and get you soon. I need to get things ready for you."

She didn't like the sound of that. When he uncuffed her, she had to make her escape. It didn't matter that she didn't know where she was. While she waited, she thought of what she needed to do, then visualized doing it. It could work.

She guessed ten minutes passed before the side door slid open. She gave herself a pep talk while she waited for him to work the handcuff off her wrist. *You can do this. You got away from him before. You can do it again, Kendall. Be brave. Be strong.*

"I've waited a long time for you," he said as he backed out of the van.

Now! She reared up and pushed him with every bit of strength she had, which with the adrenaline rushing through her was more than normal. She felt like Superwoman when he stumbled and fell on his back. Yes!

She jumped out of the van, flew past him because hell yeah, she was Superwoman. Not bothering to try and get her bearings, she just ran straight ahead. She didn't stop, not even when he fired his gun, the bullet whistling by her ear.

"I'll shoot you in the back if you don't stop," he yelled.

Not happening. She could hear his feet pounding on the ground behind her, and he sounded too close. Ignoring the burn in her leg muscles, she ran faster. He fired the gun again. She prayed he wasn't aiming at her, that he was just trying to scare her into stopping.

Although it was dark, she could see the outline of trees a few yards ahead. If she could just get to them, she could lose him. Her heart was pounding like a racehorse, her lungs and legs burned, but she didn't stop. A few more feet and she would reach the trees. She could hide until daylight.

Just as she reached her goal, something heavy hit her from behind, and she hit the ground, hands first. Excruciating pain shot up her left wrist and arm. "Hurt," she said. Gasping for breath, she turned to see him standing over her, a triumphant sneer on his face.

"You should have never tried to run, Kendall," he said coldly, grabbing her by the hair and yanking her up. "You belong to me, remember that."

With her hair still in his fist, he dragged her toward the cabin. What would he do to her if he got her inside? She didn't want to find out. She rushed at him and fought him with everything she had, clawing at his face as she tried to bring her knee up to where she could hurt him the most.

He laughed cruelly as he sidestepped, avoiding her knee. "You're only making it more exciting for me when you fight me." His grip on her hair was unyielding and brutal, and he dragged her across the yard and into the cabin. Once inside, he let go of her hair, turned back to the door and locked it with a key.

He held up the key for her to see. "Both doors are locked with this, so you can't get out, and the windows all have bars on them." He put the key in his pocket. "You can't escape."

She stepped backward, putting distance between them. "What do you want with me?"

"Right now, I want you to go in the first bedroom on the right and put on the clothes laid out for you on the bed."

What the hell? "No."

He sighed. "You can change your clothes in private, or I'll do it for you."

Afraid he would do just that, she glanced behind her. The entrance to a hallway was between the living room and the dining room. At least, she'd be alone if she went to the bedroom. She could try to find a weapon of some kind. If she could knock him out, she could get that key in his pocket.

"I need to use the bathroom."

"There's one attached to your room."

Her room was in *her* house, not this one. She didn't want to turn her back on him, so she backed up to the hallway entrance before turning around. He watched her with an intensity that made her skin crawl. John, as he'd told her to call him, took a step as if to follow her.

"I won't change in front of you."

"Then you'd best go do it yourself. You have ten seconds before I rip off the clothes you're wearing."

She blinked. What kind of sick game was this?

Did she have a choice? Still afraid to turn her back to him, she stepped backward until she was in the room. And there wasn't a lock on the door. She pressed her forehead against the wood. Cooper had to know she was missing by now and was looking for her. She didn't know how he'd ever find her, so it was going to be up to her to escape.

She scanned the room, looking for a chair she could put

under the knob, but there wasn't one. The only furniture was a white dresser and a bed. That was it. The pink bedspread and white lacy canopy was something a young girl would love. Did he have a daughter?

She walked to the bed, and when she saw what she was supposed to put on, her stomach somersaulted, and she swallowed hard. The pink dress with ruffles was something she would have worn as a seven-year-old, except it was in adult size. Next to the dress was a pair of Mary Jane shoes and white socks with a row of lace. He was trying to make her a little girl again. She couldn't put these clothes on.

The dress mocked her, a cruel reminder of a day she'd had nightmares about for years. Her hands shook as she reached for it, the fabric feeling like lead in her grasp. She threw the dress and shoes across the room.

"So creepy." She walked to the bathroom. That door didn't have a lock on it either. She closed it anyway, did her business and, after washing her hands, she splashed water on her face. Back in the bedroom, she stared at the dress on the floor. What would happen if she refused to put it on? Did he mean it when he'd said he would do it if she didn't?

The idea of him undressing her was motivation enough to do it herself. When she unbuttoned her jeans, pain shot from her wrist up her arm. She held her hand out. Her wrist was swollen but she could move her hand around, so it wasn't broken. Using only her good hand, she managed to change into the dress and Mary Janes.

In no hurry to leave the room, she sat on the edge of the bed. She was both terrified and creeped out. So many questions. Why had he come back for her after all these years? Why did he make her dress up like a little girl?

What did he plan to do with her? Was he the man who'd taken Livie? He had to be.

The knock on the door startled her, and she yelped. When she didn't answer, he opened the door. His gaze raked over her, and he smiled. His creepy smile and the weird glint in his eyes made her skin crawl. One thing she knew, he wasn't right in the head.

She wanted to pull the cover from the bed and wrap herself in it, but she stood, trying to maintain some semblance of composure despite the fear coursing through her veins. "Why am I here? What do you want with me?"

"You're here because you belong to me," he said, his voice dripping with malice. "And as for what I want with you… Well, let's just say I have big plans for you."

She clenched her fists, trying to muster up some courage. "I don't belong to you. You can't just take someone and claim them as your own."

His laughter filled the room, echoing off the walls. "Oh, but my dear, I can. And I have."

Chapter Twenty-Seven

Cooper called Harlow's cell phone while he waited for Grayson's plane to land. He needed to talk to Livie. "Hey, Princess," he said when Harlow gave her the phone.

"Daddy! Did you come home?"

"No, not yet. Your mommy and I still have some things to do in Decatur before we can come back." He loved that she thought of Myrtle Beach as home.

"But I miss you, and I want to play baseball with you."

"And we will. I'll be home in a few days."

"How many days is a few?"

Talking to young children was tricky. He didn't want to commit to how many because he didn't know. It depended on what happened in the next few hours. "Uh, no more than a week."

"A week is a long time, Daddy."

"I said no more than that, but I'm hoping it's sooner because I miss you."

"Okay. I miss you, too. Can I talk to Mommy?"

She would ask that. "Mommy's not here right now, but I'll tell her to call you as soon as she can."

"Where is she?"

"At the grocery store." He hated lying to his daughter, but he didn't have a choice. "I have to go, Princess. I love you."

"I love you, too, Daddy. Sooooo much."

"Let me talk to Harlow now."

"Okay."

"Hey," Harlow said, coming on the line. "Has Grayson landed yet?"

"Should be any minute now. Is Livie behaving herself?"

"She's a sweetheart, Cooper. I love having her here, and she and Tyler get along famously."

"Good. I just wanted to say thank you for keeping her. Knowing she's safe with you in Myrtle Beach is a great weight off my mind."

"Don't you worry about her. Just go find her mommy and bring her home."

"That's the plan. We'll let you know as soon as we have her back."

A Gulfstream landed as he disconnected, and he walked out of the FBO's lobby to wait for Grayson. As soon as Grayson exited the plane, they got in Cooper's truck. He already had the address to Schroder's cabin in his GPS, and according to the GPS, they had an hour-and-a-half drive. They were already two hours behind, and he didn't let himself think of what Kendall might be going through. If he went there, his emotions would distract him, and that wouldn't help her.

"I have some more intel," Grayson said.

"Let's hear it."

"Schroder took a leave of absence. Claimed a family emergency."

"Which put him in the wind, with no one wondering why he's not showing up for work."

"Exactly. There's more, and this part might explain his

actions. I don't know, but it's disturbing. Schroder had a sister who died under mysterious circumstances thirty years ago. There was an investigation, but nothing could be proved, so her death was listed as undetermined."

"Was there a report? Anything that hinted at what happened?"

"Both the father and the son were suspects. They alibied each other. The detective on the case is retired, but I was able to talk to him on my way here. He said the family was extremely wealthy, but they were strange. The mother seemed afraid of her husband, and the boy, young Schroder, gave him the creeps. As for the father, his word was the law in the family.

"He talked to the neighbors on the street, and they said the family was odd. It was only Schroder and his sister, and they were rarely seen. They didn't play outside like the other kids in the neighborhood, and they were homeschooled."

"Is there anything in Schroder's background that might be suspicious in hindsight?"

"Just the detective's instincts that said something was hinky about the whole family. That was the exact word he used...*hinky*. Back then, DNA was only starting to be used, but he said his small police department didn't have the knowledge or funds for it. In the end, he didn't have enough proof to make an arrest."

"But he believes it was either the father or the son who killed the girl? How old was she?"

"Seven. He says he's positive it was one of the two. That this case has haunted him for thirty years."

"You said Schroder's forty-six now, so he would've been sixteen at the time. Plenty old enough to commit a murder. Are the father and mother still alive?"

"No, they died in a house fire two years after Lisa, that's the daughter's name, was killed."

"Like that's not suspicious."

"There was an arson investigation, but in the end, it was reported as an electrical fire. The arson investigator did write in the report that it was possible the wires had been tampered with, but he couldn't say for certain."

"Schroder would've turned eighteen by then. Did he wait until he was legally an adult and didn't have to worry about Child Services to do it?"

"If he did do it that would make sense." Grayson's phone chimed. "It's Jules. Hey, Jules, I'm with Coop and putting you on speaker."

"Got yourself in the middle of a strange one," Jules said.

Cooper couldn't disagree. "You have more intel for us?"

"Yeah. I have to say this is turning out to be a fascinating story, and I'm hooked, so I did some more digging. It turned up a former girlfriend of Schroder's and I called her. They dated in college, and she said he was fun at first. After a while, though, she said he started getting weird."

"In what way?" Cooper asked.

"Talking about angels. He'd see a little girl and say what a pretty angel she would be. She said he also talked about his sister a lot, that she was an angel now and wasn't suffering anymore, that she never cried anymore. She said he started weirding her out and she stopped seeing him."

All of this was really disturbing. "I have a bad feeling about this whole thing and why he wanted Kendall."

"Yeah, same here," Grayson said. "We're dealing with a mentally disturbed man. Thanks, Jules. We appreciate your digging deeper on this."

"It's like a bad B movie, the kind you can't stop watching even if it is awful. I'll call if I learn any more. Go find your girl, Coop."

"That's the plan."

A chilling picture of Schroder's past and potential motives painted a disturbing image of a man teetering on the edge of sanity. And he had Kendall. "Something's been nagging at me. I think it's possible that this is the man who kidnapped Kendall when she was seven."

Grayson darted a glance at Cooper. "Kendall was kidnapped?"

"Yeah, right out of her front yard. She managed to get away and found help. The man who did it was never caught. I don't know. That was over twenty years ago. Maybe it wasn't him, but I can't get the possibility out of my mind."

"It would make sense as to why he's fixated on her."

"What I keep thinking." Cooper had the sense that time was running out. He glanced at the GPS. They still had thirty-five minutes to go. He was already fifteen miles per hour over the speed limit and didn't want to press his luck by going any faster. The last thing they needed was to get stopped considering all the weapons they had on them and in the truck.

"When I left, Tyler was teaching Livie a bunch of jokes to tell you when you get back home," Grayson said.

"Probably all the ones I taught Tyler." Cooper knew his friend was trying to distract him from worrying about Kendall. It wasn't going to work, but he'd play along.

"I'm sure, but you'll have to pretend you've never heard them."

"Of course. I'd never want to disappoint Livie."

There were a few minutes of silence, then, "You want to keep them. Am I right?"

"You are. I'm going to be in my daughter's life, but just how is the big question. It depends on Kendall. I'm hoping she'll be willing to move to Myrtle Beach."

"And if she's not?"

"I don't know. I'll cross that bridge when I come to it."

"She has feelings for you. That's obvious from the way she looks at you."

"I want to believe she does." But enough to upend the life she'd built and move to Myrtle Beach? And if she wasn't willing to move, would he give up everything he'd worked for since he and his brothers had created The Phoenix Three? Because he couldn't imagine not having Kendall and Livie in his life on a daily basis.

Chapter Twenty-Eight

"Why, John? Why did you kidnap me when I was a child? Why do it again?"

His brows scrunched together. "Why are you calling me John?"

"You said that was your name."

"No, I didn't. Why are you messing with my head?" He slammed his hand against the wall, causing her to jump. "Stop it. I know what you're trying to do, and I won't fall for your tricks again."

The man was seriously unhinged. "What should I call you?"

"My name."

"I'm sorry, but I think I've forgotten it."

"It's Chad."

"Chad. That's a nice name." Maybe if she humored him, she could make him think she wouldn't try to escape. "Why did you kidnap me when I was a child?"

"I was going to send you to my sister. Lisa's an angel in heaven and I wanted her to have a friend."

He'd intended to kill a little girl...her? "And now?"

"I think I'll keep you for myself."

"You can't just decide to keep someone." She understood now his talk about angels in the emails he'd sent her. She almost asked what happened to his sister but thought better of it. It might set him off. Not that he wasn't already scaring her, but if his sister's death was a violent one, who knew how he'd react being asked about it.

His expression turned mulish. "You're mine, and I can keep what's mine."

There was one thing she wanted to know, and also, if she kept him talking, it would give Cooper more time to find her. "How did you find me again?"

"Funny story that. It was by chance. I've been a fan of your podcasts almost from the beginning. There was something about you that drew me in. Then I got to thinking about the name you used, Kendra Hartley. That was too close to your real name to be a coincidence, so I did some investigating."

Why hadn't she used a name that was nothing like hers?

"I came back to get you after you escaped, but your family had moved away, and there wasn't a forwarding address."

Yes, her parents had feared he might come back for her. A week after her kidnapping, they'd moved into a gated community where it felt safer. Now, she thanked her parents for their foresight.

"I made you dinner." He turned and walked out of the room.

She stood where he left her, indecision warring within her. Should she play along with his delusions, maybe find an opportunity to steal the key from him, or should she refuse to do anything he said? She certainly didn't want to sit down and have dinner with him, but what would he do if she refused?

Before she could decide, he appeared in the doorway.

"Don't try my patience, Kendall. I can treat you like a queen, or I can keep you caged like an animal. It's your choice."

Would he actually put her in a cage or was that just a figure of speech? She didn't want to know. She had to be smart about this and make him believe she wanted to be here in the hope that it would buy her the time Cooper needed to find her. Or until she could get her hands on that key.

"Which will it be?"

"I am hungry, so I'll come eat." She wasn't sure she could eat anything, but she followed him to the dining room. The table was set with two plates across from each other, and on the plates were mac and cheese and... Was that Vienna sausages?

He pulled out a chair. "I'm not much of a cook, but this will do for tonight."

Once they were seated, he forked a sausage and put it in his mouth. She hated Vienna sausages, so she ate a little of the mac and cheese. While his attention was on his food, she studied him. He was an average-looking man. Brown hair, brown eyes, slender in build, and medium height. If she passed him on a sidewalk, she wouldn't pay any attention to him.

It was his eyes that disturbed her. There was a darkness in them, a hint of madness. What was the best way to deal with a man who she was coming to believe was mentally ill? Try to humor him, to make him think she was agreeable to being here with him? That felt like the best option. Until she could get that key from him, anyway.

"I can be a generous man when I want to be," he said, breaking the silence. "But you must understand that disobedience will not be tolerated." He set his fork down.

"Lisa didn't learn to be obedient. She was always testing father. Then one day she pushed him too far, and he taught her a lesson."

"Lisa was your sister?"

"Yes."

"What happened to her?" she asked, but she didn't think she wanted to know.

"She was bad again and made father angry. He hurt her, and she cried. She wouldn't stop crying, and when she begged me to make it stop hurting, I did."

"How did you make the hurt stop?"

"I put my hand over her mouth and nose until she stopped breathing. I made her an angel and sent her to a beautiful place where she wouldn't hurt anymore."

She barely managed not to gasp. Dear God. He'd killed his sister.

He massaged his forehead. "Stop making me talk about this."

While he had his eyes closed as he rubbed at his head, she eased her fork off the table and slipped it down the front of her dress. It wasn't much of a weapon, but it was something she could use to fight back if he tried to hurt her.

"I need to think," he muttered, more to himself than to her.

She reached over and picked up his plate, putting it on top of hers so he couldn't see that she hadn't eaten any of the food. "Why don't you go sit in the living room and think while I clean up?" Maybe there was a knife in the kitchen she could hide on her. She grabbed his fork, setting it on top of his plate, then picked up the dishes as she stood.

"Leave them." He pulled the plates from her hands and dropped them onto the table. "Come in the living room with me."

She breathed a sigh of relief that he didn't notice there was a fork missing. Unfortunately, she wouldn't be able to look for a knife. He gestured for her to go first. She didn't like having him behind her, but she walked ahead of him. In the living room, she perched on the edge of an upholstered chair, and he dropped onto the sofa. She clasped her hands in her lap and waited.

The fear she was trying to keep at bay threatened to consume her as she sat there, waiting for him to speak. Her dread intensified with each ominous tick of the clock on the wall until it took everything in her power not to snatch that clock down and smash it to pieces.

His head bobbed, and she wondered if he was falling asleep. If he did, she could sneak the key out of his pocket and make her escape. While she waited for him to say something, she thought about what he'd revealed.

It sounded like his father had physically punished Lisa. She had the impression it hadn't been the first time he'd done so. Had he hurt her so badly that she'd begged her brother to end her life, or had she just wanted him to do something to make her feel better? If it had happened as he'd said, Kendall thought Lisa was only asking for relief. Maybe an aspirin or something like that.

"I'm glad you escaped so I could find you again. Now I can keep you for me and not give you to Lisa."

Because it had been so quiet for a good ten minutes, she startled when he spoke. He reached into his pocket, pulled out the key and turned it over and over. That was her freedom, and her gaze locked on that silver piece of metal, mocking her with how close it was, yet out of reach.

Even if she managed to get it from him, she wouldn't be able to get the door unlocked before he tackled her. Unless… If she stabbed him in the eye with her hidden fork, would it wound him enough to give her time to escape?

It was so tempting to at least try, but if she failed, he would have her only weapon. And she didn't even want to think about how he would punish her for that. She needed to be patient, take him by surprise when he least expected it. She yawned widely. "I'm really tired. I'd like to go to my room."

After one last twirl of the key, he dropped it back into his pocket. "I'll give you tonight, but it's the last time you'll sleep alone."

Time was running out. She had tonight to think of a way to get the key. Without waiting for permission to leave, she stood and headed for *her* room. She closed the door, not happy that it didn't have a lock.

A shower would be great, but she wasn't about to get naked and risk his coming into the room. And these clothes he'd made her change into had to go. She quickly took off the dress and put the jeans and T-shirt she'd arrived in back on. The fork she'd stolen went under the pillow, where she could easily reach it if needed.

She did get in the bed since there wasn't a chair she could curl up in, but no way was she going to go to sleep when the door didn't lock. She lay there, listening for any noise outside the door. When she heard footsteps in the hallway, she reached under the pillow and grasped the fork. He stopped outside the door, and she slipped her hand holding the fork under the covers.

The door swung open, and he stood in the doorway, his silhouette outlined by the dim light filtering in from the hallway. For a long time after she was kidnapped, she had nightmares about a monster coming into her room to get her. Now, the nightmare was real.

"Where is it?" he said.

He meant the fork. "Where's what?" She hated the quaver in her voice. He must have cleaned up the dinner dishes and realized one of the forks was missing.

"Don't try to play games with me, Kendall. You'll lose." He came next to the bed and held his hand out. "Give it to me."

"I don't know what you want. Give you what?" She tightened her grip on the fork.

Suddenly, he reached for the cover and pulled it away from her. She didn't have time to think. It was now or never. Fueled by adrenaline and fear, she rolled over so she could push herself up, and because she was standing on the bed and taller than him, she slashed the fork down to his face with all her might. The tongs embedded into his cheek, and as he screamed, she did her best to tear open his cheek.

"Fucking bitch," he shouted.

When he tried to take the fork from her, she let go of it, reached into the pocket she'd seen him put the key in and wrapped her fingers around it. He pulled the fork away from his face, tossed it across the room and then pulled her off the bed.

"You'll pay for that," he said.

Afraid she'd drop the key, she stuffed it into her jeans pocket. She didn't think he knew she'd taken it. She hoped he didn't. He grasped her arm, his fingers so tight, she was going to be bruised. Small price to pay for getting the key.

"Let go of me." She tried to pull away from him, but he dug his fingers into her skin. Wherever he was taking her, she didn't want to go. She jerked her arm, managing to get away from him. If she tried to use the key right now, he would get it away from her, so she ran for the kitchen, hoping to find a knife.

Before she could get to her goal, he tackled her from behind, taking them both to the floor. With his weight on her back, she struggled to breathe, but she refused to give up without a fight. She reared her head back as hard as she could, and when she heard bone crunch, she gave a grunt of satisfaction.

He wrapped his hands around her throat and squeezed. "I'm going to kill you."

Oh, God. He really was, she thought as she tried and failed to suck air into her lungs. As her vision faded to black, she murmured one last word. "Livie."

Chapter Twenty-Nine

"This is it," Cooper said as they turned onto a dirt lane. He pulled the truck off the road as far into the trees as he could. To have the element of surprise on their side, they would walk in.

After they exited the truck, Grayson grabbed the duffel bag he'd brought and went to the back. He opened the tailgate, set the bag on it and opened it up. They loaded their bodies up with weapons. Guns, knives, smoke bombs and flash grenades. Probably overkill, but better to be prepared for anything over not being prepared for the unexpected. Then they each put on a Kevlar vest and coms.

They set off into the trees, moving silently as they approached the house...actually a good-size log cabin. Lights were on inside, and they eased up to a window. Cooper peeked around the side of the sill. His blood turned to ice at what he saw. Kendall was face down on the floor, not moving. Schroder was pacing around the room with a gun in his hand and seemed to be muttering to himself.

"She better be alive, or he's a dead man," he said. They didn't have time to make a plan. "I'm taking the front. You come in through the back."

Grayson nodded, and they split up. Cooper eased onto

the deck, and when he reached the door, he tried the knob. "This one's locked," he whispered.

"Back here, too," Grayson responded.

They both had lock-pick kits and within minutes the two doors were unlocked. "I'm going to go in, gun drawn," he told Grayson. "With his attention on me, you ease in behind him. We go on my one."

"Roger."

Cooper took his Glock from its holster. "Three, two, one!" He eased the door open and stepped inside with his gun raised. Schroder's attention was on Kendall, and he was still muttering. Cooper couldn't make out the words, but he didn't have a good feeling about the man. Schroder was losing it, and it was never a good thing when a man's mind was twisted. There was no predicting how he might react.

Suddenly, Schroder pointed the gun at Kendall, still unmoving on the floor. "I wasn't going to make you an angel, but you had to go and be a bad girl."

Cooper didn't want to kill the man, but he would to protect Kendall. He hesitated because if he shot Schroder, there was a risk the man's finger would jerk on the trigger of the gun he was pointing at her. He needed to get the man to point the gun at him, then if he had to kill Schroder, he would.

Schroder suddenly stopped muttering and turned his gaze toward Cooper. His eyes widened, and a flicker of recognition passed over his face before being replaced by a look of pure malice. "You! I saw you with her, but you can't have her. She's mine."

"I just want to talk to you." He glanced at Kendall, his relief immense when he saw her back rise and fall. She was breathing! Grayson was sneaking up behind Schroder, and to keep the man's attention on him and not what was happening behind him, Cooper said, "Put the gun down on the floor, Mr. Schroder, and you can walk out of the house right now." Cooper felt no guilt for the lie.

With his weapon still pointed at Kendall, Schroder looked from him to her, then back to him. "I don't think so. I kill her. You kill me. Then Kendall and I will be angels together in heaven. Perfect ending to this story."

The man actually believed that and his intention to die today with Kendall was there in the madness shining in his eyes. "You don't want to do this," he said, hoping to keep Schroder's attention on him and not on Grayson, who was sneaking up behind him. "Just put the gun down on the floor and let's talk about how you can walk away from this."

A floorboard creaked when Grayson was only a few steps from Schroder. Cooper would never know if Schroder meant to fire the gun or if it was a trigger reaction to the noise behind him.

The gunshot echoed through the cabin, its sound deafening in the quiet room. Kendall's body jerked as the bullet hit her. A second gunshot sounded from Cooper's weapon, and Schroder's eyes widened in surprise as he crumbled to the floor.

Cooper kneeled next to Kendall and set his gun on the floor. She was bleeding from her left shoulder. Not a kill shot, but she wasn't moving. He gently turned her over, and when he saw the bruises and fingerprints on her neck, he almost picked up his gun to kill Schroder all over again.

"He's dead," Grayson said from Schroder's side.

"Good." There wasn't an exit wound, so the bullet was still inside her. "We need to get her to the hospital. We're too far out to wait for an ambulance." How he was even speaking coherently, he didn't know. There was a blood-red rage inside him at seeing what had been done to her.

"He's not going anywhere, so we can leave him here for now," Grayson said. "Let's go. Give me your keys."

Cooper dug his truck keys from his pocket and handed them over, then he scooped Kendall up. He followed Grayson to the truck, got in the back and held her across his lap. "There's a small first aid kit in the console. I need something to press over the wound to stop the bleeding." It was only because of his years of military training that he was able to stay calm. Going ballistic—which was appealing right now—wouldn't help her.

Grayson handed over a pack of gauze. "Here."

He tore the package open with his teeth, then pressed several squares over the wound. "Kendall, open your eyes. Please, baby."

"Okay, I've got the closest hospital on the GPS. It's twenty-five minutes from here."

"Make it in fifteen."

He kept talking to her while Grayson sped them to the hospital. He also half listened to Grayson's conversation with their FBI friend Sean Danvers. Grayson gave Sean a rundown of the events leading up to Schroder's death, then asked him to contact the local police.

"He's going to notify the police and send one of his agents out of the Atlanta office up here," Grayson said after disconnecting. "We'll have to give statements. Kendall will, too, when she's able."

"Whatever. All I care about right now is getting her to the hospital." He lifted the gauze. The wound was still bleeding but not as heavy as it had been. "Kendall. Open your eyes."

She moaned, and her eyelids fluttered but didn't open.

How long had she been deprived of oxygen? He tried not to think of the damage that might have been done to her brain. She was going to be okay. She had to be.

"I don't know why she won't wake up. It's obvious he tried to strangle her from the marks on her neck, but she should be conscious by now." That she wasn't scared the hell out of him. "Kendall. Wake up." He put command in his voice, hoping that would bring her around, but there was no reaction. "Baby, open your eyes for me." He trailed his fingers over her face.

"No," she cried. "No!"

She sounded like someone with an awful cold. Had Schroder damaged her voice box? Suddenly, she was fighting him like an enraged cat, all teeth and claws. The only thing he knew to do was hug her to his body to keep her from hurting herself.

"Hey, hey. You're safe now, Kendall. You're safe."

"I think she's afraid to wake up," Grayson said. "She doesn't realize it's you holding her."

She quieted, sinking back down into whatever black hole she was hiding in. He stopped trying to wake her up. If she thought she was safe wherever she'd taken herself, he would let her stay there until they could get to the hospital and doctors.

"Do you think the hospital here has doctors who know how to deal with this?" he said. "Maybe we should arrange a medical flight to an Atlanta hospital."

"Let's get her to the hospital here, then decide if we need to do that. We'll be there in three minutes."

He also needed to call her father, but he'd wait to do that after they learned what they were dealing with. He didn't think the shoulder wound was life-threatening or would even cause long-term damage. The location where the bullet had entered wasn't where it would have hit any vital organs. They'd have to get the bullet out, and maybe she'd need some physical therapy, but it was the possible brain damage from being choked and her mental state that had him worried.

"We're here." Grayson stopped the truck at the emergency entrance and jumped out. He opened the back door. "Let me take her until you get out."

"I've got her." Refusing to let go of her, he slid out of the truck.

"Okay. I'm going to park the truck, then come in."

Cooper nodded. The door slid open as he approached, and he ran up to the desk. "I need a doctor. Now!"

The woman took one look at Kendall before picking up the phone. "Code Blue. Code Blue. Front Desk."

A man and a woman appeared, pushing a gurney between them. "Are one of you a doctor?" he asked as he eased Kendall onto it.

"I am," the woman said. "Dr. Hasting. What happened to her?"

"She was strangled and shot in the shoulder. She's been unconscious since I found her."

"You'll have to wait out here, Mr...."

"Devlin. Cooper Devlin. Please help her."

"We will."

He watched helplessly as they rushed her away. When he couldn't see her anymore, he closed his eyes and prayed. A hand landed on his shoulder, and he glanced at Grayson. "I need to call her father." It was a phone call he dreaded. "I promised her I'd keep her safe, and I didn't."

"Stop that right now. Only one man is to blame and he's dead."

"I wish he wasn't so I could kill him again."

"And I'd help you. I'll go get us some coffee while you call her father."

He walked outside to make the call.

"Hello," her father said. "Is this Cooper?"

"Yes. We found her."

"Is she all right?"

"No. She's unconscious. He tried to strangle her and then he shot her in the shoulder. She's in the emergency room with the doctor. They'll probably take her to surgery to remove the bullet."

"I'm coming there. What hospital?"

"Why don't you wait awhile? This is a small hospital, and I'm probably going to arrange a medevac flight to take her to Atlanta where we can get her specialized care." Someone who understood trauma and probably PTSD. He had a sinking feeling she was suffering from the disorder.

"I want to be with my daughter."

He inwardly sighed. "I know you do, Frank, and you should be, but you could be halfway here while we're flying her to Atlanta. I'll keep you updated as soon as the doctor here tells me something. I'm not leaving her side, okay?"

"I shouldn't have let her answer the door knowing he was after her."

He got Frank's guilt more than the man could imagine. He shouldn't have left her unprotected, even though he'd thought she'd be safe at her father's. "You couldn't know he'd be brazen enough to come to your door. This is on him, not you." Easy words for him to say to someone else because protecting her had been his job.

"I'll wait, but not too long," Frank said. "Call me as soon as you know something."

Cooper promised he would. After disconnecting, he

went back inside. "He wanted to come here now, but I talked him into waiting until we know if we're going to move her to Atlanta."

Grayson handed him a cup of coffee. "In his place, I'd want to be with my daughter, too, but it's best he waits until we know something." He glanced over Cooper's shoulder. "Is that the doctor?"

"Yes." He hurried to Dr. Hasting. "How is she?"

Chapter Thirty

"She's waking up," a male voice said.

Oh, God, he was here. He was going to kill her. Kendall tried to scream, but her throat wasn't working. She tried to get away, but he held her down.

"We need to calm her down."

That was a woman's voice. Had he kidnapped another woman?

"Give her five milligrams of haloperidol," the man said.

"Easy, Kendall. You're safe."

No, she wasn't safe. She never would be. Something pricked her arm. He was poisoning her. She reached for that black box where he couldn't find her. She would be safe there. The darkness settled over her, and she breathed a sigh of relief that she was invisible now.

SOMETHING WARM HAD her hand. That bothered her. What was it? Where was she? Her eyes fluttered open, and she blinked rapidly against the light. She tried to move, but her limbs felt heavy, as if they were weighed down by invisible chains. Panic rose in her chest as she realized he had her hand. She tried to pull away, but his grip tightened.

"Please, let me go." She'd said that, but that wasn't her voice.

"Kendall, hey, baby."

She knew that voice. As her vision cleared, she realized she was in a hospital room. The antiseptic smell assaulted her senses, and the steady beeping of the heart monitor echoed in her ears. She turned her head slightly and saw Cooper sitting in a chair beside her bed.

"There she is," he said. He reached across her and pushed a button. "The doctor will be here in a minute. How do you feel?"

"I... Why do I sound funny?" And why did her throat hurt when she talked?

"Let's wait until the doctor sees you, and then I'll answer all your questions."

A nurse came in, took one look at her and smiled. "I see you're back with us. I'm Corina. Dr. Andrews will be here in a minute. While we're waiting, I'll get some vitals."

While the nurse took her blood pressure, Kendall kept her eyes on Cooper. If he was here, she was safe. "He came back." She knew he would keep coming for her. Tears filled her eyes. "He'll come back again."

Cooper shook his head. "He's never coming back. I promise. It's over, Kendall."

He'd promised he wouldn't let the man hurt her, and yet, he had. Chad, she remembered the man saying. Cooper didn't understand. It would never be over. She could hide, but he'd always find her.

"Why do I sound funny?" she asked again. "Tell me now."

He glanced at the nurse before looking back at her. "Your voice box was damaged. It's just temporary. You'll sound like yourself soon."

That puzzled her. She tried to remember how she'd damaged her voice box, but it hurt to think, so she decided she didn't care.

"I hear our girl is awake," a man said, coming next to her bed. "Glad to see you back with us, Kendall. I'm Dr. Andrews. Let's take a look at that wound."

What wound? When he reached for the edge of the hospital gown, she pushed his hand away. "Don't touch me." Her eyes darted around the room. "Where am I?"

"You're in the hospital in Atlanta," Cooper said. "You were shot in the shoulder, Kens. Dr. Andrews just needs to make sure everything looks okay. He's not going to hurt you."

She was shot? How did she not know that? She was in Atlanta? How did she get here? Livie! How could she have forgotten about her daughter? "Where's Livie?"

Cooper took her hand again. "She's at Grayson's house. She's safe and having fun with Tyler and Ruby. Let Dr. Andrews take a look at the wound, okay?"

"Okay," she whispered even though she didn't want anyone touching her. When the doctor folded over her gown, she closed her eyes. The temptation to go back to that dark place where he couldn't find her was impossible to resist and she let the blackness take her.

"I THINK WE'RE going to find that she's suffering from an extreme case of PTSD," a woman said, her voice penetrating her hiding spot.

Whom were they talking about?

"Physically, she's in good shape. The shoulder wound is healing nicely, and there's not any permanent damage to her voice box."

That was the doctor. Dr. Andrews, she thought he said. Were they talking about her?

"It's been three days. If she's fine physically, why isn't she waking up?"

She knew that voice. Her father was here.

"Because she doesn't want to," the woman said.

"She's been through an extremely traumatic experience. I've seen PTSD firsthand with soldiers I served with, and I think Dr. Croft is probably right. Right now, Kendall feels it's safer to hide."

That was Cooper. If her father and Cooper were here, she was safe. She could leave this dark place. They wouldn't let the monster take her.

"So, what do we do to help her?" her father said.

She needed to tell him it was the same man who'd taken her when she was a little girl. That was important for him to know. She strained to push through the fog that clouded her mind.

"She's trying to wake up."

That was Cooper. His strong, warm hand wrapped around hers. She forced her eyes to open, and they instantly found his.

"Welcome back," he said.

"It was him."

He squeezed her hand. "We know."

"No, you don't understand. It was the same man. The one who took me when I was little." She told them what they needed to know, and now she wanted to go back to that place where her mind was able to go blank. She closed her eyes.

"Kendall, open your eyes," Cooper said, command in his voice that she wasn't able to ignore.

"What?" She was irritated that he wouldn't let her go back to her safe place.

"I need you to stay with us. You're safe."

"No, I'm not. He's going to come back."

"He's dead. He'll never come back."

Was he just saying that? She searched his eyes for the truth. "Is he really?"

"Yes. He'll never hurt you again."

She'd never wished anyone dead before, but she hoped he was burning in hell. She turned to her father. "It was him."

"The man who took you as a child?" Cooper said, bringing her attention back to him. "You said that earlier. Are you sure?"

"Yes. He admitted it." Her gaze scanned the people around her bed. She knew her father, Cooper, and she remembered Dr. Andrews, but she had never seen the woman before. "Who are you?"

"Dr. Croft," the older woman with kind eyes said. "I'm a psychologist. I thought we might spend a little time together this afternoon. Would that be all right with you, Kendall?"

"Why?"

"You've been through quite an ordeal, one that would be difficult for anyone to deal with. Sometimes it helps to talk to someone about it."

"I want to go home."

"Let's give it one more day," Dr. Andrews said. "I'll make you a deal. You talk to Dr. Croft this afternoon, and I'll let you go home tomorrow."

She shrugged. "Fine." She didn't want to talk to anyone, but if that was what it took to go home, she'd do it.

Dr. Andrews touched her hand. "I'll be back this evening to check on you, but you're doing good, Kendall." He nodded at the others in the room before leaving.

"I have another appointment, but I'll return at three and

we'll talk," Dr. Croft said. "Would you like anything special? Coffee or tea, maybe?"

"No, thank you."

After she left, Kendall closed her eyes and refused to open them even though both Cooper and her father tried to get her to talk to them. She just wanted everyone to go away.

Chapter Thirty-One

Cooper didn't know what to do. Kendall was home, staying with her father, but she was not okay. Her father was as worried about her as he was. It had been four days since they'd brought her home from the hospital, and she spent most of her time in her childhood room. At meals, she picked at her food, barely eating enough to survive. Most disturbing, except for that one time at the hospital, she hadn't asked about Livie. It was time to change things up.

"I want to take her to Myrtle Beach," he told Frank.

Her father glanced down the hallway at the closed door Kendall was hiding behind. "Maybe she just needs a little more time."

"Every day, she looks worse and eats less. If that keeps up, we'll have to hospitalize her. That's the last thing I want to do." Over the past four days, he'd gotten to know the man, and liked him a lot. He was the kind of father Cooper wished he'd had. "I talked to Dr. Croft this morning, and she agrees that a change might do Kendall good. She gave me a name of someone in Myrtle Beach Kendall can talk to."

"What if she doesn't want to go?"

"I'm not going to give her a choice, Frank."

The man's troubled eyes met his. "What gives you the right to make decisions for her? I'm her father. That right should be mine."

"I'm not trying to take away any rights you have as her father, but I've had friends, soldiers I served with, who had PTSD. I have some experience with the syndrome, and one thing I learned is that sometimes a little push in the right direction can make all the difference. Closing herself up in that room every day isn't helping her."

Frank sighed heavily. "I just want her to be okay again. I miss seeing her smile, hearing her laugh."

He placed a hand on Frank's shoulder. "She'll smile again. She just needs a reason to."

"Maybe I should come with you."

"I think for a few days, she needs to..." How did he put this without hurting the man's feelings? "For a few days, she just needs to focus on herself. Maybe sit on the beach, feel the sun on her face, watch Livie play. Why don't you plan on coming up next week?"

Frank looked at him as if trying to see into his mind. "Maybe I will. You'll take good care of my girl?"

"I will. I care for her very much, and I want to see her laugh again as much as you do."

"Are you going to take Livie away from her?"

"Never. That's a promise." He did want to keep them with him in Myrtle Beach, but until Kendall agreed to that, he'd keep that to himself.

"Maybe she does need to get away. What if she refuses to go?"

"She won't." He wasn't going to let her refuse. "I'll go talk to her now."

"I guess you mean to leave today?"

"Yes." He walked down the hallway to her door. He

knocked, and not receiving a response, he shrugged as he opened the door and went in. She was sitting by the window, staring blankly at the world outside.

He kneeled next to her. "Hey. I want to talk to you about something."

"I don't feel like talking," she said, not looking at him.

"You don't have to. I'll do the talking. We're driving back to Myrtle Beach today." She didn't respond. "Livie misses you."

"She needs to come home."

"No, she's happy there, so we're going to her." He thought she didn't really care whether Livie came home or not, and that concerned him more than anything. Livie meant everything to her, and this apathy was a clear sign of PTSD. He stood and got her suitcase out of the closet. She ignored him as he packed her things. If he had to pick her up and carry her to his truck, he would.

After he loaded her suitcase in his truck, he returned to her room. "Time to go, Kendall." When he'd talked to Dr. Croft, she'd told him not to treat Kendall like a wounded bird to be tiptoed around. The doctor had said that would only give her permission to hold on to her depression. He agreed.

She darted a glance at him. "I'm not going." Her attention returned to the view outside the window.

Her father came into the room. "Go with him, Kendall. You have to be tired of staring out that window. A change of scenery will be good for you. I love you, honey." He leaned down and kissed her cheek, then walked out.

Cooper understood how hard it had been for Frank to send her off, and he was grateful for the trust her father was giving him. "Let's go," he said. "Livie misses you, and she's starting to think you've abandoned her."

"I would never."

"You know that. I know that. Livie doesn't. You have two choices here. You can walk out on your own two feet, or I can toss you over my shoulder and carry you out."

"I hate you."

"No, you don't."

"Do, too." She stood and strode out of the room.

Although small, there was a bit of fire there. Because she had her back to him and wouldn't see, he smiled. He lost his smile when she froze as soon as she stepped outside.

"I can't do this," she said as her eyes darted around.

He put his arm around her shoulders. "There isn't anyone out here. You're safe, Kens." Keeping her tucked next to him, he walked her to his truck.

The drive back to Myrtle Beach was quiet, with Kendall staring out the window lost in her thoughts.

THEY REACHED MYRTLE BEACH at dinnertime, and Cooper went through a fast-food drive-through, getting a bucket of chicken and some sides. Once inside his apartment, she went straight to the bathroom, closing the door behind her. He put her suitcase in the room she shared with Livie, then went to the kitchen and set out plates and silverware.

"Come eat," he said when she appeared.

"Not hungry."

"I am, and you can at least keep me company." When she turned—likely to shut herself up in the guest bedroom—he caught her arm. "Please. Just sit with me."

She sighed but went to the table.

He didn't know what was going on in her mind because she refused to talk about it. The man who'd taken her as a child had come back like the worst bogeyman ever. He did know what it was like to be terrified and fearing for your life. She was crumbling the biscuit he'd put on her plate. She wouldn't talk, so he did.

"When I was kidnapped, I thought I was going to die. Grayson and Liam came from money, and when their ransom was paid, they'd get to go home. Me?" He laughed, but it wasn't a funny laugh. "The joke was on the kidnappers. Money was something other people had. Even if they'd asked my father for only a hundred dollars and he had that much money in his pocket, he would have laughed in their face. Then he would have gone down to the corner bar and stayed there until the money was gone and he got kicked out."

"Were you scared?"

"Terrified out of my mind." Her attention was on him now and not whatever dark thoughts she'd been having, so he continued. "There were two men, and they kept us in a room for two weeks, only giving us enough food to keep us alive." He'd told her a bit about that time, but not any details. He wasn't even sure she remembered the little he had shared.

"How did you get away?"

"That's where Liam and I got lucky to have been kidnapped with Grayson. His father had been a Navy SEAL, and he called in a favor. Sent a couple of former SEALs to rescue us."

"You rescued me."

"I'd give anything if I'd found you sooner, Kendall, before he hurt you." He took the half-destroyed biscuit away from her and dropped it on the plate. "Come here." Not giving her a chance to refuse, he pulled her to him so that she was sitting on his leg. He wrapped his arms around her, and she leaned against him. "I know about dark places in the mind because I spent a lot of time there, even after I was safe. Tell me about yours." When she stayed silent, he rested his chin on her head. "Talk to me," he softly said.

A long moment passed, then, "I thought I died. I wanted to die."

He flinched at hearing she'd wanted to die. There was more, so he just held her and waited.

"I wanted to disappear, to fade into nothingness and escape the nightmare I was in. If I was dead, the monster couldn't hurt me anymore." Tears streamed down her cheeks as she lifted her face to his. "I was being selfish, not caring if Livie lost her mother. I'm so ashamed."

"You listen to me, Kendall. You aren't selfish. You were a victim trying to survive a nightmare no one should ever have to endure. You're a survivor, and that takes strength beyond measure." A tremble traveled through her, and he tightened his hold on her. "I thank God that you did survive."

Tears flowed down her cheeks, and he held her as she cried. Her tears seeped into his shirt, her body racked with sobs. He hadn't seen her cry since she was rescued, and she needed this. He didn't know how long he held her while she fell apart, but when her cries subsided, he put his finger under her chin and lifted her face so he could look into her eyes.

"You're not alone in this. You have your father, Livie, me, my brothers and their ladies to lean on. To listen to you when you need to talk. I'll hold you when that's all you need." He brushed his lips over hers. "I think that's enough talk for tonight, though. How about I run you a bath, bring you a cup of tea and then I'll hold you through the night so you know you're safe. In the morning, we'll go get Livie. All that sound good?"

She swiped her hands over her cheeks, wiping away her tears. "Yes, it sounds nice."

"Good." Careful not to hurt her shoulder wound, he lifted her to her feet, then took her hand and led her to the bathroom. He believed she'd had a breakthrough tonight, but there would be other dark days. What happened to her wasn't going to just disappear like a miracle, so he'd convince her to talk to the psychologist that Dr. Croft had recommended.

THE NEXT MORNING, Kendall chose not to go with him to get Livie, saying she wasn't ready to talk to anyone. That was fine. He wasn't going to push her into doing anything she wasn't ready for. He thought—hoped—that Livie would be good medicine for her mother.

He arrived at Grayson's to find his daughter, his dog, Tyler and Einstein the cat inside a blanket fort in the living room. He wanted to talk to Grayson and Harlow for a minute before Livie knew he was here, so he motioned them to follow him to the kitchen.

"How's Kendall?" Harlow asked, keeping her voice low so the kids in the living room couldn't hear.

"Not so good. She's struggling, but she did talk a little for the first time about what she went through. I'm hoping that's a good sign. The psychologist in Decatur she talked to recommended one here, and I'm going to encourage her to make an appointment."

"If there's anything we can do, you only have to ask," Grayson said.

"Thank you. I think having Livie home will help her. I really appreciate you letting her stay here while we were gone."

Harlow smiled. "Your daughter is a delight. Anytime you need us to keep her, we'll be happy to."

"Is Kendall going to stay here?" Grayson said.

He shrugged. "I wish I knew. That's what I want, but I don't know where Kendall's mind on that is right now. For now, I'm going to take my daughter and dog home. Is there anything going on I need to know about?"

"No." Grayson squeezed his shoulder. "Take a few days off to spend with your family."

He went to the living room and peeked into the fort's opening. A laugh escaped. Ruby had a lace handkerchief on her head and a silk rose under her paw. Einstein had a bow tie clipped to his collar.

"Daddy!" Livie squealed, jumping up and flying into his arms. "You're home."

"I sure am. What's going on here?"

"Ruby and Einstein got married."

"They did? That's…uh, great." He was sure the animals were thrilled to be wedded.

"Yes. Where's Mommy?"

"At home waiting for you."

"Oh, goody. Let's go."

He collected Livie and Ruby and took his family home.

Chapter Thirty-Two

Kendall sat in a beach chair behind the apartment building, watching Cooper, Livie and Ruby play baseball. They'd taught Ruby to run after the balls Livie hit and bring them back to Cooper.

It was a picture-perfect spring day, the monster was dead and could never hurt her or Livie again, and there was a man in her life who obviously cared about her. She should feel happy. She didn't feel anything. She was dead inside.

Why couldn't she get past the numbness that had settled deep within her chest like a heavy stone? She closed her eyes, trying to ignore the sounds of her daughter's laughter coming from the makeshift baseball field. She felt disconnected from it all, as if she were watching her life unfold from a distance.

You survived the nightmare, so just get over it.

A gentle touch on her shoulder made her jump, and she opened her eyes to see Cooper squatting next to her. "Are you okay?"

She forced a weak smile and nodded, not knowing how to explain this emptiness inside her. She was blessed. She really was. The sun was warm on her face, a beautiful man was looking at her with soft eyes, and her daughter was happy as she played chase with Ruby, laughter trailing behind her. Yet, she couldn't find her happiness. What was wrong with her?

"Livie asked if we could have pizza for dinner. I thought it might be good for us to get out for a little while. Go have pizza and maybe ice cream after."

"Sure. Sounds great." Maybe if she pretended she was happy and having fun it would become real.

TURNED OUT PRETENDING to have fun for a few hours had taken her mind off all the dark thoughts crowding her head. She'd enjoyed herself, which had been a welcome surprise. Both Livie and Cooper had been entertaining with their jokes and teasing. She'd laughed several times, and that had been a gift.

Now, though, she was in bed with her daughter out cold next to her. She huffed an annoyed breath as sleep evaded her. Part of the reason was the nightmares she was having. If she didn't sleep, she wouldn't go back to that cabin in the woods.

Eventually, she did sleep. And the nightmare did come. She shot straight up, gasping for breath. She wasn't in the cabin. The monster wasn't choking her. Moonlight filtered through the edges of the blinds, casting eerie shadows on the wall. She eased out of bed, careful not to wake Livie.

Ruby lifted her head from where she was sleeping, and Kendall patted the mattress. "Why don't you come up here next to Livie?" The dog didn't hesitate to jump up and stretch out next to Livie. Leaving her daughter in the care of Ruby, Kendall quietly left the room.

At the door to Cooper's bedroom, she paused. She should return to her own bed, but she didn't want to. He made her feel safe, and she desperately needed that. Taking a deep breath, she opened the door. As soon as she stepped inside, she stopped. A lamp on the night table was on, and Cooper was leaning against the headboard, reading a book.

His eyes lifted from the pages to hers, and he smiled. "Can't sleep?"

She shook her head.

"Come here." He set the book on the table, then scooted over and lifted the covers.

How did he always seem to know what she needed? She slid into the bed, and he pulled her close to him. He only had on boxer briefs, and she had on her favorite bedtime T-shirt and panties. The last time she'd been in his bed, they'd had sex, and she belatedly wondered if he thought that was why she was here again. It wasn't.

"Turn on your side and back up to me," he said. When she did, he wrapped his arm around her waist and spooned her. "Did you have a nightmare?"

"Yes." Realizing he wasn't expecting sex, she relaxed. "I keep dreaming about him choking me. It's so real, like I'm living it all over again."

"You need to talk to someone, Kens. Dr. Croft recommended someone here who she thinks you'll like. Let's call tomorrow and make you an appointment."

"I don't know. I really need to go home."

The arm he had around her tensed. "Let's talk about this tomorrow, okay? For now, I've got you, so try to sleep."

"Okay." And amazingly, she did sleep without any nightmares.

"LIVIE AND I are going home." It was time, but from Cooper's scowl, he didn't agree.

He set his coffee cup down. "I thought we'd talk about this before you decided."

She shrugged as she pushed away her half-eaten plate of scrambled eggs. "What's there to talk about? The threat is gone, and our home is in Decatur. As is my job." She needed to get back to normal, back to her second graders. Back in her own bed. Maybe if she returned to the life she knew, she'd start feeling something again.

After waking up from the best sleep she'd had since being kidnapped, she'd decided it was time to go home. If she stayed any longer, she'd let Cooper become her crutch. She felt safe with him, but she had to resist the lure of using him as a shield between her and the big, bad world. She couldn't let fear take over her life.

"What there is to talk about is us," he said. "I thought we had something between us besides being just the parents of a beautiful little girl. Am I wrong, Kendall?"

"I don't know." Stupid tears burned her eyes. She squeezed them shut. "I just don't know."

He reached across the table and placed his hand over hers. "How can you not know? You either feel something for me or you don't."

Anger surged through her. Why couldn't he understand? "I don't know because I don't feel anything," she yelled. "Not a damn thing," she said with a quieter voice. *Not true,* her inner voice said. *You just felt anger.* She pushed the thought aside, afraid if she acknowledged she might have felt something, she'd let him persuade her to stay. If she was going to find herself again, she had to go.

Hurt flashed across his face before he let out a resigned sigh. "I'll drive you back to Decatur under one condition—that you promise to make an appointment with Dr. Croft."

"I will. I promise. Will you take us today?" She had to go before he could talk her into staying.

He pushed away from the table. "If that's what you want."

"It is." There was a coldness in his voice that he'd never used on her before, and she wanted to tell him she was sorry she couldn't be what he wanted, but she didn't. She had expected relief after making her decision to leave, but instead a profound emptiness settled in her chest. Was she making a mistake?

No, she wasn't. He was a good man who deserved a woman who could love him, who could make him happy. That wasn't her. She went to the living room where Livie was watching cartoons and sat on the sofa next to her.

"Guess what?" When Livie's gaze didn't leave the cartoon, Kendall picked up the remote and turned off the TV.

"I'm watching that, Mommy."

"Well, we need to pack up our things. We're going home today."

"Is Daddy and Ruby going to live with us?"

"No, sweetie, Daddy lives here." She glanced over to Cooper, who was standing a few feet away, his hands stuffed in his pockets. "He's going to drive us home, though."

Livie's expression turned mulish. "I want to live with Daddy."

Well, that hurt. "Daddy will come see you when he can, but you can't stay here. Don't you want to see Papaw? I know he misses you."

Livie scooted away from her. "Papaw can come see me here."

"We're going home, Livie." She should have realized that Livie wouldn't want to leave her newfound father, but she hadn't even given that a thought when making the decision to go home. That just proved how messed up she was, that she hadn't considered her daughter's feelings and what she wanted.

"No!" Livie jumped up and ran to Cooper. "I want to stay with you, Daddy."

When Livie started crying and Cooper picked her up, Kendall realized she had underestimated Livie's attachment to him. Guilt settled heavy in her heart as Livie clung to him and tears streamed down her face. It was too much. She escaped to the bedroom.

She needed to pack, but she didn't have the energy. Sometime later, Cooper came in and caught her sitting on the bed, staring into space. She jumped up and grabbed Livie's pajamas to put in the suitcase.

"Where's Livie?" she said while keeping her eyes on the pajamas as she folded them. If she looked at him, she... She didn't know what she'd do. Cry? Jump on him and wrap herself around him and beg him to give her time? But that wouldn't be fair to him. What if she was never ready to have him—or any man—in her life? No, she couldn't do that to him.

"Livie cried herself to sleep. Ruby's watching over her."

"Okay." She dropped down onto the bed. Her daughter had cried herself to sleep. Kendall thought she might cry herself. She was the worst mother in the world. He stepped close to her, too close. She could smell his spicy scent, feel the heat from his body. Her hands fisted the pajamas to keep from reaching for him.

He kneeled in front of her. "Kendall, look at me."

"I can't," she whispered.

"Why?"

There were a thousand reasons why...or maybe there was only one. That one was because she was hurting him, and she couldn't bear to see the pain she was causing in his eyes. *That means you're feeling something,* the stupid voice in her head said.

"Why can't you look at me? Tell me. You owe me that much."

She took a few seconds to school her face before lifting her eyes to his. "I'm looking at you. Happy?" Oh, God, why was she being so mean? He deserved better than that from her.

"No, I'm not happy. I'm guessing that right now you don't want to hear this, but I'm going to say it anyway. I'm in love with you."

She recoiled at hearing those words. "You can't love me. I have nothing inside me to give you."

"That's it, then? You're just going to give him the win? Let him take away your chance to be happy?"

"I guess so." She wanted to explain it to him, but she didn't understand it herself. There was no reason for her to feel so lost, yet she did. "I'll be ready to go in a few minutes, as soon as I finish packing."

"You're not going home." Cooper took her hands in his. "Did you hear me, Kendall? You're not going home."

Her eyes narrowed. "Yes, I am."

"Tell me something. How long have you been sitting here?"

"What's that got to do with anything?"

"Just answer my question."

"I don't know. Five, maybe ten minutes."

"Try two hours."

"No, it's only been a few minutes." He was wrong; he had to be.

"Two hours, Kendall, while our daughter cried herself to sleep. She cried loud enough for you to hear her, but you didn't, did you?"

Heat burned her neck and her cheeks. She was a terrible mother. Embarrassed and heartsick, she pulled her hands away from Cooper's and pressed them over her face.

"Here's the thing. I can't let Livie go home with you, not when you're not capable of taking care of her right now. What if she hurts herself and you're zoned out like you just were? You're a wonderful mother. I don't doubt that, but you're not yourself, and until you are again, she can't be alone with you."

"I'm sorry." He was right, and she wouldn't risk her daughter's safety because of her pride. She dropped her hands and met his gaze. "She can stay here with you."

"She's going to, and so are you."

"No, I—"

"It's not up for debate. You're suffering from PTSD, a severe case, I'm guessing. I called Dr. Croft before I came in here, and she agrees. Because you are, I'm making some decisions that are in your best interest. I made you an appointment for tomorrow with the psychologist here that Dr. Croft recommended. I also talked to your father, and he said if you come home, he'll put you in his car and bring you right back here."

"Who do you think you are?" She didn't have to stand for this. Yet... And yet, there was relief that he was taking charge because deep down, she knew she needed help. It was just hard to acknowledge it and admit it.

"I'm a man who loves a beautiful woman, a man who will do anything to help her through this. You don't have to do it alone, Kendall. Let me be here for you, let me take care of both you and Livie until you get past this. Because you will. I promise."

Tears slid down her cheeks as she nodded. For the first time since the monster came for her, she felt a glimmer of hope that maybe, just maybe, she could find her way back from the darkness that was consuming her.

Chapter Thirty-Three

Cooper waited for his bedroom door to open as it had every night for the past three weeks. Why she insisted she was going to sleep in the guest bedroom each of those nights was a mystery since she always ended up in his bed.

She'd made significant progress since the day he'd told her the way things were going to be. Because she had, he was stepping back from the heavy hand he'd felt he had to use for her own well-being. She loved Dr. Lydia Slater, the psychologist Doctor Croft had recommended, something he was thankful for. She was still having nightmares, but not every night, so also progress there.

The one thing he was hesitating to bring up was their future. Would she stay with him? She hadn't talked about returning to Decatur. She had talked to her boss, the principal of her school, to request a leave of absence, which had been granted. So, there was a job waiting for her if that was what she wanted. He prayed that was not what she wanted.

Thinking positive, he'd secretly started house shopping. Grayson and Liam lived on the beach, which was nice for visits. Cooper wasn't a big beach fan. He wasn't crazy about the sand and all the tourists on the beach during the season. He wanted a house in a nice neighborhood. Four, maybe five bedrooms with a big enough backyard to play baseball with Livie and the friends she would make. He had several he'd looked at online marked to go see.

As he expected, his bedroom door eased open. He put his book on the side table, then lifted the covers for her. On previous nights, they hadn't talked. She would slide in next to him, and he'd pull her against him, spooning her. He'd wrap his arm around her waist and hold her while she fell asleep. In the morning, she'd be gone when he awoke.

"Cooper?" she softly said after she was tucked against him.

Well, then, tonight was going to be different. "Yeah?"

"Make love to me."

Okay, very different. "Are you sure you're ready for that?" As much as he wanted her, he had to ask.

She turned over to face him. "I'm very sure."

He searched her eyes for any sign of hesitation or fear, but all he saw was determination and longing. Without a word, he leaned in to capture her lips, letting his love for her speak through the kiss and gentleness of his touch on her body as he trailed his fingers to the top of her camisole.

When she pushed away and sat up, he wanted to punch himself. It was too much, too soon. "I'm sor…"

She pulled the camisole over her head and tossed it to the floor, then did the same with her sleep shorts. "Now, where were we?"

He laughed, glad he wasn't going to have to punch himself in the face. "I believe we were here." He pressed his mouth to hers again.

"Wait." She leaned her face away. "I don't want to be the only one naked. Lose your pants."

"Yes, ma'am." He'd always been good at following orders, and this command was one he'd happily obey. His sweatpants joined her clothes on the floor. "Now, stop interrupting me because my mouth desperately needs yours."

She giggled, and it was the sweetest sound he'd ever heard. His fear that she wasn't ready for intimacy melted away with that giggle. As his lips met hers once more—and knowing she was beginning to heal—a wave of electricity coursed through him, igniting a passion that had been simmering below the surface, waiting for this moment when she came back to him.

With his kisses, he gave her a silent promise of his love. She responded by arching into him, then she softly gasped as he kissed his way down her neck to her chest. The heat between them intensified as he worshipped her breasts, fueled by desire and a connection that ran deeper than just physical attraction. He loved this woman with every bone in his body, with every breath he took.

His hands roamed over her body, rediscovering every curve and plane as if for the first time. She seemed as eager to relearn him as her hands traveled over his chest, down to his stomach, then down to his erection.

"Ahhh…" He pulled her hand away. "I'm going to embarrass myself if you touch me right now." He hadn't touched himself since the last time they'd made love. It hadn't felt right for him to feel pleasure when she was in such a dark place. "Let's save that for the next time."

"But—"

"No *buts*. This time is all for you. Our next time I'm all for making it about me."

She smiled. "Deal."

"I've missed you, Kens. Missed your beautiful smile. Missed kissing you. Now, where was I? Ah, I remember. I was worshipping these beautiful babies." He swirled his tongue around a nipple, then gently bit down. Her moan told him she liked that, and he moved to her other breast.

"I'm going to make you moan all night long," he said as he trailed kisses down her stomach. He slipped his hand between her thighs, seeking her heat and the wet proof of her desire for him. When he found what he was searching for, he smiled against her belly. "I love how soaked you are for me."

"It's your fault."

He chuckled. "That's one thing I'll gladly take the blame for. I've made you moan, now let's see if I can make you scream my name." He loved her with his mouth and with the touch of his hands over her silky-smooth skin. The taste of her was addicting. He memorized all the places that made her shiver. And when she did scream his name, he wrapped his arms around her thighs and held her until her body calmed.

"We're only just getting started," he said as he slowly kissed his way back up her body.

She dug her fingers around his arms and pulled. "I need you inside me."

"I need that, too, baby." More than she could possibly imagine. He reached for the drawer to get a condom. Did she even realize her tongue was tracing her upper lip as she watched him put it on and how hot that was?

He braced his hands on each side of her head and stared into those baby blue eyes. "Are you ready for me, beautiful girl?"

"Yes," she breathed, her voice barely above a whisper.

He leaned down to capture her lips in a passionate kiss as he eased into her. "Wrap your legs around me." He stilled for a moment, savoring the feeling of being inside her, of being connected to this woman he loved.

She trailed her hands up and down his back as he

began to move, slowly at first, just savoring this moment of finally being with her again. He began to move faster, deeper. The heat between them intensified as her body responded to his every thrust.

He whispered her name against her lips, feeling a sense of completeness he had never experienced before. Each brush of his skin against hers felt like an electric shock, sending waves of pleasure coursing through his body and causing his heart to beat madly against his chest.

Her nails dug into his back, the sensation a mix of pain and pleasure that sent a jolt straight to his groin. She arched her body beneath him, her breaths hitched, and her moans grew louder with each thrust until finally, she cried out his name. With one final stroke, he climaxed with her. He held her close and stroked her hair, never wanting to let go of this moment.

"I've missed you," she murmured, her fingers tracing the lines of his face.

He kissed the corner of her eye. "I've been right here."

She smiled. "I know. Thank you for waiting for me to come back."

"Know this, Kendall. I'll always be here, always wait for you."

Every night for the past three weeks, he'd fallen asleep with his arm wrapped around her waist and her back against his front. She'd told him that was when she felt the safest, when he held her like that. It hadn't been easy, but he'd patiently waited for her to want him. He would have waited however long it took and wasn't expecting it this soon. He sure wasn't complaining.

And as they lay entwined in each other's arms, he knew with unwavering certainty that this was where he was meant to be, here with her, now and always.

"I love you, Kendall."

She didn't say it back, but she gave a soft sigh as if the words pleased her. That was okay. She would say them when she was ready, and being a patient man where she was concerned, he'd wait for that day.

Epilogue

Four Months Later

Kendall smiled as she watched the man who hadn't given up on her pitch the ball to Livie. It was the boys against the girls. To help even the odds, the guys had to use a plastic toy bat. Grayson was guarding first base, Tyler second, and Liam third. If a ball was hit in the outfield, Ruby left her post of guarding baby Erin and raced after it for both teams, bringing it back to the pitcher. The game was silly and ridiculously fun.

That she was laughing and having fun was something of a miracle. It hadn't been that long ago that she hadn't been sure she'd have the strength to climb out of the black hole that had held her captive. She had Dr. Slater, whom she now saw every other week, to thank for that. And Cooper. Always and forever him. She hadn't been herself, and instead of letting her sink into that black hole so deeply that she'd never climb out, he'd been there for her. He'd been what she'd needed without her asking.

A baby's cry filled the air, and Quinn, their best batter and up next, said, "Someone's hungry. I'm out."

"I'm out, too," Liam said.

Kendall grinned. There wasn't a reason for him to be out. Unlike Quinn, he didn't have the tools to feed his daughter, but whenever his baby girl cried, he couldn't resist going to her. Ruby, too. As soon as the dog heard Erin, she forgot her outfielder's job and raced to the baby she considered her responsibility to protect.

Cooper shook his head. "Apparently, the game is over. Time for burgers and hot dogs."

They were at Cooper's new house. "Yours, too," he told her each time she called it his house. He'd refused to buy it until she and Livie had approved it. She'd never returned to Decatur, had no wish to. Her place had sold three weeks after listing it, but Cooper had refused to take any of her money to put toward the new house...their house. He'd been very adamant on that. She'd resigned from her teaching job and had been hired by the elementary school three miles from their new home as a second-grade teacher. She was excited to get back in a classroom when school started in two weeks.

Life was better than she'd ever believed it could be. The only thing she missed was her father, but he came to Myrtle Beach once a month, and she and Livie visited him when they could.

Her new friends were amazing. The guys were a blast, always giving each other a hard time. The women, Harlow and Quinn, were the sisters she'd never had. This wonderful life was hers all because of a night she hadn't wanted to be alone with her memories and had met a soldier she'd never thought she would see again.

COOPER SAT IN the corner of Kendall's podcast studio. The first thing he'd done after they'd bought the house was turn one of the five bedrooms into a studio for her. He'd wondered if she would want to continue the podcasts after what she'd gone through. She'd been adamant that she wanted to more than ever.

Tonight, she was doing a special podcast, and she'd asked him to sit in. He knew how hard this one was going to be for her, and that she wanted him nearby during it made him happy. "I can do anything with you by my side," she'd said, and his chest had swelled a little.

She glanced at him and smiled, then began to speak. "Good evening, friends. This is Kendra Hartley with another episode of *Find This Child*. These podcasts are special to me, and because I want you to understand why, I'm going to tell you my story.

"It starts when I was kidnapped. I was seven years old when the man I call the monster took me from my front yard where I was playing, a place where I should have been safe."

She looked at him again, and he tapped a finger over his heart. "Love you," he mouthed. Damn, but he loved the way she smiled and the light in her eyes each time he told her he loved her. His girl was brave and courageous, and he couldn't be prouder of her for doing this.

"I wasn't safe, though," she said, her gaze still on him. "The man who took me when I was a child found me again and kidnapped me a second time. If a group of amazing men who call themselves The Phoenix Three hadn't found me and rescued me, I wouldn't be here today.

"I was one of the lucky ones. I got away from my kidnapper twice. But what if I hadn't? Those children who disappeared into thin air are why I do this, because I could have been one of them. My parents might have never known what had happened to me, and the thought of that is why I do this. In the hope that some of these children's families have closure, and if we put any of these monsters in prison, all the better."

When her voice wavered, he pulled his chair over until he was sitting behind her, and then he trailed his hands down her arms to her hands and linked their fingers, giving her silent support.

She shot him a grateful smile over her shoulder before continuing. "My kidnapper won't be taking any more children, but we still have work to do, so tune in to my next *Find This Child* podcast. Good night and God bless."

After she signed off, he spun her chair around. "I'm proud of you, Kendall."

She grinned. "I'm kind of proud of myself."

"You should be. I love you, you know."

"I do know." Her expression turned serious. "I've noticed something."

"What's that?"

"Every day, you tell me you love me. I've never said it to you."

"Do you want to?" His heart pounded in his chest as he waited for her answer.

"Yes." She slipped her hands into his. "First, thank you for not making me feel guilty for not saying it. I wasn't ready before, but I am now."

"I was willing to wait for however long it took you to feel ready."

"You don't have to wait any longer. I love you, Cooper. So much."

"Say it again." *Say it all night long.*

"I love you. So much." She blew out a breath as if she were nervous, then she scooted off her chair and dropped to her knees.

"Kendall?"

She still had her hands in his, and her eyes were locked on his. "Will you marry me?"

All right, then. She'd managed to surprise him, but it was the best of surprises. "I'll marry you tomorrow if that's what you want."

"Maybe not tomorrow but soon."

"Just say when, and I'll be there." With a heart bursting with love for this woman, he stood with her in his arms and carried her to their bed. Some minutes later, when they were joined as one, he looked into her eyes and said, "Every day of our life together, I will cherish you. I'll protect you with my dying breath. I'll be the best father possible for Livie and our future children. I'll be your friend and your lover. I love you, Kens. Today, tomorrow and into eternity."

She smiled. "I love you, too. I had no idea at the time how lucky I was to meet a soldier in a place called of all things The Tipsy Turtle."

"It was meant to be, that soldier and the beautiful, sad woman," he said. "And they lived happily ever after."

And he knew they would.

* * * * *

COMING SOON!

We really hope you enjoyed reading this book. If you're looking for more romance be sure to head to the shops when new books are available on

Thursday 23rd April

To see which titles are coming soon, please visit
millsandboon.co.uk/nextmonth

MILLS & BOON

OUT NOW!

Available at
millsandboon.co.uk

MILLS & BOON

LET'S TALK
Romance

For exclusive extracts, competitions and special offers, find us online:

- **f** MillsandBoon
- **X** @MillsandBoon
- **◉** @MillsandBoonUK
- **♪** @MillsandBoonUK

Get in touch on 01413 063 232

For all the latest titles coming soon, visit
millsandboon.co.uk/nextmonth